To my big brother, Ken. Love ya, Stosh!

Testimonials

Praise for *Bad Pennies*

"*Bad Pennies* continues the rollercoaster ride of *Project Suicide*. There are suspenseful surprises right up to the thrilling climax."
—Dr. William Carl, award-winning author
of *The Assassin's Manuscript*.

"In this sequel to *Project Suicide*, drunken anti-hero Deacon Creel launches us onto a wild ride of thrills, twists, and surprises. Plan on being up all night to finish it!"
—Laura Vosika, author of the *Blue Bells Chronicles*

Praise for *Checkout Time*

"A well-written, fast-paced thriller!"
— John McManus, author of *Bitter Milk*,
and *Fox Tooth Heart Stories*.

"A gripping story with explosive action, high-stakes hookups, and a ticking time bomb of suspense."
— Douglas Boatman, author of the *Ted Danger* mysteries

Praise for *Project Suicide*

"John Bukowski's debut thriller, *Project Suicide*, keeps you on the edge of your seat. I can't wait to read his next book."
— Larry D. Sweazy, multiple award-winning author
of *The Broken Bow*.

"*Project Suicide* is a roller coaster ride filled with unforeseen twists, dips, and dives right up to its stunning climax."
— Matthew Clemens, coauthor of
the *Reeder and Rogers* thrillers.

Chapter 1

Amy Robbins' heart sank when she saw the headline. **Homeless man dies in Columbus house fire**. She anxiously scanned the story, then sighed in relief. It was not Deacon Creel. She slashed a large X through the newsprint, then turned to the obituaries.

This was now her routine. Scan the headlines and daily obits. Check the police blotter in the Messenger twice a week. Walk the downtown alleys, look in the bars. Visit night court to see who was on the evening's docket. This had been her existence for the past year.

Ever since the Project Suicide fiasco that almost cost her and Deacon their lives, she was a woman of leisure. The government hush money meant she didn't have to work, and her honorable discharge from the Marine Corps removed her reason for working. So, she had time for a new hobby: finding Deacon Creel. But where to look?

All the government reps told her was that Creel had eschewed their bribe in favor of $500 and a ride to the bus station. They didn't know which bus he'd taken, but Amy made an educated guess. That's how she'd found him last year, drunk and disorderly in Columbus, Ohio, Municipal Night Court. He'd stood before the judge, insolence in his steel-blue eyes, greasy brown hair and forty-eight-hour shadow attesting to his skid-row lifestyle. She'd paid his fine, cleaned him up, then tucked him into bed. The next morning, he was gone. In his place was a one-line note: *Do yourself a favor and don't look for me.* But she had looked.

A small, basement efficiency on the Cap City's west side became her base of operations. The place was cramped, with the gloom and damp common to many basement apartments. The radiator provided insufficient heat in the winter and there was no

AC to help with the summer humidity. But it was cheap, and furnished. It was all she needed.

Amy took a deep breath, steeling herself for what she might find in the obits. She exhaled, swigged some Pepsi, then started running down the list of deaths. The doorbell rang. Amy put her bottle on the cluttered kitchen table and headed toward the door.

"Whatever you're selling, I don't want any."

Before opening the door, Amy lifted the curtain to peek out the barred windows that provided her with a view of a concrete stairway and the feet of people passing on the street above. She dropped the curtain in surprise and whispered, "What is *he* doing here?"

Amy cleared her throat. "Yes?"

"Ms. Robbins?" the familiar voice replied.

Amy shook her head. Of all the people in the world, he was the last one she thought she'd ever see—or wish to see—again.

"I, I'm sorry, but I really don't have time right now." The excuse sounded lame, even to her.

"Just for a moment." There was a pause. "I need to talk to you." Another pause. "*Please*?" The voice outside her door sounded pained, almost desperate.

Amy sighed again and undid the deadbolt. July heat rolled into the gap provided by the safety chain. In that gap, she looked once again on a familiar face. She said the first words that came to mind. "Bunsen Honeydew."

Dr. Josiah Metternich visibly blanched. He cleared his throat. "May I please come in, Ms. Robbins."

Amy undid the chain and stepped back. As Metternich entered, she noticed how much he'd changed.

The former chief of the clandestine biowarfare group known as Unit 13 still reminded her of the director of Muppet Labs. But he seemed smaller, diminished somehow. The round, bald head sat upon the shoulders of a broken man. The pig eyes behind the wire-framed specs had lost their confident gleam. The expensive suit hung loosely, as if the man inside had lost weight. The clothes looked rumpled, as if he'd slept badly in them.

Metternich glanced about the apartment, head nodding. He started to say some pleasantry, but Amy cut him off.

"It's all I need," she said.

He nodded again and smiled.

"Can I offer you something?" Amy said. "I'm afraid there's no coffee, but perhaps water or a soft drink." She pointed at her Pepsi bottle.

Metternich shook his head. "May I sit down?"

"Certainly." Amy shoved bedding to one side of her fold-out sofa and pointed.

Metternich loosened his tie as he sat.

"If you're looking for Deacon," Amy said, "I don't know where he is."

Metternich smiled sadly. "And if I'm not looking for him?"

"I still don't know."

Metternich smiled again. It was almost painful to watch.

"No," he said. "I'm not looking for Dr. Creel."

"Then what can I do for you?" Amy turned to retrieve her soda.

"We already know where he is."

Amy spun about, the dewy bottle almost slipping from her grip. "What? Where?"

"Dayton, Ohio," Metternich said. His pudgy fingers formed air quotes. "A *gentleman's* hotel at Third and Euclid." That sad smile again. "Day rates. Nearby access to discount liquor."

"But how? I mean, how did you find him?"

Metternich shrugged. "We have methods."

"But I don't know…You said *we*?"

Metternich nodded. "Yes, I am once again in the employ of the federal government." He raised a cautionary hand. "Now in more of an advisory than supervisory role." Another pained smile. "The change in title goes with the demotion. You see, I know far too much about…" More air quotes. "*Things* to dismiss me altogether."

Amy put down her bottle, her back to Metternich. "Can I see him?" She was afraid to hear the answer.

"I'm hoping you will," Metternich said. "*We're* hoping you can talk some sense into him."

Amy turned slowly, her brows raised with the question that filled her head.

"Yes," Metternich said. "His country needs him once again." Before Amy could speak, he raised a hand for silence. "And *I* need him."

Amy's brows raised another question.

"Yes," Metternich said. "I *personally* need him." The big man swallowed hard. "I need him very badly."

¢¢¢

Amy sat next to Metternich on the old sofa. Tears leaked from his eyes. Amy almost took his hand in comfort, then remembered his part in Project Suicide and grabbed her Pepsi instead.

"I don't understand," she said. "I thought the project was cancelled, the materials destroyed."

Metternich nodded. He sleeved away his tears. "Yes." He sipped the water he'd asked for . "All records were destroyed. The weaponized material likewise."

"So," Amy said, "how can it be happening again? Why do you need Deacon?"

Metternich retrieved a hankie and blew his nose. "We don't know." He turned to her, his red eyes visible behind his spectacles. "Someone, somehow, has resurrected it. Which leaves us right back where we were a year ago."

Amy rose, waving both hands. "But surely, someone besides Deke knows the formula *now*." She started pacing. "Even with the records destroyed. Somebody *must* know." She turned to Metternich. "Somebody had to have synthesized the antidote after Deacon provided the formula."

"That was handled by the Unit 13 lab director, Raymond Treadaway. He transferred to National Institute for Allergy and Infectious Disease after the unit was closed down."

"Then why can't he remake it? Has he forgotten the formula?"

Metternich met her gaze. "Raymond Treadaway is dead."

"What?"

"They found him at his desk two weeks ago. He'd stayed late one Monday evening. When he hadn't clocked out by twenty-one-hundred hours, the guards checked on him."

"How?" Amy gasped.

Metternich cleared his throat. "An overdose of sleeping pills."

Amy plopped on the sofa, the strength drained from her. "Had he been depressed?"

Metternich shook a negative. "He had apparently been looking forward to the birth of his first grandchild." Metternich wiped his nose. "His only health problem appears to have been a mild cold he developed a few days earlier."

Amy stared past Metternich. "Just like before," she whispered.

"Yes," Metternich said. "Just like before."

¢¢¢

As they sat in Amy's shabby apartment, Metternich provided more specifics about Project Suicide, the therapy that was perverted from an Alzheimer's cure to an assassination drug. From her own experience, Amy knew this assassination potion had been used to clear the way for Cathleen Harris, a highly placed Russian mole, to ascend to the vice presidency. Amy and Deacon had saved the country from suffering a Harris presidency, although Amy still bore the guilt of her part in Harris's death.

All this was old news, with Metternich just filling in details. But something still bothered Amy. From what Deacon had told her about his former boss, the man's grief and remorse seemed out of keeping with merely a professional dressing down or the death of one colleague.

"One thing I still don't understand," she said. "You spoke of needing Deacon's help. That you *personally* needed it."

Metternich's face drooped like heated wax. He shoved the hanky he'd been holding into a breast pocket and retrieved his wallet. He opened the expensive crocodile billfold and handed Amy a photo.

"That is Mrs. Metternich," he said. "My wife, Claudia. That picture was taken a few years ago on our thirtieth anniversary."

Amy examined the smiling photo of a woman in her fifties, her looks still handsome in a grey-haired, matronly way. "Pretty," she said.

Metternich nodded as he replaced the photo in his wallet. Then his pudgy fingers retrieved a cell phone. A few clicks later, he handed the phone to Amy. "That's Claudia now."

Amy saw a frozen image of a woman in a hospital bed. She looked much older, her eyes sunken from recent weight loss. But that was not the most striking thing about her eyes. They had been pretty in the wallet photo. In the cell phone photo they had a feral quality, a look of desperation not unlike that of a trapped animal.

Metternich cleared his throat. "Press play."

Amy looked at him. He nodded. She pressed play.

The image on the phone leapt up from the hospital bed, teeth gnashing. Amy stepped back, holding the cell at arm's length, half-expecting the woman to spring outside the plastic and attack.

Amy could now clearly see that Claudia Metternich was bound to the bed, her body bucking against nylon straps. Out of frustration, she snapped at the air like an angry dog, flecks of blood frothing up where she bit her lips and tongue. Then she stopped thrashing and strained upward, eyes bulging toward the camera. Those eyes held a panic and desperation that Amy had rarely seen outside of combat situations. The video had no sound, but it was easy to read, "Please let me die" on the woman's lips.

Metternich took back the phone and killed the image. "They must keep her heavily sedated or else…" He motioned with the cell. "Intravenous fluids and IV feeding are the only things keeping her alive."

Amy stared at him, her mind filling with questions. She said only, "I don't understand."

Metternich repocketed his cell and retrieved his hanky. "Claudia had complained of a summer cold. Nothing unusual about that." He blew his nose and smiled sadly. "We were worried it was COVID." He shook his head. "Then she tried to kill herself the first time."

"First time?"

Metternich nodded. "There were three attempts. The first one, pills." He began weeping again. "They scheduled her for psychiatric counseling. But before her initial appointment …"

"She tried again?"

"Walked in front of a pickup truck. Walked right out from between parked cars." He shrugged. "The driver swerved. Claudia received only a glancing blow that knocked her unconscious. When the ER doctor revived her, she grabbed a scalpel from a nearby tray and tried to slit her wrists." Metternich buried his face in his hanky.

"She'd been given the suicide drug?" Amy asked. "How? Why?"

"No one knows," Metternich blubbered, face still buried in his hankied hands.

Amy placed her arms around him. "Shh."

When his sobs slowed, he squeezed her hand, then stared straight ahead. "That's why I need Dr. Creel."

"But," Amy said, slumping back in disbelief, "I thought Deacon's antidote was a sort of vaccine. It had to be given *before* infection."

Metternich turned to her, his eyes filled with fear and fierce determination. "Yes. But there must be a way to reverse the process. A *true* antidote."

"But Deacon …"

"Is the most brilliant scientist I have ever known, in or out of government," Metternich said. "He created the preventive, this Creel-1, when no one else could. If anyone can find a true cure, he can." He grasped Amy's hands in both of his trembling ones. "That's why you have to help me convince him to get back to work." Tears again streamed down his cheeks. "He's my only hope."

Chapter 2

Deacon Creel woke from the nightmare, face drenched in sweat. He hung for a moment in the nether world between dream and reality, then the first spasm hit. Fingers leveraged atop the rim of a garbage pail, he managed to jerk himself erect, body and mind swaying. Then he threw up the remains of the chili dog and beer he'd consumed last night. At least he'd managed to force the lid off the trash can, so the puke ended up inside the receptacle instead of on his shoes.

The initial wet heave was followed by several dry ones. His stomach had just started to settle when he caught a whiff of vomit and old garbage wafting from the can. He heaved again, then turned away, body leaning against the wall, face pressed against cold, alleyway brick.

Deacon coughed and spat, trying to expel the acrid bite of puke, chili, beer, and bourbon. He pressed his palms to the brick, seeking support against the swaying night. Both his stomach and the alley settled down. The dream imagery had largely fled, leaving behind only an after image of dark hair smeared with blood and brains. A burp of bile threatened to bring on another heave, but he closed his eyes and let the urge pass.

"Hey fella? You okay?"

Deacon sensed a flashlight beam spotlighting his closed lids. He recognized the authority in the youngish voice. He didn't need to open his eyes to know who'd spoken to him.

"Fine, officer," Deacon said. "Can I help you?" Deacon opened one eye.

The flash beam dropped to chest level so Deacon could get a look at the blue suit addressing him. The Dayton cop looked about mid-to-late twenties, with the square jaw and jarred head Deacon had learned to expect from young cops. The boy grinned as he shook his head. "Looks like you had quite a night. Or was it a couple of days?

Deacon spat away a fleck of vomit. "You want anything—in particular?"

The cop's grin hardened. "Yeah. ID. You got any?"

"Yeah," Deacon answered.

The flashlight beam bobbed. "Wanna show me?"

Deacon started to reach into his back pocket when the cop cautioned, "Slowly." Deacon noted that the cop's hand was now on the butt of a black-framed semi-automatic pistol. *Is that really necessary?* he thought. What he said was, "Fuck you."

The cop lifted his eyes to heaven. "You gonna be a problem for me, tough guy?"

Deacon faced the cop as steadily as he could, the alley tilting momentarily. "Not unless there's some law against puking in a garbage can that I don't know about." He burped more bile. "They pass that as part of the Inflation Reduction Act?"

The young cop smiled briefly. Then someone spoke from behind Deacon.

"No. But there are laws against drunk and disorderly, vagrancy, and smarting off to law enforcement."

Deacon turned to face the cop's partner who'd come down the alley the other way. This cop was five to ten years older, with ten to twenty more pounds on him. He sported three stripes on his shirt sleeve.

"Hey, sarge," Deacon said. "I didn't see you there. Sorry, but I don't have any donuts to offer you."

The older cop smirked, then shoved Deacon against the brick with his billy club. "Looks like we got us a smart-ass, Tony."

The cop's breath smelled of grease, garlic, and overdue dental work. Deacon felt another heave building.

"Come on, Hal," the younger cop said. "Leave him alone. He's just a drunk."

The sergeant grinned in Deacon's face, then backed off. He motioned with his club. "Let's see the ID, Cecil."

Deacon reached slowly into his back pocket and handed over his wallet.

As Officer Tony played his flashlight across Deacon's face, Sergeant Hal played his on the open wallet. "Deacon Creel?" He looked up. "*Dr.* Deacon Creel?"

"But you can call me Deke."

Sergeant Hal studied the ID. "This your current address?"

"Not anymore," Deacon said. "I checked out last night." He smiled. "Little disagreement about the rent."

The older cop searched the wallet contents, laughing as he dropped a Trojan to the alley. Then he pulled out Deacon's cash. "That it? Two bucks?"

"I didn't know I had that much," Deacon replied.

"And no credit cards?"

Deacon shrugged, his stomach finally settling. "Must have left them in my tux."

Sergeant Hal smiled and shook his head. "Well, since you've got no visible means of support, we'll give you a night's accommodation on the city." His smile widened. "We got a nice, dirty cell with a couple stinking druggies in it, but I guess there's room for one more."

Deacon held up both palms. "If it's all the same to you, I'll pass."

The older cop pocketed Deacon's wallet, then signaled with his baton. "Didn't ask you, Doc. Now come with me." The cop gripped Deacon's arm so tight it hurt.

The rest was a blur of misplaced anger and repressed emotions. Deacon briefly registered that he'd reversed the cop's grip and placed him in a choke hold. Then the world dimmed out as something struck the back of his head.

¢¢¢

Deacon swam toward consciousness with a headache that made him wish for sleep—or maybe a double shot of bourbon. He started to reach toward the knot on his skull, but his hands were manacled together behind his back.

"Take it easy," said a young male voice.

Deacon saw the junior cop named Tony smirk and add, "Sorry about that rap on the skull, but nobody assaults my partner." The cop looked toward the front seat and said, "Even if it is Hal."

"Thanks a lot, partner," Sergeant Hal said.

Tony laughed as he squeezed a blue and white bag, then reached toward Deacon's head. Deacon instinctively flinched back.

"Steady, there, pal," Tony said. "This insta-cold pack will help."

The icy cold felt heavenly against the lump still rising above Deacon's collar.

"Oh. That's a nasty one," Tony said. Then he spoke to his partner in the front seat. "We better get him to an ER, sarge."

"He just got a rap on the noggin," Hal said, still driving. "What's the big deal?"

"No big deal," Tony replied. "But you know procedure. Could have a concussion or something. Maybe something got knocked loose."

Sergeant Hal chuckled as he turned the corner. "You gotta have something up there for it to get knocked loose."

"I don't need a hospital," Deacon said.

Deacon's contrariness seemed to bring on the sergeant's own. "We'll tell you what you need." Then Sergeant Hal grabbed the mic on his shoulder and said, "I'll report in that we got us a wise-ass tough guy going to the medic." He grinned at Deacon from the rearview mirror. "Before he goes into the can for six months."

¢¢¢

The cop car pulled into the lot behind 335 West Third Street. It looked like any other municipal lot in any other mid-sized, Midwestern city. Deacon noted the blue-and-white police cruisers, the brown and grey smattering of nondescript unmarked cars, and the van labeled SWAT.

The trip to the ER had been perfunctory. A quick exam by a PA followed by a quick skull film. A cold compress was applied. Pain medication dispensed. Then it was back in the cruiser, braceleted hands behind back, for the trip downtown.

Sergeant Hal pulled into an open space. "Let's go."

Deacon saw Officer Tony roll his eyes. "Hey sarge? Why don't we just let him go?"

Sergeant Hal turned back with a grunt. "*Huh*?"

Tony shrugged. "He's just a drunk. Let him go home to sleep it off. Save us some paperwork." He eyed Deacon. "Besides, seems sober now."

The sergeant gave his partner the skunk eye. "Your 'just a drunk' assaulted a cop." Hal unbuckled his seat belt and popped the door latch. "Drunk or sober, that's six months."

"Come on, Hal. I paid him back for that with the billy." Tony turned to Deacon and mouthed "say you're sorry."

Deacon cleared his throat. "Sorry about that sarge. I guess alcohol and PTSD don't mix."

Tony winked at Deacon as Sergeant Hal looked out the window, thinking. "What do you say, sarge?"

Hal thought for a moment, then said, "I say, the people upstairs tell me to take him downtown, I take him downtown. Now let's go."

Tony undid Deacon's seat belt and said, "You heard the man. Let's go."

¢¢¢

Deacon sat in the interrogation room drinking coffee and thinking what the hell? He'd expected fingerprinting followed by the cell with the smelly junkies that Sergeant Hal had promised. Instead, the desk sergeant said to take the cuffs off and put him in Interrogation One. So, Deacon waited.

The pain pills had quieted the knot on his head and his hangover. The warmth of the coffee settled his stomach. He felt like he could eat something. Deacon looked up at the eye in the sky and started to raise his hand. But the door opened before he could ask for an egg sandwich. The person who came in stole his breath along with his appetite.

"Hi, Deke."

The sight of Amy's dark hair and round, dark eyes drenched Deacon in a tidal wave of déjà vu. He remembered their perilous journey last year. He remembered their one night in bed together. He recalled dozens of nights with his fiancé, a woman who could have been Amy's twin sister, a woman who was now dead. He swallowed hard.

"Hi, Amy. What brings *you* here?" He tried to smile. "Unpaid traffic tickets?"

"Are you alright?" she asked.

He shrugged. "Lump on the head and a hangover. Assaulting a police officer. Same old, same old."

Deacon's half-hearted smile vanished as she ran to embrace him. He again felt the firm curves under her clothes. He again smelled the green apples that were as much a part of his memory as their night together. He hugged her back.

"I was so worried," Amy whispered in his ear. "I didn't know, I thought you were…"

Deacon let her fragrance wash over him. "You know bad pennies always turn up."

She pushed him to arm's length, a scowl on her face. The same scowl he'd seen during their life and death escapes last year.

"That's not funny," she said. "Sometimes … sometimes bad pennies get taken out of circulation."

Deacon touched her cheek, his fingertip wet from a single tear. He smiled. "It's good to see you."

Amy smiled back. Then her face darkened. "I guess you know why I'm here."

Deacon motioned her to the other chair. "I'm guessing Bunsen Honeydew came to see you." Deacon gulped dregs of coffee that now tasted vile. "Or did he send one of his minions?" Her look of disapproval soured his stomach.

"He needs you, Deke. The country needs you."

Deacon crumpled his empty cup and tossed it. "Where have I heard *that* before?"

"From me," Amy said. Her face remained calm and determined. "From Joe Metternich."

Deacon nodded and wished for a drink. "And from Nelson Barzoon. And Cathleen Harris." He scrunched his face in thought. "Let me see. Any other bad guys I forgot?"

"Lisa," Amy said simply.

Remorse hit Deacon like a roundhouse from Mike Tyson. He tried to swallow the knot in his throat. "Below the belt, marine force specialist."

Amy took his hand. "I'm no longer in the Corps, but I still believe in its principles."

Deacon tried to pull his hand away, but Amy held him fast.

"Duty. Honor." She spat the words, her grip tightening with each one. "*Country.*"

Deacon felt a tear roll down his own cheek. He squeezed her hand. "Good words, Amy. But I'm not sure they apply anymore."

She gently placed her other hand atop his and smiled. "Yes, they do, Deke. They still do. They always will, no matter how messed up government becomes." She paused to look into his eyes. "Those ideas still matter. Which is why *you* have to help."

"After what they did? After what *he* did?"

Amy touched a finger to his lips. "It doesn't matter what they did or what Joe Metternich did. Only what you *have* to do." She leaned forward and kissed him.

Deacon kissed her back. A silent message was passed and received. She knew him too well now. He couldn't refuse her call to duty. Or maybe he just couldn't refuse her.

Deacon exhaled as their lips parted. Amy smiled.

"Fine," he said. "Let's go get some breakfast. Then I'll talk to Herr Metternich." He waved at the surveillance camera. "Waiter! My check, please."

Chapter 3

Deacon and Amy stood outside suite 406 at the Dayton Radisson Hotel. Officer Tony and Sergeant Hal stood next to them. Deacon studied the Sergeant's name plate. "Listen, Officer Lipshitz."

Sergeant Hal grimaced. "Lipsitz."

"Right," Deacon said with a smirk. "You and Officer Movello don't need to hang around."

"Call me Tony," the younger cop suggested.

"Right. You and Tony can leave now. It was nice having your company at breakfast." Deacon pointed to the suite door. "But as you can see, we found the place."

Sergeant Hal crossed his hairy arms. "My orders are to see to it that you meet with this Metternight guy."

"Metternich," Deacon corrected.

"Whatever. So, we'll stay right here until you go inside."

Deacon shook his head and smiled at Amy. She shrugged. Deacon knocked on the door.

There was a brief pause and the clink of glassware. Then a voice said, "Just a moment." They waited. The door opened.

Deacon started to walk in, but Sergeant Hal nudged him aside.

It was a luxurious suite as such things go, at least for Dayton, Ohio. Josiah Metternich walked toward a coffee table; sitting on top were a carafe, several cups, a glass jug of orange juice, and a plate of assorted pastry. Metternich was dressed in office attire, sans the suit jacket. He held a *USA Today*.

"Yes, please come in." Metternich motioned them forward.

Sergeant Hal led the way. He looked at Metternich and then at a sheet of paper from his breast pocket. "Are you Josiah Metternich?" He said both names slowly, stumbling a bit on the pronunciation.

"Yes. Yes, of course," Metternich said. "I sent for Dr. Creel and Ms. Robbins." He cleared his throat. "That is to say, I *invited* them." Metternich walked forward and extended his hand. "Thank you, Officer …" He squinted through wire-framed specs at the cop's name plate. "Lipshitz?"

Deacon coughed to suppress a giggle.

Hal cleared his throat. "That's *Sergeant* Lipsitz, Doctor."

"Quite right, quite right," Metternich said, shaking the cop's hand. "Thank you so much for fetching, I mean escorting them here." He pointed to Officer Tony. "You and your partner both. I'll be sure to pass on my thanks to your superiors." Metternich paused, waiting for the cops to leave.

"I'll need to see some ID, Doctor."

Officer Tony rolled his eyes. "Geeze, Sarge."

Sergeant Hal glared Tony into silence.

"Of course, of course," Metternich withdrew a leatherette billfold from his vest pocket and opened it to an impressively official ID.

Sergeant Hal compared the ID photo to the man, then nodded. "Thank you, Doctor. I remand them to your custody."

Deacon smirked as Officer Tony shook his head.

"So noted," Metternich said.

Sergeant Hal sternly pivoted toward the door. The younger cop followed.

"Bye, Tony," Deacon said. "Take care."

Officer Tony smiled, nodded, and left, closing the door behind him.

"Nice guy partnered with a putz," Deacon muttered.

Metternich cleared his throat. "My apologies for that." He waved toward the sofa. "Please have a seat." His wave encompassed the coffee table. "I took the liberty of ordering a few refreshments. Help yourselves."

"Just ate," Deacon said.

"Do you have Pepsi?" Amy asked.

Metternich frowned. "No. I'm afraid, I … wait a minute." He reached into his pocket for a wallet. "There's a machine down the hall. Won't take a moment."

Amy raised a restraining hand. "No, that's alright. Coffee will do." She stepped forward to get a cup.

"Are you sure?" Metternich said. "No trouble at all."

How much things had changed, Deacon thought. Instead of barking orders and pompously posturing, Metternich was now solicitous to the point of servility. A personality transplant from martinet to sycophant. Even his appearance had changed.

It had been almost a week since Metternich visited Deacon at the Euclid Arms. At that time, Deacon noted how the man seemed a nervous, diet version of Bunsen Honeydew. The past seven days had not improved his appearance. Metternich's dark suit was even more rumpled than before, as if he had tossed and turned in it. Redness now rimmed the pig eyes behind his specs. His air of superiority had leaked away as well. The man now sagged like a leaky balloon.

"Well." Metternich cleared his throat and waved. "Please have a seat, Dr. Creel. Ms. Robbins."

Deacon remained standing. "Let's cut to the chase, Joe. I'm not here for you. I'm here because Amy made a good case for duty and country."

Metternich started to speak, but Deacon waved him off.

"I don't know how you guys fucked this up, but based on last time, I'm not surprised that you did."

"Things are different now," Metternich protested.

Deacon held up both palms. "I don't care if they're different or the same. It doesn't matter." Deacon paused for a deep breath, then continued in a calmer voice. "I'm willing to rederive the formula again."

Metternich smiled. "Thank you, Deacon, my…"

Deacon glared at him.

"I mean, *Dr*. Creel. But we have people to do that if you provide the formula. What we really need … what I really need."

Deacon shook his head slowly. "Oh, no, Doctor. *I'll* rederive Creel-1. Personally. So that there are no screw-ups like last time."

Metternich tugged at his collar. "Very well. Unit 13 has been shut down, but we can arrange offices for you at some other agency, maybe National Cancer Institute, NIAID, or even NIEHS."

"Oh, no," Deacon said. "No, no. Alice isn't going through that alphabet looking glass of yours. Not again. I'll choose my own workspace."

Metternich sat down with a sigh. "Fine. Where do you have in mind?"

"Right here," Deacon said.

Metternich looked up. "The Radisson?"

"Dayton," Deacon said. "University of Dayton. It's summer semester, so things should be pretty much vacant until September."

Metternich stood, a little of his old bluster returning. "But the government has no jurisdiction here."

"Find some," Deacon said.

"And what about laboratory facilities?"

"The ones at UD will do just fine," Deacon finished. "Creel-1 requires only standard techniques."

"Well, well, what about security?"

Deacon laughed. "Let me handle security." Metternich started to protest but Deacon cut him off. "I dealt with your security at Unit 13. It almost got me killed." He pointed at Amy quietly sipping her coffee. "Almost got her killed." Then he paused before adding, "Almost got the president killed."

Metternich started to speak, his face bulging with restrained objections. After a moment, he exhaled, shoulders sagging. "I suppose it can be arranged. I'll need a little time. Twenty-four hours, anyway."

Deacon rubbed three days of stubble. "That'll give me time to clean up and get some rest." He turned to Metternich. "I assume we'll have rooms here at the Radisson?"

Metternich nodded. "Register under my account. We can fly down any expertise you need from Maryland."

"I'll get by with staff and grad students from UD," Deacon said. "I'll just need Ray Treadaway to handle the synthesis."

Deacon saw Amy blanch. He turned to Metternich. "Problem?"

Metternich tugged his collar again. "Dr. Treadaway is dead." He cleared his throat. "Suicide."

Deacon plopped on the sofa, strength leaching from him. "Damn."

"I'll arrange for a replacement," Metternich said. "But in the meantime, there's something more."

Ray Treadaway, Deacon thought. Ray, the faithful worker bee. Ray, who minded his business, put in his time, went home to his family. Ray, whose daughter had gotten married last year, probably waiting on a grandkid or two. Anger simmered within Deacon. Ray, who was a few years from retirement. Ray, whose only mistake had been to work for the likes of Joe Metternich and Nelson Barzoon. Simmer turned to boil.

"In addition to resynthesizing Creel-1," Metternich added, "we'll need you to, well, that is to say, I'd *like* you to …"

"Fuck you," Deacon spat.

Metternich flushed as Deacon flew from the sofa, their faces inches apart. "Fuck what *you* want. What *you'd* like." Deacon's words and hot breath struck Metternich but were poor substitutes for the fists Deacon wished to pound the bureaucrat with. "Fuck you and all the government pricks who use people like so much lab equipment." Deacon jabbed a finger into the ex-director's slack flesh. "I'll rederive Creel-1 for you. I'll place it in your sweaty little hand." Deacon slapped his palm and smiled. "I'm sure you have a pilot plant all ready and waiting to make it in quantity."

Metternich nodded. "In Rahway, New Jersey."

Deacon laughed. "Naturally." He turned a stony stare on Metternich. "I'll get you your vaccine. Then I'm done. My involvement ends. Is that clear?"

Color drained from Metternich's face. He closed his eyes as a tear dribbled down his cheek. "Very well."

Deacon's anger ebbed. He edged toward the door. "Now, if that's all, we'll register and get cleaned up." He turned toward Amy, expecting to see her meekly following. Instead, her eyes glared fiery brown as she clunked her empty cup on a table. Deacon stopped halfway to the door, "Coming, Amy?"

"That's *not* all, Deke." She turned to Metternich. "Tell him."

Metternich stood there, eyes closed, silently weeping. He shook his head.

Deacon huffed. "He has nothing more to tell me. Let's go." He turned again to the door. "Come on, Amy."

"No," she said.

Deacon stopped and looked at her.

"There is more to *say*," she said. "More that you have to *do*."

Deacon laughed. "I don't *have* to do anything. I think I've done more than enough. After what they did." He jabbed a finger toward Metternich. "After what *he* did, I think I've paid my dues. I've earned the right to retire and leave them to the stinking mess they created. Now let's go."

Deacon grabbed Amy's arm harder than he'd intended.

She slapped him, probably harder than she'd intended.

Deacon stood there, face stinging, staring in disbelief at the fire in her eyes.

"Deacon Creel," Amy yelled. "Stop being a pompous bully and listen." Her tone and fire quieted. "Please."

¢¢¢

Nelson Barzoon pressed his whitened fingers against the table, then slammed the knife into the wood. The edge of the blade nicked the webbing near his thumb. The exquisite pain drove away thoughts of suicide, but only temporarily. They'd be back. They always came back, and had been since two days after his flight landed in Moscow.

He'd arrived in Russia with samples of the weaponized suicide drug (formula 606) and the Creel-1 antidote, along with the formulas for their production. After he'd debriefed his handlers, he'd checked into the Moscow Four Seasons for some rest and recreation. That's when the first wave of melancholy struck. Barzoon spent twenty-four sleepless hours drinking and trying to deny what he felt. That life was no longer worth living. That death was the preferred option, one to be exercised as quickly as possible.

Barzoon had run a hot bath and lay in it, razor blade poised over booze-distended veins bulging in the steam. The blue of the veins looked as calm and comforting as the Mediterranean. He arced the blade up, preparing to add force that would sever an artery. But his backward-traveling hand had tumbled a fragrance bottle to the floor. The sound of breaking glass had startled him as the air filled with a sweet, aromatic chemical. For some reason, the smell had reminded him of breath spray. Then, lying in the tub, Barzoon realized why.

His mind had flown back in time, back to Cathleen Harris's inaugural party. He remembered Deacon Creel puffing breath spray into his own mouth, then puffing in Barzoon's direction as well. At the time, it had appeared to be only a demonstration of how Creel and his breath spray posed no threat. But as he thought about it while lying in the tub, Barzoon remembered that Creel had grimaced, as if the taste was far worse than simple breath spray. As Barzoon thought further, he realized that the sweet, chemical odor was unlike any breath spray he'd ever smelled.

In a blinding moment of clarity, Barzoon realized what had happened. He'd jumped from the tub, slipping on the wet floor and landing with a whoosh of exhaled breath. The world around him dimmed. When consciousness returned, he saw only one smiling face in his mind's eye—Deacon Creel's. In that expensive Moscow hotel, Barzoon had vowed to stay alive until he could wipe the smirk from Creel's face. He'd made a promise to stay alive for revenge. Now, in a much cheaper motel room, that hadn't changed.

Barzoon pulled out a hanky and wrapped it around the bleeding wound. Then he took a pill from one of the bottles on the sink and washed it down. The tap water tasted rusty, which fit the red ring in the basin, which fit the mildewed caulk on the bathtub seams. A semi-truck blatted on the highway outside. Not at all the kind of high-class room Nelson Barzoon usually occupied, but good enough. Only revenge mattered now.

He grabbed the pill bottles and headed toward the bed. Heavy doses of Prozac, buspirone, and mirtazapine kept him going. He popped Xanax for acute flare-ups. But even with the constant mood elevators, the suicidal thoughts were never far away. They hid in the recesses of his mind like a genie waiting to be called to the bidding of its dark master. Even now, as he dropped the pill bottles into his shaving kit and withdrew a stick-on bandage, death had a sweet sound, an even sweeter taste.

Barzoon shoved the last of his clothes into his suitcase. There were only basic items: socks, briefs, and T-shirts bought at a department store. He no longer wanted the expensive, tailored clothing of his old life. That life was gone, burned away like slag in a smelter. Low-cost simplicity was what he valued now. It made the money last longer. Long enough to accomplish his mission. Then he'd give in to the genie and his promise of sweet relief.

He picked up the vial of weaponized 606 and placed it carefully in his shaving kit. The kit went into the center of his luggage so it would be padded by the surrounding clothes. Then he closed the suitcase and quickly scanned the room. He'd leave nothing behind. He'd never be back this way. The former Nelson Barzoon was on a one-way trip, a kamikaze mission.

He hefted the suitcase and headed toward the door. For the thousandth time, Barzoon wondered how Deacon Creel had avoided his own fate. Creel had breathed the weaponized 606, had received an even bigger dose of suicide drug than Barzoon. And for the thousandth time, Barzoon realized that Creel must have taken the preventive. That was the only explanation. But had those around him taken it? Barzoon thought of a slim figure with dark hair and even darker eyes. Had Creel given her the preventive? He smiled. If not, Barzoon would see that she got a dose of eternity. Let Creel watch her suffer and succumb. Let Creel endure the loss, the guilt, the torment. Then and only then, would Nelson Barzoon end Creel's miserable life. Only then would he get his revenge. Barzoon tapped the pistol in his pocket, then left for the three-hundred-mile trip north.

Chapter 4

Amy stroked the softness of the robe clinging to her freshly showered body. She looked around at the hotel room with its plush carpet and Monet prints. Not as nice as Metternich's presidential suite upstairs, but much better than what she was used to. Travel within the Corps had usually been cheap motels or bachelor's quarters with hot and cold running roaches. Her barracks overseas had been even worse.

She thought back on the series of events that brought her to this fancy hotel in Dayton, Ohio. Casually meeting Deacon Creel on a transport aircraft last year; him drunk, she assigned to get him presentable. Then the surprise of being named his aide-de-camp. Watchdogging his drinking. The whole Project Suicide shitshow. Getting almost run over outside a bar. Machine guns chattering at her family cabin. Running from the law. Lisa Reilly's betrayal. Cathleen Harris's inaugural party. Amy's face flushed at the shame of letting the new VP die. Was it indeed for the greater good? She might never know.

A knock on her door broke Amy's musing. She toweled off her short, dark hair as she walked to answer.

"Yes," she called.

"It's me."

Amy didn't need to ask who me was. She undid the deadbolt and let Deacon in.

"All freshened up?" he asked.

She nodded. "I thought you were doing the same."

Deacon rubbed his cheek stubble. "In a bit. I, um, wanted to say something first. Get it off my chest."

Amy motioned to the loveseat. Deacon shook his head and began to pace.

"I, I, back there, with Joe, I mean. I was, well …"

"A pompous bully?"

Deacon smiled sadly. "Just what my mom used to say when I'd rant about kids in high school or college. They were all older and …" He shook his head. "Anyway, I guess what I'm trying to say is."

"Apology accepted," Amy said.

Deacon smiled and nodded. "Thanks." He cleared his throat. "I also wanted to invite you to my room for dinner later. After you've rested up. We can order room service on Joe's credit card."

Amy smiled back. "I'd like that."

"Good. Say, seventeen-hundred hours?"

Amy snapped off a quick salute.

Deacon turned to leave. He put his hand on the doorknob, then looked back. "I just meant dinner. You know? You don't have to think that I expect anything more than that."

Amy batted her Linda Ronstadt eyes. "Why whatever do you mean, Dr. Creel?"

Deacon blushed and started to stammer.

Amy walked up and kissed his cheek. "Let's see how dinner goes."

¢¢¢

Deacon's room was identical to her own just two doors down the hall. Amy sat on his loveseat, the coffee table in front of her cleared in preparation for room service. She and Deacon were dressed in the matching outfits Metternich had sent over: new chinos and blue polos.

Deacon poked around the cabinet under the TV. "Want a drink?" He asked. "We've got rum, scotch, bourbon, Kahlua…"

"I don't think I should," Amy said. "Maybe you shouldn't either."

Deacon looked sternly at her, then smiled. "Just one, marine force specialist. I'm not planning on going in the tank."

"Do you ever *plan* on it?"

He thought for a moment, then said, "Sometimes." After a pause, he added, "But not tonight."

"I'll have a scotch, then," Amy said. "Rocks."

Deacon pulled out tiny bottles of Dewers and Jim Beam. "For rocks, I'll need to get some ice." He walked toward the door.

"Neat is fine," Amy said.

His look asked if she was sure. She nodded. He shrugged, filled the two glasses, then sat in a straight-backed chair opposite her. "Cheers," he said.

Amy sipped. The fire of the scotch warmed her as much as the shower.

Deacon sipped his bourbon. "I figure Joe owes us one expensive dinner before I get started."

"So, you begin work tomorrow?"

Deacon nodded. "I've got a meeting with the chair of the UD biology department at zero-eight-thirty. He's going to set me up with lab space and recommend some staff to assist with derivation." Deacon sipped, deep in thought. "Hope he has someone as good as Ray for synthesis. Or as good as Lisa for ..." At the mention of the late Lisa Reilly, he stopped speaking and gulped the remains of his liquor.

"Let it go, Deke."

Their eyes met for a moment, then he turned away.

Amy changed the subject. "How long do you think the work will take?"

"What? Rederiving Creel-1?"

Amy nodded.

Deacon shrugged. "A few days." He tapped his head. "The formula is up here. The synthesis is straightforward, if a little complicated. Assuming the staff that Joe digs up know their stuff, shouldn't be much. Then it's up to Joe to make as much as he wants." Deacon pointed to himself. "And since I was already a guinea pig, they won't even need testing on human subjects." He leaned back and closed his eyes. "Although I'm sure Joe will have some volunteers standing by—secret service probably."

"And the other work," Amy asked. "The, ah, cure for Claudia Metternich."

Deacon shrugged. "I don't know."

"How many do you think there were?"

"Hmm," Deacon opened his eyes. "How many what?"

Amy put down her drink. "How many suicides, besides that lab director."

"Ray Treadaway," Deacon said.

"Yeah. Besides him and Claudia Metternich. Although I guess she isn't technically a suicide *yet*."

Deacon sat up. "Yeah. Hers is the first case of survival. At least that we know of."

Amy nodded. "How many do you think?"

"I don't know," Deacon said, rising to get another drink. "But enough to get Joe and his bosses worried again." He uncapped the tiny bottle and upended it into his glass.

"That's two," Amy said.

Deacon turned and smiled. "Three and I'm out? Is that how it works marine force specialist?"

"That's how the game is played, commander."

"Fair enough, Amy," Deacon said. "So why don't we order dinner." He picked up the room-service menu. "What looks expensive?"

¢¢¢

Officer Tony and Sergeant Hal stood outside room 311. Hal grabbed the single straight-backed chair and straddled it, backward fashion. "Stupidest ass assignment I ever heard of. Wet nursing some scientist and his tootsie."

Tony glanced back at the door. "Keep it down, Sarge. They're right inside."

Hal shook his head. "What are they gonna do, take me off the assignment? Good."

Officer Tony tapped Hal's shoulder. "It's a security detail, Hal. You've had them before. Guarding some bigshot witness in a hotel or hospital room. What's the big deal?"

"The big deal, hotshot, is that none of those assignments had me playing nursemaid to a pompous, drunken prick who tried to put me in a choke hold."

"*Did* put you in a choke hold," Tony corrected with a smirk.

"Fuck you."

Tony heard the elevator bing down the hall. "Here comes their supper. Why don't you head home, let me handle the first shift."

Sergeant Hal stood up and adjusted his belt. "I've been around too long to fall for that, sonny. Once the food gets inside, *I'll* stay and *you* go home. You can come back for the midnight-to-eight shift."

"You're all heart, sarge."

"Good evening, gentleman."

Tony glanced up at the waiter rolling the dinner trolley. The guy looked a little long in the tooth for the job—grey sideburns and plenty of laugh lines, although maybe in this case they were frown lines. This guy didn't look like he laughed much, more like he spent his time looking down his narrow nose at lesser people—

and *him* a waiter. Tony shook his head. A small streak of blood tinged the collar of the slightly oversized uniform the waiter wore. "Must have cut himself shaving," Tony muttered.

Place settings were visible in a lower tray of the cart. The upper tray held two large stainless covers. With a flourish, the waiter lifted the lids off both platters. One held a sirloin two inches thick, red juice oozing out the side. Next to it sat a whole lobster. The other tray held a mountain of French fries next to a side of broccoli. Tony nodded to the old waiter, his stomach rumbling.

The waiter nodded back and started to replace the covers. But Hal edged past him and grabbed a handful of fries.

"Geez, sarge," Tony said.

Hal looked at him, then at the waiter. "I'm the official taster." He shoved the fries into his mouth and grimaced.

"Problem?" the waiter asked.

"For a fancy place, these aren't very good. Taste funny."

The waiter clacked the lids in place, then shoved the cart at Hal. "Since you're the food critic, perhaps you should serve them." He handed the room-service card to Tony, then turned to go.

As the waiter left, Tony noticed him snatch a steak knife from beside the tray. The guy's knuckles whitened on the handle as his whole body tensed. Tony found himself reaching for his service pistol, somehow sure that this waiter was going to shove the blade into Hal's chest. A moment later the waiter paled and dropped the knife. Tony watched in amazement as the waiter stumbled toward the elevator.

"What was *that* all about?" Tony asked.

Sergeant Hal shrugged, still chewing. "Must not like anyone touching the food."

¢¢¢

Nelson Barzoon slumped against the wall of the elevator. He wiped cold sweat from his forehead, then reached into the pocket of the uniform he'd taken off the dead waiter. He pulled out a bottle of Xanax and dry swallowed a tablet.

Hopefully, no one would find the waiter's body until morning. By that time, the drug will have been delivered. Then just a few days. He felt the calmness of the anti-anxiety med taking effect, or maybe it was his own will taking charge. Yes, just a few days.

Perhaps Creel would notice Robbins' summer cold, order her some chicken soup. Perhaps not. But he'd be sure to notice when she died. Barzoon smiled. After that, after the anguish and guilt washed over Creel, they'd meet eternity together.

¢¢¢

"Do you have any ideas on how to reverse the suicide drug?" Amy asked. "Once it's in someone, that is?"

Deacon pondered this, then tapped his head. "I've noodled a couple of thoughts in my spare time. I've had a lot of that lately." He lifted his glass to take a sip, but it was empty. "Something along the line of targeted monoclonal antibodies."

"Like in cancer treatment?" Amy asked.

Deacon nodded. "It should be possible to develop monoclonal antibodies to attack 666, remove it from the site of attachment in the brain. Patient might lose a few neurons in the process, but it should work." He tapped his skull again. "Still thinking on it."

There was a knock on the door. Amy started to rise, but Deacon waved her off. "My room. I'll get it."

He opened the door and saw Officer Tony, Sergeant Hal, and a room-service trolley. "Officers? Is that for us?" He poked his head out to glance down the hall. "No waiter?"

"He left," Tony said, handing Deacon the room-service chit and a pen.

Deacon frowned and signed. "A bit unusual, isn't it?"

Tony took back the chit and shrugged. "I can drop this at the desk when I leave."

Deacon smiled at Hal. "So, we'll be under the watchful eye of the good sergeant this evening?"

Hal shoved the cart at Deacon, who stopped it with his hands. Their eyes met, Deacon's smirking and Hal's glaring.

"Until I come back at midnight," Tony said. The younger cop shoved Hal aside and grabbed the handle of the cart. "Want me to take it inside and set you up before I go?"

"That's okay," Deacon said. "We can handle it." He extended a hand to Tony. "But thank you for the offer."

As they shook, Deacon saw Hal roll his eyes. Then the older cop said, "If you're gonna leave, Tony, you better get to it."

Tony looked at Deacon and doffed an imaginary cap. Then he turned and left. Deacon smirked once again at Sergeant Hal's scowl before rolling the trolley into the room and closing the door.

"Smells good," Amy said, as Deacon trundled the cart to the coffee table.

Deacon grabbed a towel off the trolley and tucked it over his arm, waiter fashion. "Allow me, Madam." He pulled plates and napkin-rolled setups from the lower shelf of the cart and placed them on the coffee table. Then with a magician's flourish, he whipped off the two steel covers. "Ta da!"

Amy laughed.

"Shall I serve?" Deacon said.

"Yeah," Amy said, sitting on the loveseat. "I'm starving." She reached across and grabbed some fries.

Deacon frowned in mock surprise. "With the fingers?"

Amy laughed and raised the fries toward her mouth. "Yeah. Although if I did that at my mom's table, I'd be committing suicide."

Chapter 5

Deacon smiled as Amy laughed and grabbed French fries. It was good to see her relaxed. He remembered how nervous she'd been at the Empyre Club for Harris's inaugural ball. How nervous they'd both been, both pretending to be someone else. His mood darkened as he thought again of the late Lisa Reilly. How she'd betrayed him. How he'd killed her for it. He tried to shake off the guilt as he looked back at Amy; her face scrunched in a grimace.

"This food smells funny," Amy said. "Almost flowery." She shrugged and raised the fries. "Waiter must have had on some killer cologne."

Deacon swung hard and slapped the potatoes from her startled hand.

"Hey! What the hell?"

Deacon raised a cautionary palm. "Put your hand down."

"What?" Amy asked.

"Hands down," Deacon shouted. "Now! And don't touch your face." He ignored Amy's angry stare and sniffed the fries. He recognized the telltale odor. It wasn't as strong as when he'd puffed the suicide drug into his own face at the Empyre Club. But it was there. Unmistakable.

"What's gotten into you?" Amy asked.

Deacon pointed at the bathroom. "Go wash your hands." He snapped his fingers and pointed again. "Now."

"Why?"

"Don't ask questions, just do it. And for God's sake, don't touch your face."

Amy rose and looked at him as if he was insane. That was okay, as long as she obeyed.

"Wash thoroughly," he added. "Like you were scrubbing for surgery, marine force specialist."

Amy shook her head and headed toward the lav. Deacon heard the water running. "You want to tell me what's going on?" Amy yelled.

"Later," Deacon yelled back, heading toward the door.

Deacon clicked off the lock and swung the door wide. Sergeant Hal looked up from the chair in the hall. The cop had some type of video game on his glowing cell.

Hal raised his brows. "Yeah?"

"The waiter," Deacon shouted. "What did he look like?"

"Huh?"

"The waiter who brought the food. What did he look like?"

Hal shrugged. "Middle-aged guy. Maybe a little older. Grey in his hair. Thin nose. Uniform was a bit big on him." Hal pointed to his collar. "Had a smudge of blood where he must have cut himself shaving. Why?"

"Anything unusual about him?"

Hal shook his head. "Just a waiter. Seemed a little frazzled is all."

"Frazzled how?"

Hal spread his hands wide. "I don't know. Like maybe he hadn't slept well. Or had a fight with the missus." Hal smiled. "Or these days, maybe had a fight with the *mister*. You know, frazzled."

Deacon nodded and started to reenter the room. Then he turned back to Hal. "Did you or Tony touch any of the food he brought?"

Sergeant Hal paused for a moment. Then he shook his head. "Nope. We just looked under the lids to make sure everything was kosher." Hal smiled again. "Surf and turf. Nice. But no dessert?" After a beat, he winked at Deacon. "Or is that for later?"

"As you were, Sergeant."

Hal laughed as Deacon slammed the door.

¢¢¢

Deacon paced the room. "I should have known better than to get involved with you again. I should have known better."

Joe Metternich sat on the love seat, shoulders slumped, hands tented together. "I don't understand how this could happen." He looked hard at Deacon. "Who?"

"That's the million-dollar question, Doctor."

Metternich spread his hands wide. "How did *whomever* even know you're here?"

"And that's the daily double," Deacon responded. He turned to Amy. "You better go to your room for a shower and clean clothes."

Amy held up her hands. They were rosy from washing. "I scrubbed until they hurt."

Déjà vu washed over Deacon as he stopped pacing and stared at her. It was as if he was looking at Liz again—Amy was a dead ringer for his ex-fiancée. The old guilt flooded back with the memory.

"I don't care. I don't want you touching your face until you've showered just as hard. He stabbed a finger at her. "Scrub hard. *Everywhere*. You understand?" He resumed pacing. "And change clothes. Throw the old ones out … *before* your shower."

Amy snapped off a salute and stalked toward the door. She stopped long enough to ask, "Is it alright if I leave some nipple, sir."

Deacon flinched, then smiled. "Wouldn't want to lose those. Carry on, marine force specialist."

Amy shook her head and left. Through the open door, Deacon saw Sergeant Hal leer as his eyes followed her down the hall.

"Deacon?" Metternich cleared his throat. "I mean, Dr. Creel. Is that necessary?" Metternich pointed to where the room-service cart had been. "The hazardous substance unit has removed the threat. There isn't even residual odor, which is in and of itself not dangerous."

Deacon slumped into the room's easy chair. "Maybe some weaponized 606 got on her clothes or something. I don't want to take any chances."

Metternich rose with a grunt and shambled toward the window. He looked tired, as if he hadn't slept. Deacon found himself feeling sorry for his former boss, because he knew the reason for those sleepless nights. He'd had them himself. He still did.

Metternich parted the drapes and looked into the twilight. "I'm bringing in federal security in addition to your police detail."

Deacon started to say something, then stopped himself. Joe was right. The poisoned food had proved that much.

Metternich turned. "I had the U.S. Marshal's Service leading the search for you. Headed up by a deputy named Tremaine. I've called them back in now as security. Here and at UD." Metternich let the window curtain drop. "After all, that's their job, finding people and guarding people. In this case, you and Ms. Robbins." He turned to Deacon. "Alright?"

Deacon paused long enough so he wouldn't be seen as agreeing right away. "If you insist."

Metternich smiled sadly. All his smiles seemed sad now. "I do."

"I hope this Tremaine guy is good."

Metternich nodded. "Oh yes … *she* is."

¢¢¢

Nelson Barzoon slumped on the cheap hotel bed and popped another Xanax. He was having difficulty hanging on. If the plan had worked, if Robbins were sleeping in blissful ignorance of the fact that she'd be slitting her wrists in a few days, he could hang on, if just for those few days. Now?

He pounded the sheets and bit his lip. The pain drove away the urge momentarily. He tasted blood.

Perhaps he should just confront Creel directly. Look him in the eye before shooting him. Barzoon imagined pointing the gun at Creel, seeing the look in his eyes when he knew he was about to die. The satisfaction of watching Creel's skull explode. Then the orgasmic relief of turning the pistol on himself.

The thought of shooting himself was so strong, so sweet, that Barzoon white-knuckled the pistol in his pocket. He willed his fingers to release the grip. Will was about all he had left.

He breathed deeply, trying to relax. He told himself that the added security made shooting Creel difficult. So, there was really no choice but to hang on for now. Hang on and bide his time. Then a thought struck. He smiled when he realized how it could be done so much more enjoyably than he'd originally intended.

<h1 style="text-align:center">Chapter 6</h1>

Sergeant Hal Lipsitz sneezed into a red bandana that needed laundering.

"Gesundheit," Officer Tony Movello said.

"Damn summer cold," Lipsitz replied, before sneezing again.

"You okay, sarge?"

"Yeah," Lipsitz said as he wiped his nose.

"Why don't you take some sick time?" Movello asked. "You've earned it."

"I said I was fine," Lipsitz growled. He cleared his throat.

"Go on," Movello continued. "I can handle it. It's not like I won't have help." He pointed to a guy in a dark suit standing guard down the hall. From their vantage point at the top of the stairwell, Movello could see a similar guy downstairs guarding the front door. "Enough suits around here for a presidential press conference." He thought for a moment. "What do you think? FBI? Secret service?"

Lipsitz shook his head, then blew his nose. "That one downstairs showed me his ID. U.S. Marshals service."

"Marshals?"

Lipsitz nodded and shoved the hanky into his service trousers. "Yeah. Looks like Wyatt Earp is taking over."

Movello whistled. "That Creel guy must be pretty hot shit."

Lipsitz pointed to the stairwell. "Speak of the devil. Here comes that hot shit and his tootsie now." He smiled. "She's definitely an assignment I could get behind guarding."

Movello nodded. "Ten four on that, sarge."

¢¢¢

The campus was almost as deserted as Deacon had guessed. Their security detail, Deputy Curtis Boyer, escorted them into the safety of The Science Center, the hub of scientific study at the University of Dayton.

Amy glanced about as she followed Deacon up the stairs to the second floor. The UD Science Center was a lot different than their last assignment. Unit 13 at Fort Deidenbach had been a blockhouse of dark, underground corridors that kept out the Maryland sunshine. The Science Center was all above ground, with lots of open space and windows. She'd found the atrium they passed through inviting, almost homey, very unlike most of the institutional settings she was used to. Plants dotted the high open space, and padded study benches lined the walls.

"This is nice," Amy said.

Deacon smiled at her. "Yeah. I worked here two summers off during vet school."

The stairway was open, supported by only a few strategically placed beams. Halfway to the top, they pivoted left on a landing, then continued to the second floor. At the head of the stairs, Amy saw familiar faces dressed in cop blue.

"Hello, Officer Tony," Deacon said. "Sergeant Hal."

The sergeant only grunted and pointed down the hall. Tony Movello waved, then smiled as Amy waved back.

"Aren't you going to check our credentials?" Deacon asked with a smirk. He held up the laminated card that she and Deacon had been given.

Lipsitz pointed again. "Down the hall. Conference Room 2."

Deacon saluted, and they headed left.

As they walked down the brightly lit corridor, Amy wondered what she was doing here. She was trained as a medic, a clinical specialist, not a researcher. She'd felt almost as superfluous last year when she'd been Deacon's aide-de-camp. He'd spent eighteen-hour days at meetings and in the lab, while she spent her time cleaning guest quarters and otherwise trying to stay busy. She didn't even have guest quarters to clean here.

"This is it," Deacon said. He nodded to the deputy marshal standing guard, then raised his hand to knock on the conference room door.

"Deke?" Amy said. "Why don't I head back to the hotel. I'm not needed here."

Deacon turned to her and grinned. "What are you talking about? I need you."

"For what," she said. "Fetching coffee? Security blanket?"

Deacon started to say something but caught himself. She could see from his expression that he was embarrassed. He cleared his throat. "I guess it seems that way to you, doesn't it?"

She let her eyes answer for her. Then she squeezed his hand.

He squeezed back and nodded. "Okay, I see your point. Let me introduce you around, then Officer Tony can escort you back." He knocked on the door. "You should at least meet our head of security."

"Come in." Amy recognized the voice of Josiah Metternich from inside the conference room.

Metternich looked better than when she'd first met him, as if he'd finally gotten some sleep. Amy guessed he was seeing a glint of light at the end of his long tunnel of despair. She hoped he wasn't setting himself up for a fall. Deacon was the smartest man she'd ever met. From the way Barzoon, may he rot in hell, and Metternich treated Deacon, she suspected he was among the smartest people *they'd* ever met. But he was just a man. Amy had been around medicine long enough to know that cures didn't magically appear. They required months, years, or even decades of research down blind alleys. Still, she hoped for Metternich's sake that his faith in Deacon was justified.

As she walked with Deacon, Amy watched Metternich smile and gesture toward his right. When she saw who he was pointing at, she stopped and stared.

"Allow me to introduce Deputy Marshal Theresa Tremaine, our head of security."

What Deacon was in the science department, Tremaine was in the looks department. She was one of the most attractive women Amy had ever met, the most attractive inside government (Cathleen Harris included). She looked to be no more than thirtyish, her trim body sculpted within a black suit and cream-colored blouse. The blouse was open at the neck, showing just a hint of pale cleavage. Her cheekbones were high, her lips full. Her eyes gleamed like sapphires set in alabaster framed by corn silk scrunched back with a black velvet band. Tying it all together was just a touch of makeup; Amy saw no blemishes underneath the powder on her slender, well-proportioned nose.

Tremaine reached toward Deacon and smiled. Amy rarely envied beautiful women, but she envied that smile. It was the kind of smile that opened doors and glass ceilings.

"It is a pleasure to meet you, Dr. Creel. I have friends in both the bureau and uniformed service and, well, let's say your reputation precedes you."

Amy watched Deacon smile back as the two shook hands for more than five Mississippis.

"That's nice of you to say, Deputy Tremaine."

"Call me Terri, please."

Deacon nodded. "Mine is Deke. So, you're going to be looking after me?"

Tremaine beamed. "We'll do our best, my detail and me. I'm scheduled to transfer to Secret Service in the fall, but until then, I'm at *your* service."

Deacon continued to stare like a sick calf, saying nothing, until Amy tapped his arm.

"Oh." Deacon released the deputy's hand and waved toward Amy. "This is Amy Robbins, my aide-de … um, assistant."

"Ms. Robbins," Tremaine said.

Amy got a single pump of her hand, the grip hard and challenging. Tremaine favored her only with a forced, professional smile, the kind of smile reserved for women unable to help Tremaine's career.

Amy had known other attractive women both inside and outside government. Some tried not to use their looks to get ahead, relying instead on hard work and team play. Others saw beauty as a stepladder to wealth or advancement. Amy liked to think she herself was in the former category. Terri Tremaine seemed firmly planted in the latter. Amy immediately disliked her.

"Well," Metternich said. "I've just brought the deputy up to speed on our situation. So, why don't we have her brief us on the security arrangements." He waved to the conference table. "Shall we be seated?"

As Metternich held Tremaine's chair, Deacon turned to Amy. "Why don't you head back now? Have Officer Movello escort you to the hotel."

"I think I should stay," Amy said. She stared at Tremaine, who was smiling at Joe Metternich now. "It might be important."

¢¢¢

Terri Tremaine took off her black suit jacket, revealing a sleeveless blouse. Amy noted that the arms of the deputy marshal were as perfect and toned as the rest of her. Her skin was unblemished ivory, her pits waxed free of hair. Amy wondered briefly what else was waxed and if that was government policy or a coquettish extravagance.

Tremaine shook her golden locks into order, then pointed to the large hotel diagram on the easel in front of her. "We'd need half a dozen operatives inside, working rotating shifts." She pointed to the lobby and third floor. "In addition, there'd be deputies or cops at the outside entrances, here and here, as well as unmarked vehicles front and back." Tremaine crossed arms under her pert bosom. "Usually, I'd just have local PD doing hourly drive-bys, but given the traffic volume near the Radisson, we couldn't expect a quick response in an emergency. Hence, the need to post the unmarked vehicles."

Deacon whistled. "That's an awful lot of manpower, without even counting the units here at UD."

Tremaine smiled at him again. Amy started to wonder if the deputy was just charming the celebrity or outright flirting with Deacon. Either way, Amy didn't like it.

"And impossible to keep secret," Tremaine added. "Our people would stick out like turds in the pool, if you'll pardon the expression."

Amy watched Deacon and Metternich chuckle at this crude turn of phrase and wondered why men were so easily manipulated by beautiful women.

Tremaine massaged kinks from her swan-like neck and shoulders. "I don't think we'll attract much attention here on campus. There are few students this time of year, and my deputies can dress in college garb." She pointed again to the hotel diagram. "But the Radisson is a much more challenging situation."

"So," Metternich said. "How do we handle that?"

"We don't," Tremaine said, pointing to the chart. "Not at the hotel."

"Safe house?" Deacon asked.

Tremaine smiled at him as she tapped her nose. "Give that man a kewpie doll." Tremaine grabbed a map from the conference table and started to pin it over the diagram. As she held one end, body outstretched and perfect ass to audience, she dropped the pins she was holding. "Crap."

Amy rose to give her a hand, but Deacon beat her to it, popping up as if on springs.

"Thank you, Deke," Tremaine said, scooping the pins from his outstretched hand.

"My pleasure," Deacon said, holding the other end of the map for her to pin.

When he sat back beside her, Amy muttered, "You gonna carry her books, too?"

The puzzled expression in Deacon's eyes said he was as clueless as most of the men she'd known.

Tremaine pointed south of the city. "The safe house is located in this general area." She turned her killer smile on Metternich. "Sorry, but we reveal the precise location only to those directly involved with the detail. It's an added security measure." Now she smiled at Deacon. "It's in a mostly rural area, so suspicious traffic stands out." She stabbed the map with a manicured nail. "But as you can see, there is still easy access to the UD campus via Route 48."

"How is security handled on-site?" Metternich asked.

"In teams of two," Tremaine replied. "One inside, one outside in an unmarked car. Rotating shifts that change every twelve hours. Of course, when Dr. Creel is at UD, inside security may be unnecessary."

"What about Amy?" Deacon asked. "I may be gone, but she'll still be there."

Tremaine turned to Amy, her expression perplexed rather than amused. "I assumed that Ms. Robbins would remain at the hotel. That I and my deputies would be responsible only for Dr. Creel's safety."

Deacon glared at Metternich. "Joe?"

The former director cleared his throat. "I may not have made myself clear that we'd be needing security for both Dr. Creel and his assistant."

The deputy marshal looked disappointed. It was almost as if Terri Tremaine had been looking forward to some alone time with Deacon. It was a wild idea that was probably Amy's imagination, but she couldn't help feeling it was on the mark.

"Problem?" Amy asked.

Tremaine paused, then shrugged. "Well, this complicates things a *little*, but we can make it work. The house has two bedrooms upstairs and one down, so privacy shouldn't be an issue." She smiled at Amy. "Perhaps only outside guards would be needed at night."

"Best laid plans, huh?" Amy muttered under her breath.

Deacon turned to Amy with raised brows. She shook her head and locked eyes with Tremaine. The look she got in return said this was only round one.

¢¢¢

Amy listened as the door opened downstairs. She recognized Deacon's voice and that of Deputy Boyer who had escorted her home. She'd been too upset to eat more than tea and toast before heading up to bed.

The safe house was a simple three-bedroom colonial located off Nutt Road. They'd passed a few suburban developments heading southeast, but the safe house stood alone surrounded by a dozen acres of trees and fields. The interior was dusty, with the kind of cheap furnishings common to rentals. With the exception of new kitchen flooring, nothing looked to have been updated since W was in the White House. Both upstairs bedrooms had double beds without headboards and were connected by a shared bath. There was a queen bed and another bathroom in the downstairs master.

Amy picked the first upstairs room. The furnishings were limited to a bedside bureau with a nondescript table lamp, and a similarly nondescript short dresser. The carpet was cheap and thin. There was no wall art other than a cobweb high in one corner. Only roller blinds adorned the windows.

Deacon could stay downstairs. She wasn't in any mood to talk to him or even see him tonight. So why had she waited up until quarter past eleven?

Amy knew she was being ridiculous, but it didn't change how she felt. She was mad at Deacon for playing the smitten schoolboy, which in and of itself was foolish. She hadn't seen Deacon in months, and their prior relationship was hardly exclusive. So why was she angry? Why was she jealous? Amy had had all evening to ponder these two questions. And the answer was unavoidable. She and Deacon were exclusive in her mind. Their shared experiences, their escapes from danger together, made them exclusive. Maybe Deacon didn't know that, but she did. She remembered his note, 'Do yourself a favor and don't look for me.' That advice went out the window when she'd bailed him out last year. At that time, she knew she was committed. She was angry because he should have known it, too.

But as angry as Amy was with Deacon, she hated that bitch Tremaine more. Not just because she was making an obvious, unprofessional play for Deacon, the man she was supposed to be guarding, but because of the type of woman she was. The kind that used beauty and sex to win prizes—in this case, a bad-boy genius who was already taken. Such women were in it only for the hunt. To capture the big fish that could net them advancement or prestige or maybe just an ego boost. Amy saw it in Tremaine's beautiful blue eyes. The look that said I can get whomever I go after, just see if I don't. Amy had seen it many times before in many other women. She remembered a blonde at Bethesda who went after the head of radiology. The blonde ended up with a senior nurse position, the doctor with a transfer and a divorce.

There was more talk downstairs, then footsteps coming up the steps. Amy clicked off her bedside lamp and lay still. The steps receded down the hall, paused, then came back. Her door clicked open, hallway light spilling across the bed. After a pause, the door started to close.

"Working late?" Amy asked.

The hallway door opened. "I thought you were asleep," Deacon said.

"I just turned in." Amy sat up and clicked on the table lamp. "Terri bring you home?"

Deacon shook his head. "Officer Tony. He'll be outside as our night guard." He looked around. "What do you think of the place?"

Amy shrugged. "Not bad if you like Walmart and Ikea."

Deacon smiled. "Yeah." He stretched. "Well, I guess I should let you get back to sleep."

"Why was the first day so long? You'd said it would just be preliminary stuff."

Deacon sat on the bed and smiled. "Preliminary stuff takes the longest."

"What kind of stuff?"

He shrugged. "Well, I had to meet the staff Joe picked out, check their credentials." He yawned. "Then I had to send one of them packing and select a replacement." He shook his head. "Had to oversee the lab, make sure all the reagents were fresh and the glassware clean." He shrugged. "You know, stuff."

"No more meetings with Terri about *security*?"

Deacon gave her an odd look. "There was a meeting, yes. Her, a guy named Kalinsky, Joe, Tony Movello, a couple others. Shift assignments. Why?"

"I'm surprised that Terri didn't come back with you."

"She's scheduled for next week."

"Surprised you two could wait that long. After all, there's that big bedroom downstairs so 'privacy shouldn't be an issue.'"

"Hey." Deacon shook her blanket-covered knee. "What's this all about?"

"What?" Amy asked.

He gestured about the room. "This. The third degree. Bedrooms and privacy. What gives?"

"Nothing," Amy nonchalantly replied. "I just figured the way you two were carrying on, you'd want some privacy."

Deacon looked stunned. Then he started to laugh. "Is that what this is about? You're jealous of Terri Tremaine?"

"You find her attractive, don't you?"

"Yes. I am a man with a pulse, so I find her attractive."

"She certainly finds *you* attractive." Amy batted her eyes. "Oh Deke, your reputation precedes you." Amy made a gagging face. "I thought she was going to jump you right in the conference room."

"Hey," Deacon said. "Look at me."

Amy stared down, tears welling in her eyes. "And you, you were …"

Deacon took her hand. "Amy. Look at me, please."

A tear dribbled her cheek as she looked up.

"There is nothing between me and Terri Tremaine. Understand? She's a U.S. marshal assigned to protect me—to protect us." He squeezed her hand. "That's all." Deacon leaned over and kissed her gently on the lips. "That's all."

She kissed him back.

He clicked off the lamp and slid in beside her.

Chapter 7

They had been in the safe house for more than a week. Amy spent her time straightening up, reading, or watching TV. She sometimes chatted with the deputies assigned to watch the house. They were always very polite but otherwise uninteresting. Deacon was away until seven or eight at night, sometimes later. When he came home, he was usually too tired to do more than have a drink, eat, and go to bed. Sometimes he didn't even eat, although he always had a drink or two (three was still the limit). There were no more bouts of lovemaking, making Amy wonder again if he was finding release in the arms of a blonde U.S. Marshal who looked more like Scarlett Johansson than Matt Dillon.

But tonight, things would be different. Amy stirred the spaghetti sauce on the old, enameled stove. It was her mom's recipe; it had always been part of a fantasy. For years, she'd prepared this meal for countless lovers conjured from among the men of influence she had known. The setting was always the same: spaghetti dinner, candlelight, a little black dress, and romance. Always it had been imaginary, a stress-reliever after tough exams or demanding duty. A little mental downtime with fictional lovers. Tonight was for real.

Deacon had promised to be back by six-thirty. Deputy Boyer had promised her privacy. The sauce was simmering nicely. Candles were on the table. A little black dress was laid out on the bed (a Target special, but beggars couldn't be choosers.) Tonight, Amy would erase all thoughts of the luscious Terri Tremaine from Deacon's head, leaving only room for work and the love of an ex-Marine.

Amy wondered why her feelings had grown so strong. Was it their shared life-and-death experience during Project Suicide? Was it the year afterward she'd spent searching for him, always fearing the worst? Was it his genius … or his vulnerability, the damaged past that led him to the bottle? She didn't know. She only knew that her feelings for Deacon Creel were stronger than she'd ever felt for any man. She was not about to let that go.

She gave the sauce another stir just as the phone rang. It was an old, beige wall model. Amy put down her spoon and picked up.

"Hello?"

"Hi Amy."

"Hi Deke." She looked at the kitchen clock, its round, ticking face reminding her of the old kitchen clock in her mom's house. "Dinner's almost ready. Did you pick up the wine?"

"Yeah. About that."

Amy didn't like the sound of his voice. "Don't tell me. Something came up and you're running late. Well, I can turn down the sauce and I haven't put the garlic bread in the oven yet, so I guess …"

"Yeah. Something *has* come up. We hit a snag during the synthesis." He muttered something, possibly a curse word. "Techs aren't as good as in Ray's lab, although I found one good post-doc, kid named Howard Threlkis, if you can believe it. Anyway, that set us back to zero. And now Terri wants to talk to me about some security matters."

"I see." Amy switched the phone to her other hand, sweat pooling in her palm, jealousy growing in her heart. "Another late meeting with *Terri*. Does that make two or three?"

"Are you keeping count?"

"What about dinner?" Amy asked.

"Yeah," Deacon said. "Sorry about that. I probably won't get back until nine, maybe ten. Why don't you go ahead. I'll grab something quick here."

"Grab a quick bite with *Terri*?"

"Will you stop," Deacon snapped at her. There was a pause, then he added, "Sorry. Been a long day. But I promise I'll be home earlier tomorrow. We'll do something fun."

Amy didn't answer. The acid burning a hole in her gut wouldn't let her.

"Amy? You there?"

"Yes," she said. "Fine. I'll pencil you in. That way it'll be easy to erase."

"Now look. I said I was sorry."

"Yeah. Right. But hey, my sauce is gonna burn. Maybe Dan Boyer will share it with me. At least *he* likes my company."

"Listen, Amy …"

"Bye, Deke. I won't wait up."

Amy slammed the phone into its cradle harder than she'd intended. No, that wasn't true. In her heart, she'd wanted to slam it even harder.

¢¢¢

Amy watched as Terri Tremaine exited a black SUV, shrugged into her blazer, then glided toward the safe house. The chief deputy made even these normal gestures look sultry. Amy hated her for that. It was irrational and childish, but hate was hate.

The man assigned to security last night had been Officer Tony—without his partner Hal. Amy saw Tony exit the safe house, speak to Tremaine, then point toward the brown Ford in which Amy sat waiting. Tremaine turned in Amy's direction, shielding her eyes against the morning sun. She smiled and finger-waved at Amy. Amy finger-waved back without the smile. Then Tremaine headed into the safe house.

Tony jogged over to the car and opened the driver's door. As he got in and started the engine, Amy asked, "You okay?"

"Huh?" he replied. "Yeah. Why?"

"You look a little flushed. Like you're running a fever."

Tony shook his head. "No. Must be from running to the car. I'm a little out of shape."

More like flustered by Ms. America's smile, Amy thought.

"So," Tony said. "Where are we going?"

"The Kroger up on 48. I need to pick up a few things."

Tony put the car in gear and headed down the gravel path leading to Nutt Road.

"Thanks for taking me," Amy said. "I know you've been up all night and probably want to clock off and head home to your wife."

Tony shook his head. "Not married. Just me, a roommate, and a *very* messy apartment." He smiled. "You?"

At first Amy wasn't sure what he meant. Then she said, "No, not married. But …"

"You and Deke, huh?"

Amy smiled shyly. "It's complicated."

Tony laughed and turned onto Nutt Road. "Lots of pretty women say that."

Amy thought for a moment, then said, "What do you think about Deputy Tremaine?"

"As a cop?" Tony asked with a grin.

Amy rolled her eyes in reply.

Tony nodded and wolf whistled.

Now Amy laughed. "Why do men turn into drooling idiots around women like that?"

Tony shrugged. "Nature of the beast, I guess."

"Yes," Amy said, looking straight ahead. "I've noticed. Must open a lot of doors for her. Get her just about anything she wants. *Anyone* she wants." This last sentence was mumbled, but Tony must have heard.

He looked over at Amy and smiled. "From what I can see, I don't think *you* have much to worry about."

"You wouldn't be tempted?" Amy asked.

"What? By Deputy Trimframe?"

Amy laughed. "Is that what you guys call her?"

Tony smiled. "Just a name Hal came up with." He thought for a second in silence then said, "Don't get me wrong, I wouldn't necessarily say no, but she's not really my type. She's ..." He fought for the right words.

"Out of your league?" Amy said, immediately hoping he didn't perceive that as an insult.

He shook his head. "It's almost as if she's not in any *kind* of league. She's ... too much. Too perfect. Almost not real. Like a statue or supermodel or something." He glanced over, grinning. "You on the other hand."

Amy smiled to herself. "Should I take that as a compliment?"

Tony laughed. "Yeah. A dumb, backhanded one, but most definitely, yeah."

Amy had a quick thought. Maybe two could play this game.

They turned onto Route 48. "The Kroger's not far ahead," Amy said. "I'll only be a few minutes. Then maybe we can grab a late breakfast or early lunch." Tony didn't say anything, but she could see he was thinking about it. "I'd rather not go back right away. I'm not relishing spending my day with Deputy Trimframe."

Tony slowed and angled the car into the left turn lane. He looked at Amy and said, "I'd like that. I *really* would. But I promised to stop by and see Hal. Maybe bring him some soup or something."

"Is he sick?"

"Summer cold. But it's got him down. And he's going through a divorce."

"That's too bad," Amy said. "But you're right. I'm sure he's desperate for some company."

"Sounded like it on the phone," Tony said.

Amy sat back, feeling rebuffed, embarrassed, and a bit ashamed. It had been a ham-handed flirtation. A crude attempt to generate jealousy in Deacon to satisfy her own, no doubt unfounded, insecurity. But she hadn't expected it to be refused.

"How about we make it dinner?" Tony paused then raised a dismissive hand, "I know. Sorry, but it's complicated."

"Dinner sounds like fun," Amy said.

His surprised expression said he thought so, too.

¢¢¢

The day was warm, so Barzoon left the car parked down the street and walked over. From his position behind a large oak, he could observe the small frame house on Irving Avenue. The place was old—maybe mid 1960s vintage—and could use some paint. The grass was long, weedy, and in need of cutting. There was a hedge, also in need of trimming, separating the lawn from the neighbor's drive. The owner must have other things on his mind, Barzoon thought with a smile. Then the image of hedge trimmers snapped into his brain, their shining blades razor sharp and suitable for cutting. Barzoon bit the inside of his mouth, banishing the image in pain and the taste of blood. The thought passed momentarily but would be back.

Hang on, he told himself. Please let me hang on for just a while longer. As if in answer to his plea, a Ford Mustang rumbled into view and parked in front of the house. Barzoon pushed the gleaming hedge trimmers farther from his thoughts and concealed himself completely behind the tree trunk. He heard the engine idle down then stop. A car door opened, and footsteps pounded away. When the footfalls landed on wooden steps, he peeked out from behind the tree.

The man Barzoon sought was knocking on the door. There was no answer. The man knocked again, louder, screen door rattling in its frame. Only the distant sound of a lawnmower filled the summer air.

"Hey," the man yelled. "It's me. Let me in."

When he got no answer, the man raised his fist to knock again. But instead, he backed away and looked at the locked door and curtain-covered windows. He hesitated.

"Don't give up now," Barzoon whispered, then smiled as the man bent to retrieve something from under an empty flowerpot. Barzoon shook his head and whispered, "Such lax security."

The man took the key he'd retrieved from under the pot and placed it in the lock. "I'm coming in. So, if you're doing something nasty, cover up." The man's laughter was lost as he entered the house and closed the door.

Barzoon waited patiently. He could be patient now. The gleaming blades had left his thoughts for now. He waited and listened. He didn't have to wait long, perhaps thirty seconds. Then he heard a scream carry over from inside the small frame house. Barzoon smiled and began to walk.

¢¢¢

Deacon said hello to the deputy out front and entered the house. The clock ticking over the mantle read six-forty-five. Early as promised, he thought with a yawn.

They'd finally completed the synthesis of the Creel-1 preventive and administered it to four rats. All survived. That's as far as he could go without any weaponized suicide drug to test it against. Metternich took over from here. His people in Maryland would conjugate the Creel-1 to a deactivated polio virus, so they wouldn't have to deliver the antidote directly into the spinal column. No doubt Mila Siponek was handling that just like last year.

Deacon walked into the kitchen and threw his house key into a bowl on the counter. Amy was not around.

"I'm back," he yelled, then chuckled. "Maybe I should have said, "Honey, I'm home.""

"Upstairs," Amy yelled.

Deacon walked toward the stairs. "I sent the Creel-1 off to Joe. Mission accomplished, part one, anyway." He trudged up the steps. "Couldn't test it against the suicide drug, but I suspect Joe will." He backhanded another yawn. "He claims that all the weaponized 606 has been destroyed, but I think he doth protest too much. If I know the government, and I should after all this time, they have some of the nasty suicide drug stashed away somewhere. Maybe at Snyder Labs." He reached the upstairs hall and turned left. "Anyway, it's out of my hands and in Joe's. On to phase two."

A light was on in the bathroom. "How about Chinese tonight? Uncle Sam delivers even out here in the boonies."

Amy was leaning over the sink, putting mascara onto her dark lashes. She was dressed in a short, black skirt, a matching top pulled tightly across her chest. Half boots with heels colloquially known as fuck me.

"We going out?" Deacon asked. Amy didn't answer. "*You* going out?"

Amy put down the mascara brush and picked up lipstick. "Tony is taking me out to dinner."

"Tony?"

"Yeah," she said. "You know, Officer Tony Movello, Dayton PD?"

"Yeah. Got it. I was the one that requested him for security, as I recall. Him and Sergeant Hal." Deacon paused, still trying to take it all in. "He's taking you *out*?"

"Yes, to dinner," Amy said, smacking her lips into a tissue. "I've been stuck in this house for days. I need to get out." She turned to him, her eyes even larger than Linda's of rockstar fame. "You don't *mind*, do you?"

"No. I, um, I just thought we'd order some Chinese and watch a movie. You know, relax together."

Amy smiled. "You relax. You're the one working hard all day. I need to get out and have some fun."

"Well, well …"

"Well, *what*?" Amy snapped, dark eyes flashing.

"Well, what about security?"

Amy furrowed her brow in mock concentration. "I believe that Tony is part of our security detail. After all, you're the one who requested him, as I recall."

He stared at her for another ten seconds before it all clicked in his brain. "Listen, Amy. I'm sorry about last night. I'm sorry we haven't spent much time together the last few days. I've been busy at the lab. But now Creel-1 is done." He placed a hand gently on her shoulder.

She shrugged his hand off. "I can finally have a little fun. And I'm going to. Excuse me." Amy edged past Deacon, headed for the stairs. "Tony is picking me up at seven."

Chapter 8

Deacon poured the last of the bourbon into his glass. He held the bottle upended for a few seconds as the remaining drops plopped over the ice. This third drink killed the bottle.

"Poetic justice," he said to the empty room. "Amy gets the final say again."

He gulped the amber liquid. The fire in his belly felt good, but that wasn't enough to lift his spirits. Not tonight. No, tonight would be a good night to dive into the tank, but not on three drinks. He lifted the empty bottle, inspecting it as if it would magically refill. He scanned the counter they used as a makeshift bar. Empty.

"Not even beer in the fridge," he said, sipping the whiskey.

He started back toward the sofa when the doorbell rang.

"Probably Kalinsky wanting to use the can."

With the nice summer weather, the inside guard moved outdoors, supposedly to give him and Amy privacy.

"So much for that," Deacon said as he unlocked the door. "Come on in, Dan. You know where the head is."

"Well, it's not Dan. But can I come in anyway?"

Terri Tremaine stood in the doorway holding a paper sack. She was dressed in casual clothes—jeans, sneakers, and a summer top. She looked just as good as she did in her business suit, or in a gown and tiara, Deacon thought. Her hair, no longer scrunched back, flowed freely like molten gold.

"Sure, Terri. Sorry." Deacon backed away as she entered. "I thought Dan and Pete had the duty tonight"

"Yes," Terri said. "But I relieved Dan so he could get home to his family." She smiled. "He's based out of the Southern District in Columbus, and Kathy is expecting." She glanced around. "He told me that Ms. Robbins left with Officer Movello." She paused, a look of concern on her face. "Is everything alright?"

Deacon nodded. "Sure. Amy just felt a need to get out. Been cooped up while I've been working. Tony is one of the detail, so we figured it would be alright."

"I guess," Tremaine said, with a sigh. "But you really should have run it past me."

"What's in the bag?"

"Oh," Terri said. "A little peace offering."

"Peace offering?"

"Yes. I think Ms. Robbins, I mean Amy, and I got off on the wrong foot." She reached into the bag and pulled out a bottle of Chivas Regal. "I understand she's a scotch drinker?"

Deacon nodded.

Terri smiled. "Me, too." She glanced about. "Where should I put this?"

"Oh, sorry," Deacon said. "Let me take that." He grabbed the bottle with one hand and the bag with the other. He was expecting the bag to be empty and almost dropped its weight.

"Careful," Terri said. "That's precious cargo."

Deacon tucked the bag into his shoulder and headed to the kitchen. "You bought her two bottles of scotch as a peace offering?"

"No," Terri said, following him into the kitchen. "The other one's for you."

Deacon put the items down, reached into the bag, and pulled out a fifth of Maker's Mark.

"I believe that's your brand?"

"Yeah. How did you know?"

Her sly smile lit the kitchen. "I'm in law enforcement. I have sources."

Deacon eyed the bourbon. Amy held him to three drinks, and his third was almost gone. But Amy wasn't here. She was on a date. He'd worked hard all week on the project she'd begged him to take on. Now she was on a fricking date. He pulled the tab that ran around the waxed cap. "Care to join me?"

"Technically, I'm on duty. But I guess *one* wouldn't hurt." Terri winked and headed back to the living room.

"Want ice in yours?" Deacon called out.

"Yes," Terri said. "But don't drown it."

Deacon reached into the cubes in the bucket on the counter. He snatched up two, shook off the water, and dropped them into a glass.

He did the same for his drink. "Thanks for giving us some privacy." Deacon unscrewed the Chivas and poured in three fingers. "I know the plan was one guard inside and one outside, but there doesn't seem to be much action around here." He poured four fingers of Maker's into his glass while muttering, "Inside or outside."

Terri was sitting on the sofa, her feet curled under her. Deacon noticed her shoes were sitting on the floor. He also noticed that she had perhaps the most perfect ass he'd ever seen, a fact usually reserved for thoughts of his late fiancé.

"No problem," she said, reaching for her glass. "We try to make subjects as comfortable as possible. Give them what they want." She paused, then continued with her killer smile, "If we can."

Deacon sat on the other end of the sofa and sipped his drink. The bourbon slid down his gullet like liquid smoke. He closed his eyes and let it flow.

"Has it helped?" Terri asked.

"Hmm? What?" Deacon opened his eyes.

Her brilliant blues were locked on his. "The privacy? Has it helped ease the …" She twirled her blond hair, eyes skyward in thought. Then she locked eyes with him again. "The tension. Stress." She laughed; it was soft and lyrical. "Whatever it is that's making things difficult between you and Amy."

"Well," Deacon said. "I wouldn't say difficult." He gulped half his drink. "It's just my long hours, I guess. I mean, I think Amy feels a bit lonely and maybe …" He finished his bourbon. "Useless. Ignored. Maybe a little …"

Terri reached over and took his hand. "I know what you mean." She squeezed once, her touch soft and gentle. "It's the same for powerful or important men everywhere. Women find themselves playing second fiddle to their partner's vital work."

She removed her hand. Deacon found he missed the contact.

Terri sipped. "It's hard for them. I've seen it before."

The last was said nonchalantly, but Deacon felt it carried deeper meaning. He lifted his drink, but only ice clunked against his teeth. He raised the glass. "Can I get you another?"

She shook her golden hair and smiled. "I'm good. But please, don't let me stop *you*."

Deacon looked down at the remains of his fourth drink. The lonely ice seemed to be calling to him. A familiar voice in his head cried a warning. "No," he said. "I guess I shouldn't."

Terri shrugged, then sipped. "It's not like you have to drive anywhere. And you've had a long week." She winked. "I should know, I've been watching you." She lifted her glass in salute. "I won't tell if you don't."

Deacon saw her smile. It was just an ordinary smile, just a lifting of the lips, a twinkle in the eyes. Yet, it seemed to say more, to offer more. He wasn't sure what *more* entailed. Maybe another drink would help him understand. "Well, I guess one more wouldn't hurt."

Terri's smile brightened. "I'll fetch the bottle."

"So," he said, when she returned with the bottle. "What got you into federal law enforcement instead of modelling or … That is to say, you are a lot more … well …"

She poured his drink, her eyes on his. "I think the word you're looking for is attractive." She laughed at his fluster. "Yes, of course I know I'm attractive, *very* attractive. Women always know how they look to men, even in this day of curves are beautiful and every girl is a ten in her own mind." She sat closer to him this time, legs tucked, small feet under perfect ass. "Sometimes my looks are a help, sometimes a nuisance." She shrugged. "I try to maximize the help, ignore the nuisance."

"It must be hard," he said. "Hard to ignore in a profession dominated by men." The booze was making him warm, comfortable, and loquacious. It was also making him a little horny.

She sipped, eyes peering over the lip of her glass. "It helps to be good at what you do."

"*Are* you good?"

She smiled. "*Very* good." She licked her perfect lips. "I graduated top of my class at Glencoe. I've received notes of merit for marksmanship, defensive driving, and interrogation." She batted her eyes. "The looks help with interrogation." Deacon watched her throat bob delicately as she took another dainty sip. A slight flush rose on her cheek. "In fact, I am slated for transfer to secret service this fall."

"Promotion?" he asked. He tried not to stare at her, but failed.

She nodded coyly. "Mmm. Presidential detail no less."

Deacon felt his own cheeks flush. He felt heat and stiffness lower down as well. "So, I'd think it safe to say that you are good at many job-related tasks."

That subtle smile again. It was a little thing, just a lift of lips and twinkle of eyes, yet it spoke of everything nice. "Not just job related." She pointed a slender finger. "How about I freshen your drink and we talk about it?"

¢¢¢

Amy sipped beer that tasted as bitter as her mood. The Pier 27 brewpub was brightly lit, with lots of people talking and laughing. Amy wasn't one of them. Bob Seger was playing her favorite song about old-time rock 'n' roll, but she barely heard it. Her mind was otherwise occupied with feelings of anger and shame—the first directed at Deacon, the second herself.

He'd canceled last night when she was all prepared to live out a fantasy with him. Then he waltzed back today expecting her to be at his beck and call. After all that had happened, all they'd been through, he was still treating her more like an assistant, his aide-de-camp. Except that now she was an aide-de-camp with benefits. Maybe that's all she ever meant to him—ever would mean.

Maybe her anger was justified, maybe just residual hurt feelings. But was that an excuse for doing what she was doing now, stringing along a nice guy like Tony just to make Deacon jealous? And why exactly was *she* jealous when there was no evidence that Deacon had ever done anything with Terri Tremaine, or ever would?

All true. All logical. Then why was she still hurt and angry?

"Are you okay?" Tony asked.

"Huh? What? I mean, why do you ask?"

"Well, you've barely said two words since we got here. Or in the car for that matter."

Amy shook her head and managed a smile. "I'm just tired I guess."

"Maybe this wasn't such a good idea." Tony pointed around the room. "Coming *here*. Not exactly a fancy place to take someone who's been cooped up all week." He shrugged. "But it was close, and I figured." He shrugged again.

"It's fine." She laid her hand on his. "I'm not a fancy lady, Tony."

He clutched her hand. "No, I didn't think you were." He smiled. "But you are a pretty one. *Very*."

Amy squeezed his hand in thanks, then released it. She grabbed her beer and drank. It tasted no better but was something to fill the awkward moment.

Tony sipped his own beer, watching her, then waved to someone at the counter. "I think our food is ready. I'll go get it."

Amy shook her head and held up her glass. "This is fine. I'm not very hungry."

Tony's shoulders slumped. Then he straightened up and said, "Just give it a taste. You might surprise yourself. The burgers here are supposed to be the best in town." He smiled.

Amy didn't answer.

"Uncle Sam is paying for it."

Amy smiled back and nodded. No sense ruining his evening, too, she thought.

As he headed to the counter, Amy again felt that shame. For the tenth time, she thought she had made a mistake. This was not like her—none of it. Not the petulance. Not the scheming. Not using one guy to make another jealous—or to punish him. None of it was like Marine Force Specialist Amy Robbins. It wasn't duty, honor, country. And it wasn't the woman Deacon had fallen in love with—even if he didn't know it yet.

She'd need to end this … date. She'd let Tony finish his burger, then ask to head back. There would be no trip to his messy apartment. No good night kiss. No anything.

Tony returned with their platter of food. "Mmmm," he said. "Doesn't that smell good?"

And it did smell good. It smelled heavenly. Amy's stomach grumbled. She hadn't eaten much today, shame butterflies making that impossible. Now that she'd made her decision, come to her senses, she was hungry.

"This is yours," he said, handing her a plate. "Well done."

Bacon and cheese glistened back at Amy from atop the burger grease. Lettuce and tomato sat on the other bun. She grabbed the ketchup bottle from the counter and gave it three good shakes before squirting it on burger and fries. As she bit in, she noted a slightly sweet and flowery aftertaste, but that disappeared amid the heavenly flavor of seasoned meat juices. She looked up at Tony. He was smiling.

"Told ya."

Amy chuckled past the food trying to choke her. She nodded as she swallowed. "Yep, best in town."

¢¢¢

It was after eleven as they walked from the brewpub to the car. Amy felt full, more than a little buzzed, and better. She'd told

Tony that her and Deke were still her and Deke. He'd seemed to take it well, no doubt a cop lothario used to strikeouts as well as home runs. So, instead of any moves, he'd launched into cop stories. She'd laughed for hours as he kept filling up her beer glass. He kept asking if she was okay, if the beer was going to her head. She'd answered yes to both questions. She was glad she wasn't driving.

"So, I told the perp, "How can you explain the fact that we found the dope in *your* pants pocket.""

"What did he say?" Amy asked.

Tony pulled the key fob from his jeans and clicked open the car doors. Then he looked at Amy, his face deadpan. "These are not my pants."

Amy bent in laughter, almost falling over in the unaccustomed three-inch heels. It really was a shame that she was in love with Deacon. Tony was a nice guy who made her laugh.

He patted her on the back. "You feeling okay?"

"Yeah," she said, wiping tears from her eyes.

"You feeling, I don't know, sleepy?"

She furrowed her brow at the odd question. "No. Why should I feel sleepy?"

He shrugged. "Um, I don't know. I just thought, with all that beer, you might want to, maybe … take a nap on the ride back."

"A nap?" Amy giggled. She usually wasn't a giggler, but the beer had taken hold. "No, I'm fine."

He scanned the lot as if he were looking for something or killing time.

"Are *you* alright?" Amy asked.

"Me? Yeah, why?"

"You look a little nervous." She leaned forward and pecked him on the cheek. "In case you were worried about the goodnight kiss."

He smirked, shyly. "No, no, it's not that." He looked at his watch. "It's not too late. Maybe, you want to ..." He shrugged again. "Maybe take a drive or something? Nice night."

"Maybe, park somewhere?" Amy asked. She shook her head. "No. Take me back to Deacon, Romeo." Amy turned toward the car, then stopped. "Shit. I left my purse in the pub."

Tony started to say something when a car illuminated them with its headlights. Amy shielded her eyes, waiting for the car to move past and into the distance. But instead of driving away, it stopped. She heard a door open. The driver got out, his face clearly visible in the reflected dome light.

"You," Amy gasped. It was the last face she expected to see.

The driver said, "Good evening, Ms. Robbins. I'll need you to come with me." He raised his hand, revealing a short, dark pistol, kind of like the one James Bond used to carry. "As for you, Officer Movello, drop your weapon."

Tony withdrew his Glock from its behind-the-back holster and clattered it to the pavement.

The driver then pointed the pistol directly at Tony's head. Amy had seen enough combat to know when someone was intent on killing.

"No," Tony screamed, his hands raised defensively. "No! You promised!"

Chapter 9

It was impossible, Amy thought. She couldn't be seeing who she was seeing. But even in the glare of the headlights, she knew it was him. The smug, ivy-league grin was gone, replaced by a grimace of cold determination. Instead of a tailored, three-piece suit, he wore a polo shirt and chinos. But there was no mistaking Nelson Barzoon.

"No!" Tony repeated, his eyes big as saucers. "You said …"

Amy was shocked, surprised, and still quite drunk. But she was also a combat veteran. As a medic, she'd needed to keep her wits when others about her were losing theirs. And she needed more than a little courage to accomplish that. And from her time on the run with Deacon, she'd learned to tap into the logical part of her mind. To focus on what needed to be done, morality or consequences be damned. To judge the situation for what it was, not for what she hoped it would be. Hope was a great thing, but it could also get you killed.

Tony stood like a deer in the headlights. Amy could tell he was clinging to hope that Barzoon would let him go. She didn't know why the young cop thought this, but she could tell from experience that his hope was no match for bleak reality. Terrorists didn't put down their RPGs or AKs because you hoped they would—they fired.

Amy was moving before the shot rang out, her battle-honed instincts taking over. She launched her one-hundred-thirty pounds headfirst into Barzoon. The rest was a topsy-turvy kaleidoscope of sensory inputs. The flash and roar of the unsuppressed pistol. The sonic whipcrack as a round sang past. The headlamps and overhead kliegs sparkling off a dozen windshields. A high-pitched cry penetrating through the ringing in her ears. The smell of burnt powder. The nauseating pain as her skull connected with Barzoon.

Amy had always imagined Nelson Barzoon to be relatively soft, his body conditioned only by rich food, alcohol, and an occasional game of squash. But this current version of the man was thin and hard.

Pain flared through Amy's neck and shoulders as she drove Barzoon to the pavement then tumbled over him, her body continuing to roll. She barely noticed the darts of pain where the pavement scraped her legs, then scampered to her feet and scooted toward Tony.

The cop was lying on the pavement, black blood oozing from a hole in his right shoulder. She pressed her palm flat against the bleeding wound, then tried to stand Tony up. She needed to get them to the relative safety of the pub before Barzoon was back on his feet.

"Tony," she yelled. "Come on."

The cop moaned groggily and rolled to his side.

Amy tugged on his good arm. "Get up, Tony."

Tony moaned, then rolled again, this time to his wounded side. Pain jerked him into a half-sit. Amy saw her opportunity and yelled, "Up, goddamit." She tugged hard on his arm and they both rose. Amy slammed her palm back over the wound and wrapped her other arm around Tony. "Move it!"

A second pistol shot rang out. Amy felt hot wind as the round whistled through the narrow space between their cheeks. Tony must have felt it, too, because he stumbled forward. With Amy's support, his stumble became a jagged run. The first few steps were slow and hesitant, like participants in a three-legged race learning a rhythm. Then they shot forward.

Someone shouted from the pub. "Hey! What's going on out here?"

Barzoon fired again. Amy cringed as she heard someone scream. The medic in her wanted to stop and help the newly wounded person, but her battle reflexes said that would be a good way to die. So, she and Tony kept moving.

Amy's vision dimmed as they left the glare of Barzoon's headlamps and headed into the shadows cast by parking-lot lights. She held onto Tony and ran toward the neon of the brewpub sign. Another shot rang out, followed by a hollow pop as the bullet broke the sound barrier whizzing past her ear. The lights of the bar no longer seemed safe, so Amy led them darting past the building and into the darkness beyond.

¢¢¢

She supported Tony as they staggered through the halo cast by the single bulb over the pub's back door. She almost fell, but held onto him and kept moving. Cursing the heels and her decision to wear them, she kicked off one and then the other. Going barefoot was easier, if she ignored pebbles and grit digging into her feet. But Tony was slowing, spent adrenaline and loss of blood sapping his strength.

"Don't pass out on me," Amy panted as she tugged him along.

Darkness enveloped them as they crossed an unlit alleyway. In the shadows, she could vaguely make out what seemed to be a hedge with an arbor-like opening. Beyond that was the backyard of a two-story house. No light shone from the windows, but a house meant people and a telephone. So, she tugged Tony toward the arbor.

Inside the narrow bower, it was darker yet. Gossamer filaments snatched at her face as she entered. Amy paused inside the relative shelter of the yard, slapping at sticky spiderwebs and leaving streaks of Tony's blood across her cheeks. Like his, her adrenaline was wearing thin, her beer buzz returning. Her vision spun, so she held out both arms for balance like a tightrope walker. The spinning stopped, but Tony didn't. Without her support, he grunted and dropped to his knees.

Amy dropped beside him. "How you doing, Tony?"

The cop managed a wan smile. "I've been better." His voice sounded weak and far away.

"Don't pass out on me. We're almost there." She pointed to the back porch.

He nodded and tried to stand. He made it halfway, then ended up back on his knees.

"Careful," Amy said. She grabbed his arm; it felt cool and clammy, the pulse fast and thready in his wrist. "Shock," she said. "Need to staunch the bleeding." She looked around for bandage material, but there wasn't any. Amy sighed, crossed her arms, and whipped the sweater over her head. The sudden motion made her vision swim, but she managed to shove the sweater inside Tony's polo shirt and onto the hole in his shoulder.

He moaned as she applied pressure. "Hold that," Amy said, taking his good hand and pressing it against the wound. Tony looked at her. He managed another smile before his eyes went white and he fell onto the grass.

"Shit," Amy said. "He's in shock. He need fluids—and soon."

She kneeled there for a moment, panting. Her neck and shoulders ached from contact with Barzoon. More pain radiated from the scrapes on her palms, legs, and feet. She felt woozy from the fight, flight, and beer. But she was an ex-marine medic and needed to do her job. She closed her eyes and the wooziness improved. She opened her eyes and looked down at her patient.

"You wait here, pal, while I get the calvary."

Amy sprang up and dashed toward the back porch.

¢¢¢

Amy pounded on the back door, the rapping like thunder in her ears. She looked back but saw only Tony and no one else. She errantly wondered what he'd meant talking to Barzoon like an old buddy who'd been double crossed. She didn't like the implications of that, but she didn't have time to worry about it now.

Amy tried the doorknob. Locked. She looked back one more time, then trudged off the porch and around the side of the house.

The cool grass soothed her bare feet, but it didn't do much for the dozen other pains punishing her body or the goosepimples dotting her skin. As she moved into the light of a streetlamp, she realized that she must look a sight, bruised, scraped, and dressed only in miniskirt and bra. Nothing she could do about that now.

The front porch was deserted, as was the street. Amy staggered up two concrete steps onto the porch and pushed the bell. No sound radiated from the house. "Broken doorbell," she muttered. "Perfect." She cupped her hands and peered through the glass. There was no light or movement. Nobody home.

Amy flinched as a light came on behind her. A window in a house across the street glowed yellow. Amy lurched in that direction.

She'd made it only to the curb, hopping and stumbling on bare feet, when she was suddenly bathed in light. Two more steps and she was in the street, headlamps racing toward her. Amy froze, raising her arms protectively in front of her face. The car swerved right and screeched to a halt. The door popped open, and a man staggered out.

Amy's night vision was gone, replaced by a bright afterimage from the headlights. Someone grabbed her. In her mind, she saw the hard, unfeeling face of Nelson Barzoon.

Martial arts training allowed her to break the man's grip and deliver a blow to his neck. But her punch lacked power and unbalanced her. For a moment she seemed to hang suspended, then she tumbled backward. The world blinked like a camera shutter, then flared back just as quickly. The white dots left her vision, and she could see the man's face. Instead of Nelson Barzoon, there was a chubby guy of about forty, with glasses and a crew cut. He was wearing a checked sport jacket over a white shirt. His askew tie had a large grease stain.

"Jee-sus:" he yelled, grabbing his throat where she'd punched him. "Are you nuts? You run out in front of my car, then karate chop me when I try to help? What the …?"

Amy could tell that the man had been drinking. Beer breath from his tirade wafted toward her. She could tell by the look on his face he was scared to death. She could also tell that he finally realized that she was bruised and half-naked.

"Hell?" he finished.

Amy reached out her hand. "Help me up,"

The man complied, although his expression said he was moving on autopilot.

She stumbled against him as he pulled her up. The night had cooled, and Amy found herself huddling against his warmth. After a moment, the guy cleared his throat and pushed her away.

"You got a name?" Amy asked.

"Carl. Carl Sinclair." He looked her up and down. "What the hell happened?"

Amy smiled. "It's complicated." She looked around at the deserted street and thought she saw a curtain move on the house with the lighted window. "How far to the nearest hospital?"

"Maybe twenty or twenty-five minutes."

"Shit," Amy said. "Nothing closer?"

Carl shrugged.

"Come on, anything with a doctor in it."

"There's an urgent care about five minutes away. I think they stay open until midnight."

"What time is it now?" Amy was almost shouting as she grabbed Carl's sleeve. "Well?"

The confused motorist looked at his watch. "Quarter of."

Amy tugged him toward the backyard. "Come with me."

"Where we going? My car is over there." He pointed.

"But my patient is over here."

"Huh?"

Amy pulled Carl after her. "A guy's been shot and you're going to help me carry him."

"Shot?" Carl yelped, pulling back his arm. "Hey, I don't want to get involved with a shooting."

Amy turned back, her teeth ground in grim determination. "You're gonna help me get Tony to a doctor. Or I'm gonna hurt you more than that love tap to the neck. You got that?"

Carl raised his palms in surrender. "Okay." He followed as she walked briskly to the back. "But if I help you, um, can we leave the cops out of it?"

Amy kept walking. "What's the deal, Carl? Unpaid traffic tickets?"

Carl paused, then stammered, "DUI."

Amy shook her head, the world swimming a bit. "I'll try to keep you out of it. On one condition."

"Name it."

"Give me your sports coat, I'm freezing."

¢¢¢

Carl's Kia screeched to a halt outside the Parkview Urgent Care clinic. The lights were on, the place still open. Amy sat in the back with Tony, applying pressure to the wound. The bleeding had slowed, but Tony didn't look good, and he was drifting in and out of consciousness.

"We're here," Carl said. "It's not much. Just a doc, a nurse, and a receptionist."

Amy nodded. "They can put in an IV and treat for shock." She checked Tony's pulse; it was thready. "He's lost a lot of blood, but hopefully the fluids will bring him around." She tapped Tony's cheek. "Hey? Hey?"

The cop's eyes fluttered open.

"We gotta get you inside," Amy said. "Can you walk?"

Tony blinked. His color was pale, his words mushy. "I don't … I think so."

"Carl," Amy yelled. "Give me a hand."

"Where am I?" Tony asked.

"Emergency clinic," Amy said, as Carl opened the back door. "What? Why?"

"*Why?*" Carl said, looking at Amy. "Is he kidding?"

"No," Amy said. "He's in shock. Help me get him out."

Carl shook his head. "How did I get involved in this?"

"Quit your bellyaching," Amy eased the wounded cop out of the back seat. "Look at it this way. How often do you get to be a good Samaritan?"

¢¢¢

Nelson Barzoon sat in his car and watched the emergency clinic. A county cruiser was parked near the entrance, its wigwag lights flashing. Barzoon had heard the call on the police scanner and came right over, hoping to beat the cops here. He hadn't. Not exactly ideal, but beggars as they say. He dry-chewed a Xanax and listened to the drone of an ambulance in the distance. He'd need to act quickly.

It might not be Robbins; the police call didn't say. But whether it was or wasn't, he'd need a cover story, a reason to be snooping around the clinic at 1 a.m.

Barzoon popped another mood elevator and chewed. The pill tasted dry and chalky, like old bones in a sepulcher. The image of a crypt sprang into his head unbidden, something right out of Poe. The picture was cool and comforting. He could almost smell the musty odor of ancient death. The scent brought pleasure and peacefulness.

Barzoon pulled the pistol from his waistband. Its cool solidity brought the same comfort as the image.

In his original plan, Barzoon would have been satisfied with Creel's anguish over Robbins' suicide. He'd claim responsibility for it before killing Creel and then himself. But that was before the little nerd had spoiled Barzoon's play at the hotel. "You thought you'd get the best of me?" Barzoon asked the empty car. He shook his head slowly and smiled at thoughts of his new plan.

Robbins would still die, that was a certainty, as would Creel. But now, Barzoon would drag it out, prolong Creel's agony and his own pleasure. The know-it-all little shit would receive a series of love notes, a video record for his scrap book if you will. Barzoon's smile widened. Perhaps he'd share them on social media with some appropriate emojis. Praying hands. Heart. Peace symbol. Barzoon would top it off with a smiley face.

His mind filled with images. Robbins strapped to a bed, ball gag in her mouth. Her anguished eyes pleading. Muffled cries, barely distinguishable, but their meaning clear. 'Please. Let me die.' Then his mind's eye saw Deacon Creel, tears streaming down his tortured cheeks. How long would Barzoon make him wait?

A few days? A week? Each day adding a little to Creel's heartbreak and Barzoon's pleasure. And when despair was at its apogee, Creel deeply in the bottle, Barzoon would visit him. A mercy killing for Creel, sweet oblivion for Nelson Barzoon.

Sweet oblivion. Barzoon absently raised the gun slowly, his hand moving on its own. The barrel pressed against his temple, cold and reassuring. His finger tightened on the trigger. The sensation was strong, almost orgasmic. Barzoon's face flushed with joy as he added another pound pressure to the trigger. It was so close now. A mere squeeze away. Why wait?

The mental imagery suddenly shifted. Creel was no longer crying, his face drawn out in anguish. The little shit was smiling. That mocking, I know something you don't, shit-eating grin. The smile that said, I'm the winner here, not you.

Barzoon's finger froze. "No," he murmured. "You won't beat me. Not again." Barzoon shouted into the empty car. "You won't beat me again. I'll have my cake and eat a big slice of revenge before I leave." He paused, gun still to his temple. "I'll wipe that grin off your face. And you will know who has won, Deacon my boy. You will know."

Before the imagery faded completely, Barzoon slammed the pistol across his left hand positioned on the steering wheel. Glorious pain flared, extinguishing all thoughts of suicide. Bliss momentarily thrilled him as he looked at the welt forming across his flesh, blood seeping beneath the skin. He held his throbbing hand protectively against his shoulder as he reached across to open the door.

Chapter 10

Amy sat drinking Pepsi. The room was a standard exam room, the outer door leading to reception, the inner one to the treatment area. Amy ached all over, but at least she was warm and somewhat comfortable.

The nurse, Angela, and a young African American doctor named Isabela Sanford were in the treatment room with Tony. That left no one but the receptionist to treat Amy's wounds, so Amy had done it herself; as a medic, it wasn't her first time.

She'd washed her scrapes with iodine soap and applied antibiotic ointment. Gauze bandages covered her knees, shins, and elbows. A pair of the receptionist's socks covered her feet, and a spare smock from the back room covered the rest of her. The receptionist, Gaylene, had called for an ambulance, but it was going to take a while; the local medics were dealing with both a heart attack and a five-car crackup on Interstate 75.

Amy took a swig of sweet caffeine and listened to the voices in the reception area.

"Look," Carl Sinclair said. "I brought them here and already told you I don't know anything."

"I understand," the cop named Perry said. "But I still have to ask you some questions, sir." There was a pause and the rustle of pages. "You said that the woman ran in front of your car. Is that right?"

"Right. She told me that someone had been shot, so we brought him here."

"Back up a minute, sir. About the woman. She ran in *front* of your car?"

Carl didn't answer. No doubt he was nodding.

"Did you hit her with your car?"

"No!"

"How fast were you going?"

"What the hell does that have to do with anything? I stopped. I didn't hit her. In fact, she hit me!"

"She hit *you*?"

"Yeah … wait … it doesn't matter. The point is, I didn't hit *her*, and I brought the wounded guy here. That's all I know. So can I go now?"

"In a minute," the cop said. There was another pause. "Had you been drinking, sir?"

"I didn't hit her! I don't know anything about her or the guy who was shot. So, why don't you ask *him* about it? Or *her?*"

"Please, sir. No need to raise your voice. I *will* ask them when they're done being treated. For now, I'm asking you. Can I see your license and registration, please?"

Amy smiled and whispered, "I said I'd *try* to keep you out of it, Carl."

As Carl and the cop droned on, Amy heard the same front-door chime she'd heard when they'd brought Tony in.

"I'm sorry," the receptionist said. "The clinic is closed."

"The door was open," said a new voice that sounded faintly familiar.

Amy sipped more Pepsi.

"Doctor Sanford is with an emergency. As soon as the ambulance gets here, we're closing. What seems to be the problem?"

There was a pause, then the receptionist said, "Oh my. How did that happen?"

"Caught in a door," the man replied.

Amy cocked her head to one side. She thought she'd heard that voice before but couldn't place it without context. She grunted up from her plastic chair, a thousand aches and twinges reminding her to move slowly. Her beer buzz had worn off and the room hardly even swayed as she walked over and turned the exam room doorknob.

The first thing Amy saw was Carl stepping heel-to-toe while touching his nose with either hand. His eyes were closed. The Centerville cop was standing by his side, ready to catch him if he failed the field sobriety test.

"Maybe the doctor can take an X-ray and give me something for the pain," the familiar voice said. "When she's done with the emergency, that is. What kind of emergency?"

"I'm not at liberty to say, sir," the receptionist replied.

Amy ducked her head into the waiting room. She saw Gaylene behind her desk, but the man had turned away, his face hidden. All Amy could see was grey hair and a red cotton jacket over the collar of a polo shirt. A cold chill traveled from the base of her skull down her back. The man turned toward Gaylene and Amy saw his face. Fortunately, he didn't see Amy.

Carl stopped walking and opened his eyes. "Is that good enough?"

"Fine," Officer Perry said. "Now if you'll just wait here, sir, I'll need to check your license with dispatch."

The cop turned away and walked toward the door, holding Carl's license with one hand and a shoulder mic with the other. Amy heard the door chime again.

Carl watched the cop leave, anxiety written across his face, his Adam's apple bouncing.

"Psst," Amy whispered.

Carl looked around.

"Carl?" Amy called a bit louder,

They made eye contact, then Amy gestured for him to come over.

"There you are," Carl said.

"Shh, Keep your voice down."

Carl lowered his voice. "Will you please tell that cop I had nothing to do with all this?"

"You see that guy?" Amy pointed, keeping her gesture low and within the exam-room doorway.

Carl turned toward reception. "You mean the guy with the hand?" He grimaced. "Ow. That had to hurt."

"He's the one who shot Tony."

"Huh? Who's Tony?"

Amy pulled Carl into the exam room. "The guy who was shot." She shook her head. "Jesus. How many gunshot victims are we talking about?"

"You don't have to get nasty." Carl looked out the door then ducked back inside the exam room. "That guy? He shot this Tommy guy?"

"Tony," Amy corrected.

"Whatever. Then he just happened to hurt his hand and ended up in the same ER?"

"He followed us here. He must have."

Carl pointed. "Come on. Look at his hand. That's not fake." He stared incredulously at her. "Hey, it's been a rough night. I don't know exactly what happened to you, but I think it shook you up enough to start seeing things."

Amy grabbed Carl's arm. "I'm not *that* shook up. It's him."

Carl turned toward the doorway, then turned back. He shrugged. "So, come out and tell that cop when he comes back."

"I can't let Barzoon see me."

"Who?"

"The guy with the hand."

The inner door to the exam room opened. "Ms. Robbins? I'm Doctor Sanford." Sanford was an attractive woman in her late twenties dressed in green scrubs and lab coat. Her dark hair was scrunched into a makeshift ponytail. "I've bandaged your friend's wound and administered fluids and Centhaquine for shock. His BP has stabilized, but we'll need to get him to a hospital as soon as the ambulance arrives. He'll need whole blood and probably surgery. Who dressed your wounds?"

Amy grabbed Sanford by the shoulders. "Is there a backdoor to this place?"

"What?" Sanford asked.

"A backdoor to the parking lot or whatever."

Sanford raised her eyebrows. "Well yeah. To the employee parking area. But …"

"Show me," Amy said, turning Sanford back toward the door she'd just entered.

Sanford let herself be led, too flummoxed to resist.

"Is your car back there?"

"Well, yeah," Sanford replied.

"Keys in it?"

Amy heard a clink as Sanford tapped her lab coat. "In my pocket."

Amy grabbed the knob of the door to the treatment area. "Okay, doc. You, me, and Carl are headed to your car."

"What?" Sanford said loudly, tugging her arm free. "Are you crazy? I have a patient."

"Shh," Amy said, finger to her lips. "Barzoon will hear you."

"Who the hell is Barzoon?" Sanford yelled.

Amy cringed, then hurried toward the waiting room. She poked her head out just as the front-door chime rang.

Barzoon turned at the sound of the chime, his body facing Amy. His eyes flared when he saw her.

Officer Perry came through the front door as Barzoon drew his pistol. "Mr. Sinclair?" Perry said, before seeing the gun in Barzoon's hand. The cop froze, then reached for his service automatic.

Barzoon was faster, pivoting and firing one shot directly into Perry's forehead.

Amy flinched back into the exam room, the smell of burnt powder filling her nose, an afterimage of splattered brains imprinted on her retinas. She vice-gripped Sanford with one hand as she opened the inside door with the other. "Go!"

Dr. Sanford stumbled into the back hall. Amy snatched Carl's arm and shoved him after Sanford just as a second shot rang out. Amy heard a strangled yelp, as if someone else had been shot. "Shit," she muttered, before propelling both Sanford and Carl into the hall.

"Where's that backdoor?" Amy yelled.

Sanford pointed to the end of the corridor. "I can't leave. What about my patient? What about my nurse?"

Amy bulldozed Sanford and Carl toward the back door. "No time. Move!" She shoved her charges through the exit when a third shot rang out, paint and cement exploding from the wall beside her. Amy ducked and rolled through the exit doorway, then slammed the door behind her.

An ice pick rang through Amy's ears from the pistol shot. A thousand needles sang through her body from the roll. She ignored the pain and let her training take over, using her momentum to spring to her feet.

Sanford was already racing for her car. Carl stood like a startled buck.

Amy searched the lot for something to block the back door, otherwise she'd never reach the safety of the car before Barzoon was in the parking lot. In a beat of her heart that seemed an eternity, she spied a dumpster adjacent to the back exit. It was a small waste bin, but still had to weigh several hundred immovable pounds. In the glow of the single bulb over the exit, she could see wheels under it. They had a chance.

"Carl," Amy yelled as she grabbed the dumpster handle. "Give me a hand, goddamit!"

Her shouting broke Carl's stupor and he ran to her side.

"Push," Amy yelled, then threw all her weight against the dumpster. At first, nothing moved. Then Carl added his weight. The dumpster screeched a few inches toward the closed door. "Harder" Amy grunted, her aching muscles straining. The dumpster creaked again and rolled further.

Amy's strength was spent. She didn't know if she could push again. Before she could try, the clinic door sprung open a few inches and clanged into the side of the dumpster. Amy collapsed next to the steel waste bin. Carl helped her to her feet and dragged her across the lot toward the glowing headlights of a red Miata.

Amy felt like an empty shopping bag dancing in the draft of a passing car. She knew there were dozens of new aches and pains awaiting her, but for now she was numb with fatigue. The Miata's headlights flared, blinding her, and then someone tossed her into the front seat. Her head didn't quite make it, thudding against the door jamb. A light bulb popped, then blackness streamed in.

¢¢¢

Barzoon tried the exit door a second time but couldn't open it more than a few inches. Through this gap, he heard the roar of an engine and a man shouting, "Come on." A car door slammed, and the engine noise dopplered away.

Barzoon closed the exit. His last shot was only to distract, hoping to force Robbins down inside the hall. But her reflexes had been deceptively quick. No doubt, marine corps training, he thought with a smile. The smile left his lips as he heard the distant sound of a siren.

He might need to forego his plans, settle for the satisfaction that Creel would feel responsible when Robbins killed herself. For a moment, he envisioned seeing the anguish on Creel's face change to terror as Barzoon fired first into the troublesome scientist's head and then his own. Barzoon raised the gun toward his temple, but a twinge of pain in his injured hand stayed his good one. The siren in the distance grew louder. He lowered the gun, then headed for the front exit.

Chapter 11

Deacon woke to fire bells clanging painfully in his ears. It took him a moment to figure out that the pounding was only in his head, a painful gift from a four-alarm hangover. The early morning light hurt his eyes. Shutting them didn't stop the pain, and the room started to spin. Deacon slowly opened his eyes and lay still. The spinning eased, and the pain slackened. Keeping his head stationary, he scanned the room with his peripheral vision. It was early, the sun still low in the window. He was in the master, lying on the queen-sized bed. What was he doing here instead of in his upstairs room? Finally, bits and pieces from last night popped into his brain.

He turned his head suddenly, ignoring the flare of pain. No one slept next to him. He breathed a sigh, then noticed a small slip of paper on the adjacent pillow. He reached over and opened it. At first, his eyes wouldn't focus. He closed them tight, then opened them again. He read the feminine scrawl.

> *Morning Tiger. I'm still in the afterglow, but duty doesn't pause for such things. Deputy Strayer will take you to the lab in the morning. I'll send you some breakfast around nine. Your stomach should have settled by then. T.T.*

Deacon cringed, rousing butterflies in his hungover gut. "Shit," he muttered, tossing the note into a crumpled ball. And that's how he felt, like a shit.

He slowly slipped his legs over the side of the bed, the world turning topsy turvy for a moment. When reality settled, he rose and staggered to the master bath to relieve his bladder. He barely made it.

Seated on the can, listening to a steady ping on the porcelain, he had time to think. Amy had gone on a date. He didn't know why she did it—anger probably. His transgression was far worse, his reason far less exculpatory. Being drunk was a lame excuse that husbands and boyfriends had used forever. It didn't forgive the dirty deed. In fact, it ramped up his shame.

A bright thought lit his clouded mind. Maybe his slip wasn't terminal. His one hope was that Amy didn't know. If she was angry at his neglect, which was likely, she would have gone right to bed when she came home. She wouldn't have checked out the master bedroom. She may even have arrived after Terri had left. A faint glimmer of Terri's body bobbed through the fog clouding his brain. He didn't know if the memory was real or imaginary, but it stirred him just the same.

"Shit," he muttered, again.

Bladder relieved, Deacon pulled up his shorts and reached to flush the commode. His hand was on the steel handle when he remembered the note. Deacon stumbled into the bedroom and snatched up the crumpled message. As he shuffled back to the bathroom, he ripped the paper into a dozen small pieces that he flushed down the john. Only then did he wash up and get dressed.

He'd leave as stealthily as he could so as not to wake Amy. If he was lucky, she'd never know. He'd have to live with the guilt, but he carried much deeper remorse. A warehouse full.

¢¢¢

Deacon opened the coffee can, then threw down the plastic lid in disgust. Empty. A day when he desperately needed caffeine and … nothing. Why hadn't he asked Pete Strayer to stop at a drive-thru. Probably because he didn't want to acknowledge the deputy's smug grin that said he recognized a hangover when he saw it.

"Morning."

Howard's cheery hello painfully echoed through Deacon's skull. He closed his eyes and held up his palm. "Do you have to shout?"

"Sorry," said Howard Threlkis, the top biochemistry post-doc at UD. Deacon thought the kid's name belonged in a Jerry Lewis movie, maybe "The Nutty Professor Meets Revenge of the Nerds." Howard was tall and gawky, with clothes out of a 1980s thrift store. The only thing missing was tape repairs on his horn-rimmed glasses, but Deacon figured Howie would get around to that eventually. All that was on one side. On the other was a brilliant mind that reminded Deacon a little of his younger self.

Deacon rubbed his temples. "Not your fault."

"I stepped out for some coffee," Howard said, holding up a shopping bag.

"You're a lifesaver," Deacon grunted onto a lab stool. "Add some Tylenol and I'll name my first kid after you."

"I've got some generic ones at my workstation. I'll get them."

"Forget naming," Deacon said. "I'll give you the kid." As Howard scampered over to his computer, Deacon said, "Wait a minute. You stepped *out*?" He looked at his watch. "It's seven thirty in the morning. When did you get here?"

"Six," Howard said, handing Deacon two white caplets.

Deacon grabbed a clean beaker and ran water into it. "You got here at six today?"

"No," Howard said. "Yesterday."

Deacon almost choked on the pills. "You stayed here *all* night?"

Howard shrugged. "I was working on something and didn't want to stop."

"You get *any* sleep?"

"A couple hours," Howard said.

"Any food?"

Howard pointed toward the hall. "Vending machine."

Deacon shook his head. "Commendable, pulling an all-nighter. But not if you're too exhausted to work." Deacon finished the water. The fluid felt good on his empty stomach. "We've got to start synthesizing the monoclonals today."

"I was thinking about that," Howard said, pulling up a lab stool.

Deacon winced at the screech of the stool across the floor tile. "Quietly?"

"Sorry," Howard said. "How long do you think it'll take to isolate a monoclonal against Snyder Labs 606?"

Deacon closed his eyes and rubbed his temples. The pain was starting to become bearable. "Oh, a few weeks and a few dozen dead rats, give or take. A few more weeks for Joe to synthesize it in quantity."

"Right," Howard said. "Wouldn't it be quicker to use an existing monoclonal? Lots of commercial labs produce them. We could have some in a couple of days. Sooner if Dr. Metternich pulled some strings."

"Sure," Deacon said, burping up the chalky taste of acetaminophen. "Joe could probably get it this afternoon. But it'd take forever to test all the possibles for compatibility with SL 606."

"That's exactly what I was thinking," Howard said, hopping off his stool and scuttling over to the printer.

Deacon flinched at the sudden movement. "Slowly. Slowly and quietly are the watchwords today. Okay, Howie?" Howard thrust a printout under Deacon's nose. "What's this?"

"I downloaded the structures of all the chemicals linked to commercially available monoclonal antibodies," Howard said, "and developed a computer algorithm comparing them to the chemical structure of 606. These are the three closest." He tapped the paper. "This one is *really* close. See? Same ring structure. Same number of chlorines. The only difference is this side-chain functional group." He tapped the paper again. "But that shouldn't have much effect on binding affinity."

Deacon admired the kid's enthusiasm, if not his naivete. "Not so fast Einstein. Even if it binds, we don't know if it will stimulate a sufficient immune response. And even if it does that, a vigorous inflammatory response in the brain could lead to encephalitis that would make the cure worse than the disease."

Howard's eyes gleamed. "But if we conjugated something to the monoclonal, a radioisotope or something, we could kill off the impacted brain cells without a vigorous inflammatory response. Couldn't we?"

Deacon took a deep breath, his muddled brain searching for a good rebuttal. After a minute, he couldn't come up with one. "We'd lose some brain cells," Deacon pondered aloud.

"Yeah," Howard said, "but that'll mostly be tissue adjacent to major cerebral arteries. Basal brain functions and thought centers shouldn't be impacted much."

Deacon stared at the paper. Then he looked at Howard. "How old are you, Howie?"

"Twenty-three. Why?"

Deacon smiled. "You just remind me of someone."

"So, what do you think?"

"I think," Deacon said, easing off his stool, "I'll have Joe Metternich dig us up some of this monoclonal ASAP. Who manufactures it?"

Now, Howard smiled. "Snyder Laboratories."

¢¢¢

Deacon spent the morning in the office next to his lab drinking coffee and reviewing Howard's notes. The kid was good, with a level of insight bordering on genius. Deacon would find what he thought might be an error in logic, but that thought would evaporate as Howard explained his reasoning, often citing research papers with which Deacon was unfamiliar. Deacon found himself liking the kid more and more. He also found himself more than a little jealous, more than a little depressed.

Genius. Wunderkind. Those were words used to describe Deacon Creel at twenty-three. Now, the words that best applied were drunk, smart-ass, has-been. He leafed through Howard's notes, hefted them as if their intellectual import had commensurate physical weight. Deacon stared down at Howard's chemical equations and related text. Here was genius, he thought. Here was promise that might be fulfilled instead of being eroded by time and a river of liquor.

All the old insecurities came rushing back, threatening to drown Deacon's soul. And they weren't alone. Amid the flotsam were hunks of guilt, driftwood too small to cling to but big enough to dash a man to pieces within the surging torrent.

In his mind's eye, Deacon saw his mother's pale face atop her bed, her hand holding an empty pill bottle. He blinked the image away, only to have it morph into the face of his longtime friend and colleague, Lisa Reilly, her wisecracking grin replaced by a slack-jawed stare and splattered brains. His gut tightened further as Lisa became his fiancé, Liz, her hand bobbing in a pool of pink, her dark eyes blankly gazing into eternity. Liz's dark eyes became Amy's, the woman who loved him and whom he'd cheated on last night.

Someone behind him cleared her throat. "Excuse me."

Deacon wiped away tears and turned. "Speak of the devil," he whispered.

"Pardon?" Terri Tremaine said. She was now dressed in a business-like blue blazer, which somehow accentuated her beauty rather than hid it. She was washed and freshly made up.

Deacon shook his head and tried to smile. "Where's that breakfast you promised me?" He looked at the clock. "It's after ten."

"Sorry," Tremaine said.

More thoughts bobbed into Deacon's consciousness. Bourbon-soaked images that were part memory, part dream. Deacon's foggy brain had difficulty separating the two, making him wonder what exactly had happened last night. He was sure only that he'd found Tremaine highly desirable—and still did. That he'd wanted her. That they'd drank together, flirted together. The rest was hidden behind an alcoholic haze, a curtain that couldn't hide the remorse he felt. With remorse came guilt. Deacon longed for a drink.

"Something has come up," Tremaine said. Her voice was steady, but there was concern written across her beautiful face. Was she guilt-ridden too, Deacon wondered?

Tremaine cleared her throat again. "Have you heard from Ms. Robbins today?"

Deacon tried not to let his inner guilt show on his face. "No. Why?"

"She hasn't called?"

"No," Deacon answered, concern edging its way past his guilt. "What's going on?"

Tremaine didn't answer immediately. Deacon rose from his chair. "What's going on? Tell me."

Tremaine held up a palm. "We don't know yet. Not everything."

Deacon dashed around the desk and grabbed Tremaine by the shoulders. "Has something happened? Has someone attacked the safe house?"

Tremaine flinched as his fingers pinioned her flesh, then she effortlessly twisted free of his grip. "No. No one has attacked the safe house."

Deacon breathed a sigh.

"But Ms. Robbins isn't there."

"What do you mean she isn't there?"

"She never came back last night."

"What?" Deacon found himself screaming. "What do you mean? She was there this morning. I ..." Deacon suddenly realized that he'd assumed she was asleep when he left but that he hadn't seen her.

"She hadn't come back by 0400 hours, which was, um." Tremaine cleared her throat a third time. "Which was when I was relieved. I asked Strayer out front if he'd seen her."

"And?"

Tremaine shook her head.

Deacon was shouting again. "Why didn't somebody check on her?"

Tremaine held both palms up defensively. "She was with Movello, so she had security present. And, well, she was on a date." Tremaine's eyes studied her shoes. "We had to consider the possibility that it had turned into a sleepover somewhere."

Deacon stared blankly at the wall past Tremaine's head. The thought had never occurred to him. "Had it?"

Tremaine shook her head.

Deacon let out a long breath.

"But something *did* happen." She swallowed hard. "There was a shooting. She and Movello may have been involved."

"Shooting?" Deacon repeated. "Where?"

"Outside a restaurant called the Pier 27 Brewpub. Centerville PD called it in."

Deacon felt cold, detached. As if someone else was talking but he only heard the words through a bad speaker. "What about Amy? Is she okay?"

"We don't know. A woman matching her description was seen at the bar. ID in the purse she left behind confirms it was Robbins, but she was not found in the bar or at the scene outside."

Deacon felt himself floating. It was a familiar feeling he'd experienced before. When he'd found his mom. When he'd found Liz. When the antidote he'd been developing, Creel-1, mysteriously failed in front of Joe Metternich. That out-of-body feeling that presaged violence or collapse.

"Who?" Deacon heard only a whisper.

"We don't know," Tremaine said. "The shooter wasn't seen, not clearly. He drove off in a dark, late-model Ford. Possibly a rental."

"Where?' Deacon swallowed glue. "Where's…" That's the last thing he remembered before the walls closed in on him.

Chapter 12

Deacon awoke to the familiar urging of smelling salts. He shoved the hand holding the capsule away and sat up. He was still on the floor, his head propped against the wall. Howard Threlkis was smiling down at him. Deacon flinched as something cold and wet was laid upon his forehead. Instinctively, he grasped the arm of the person doing the laying. The flesh was smooth as satin, but with an inner toughness. He looked up at the serious face of Terri Tremaine.

"How long was I out?" Deacon asked.

"Less than a minute," Tremaine answered.

"What happened?" Howard asked. "Did you faint?"

Deacon scowled at him. "Yes, I fainted, Howie. Help me up."

"Careful," Tremaine said, as Deacon rose. "You okay now?"

Deacon nodded. He glared at Tremaine and asked the question he was unable to ask a moment ago. "Where is Amy?"

"We don't know," Tremaine said, tossing away the wet paper towels she'd laid on Deacon's brow. "She hasn't been found." She raised a hand as Deacon started to protest. "We have *one* lead. When the police canvassed the neighborhood around the pub, they talked to a woman who may have seen something."

Tremaine took a notebook from her blazer. "One Eleanor Forgeron of 1312 Clark Street heard a car screech to a halt outside her house. She looked out and saw two people talking by a car skewed in the road. One looked like her neighbor, the other was a …" Tremaine quoted from her pad. "A scantily clad lady of the evening." Tremaine smiled as she read. "She then put the kettle on to make a pot of tea. When she looked back outside, the car was speeding away." Tremaine looked up from her pad. "Forgeron didn't think much about it at the time. It seems that her neighbor is a bit of a carouser, out to all hours, weaving home drunk many nights."

"Her neighbor have a name?" Deacon asked.

"Ms. Forgeron didn't know that." Tremaine smiled again. "I assume that she is the neighborhood snoop, although she would probably deem herself a concerned citizen. Doesn't know names but knows everybody's business." She glanced back at the notebook. "Search of tax records said the neighbor's house belongs to one Carl Sinclair, age forty-six." Tremaine showed Deacon a grainy driver's license photo.

"Anyway, what *was* unusual was that Sinclair was speeding *away* from his house rather than toward it. And that his car was skewed across the road when Forgeron saw him talking to the supposed hooker." Her startling blue eyes left the notebook and gazed at Deacon.

"Hit and run?" Deacon asked.

"Could be. No body was found by the investigating officers, so it might be that Mr. Sinclair was rushing someone to the hospital."

"Anything at the hospitals?"

"I called the county sheriff at nine. Asked them to check."

"At nine?" Deacon shouted. "a.m.? Why the hell didn't you do that last night?"

Tremaine backed up, one hand on Deacon's chest, fending him out of her personal space. "We didn't even get a chance to talk to Forgeron until eight a.m. Then we had to get the tax records to ID Sinclair. Investigations take time. You should know that."

Deacon raised both hands and backed off as another blue-blazered marshal called over from the doorway. "Terri?"

Tremaine waved over her shoulder but kept looking at Deacon. "Take it easy," she said, then walked over to the other marshal.

"You okay?" Howard asked. He was talking to Deacon, but his eyes followed Tremaine's butt.

Deacon nodded, although he really wasn't okay. He was awash in worry and guilt, a new guilt to add to his growing list. If he hadn't neglected Amy, she wouldn't have gone out with Tony. If he had insisted on more security, maybe Amy and Officer Tony would be okay instead of missing or … A cold chill shuddered through him. If he hadn't been a drunken cheater, maybe he would have known that Amy didn't come back last night. Maybe he could have gone out looking for her. A lot of maybes. But there was no maybe about his guilt. That was real.

Tremaine hurried back. "There has been an incident at Parkview Urgent Care. Seems a guy brought in a young woman that fit Ms. Robbins description around midnight."

"Amy," Deacon gasped.

Tremaine raised her hand. "The woman was only dinged up. But there was another guy who'd been shot."

"Officer Tony?"

"Yep. According to his ID." She checked her pad. "They didn't get the name of the guy who brought them in. Then, apparently, shots were fired. There were some fatalities."

Deacon clutched Tremaine's shoulders. "Is Amy alright?"

"Hey!" Tremaine broke Deacon's hold with the effortlessness of someone trained in self-defense. "We don't know. Okay? We don't even know for sure if the woman was Amy. The only witness besides Movello was the receptionist, and she'd been shot. So, as you can imagine, things are a little sketchy."

Deacon paced as he shouted. "Why are we just hearing about this now?"

Tremaine raised a restraining palm. "Local cops were handling it. They didn't know they were supposed to notify the U.S. Marshals."

Deacon stopped pacing and closed his eyes. His heart raced. His face flushed. The world felt tight and small again. But he had no time for a panic attack or any other dramatics.

"I'm heading over there now," Tremaine said.

"I am too," Deacon said.

"Negative. This is *my* job. Yours is here."

"I'm going." The tone in Deacon's voice brooked no argument.

Tremaine shrugged and walked out.

"Um. What should *I* do?" Howard asked, eyes still on Tremaine's butt.

At least the kid's a red-blooded American boy, Deacon thought as he wrote on a pad. "When the monoclonal antibody comes in, run it through a couple of rats. If they live, start the conjugation with the radioisotope." He ripped the paper from the pad. "Here's Joe Metternich's number."

"Maryland area code?"

Deacon nodded. "He's tending to a family matter, but is available day or night. Tell him I'm putting you in charge. He should get you whatever you need."

"*Me?*" Howard said, finally looking at Deacon. "But, but …"

"You can do it, Howie. Keep plugging." Deacon shoved the paper behind Howard's pocket protector.

"But I'll need help."

"Get that other postdoc, Dion whatshisname."

"Leon," Howard said.

"Right," Deacon said, pouring a coffee for the road. "Get Leon."

"How will I know what *you* want done?"

Deacon patted the kid's shoulder. "Don't worry about me, Howie. Use your best judgment. You're a postdoc, which means you already did a dissertation. This is just another project."

Deacon was out the door before Howard could say anything more.

Chapter 13

Yellow tape was stretched across the entrance to Parkview Urgent Care. A Centerville PD cruiser and a plain brown Ford were parked in the lot, along with a CSI van and a hearse with County Morgue lettered on the side. A man in a tan sports coat was talking to a uniform; he glanced over at Tremaine's SUV as they pulled into the lot.

The uniformed cop ran over to the SUV and tapped the window. Tremaine hummed it down.

"Sorry, ma'am," the cop said. "This is a crime scene. The clinic is closed."

Tremaine flashed her credentials and said, "U.S. Marshals." The plainclothes detective must have heard because he walked over.

"It's okay, Jackson," the detective said, then peeked in the window. "You Tremaine?"

"Terri," Tremaine said.

The detective gave her the once over, barely bothering to hide a lascivious grin. "Detective Monty Pittman, Centerville PD."

Deacon got out of the shotgun seat as Tremaine exited the driver's side. She adjusted her blazer, shaking her golden hair over the collar.

Pittman eyed her again and pursed his lips as if he was going to wolf whistle. Instead, he shook his head and pointed to where a morgue attendant was wheeling out a blanket-covered body. "Meat wagon has started taking out the bodies." A lab tech walked out of the clinic with a silver case about the size of a tackle box. "CSI has already dusted for prints and checked for trace."

"And?" Tremaine asked.

Pittman shrugged. "Found lots of prints, as you'd expect from a clinic that sees lots of patients. It'll take some time to sort those out from those of the victims."

Deacon blanched. "How many victims?"

Pittman looked at Deacon, eyebrows raised.

"It's okay," Tremaine said. "That's Doctor Creel. He's with me."

Pittman nodded. "Three. Two women and a guy." He pulled a pad from his jacket. "The guy was one of ours, a Centerville cop named Perry."

"The women?" Deacon asked, holding his breath.

Pittman flipped pages. "Both clinic employees. The receptionist, Gaylene Smith, and the nurse, one Angela Perez. Smith lived long enough to give some details to the officers responding."

Deacon exhaled in relief. Two more had died, but neither was Amy.

"The weapon was a small-caliber handgun," Pittman said. "Judging by the slug they dug out of the wall, possibly a 0.380 or nine-by-eighteen Makarov." He flipped the notebook closed and looked hard at Tremaine. "So, you want to tell me why the U.S. Marshals are interested?"

Tremaine smiled. Deacon thought that one of her smiles would satisfy most male curiosity.

"What about the doctor on duty?" Tremaine asked.

"Gone," Pittman said. He flipped open his pad again. "Dr. Isabela Sanford, aged twenty-nine."

"You talked to her?" Tremaine asked.

Pittman shook his head. "Found ID in the purse she left behind."

"She was supposedly treating two patients," Deacon said. "A man and a woman. What happened to them?"

Pittman pointed. "The guy is at Miami South." He looked at his pad. "Dayton cop named Antonio Movello."

Deacon grabbed his arm. "What about the woman? She was with Movello."

Pittman stared at Deacon until he released the sleeve of his sport coat. "No other woman was found, but we can probably ask Movello at the hospital—if he's conscious." Pittman turned his attention to Tremaine. "Does this have anything to do with the shooting at the brewpub last night?"

Tremaine answered his question with a question. "Why do you ask?"

Pittman shrugged. "Quiet town like Centerville gets a parking-lot shooting and then *this*." He pointed to the clinic. "I just figure … two plus two, ya know?"

Tremaine granted him another smile. "Let's go see Movello."

¢¢¢

Deacon, Tremaine, and Pittman stood outside Room 226 talking with Dr. Slovak, the attending resident.

"Movello should be alright," Slovak said. "The bullet severed a minor artery but otherwise didn't hit anything vital; it didn't even enter the joint. His biggest risk was shock from blood loss, but the fluids they pumped in at Urgent Care stabilized him. We've given him whole blood and tied off the vessel when we removed the bullet." He smiled. "Lucky guy."

"Can we talk to him?" Tremaine asked.

Slovak nodded. "I guess so. He's a little dopey but conscious." Slovak raised a cautionary hand. "Just don't stay too long."

As Dr. Slovak walked away, the trio turned toward the hospital room. Before they'd made it inside, Pittman placed a hand on Tremaine's shoulder. "It's my case, so why don't we let me ask the questions? Okay, deputy?"

Tremaine gave forth a patented smile. "Whatever you say, detective."

Tony Movello lay in a standard hospital bed separated from a similar, unoccupied bed by a curtain. An IV dripped into his arm and the edge of a bandage was visible under his hospital johnny. His eyes were closed when they entered.

Pittman cleared his throat. "Officer Movello?"

Tony opened his eyes.

"I'm Detective Pittman." He pointed over his shoulder. "I think you already know Marshal Tremaine and Doctor Creel. We'd like to ask you a few questions. If you feel up to it."

Pittman pulled out his notepad as Tony nodded.

"Did you see the man who killed the clinic staff?" Tremaine asked.

Pittman's eyes shot daggers at her. "What happened to 'I ask the questions?'"

"You got the first two," Tremaine said, still smiling at Movello. "Did you see him, Tony?"

Tony Movello shook his head. He swallowed hard. "I must have been out of it. I just remember coming to and smelling burnt powder. Then …" He pointed to the bedside table. "Can I have a sip of water?"

Deacon held out the plastic cup with a straw in it.

Movello slurped then nodded for Deacon to put it back. "Um, what were we talking about?"

"The shooting at the clinic," Pittman said before Tremaine could interrupt. "What do you remember about what happened? Anything you can remember. What the guy looked like? Anything you heard? Any other smells? Anything."

With his good hand, Movello rubbed eyes that looked tired, the pupils dilated. "Not much. I remember getting out of a car." He held up one finger. "Being *pulled* from the car. A lot of pain. A bright light when we got inside the clinic. Then …" He shrugged, grimacing in pain despite the meds. "Then waking up to the smell of burnt powder."

"How about at the brewpub?" Tremaine asked. Pittman shot her more daggers, but she continued. "Did you see the guy who shot you?"

Movello's brow furrowed in concentration. "Yeah. I think so."

"What did *he* look like?" Pittman asked.

More brow furrows. "Thin. Middle-aged." He touched his temple. "Grey here."

"Was it the same guy at the hotel room? The one who brought the dinner when you and Hal Lipsitz were on duty?"

"Who is Hal Lipshitz?" Pittman asked. "And do you mind if I ask the questions, Doctor?"

Deacon ignored the outburst. "Was it the same man, Tony?"

Movello sighed. "It might have been. I can't remember much except the glare of the lights and looking down the barrel of his automatic."

Deacon lowered his voice and leaned closer. "What about Amy? What happened to her?"

"Maybe *I* should just wait outside," Pittman grumbled.

Movello swallowed again. "I don't know. I was with her coming out of the pub. And she was in the car on the way to the clinic—I think. After that, it gets all …" He shook his head.

A nurse came in with pills in a plastic cup. She smiled at Movello. "Here are your antibiotics, officer." She handed him the cup, then grabbed the water glass. As he sipped, she turned to Pittman. "You should leave now. Let him get some rest."

Pittman nodded. "Not getting much anyway." He looked around. "*Any* of us."

Tremaine tapped his arm as he turned to leave. "Better post a cop outside this room."

Pittman looked her up and down and nodded. "Then how about I buy you two a cup of coffee and you tell me what the hell is going on here?"

Deacon met Tremaine's eyes, then turned to leave. Movello motioned him over.

"Can you let me know what you find out about Amy?" Movello whispered. "I'm worried about her." He cleared his throat. "And I feel kind of responsible."

Deacon patted his arm and winked.

¢¢¢

Amy snuggled into Deacon's chest. It was warm and safe. He smelled of sweet sweat and a hint of soap. She sighed. Deacon cleared his throat.

"Um, miss?"

Amy woke and opened her eyes. It took a moment to take in her surroundings. She wasn't snuggling in bed. She was slumped inside a small car with no back seat. A Black woman stared intently at the road, concern and stress written on her face. Amy sat upon the lap of a man who was not Deacon Creel.

"You two want to be alone?" the Black woman asked.

Amy squirmed away from the man holding her, pain singing through the bump on her head. A thousand other aches and pains joined the chorus. "Where am I?"

"You're in my car headed toward the nearest police station. And you're lucky to be alive. We all are."

Disjointed memories struggled back into Amy's brain. "Dr. Sanford?"

"Guilty as charged," Sanford replied.

Amy turned to the man under her butt. "Carl? Right?"

"Now that we've established who everybody is," Sanford said, "who the hell are you? And why did that guy start shooting?"

"Barzoon," Amy said.

"Barzoon again," Carl said. "Who is this Barzoon guy?"

Amy watched Sanford wipe tears from her eyes. "And why was he shooting up my clinic?"

"It's complicated," Amy said. She shifted position on Carl's lap, more pain spun her head.

"You're going to have to tell it to the cops," Sanford said.

"Cops?" Amy yelped. "No. We can't go to the cops. Not yet. Stop the car."

Sanford stared at her. "Are you kidding? I'm not gonna …"

"Stop the car!"

Sanford hit the brakes and swung into a driveway. Amy saw stars at the sudden stop. When her vision cleared, she saw that they were in the parking lot of the Do Hop In diner. The lot was deserted, the place closed.

Neon flashed over the tears streaming Sanford's face. "We're stopped," she yelled. "Alright? Now why the hell can't we go to the cops?"

Amy felt faint and a bit nauseous. She wiped cold sweat from her forehead. "We can't because that may be how he found me last time."

"Barzoon?" Carl asked.

"Who the hell *is* Barzoon?" Sanford screamed.

Amy held up a hand to stop the shouting that knifed her skull. "The guy who did the shooting. That may be how he found me. At least I can't think of any other way. It was something Tony said just before Barzoon shot him. I can't remember exactly what." She turned to Sanford. "I just remember thinking Tony could be in on it. Maybe other cops."

"In on *what*?" Sanford shouted.

More pain speared Amy's brain. "I can't explain." The dizziness and nausea intensified. Amy gulped. "We just … I mean …" The neon flashed topsy turvy. "I need to lie down."

"We can go to my house," Carl said.

Amy tried to shake her head, but the dizziness wouldn't let her. "Can't. Too near the pub. Barzoon might have seen. Followed us." Complete sentences were becoming difficult. "Need to get safe house." The world went dark again.

Chapter 14

Deacon sat in a metal folding chair, sipping coffee strong enough to eat through the paper cup. He'd seen his share of police stations, squad rooms, and drunk tanks. Pittman's office was a combination of all three. There were several scuffed, grey-metal desks arrayed around a holding cell. Pittman's desk was against the far wall, its distance from the cage no doubt a sign of seniority. Several lockers sat next to a corkboard holding a pinned array of wanted posters, administrative memos, and procedural minutia. On another wall, a sign said smoking was prohibited, but this didn't remove the stagnant odor of tobacco or the residue of despair covering the walls like an overdue coat of paint.

Deacon wondered how many parents, wives, or husbands sat in this very chair desperately seeking hopeful news. He felt their anguish. Every minute they wasted here was a minute Amy might be dying—if she wasn't already dead.

"When you said you'd buy us coffee," Tremaine said, "I imagined a diner or Dunkin' Donuts." She waved about the room. "Not this."

Pittman creaked into an old desk chair but didn't answer. Instead, he swigged coffee from a chipped Star Trek mug and stared at her. "And I didn't expect two shooting incidents and a triple homicide, including a cop." He smiled grimly. "So, we all have our disappointments." His chair groaned as he leaned back. "You wanna tell me why?"

Tremaine crossed her legs. "I can only say that Dr. Creel is part of a confidential government research project." She pointed to Deacon. "And that the Marshal's service is providing security."

Pittman frowned. "Research project?" He looked at Deacon. "Just where is this research taking place?"

Deacon looked at Tremaine, who nodded. "University of Dayton," he said. "Listen, detective, we're wasting time."

Pittman raised his brows. "This is southern Ohio, not Bethesda. What kind of hush-hush government research with U.S. Marshal security goes on at UD?"

"I'm not at liberty to discuss it," Deacon said. "But you need to listen to me."

Pittman laughed. "Not at liberty. A pretty standard bullshit answer." He sat forward. "How is this Robbins woman involved in this project?"

"She's not," Deacon said. "She's my …" He almost said girlfriend. "My assistant."

"And the guy who's doing all the shooting? What's his involvement?"

"We're not sure who's doing the shooting," Tremaine said. "That's one of the reasons we need to find Ms. Robbins."

"You guys are a mountain of information, aren't you?" Pittman finished his coffee. "Looks like I'm wasting my time."

"No," Deacon shouted. "You're wasting *mine*. Amy is in danger. Maybe already killed or captured. I need for you to do *something*."

"And I need information that you won't give me," Pittman said, rising from his chair. He counted fingers into his open palm. "I've got three dead, including a cop, and a couple more injured. I've got a shooter nobody knows from Adam. I've got a scientist and a deputy marshal won't tell me jack. Anything I left out?" He shook his head and laughed. "And my only clue is the word barroom."

Deacon sat up straight, a shiver running down his spine. Maybe it was the way the detective said it, with accent on the room. Maybe it was a memory of Judge Webster scrambling a certain name in night court last year. Maybe it was a coincidence. But Deacon's spider senses didn't think so. "What?"

Pittman looked at him and nodded. "Yep. Receptionist was shot in the chest. She died on the way to the hospital. Her dying word was something like 'barroom.' So, you can see…"

Deacon cut him off. "Something *like*? What did she say exactly?"

Pittman grunted at the request, then pulled his notepad out and flipped pages. "Cop who arrived with the ambulance asked, 'Who shot you?' Receptionist replied with what sounded like …" He squinted at his own handwriting. "Sorry. *Barzoon*, not barroom. And that makes even less sense."

Deacon felt cold and hollow, blood running from his head and out his feet. He remembered Officer Tony's description. Middle aged. Grey hair. Narrow nose. "No," Deacon muttered. "It can't be. It's impossible."

"What?" Pittman asked. "You know what Barzoon is?"

Deacon nodded. "Not what. Who."

"Okay," Pittman said. "I'll bite. *Who* is Barzoon?"

Deacon met his gaze. "A dead man."

"What?"

Deacon turned to Tremaine. "I'll need you to track down a photo for me."

Tremaine looked at Pittman, then back at Deacon. "Photo of who?"

"Someone who officially no longer exists."

¢¢¢

Deacon nodded to the cop on duty, then showed the credentials Metternich had given him. The cop studied the ID, then waved to the hospital room door. Deacon thanked him and knocked. There was no answer. He waited, then raised his hand to knock again when a voice from within croaked, "Yeah?"

Tony Movello was leaning into a pillow, his hair askew, his eyes ringed with the droopy red common to drunks and druggies.

"How's it going, Officer Tony?"

"Hey, Dr. Creel."

Deacon smiled and said, "Deke."

Tony nodded, a twinge of pain passing over his features. "Right." He gestured with his good arm. "Have a seat, Deke. Almost time for dinner. Can I order you something? Coffee? Tapioca?"

Deacon laughed. "I've had hospital food, so I'll pass."

Tony smiled, tiredly. "What can I do you for?"

Deacon sat in the chair beside the bed. "Just came by to check on you. See how you're doing."

Tony shrugged his left shoulder. "As well as can be expected, as they say. Doctors tell me I can go home the end of the week, if there's no more bleeding."

"Glad to hear it," Deacon said.

Tony swallowed hard and his face drooped. "Sorry again about what happened to Amy. I mean, I hope nothing did but …" He wiped his eyes. "I just keep thinking I should have done something."

Deacon reached over and patted his leg. "You got shot, Tony. You took a bullet meant for Amy. You don't have anything to apologize for."

Tony gripped Deacon's hand. "Thanks. Still, you know how it is."

Deacon nodded. He did indeed. He and guilt were old friends, or maybe that was enemies.

"Let me know if there's anything I can do," Tony said.

Deacon raised a finger. "There is something."

"Name it."

Deacon reached into his back pocket and pulled out a folded piece of paper. "Tell me if you recognize this man." He held out the photostatic image.

Tony studied the picture for a second, then his rheumy eyes brightened. "That's the guy." He paused. "I *think*." Tony placed the photo on his knee and tapped it. "The guy in this picture is heavier and the expression is, well?" He searched for the right words. "The guy I saw looked less confident, numb, almost spaced out."

"But that's the man who shot you?" Deacon asked.

Tony nodded. "I think so. Who is it?"

Deacon refolded the paper. "A man named Nelson Barzoon. A former government big shot." Deacon smirked. "Although he's now persona non grata. In fact, he isn't supposed to be alive. It took pulling strings to even get that photo."

"I don't get it," Tony said.

"Me, either." Deacon returned the paper to his pocket. "But I may be beginning to."

"Huh?"

Deacon shook his head.

There was a light rap on the door. Before Tony could answer, it opened. A cute, slightly pudgy woman in her mid-twenties came in smiling. In her hand, she clutched the fingers of a child of maybe three. "Look who came to see daddy." She paused when she saw Deacon. "Oh, I'm sorry. I didn't know you had company."

Tony cleared his throat. "That's okay, babe." He pointed. "This is Deke Creel." He pointed again. "My wife, Vanessa, and my boy, Chip."

"Pleased to meet cha," the woman said. Deacon stood and shook her hand. Then he turned back to stare at Tony.

The cop met his gaze for a moment, then blushed and looked down.

"Yeah," Deacon said. "I guess I'm beginning to understand a lot of things.

¢¢¢

Amy woke in somebody's bedroom, dressed only in bra, panties, and a summer coverlet. She guessed it was a woman's room, although it lacked frills or obviously feminine accouterments. It reminded her of her barracks room in Iraq, neat and clean, with a few homey touches. She blinked against rays of summer sunshine, then raised a hand to shade her eyes. This little effort hurt her head, her arm, and her shoulders. But the pain was more annoying than intense; it was nothing like yesterday. Her headache throttled back almost immediately.

"Good morning."

Amy looked toward the window. The doctor from last night had parted the blinds to look outside. Amy searched for her name.

"Morning, Dr … Sanford." Amy's throat hurt. There was a bottle of water on the nightstand. She took a swig and looked about the room. "Where am I? What time is it?"

Sanford sipped from a coffee mug as she looked out the window. She no longer wore a lab coat but was still in the scrubs from last night. "In answer to your first question, my house. In answer to your second, almost noon."

"You shouldn't have let me sleep so long."

"Technically, you were passed out. You may have had a concussion."

Amy put the water bottle down. Bits and pieces of last night swam into place. The emergency clinic. Barzoon. Gunfire. Racing off in Sanford's car. "I'm surprised you brought me here. As I recall, you wanted to call the cops or take me to the hospital."

Sanford dropped the blinds and turned to Amy. The MD's face was haggard, bags under her eyes. She chuckled mirthlessly. "With what you *told* me? With what *happened* at the clinic? I was afraid to even bring you here." She shrugged and sipped coffee. "Your vitals were strong. Pupillary reflexes normal. You didn't appear to have a fractured skull or a brain bleed, so …" Sanford shrugged again.

"Did *you* get any sleep?"

Sanford's chuckle became a laugh. "With what happened last night, with what you were ranting about? I spent the night staring out the window expecting foreign spies or a gang of ninjas to swarm the place."

A thought struck Amy. "Where is Carl?"

Sanford gestured with her mug. "The guest bedroom." She walked over and put her mug beside the water bottle. "Let me see how you're doing." Sanford pulled a penlight from her pocket and checked in Amy's eyes. She then felt Amy's pulse.

Amy smiled. "Will I live?"

"Yes," Sanford said, pocketing the penlight. "But from what you were raving about, I'm wondering if I will." She rose from the bed and retrieved her cup. "So, what now? We go to this safe house you mentioned?"

Amy couldn't remember talking about the safe house. She shook her head, pain flaring then strobing back. "No. Barzoon might have had it staked out."

"Barzoon again," Sanford said. "How about this Deke guy you mentioned?"

Amy couldn't recall mentioning Deacon.

"You talked in your sleep," Sanford said in answer to Amy's puzzled expression. "From what I could gather, he's a combination of Einstein and Sir Galahad."

Amy smiled again. "With maybe a little Jim Beam thrown in."

"Do we call him?"

"Maybe," Amy said. "If I could remember his number. The cell they gave him is on my phone, but unfortunately my phone is in my purse and my purse is at the brewpub."

"So, if he's out, and the cops are out?"

Amy thought for a moment, then snapped her fingers. "U.S. Marshals."

"We call Wyatt Earp?"

Amy picked up the bedside landline. "The marshals were providing security for us. The head honcho was a bitch named Tremaine." Amy held her hand over the phone's push buttons, but her mind blanked. "How do you call information?"

Sanford walked over and grabbed the handset. "Here, let me."

Amy heard three beeps. "Ask for deputy Terri Tremaine. Tell them it's Amy Robbins calling."

"So that's your name." Sanford shook her head. "And I just know it spells trouble."

Chapter 15

Deacon walked down the hall from Tony's hospital room, the muffled coos from the cop's wife and son fading. Maybe Tony took Amy out as a kind gesture. He saw she was cooped up and figured she'd enjoy an evening's fun. It was possible, Deacon thought. But if that was true, it contradicted everything Deacon had ever known about guys, including himself. In his experience, that level of male altruism was a myth akin to the Easter bunny or sewer gators, especially when the young gal in question was single and looked like Amy. And guys that nice wore their wedding rings. No, Deacon thought, good-looking Tony was a hound with a nose for snuggling not smuggling. So? So, maybe nothing. He wouldn't be the first married guy in search of comely tail. Truth be told, Deacon himself had bedded a couple married women back in his drinking days. Days he wasn't sure had ended. So?

Deacon still didn't like it. It spoke to loyalty and honesty, the kind you expected from someone trusted to guard you and (especially) your loved ones. And yes, Deacon had to admit that Amy now fell into the latter category. The thought that she might be dead tightened the knot in his throat.

Deacon also worried about the fact that Tony had fooled him. Through his years of government and military service, Deacon had thought himself a good judge of character. He could usually tell the guys in Iraq who hung tough from those who'd cut and run, despite their peacetime bravado. Barzoon had fooled him last year, but not really. On a gut-level, Deacon had known the homeland security honcho couldn't be trusted. He just couldn't distinguish that gut feeling from the dozen other conflicting stresses and emotions wrought by Project Suicide. In the current, much less stress-filled time, he'd thought of Tony as a nice guy partnered with a putz. Well, maybe Officer Movello was just a good actor.

Deacon thought again of Barzoon, a man he assumed dead in a foreign land. What was Nelson Barzoon doing here? Deacon had sprayed him full in the face with the suicide drug, a dose that should have been sufficient to send a bull elephant happily to the nearest straight razor. And then Barzoon had escaped to Moscow. How did he get to Ohio? How did he survive? What did he want? A female voice broke through his musings.

"I've got some good news."

Terri Tremaine was at his side. Despite the hectic last twenty-four hours, she looked as good as ever. She'd showered and had changed into a peach-colored blouse under her blue blazer. Her makeup was tastefully applied.

"I could use some good news," Deacon said.

"We've heard from Sanford, the doctor from the clinic."

The knot in Deacon's gullet tightened. "And?"

"She's alive, and so is Amy."

The lump in his throat was gone, swallowed with a lot of worry. Deacon hugged Tremaine for a moment before thinking better of it and backing off. "Sorry."

Tremaine smiled. "No problem."

Deacon wiped away tears of joy. "Where?"

"A townhouse in Bellbrook. I have Kolinsky and Boyer picking them up. Once they've been checked out at Children's Hospital—that's closest—they'll whisk them back to the safe house."

"Do you think that's a good idea?" Deacon asked. "Barzoon may have marked Amy at the safe house."

Tremaine's hair waved like harvest wheat. "A *different* safe house. It's on Miller, up by the airport. We use it transporting witnesses. It's not as close to UD, but mostly freeway. I'll drive you over." The deputy looked at her watch. "Your Amy should be there in an hour or so. We can be there in half that time."

Deacon turned to follow her, then stopped. "Give me a second," he said.

Tremaine turned to him, then pointed. "Restrooms are down the hall."

Deacon shook his head. "Not that. I just want to tell Tony. No matter what else, he at least deserves to know."

Tremaine raised her brows, then said, "I'll meet you out front."

¢¢¢

Nodding again to the cop on duty, Deacon rapped on the door. The speaking inside stopped. "Come in," Tony said.

"Don't mean to interrupt," Deacon said, his hand on the knob, his body half-way in the room.

Tony waved him in. "That's okay, Dr. Cr … I mean Deke."

As Deacon entered, he said, "Excuse me, Mrs. Movello. Can I speak to your husband in private? I'll only be a minute."

The woman's pretty face blushed. "Yes, yes of course."

"You should probably take Chip home, Vinnie. I'll see you later."

"Yes," Vanessa said. "I'll get Chip a happy meal and take him home. I'll be back later." She kissed her husband on the cheek. "Rita from next door said she'd sit with Chip this evening."

Tony kissed her back. "Yeah, I'll see you later, hon."

Vanessa smiled shyly at Deacon and grabbed her little boy's hand. "Wave bye, bye to daddy."

Little Chip waved little fingers and said, "Bye, bye, da."

Vanessa beamed. She turned to Deacon. "Nice to have met you."

"Likewise," Deacon said as she walked her son out the door and closed it. "Nice family."

"Yeah." Tony said. "Um, listen …"

Deacon interrupted. "I thought you'd like to know that Amy is safe." He nodded to the door. "I figured it was best to tell you in private."

Tony sighed in relief. "Thank God." He cleared his throat. "Listen, Deke. About last night. I just took Amy out, you know, as a friend."

Deacon waved him off. "No explanations necessary. It's enough that she's okay. I'm on my way to see her now."

"Where is she?" Tony asked.

"Safe house," Deacon said. "I should see her in less than an hour."

Tony nodded. "Give her my best. And, um, tell her how sorry I am about, well, how things turned out."

"I will," Deacon said. Then Deacon left, but he still had an uneasy feeling.

Chapter 16

Deacon eased off the warm, tautness of her. Amy squeezed his back, prolonging contact for a moment while kissing him gently on the mouth. Then her hand slid off him as he slid off her stomach.

As his weight left her, she exhaled loudly. He stroked her shoulder. "Was I crushing you?"

Amy giggled. "A little. But I didn't mind." She blew a lock of hair from her forehead. "You can crush me anytime."

Deacon smiled but Amy turned more serious.

"Listen, Deke. About that, um, date with Tony. It didn't mean, well I mean, I was just, you know." She swallowed hard. "I know it was stupid, but I was trying to make you …"

Deacon touched a finger to her lips. "Shhh. No apologies necessary. I guess we've both been stupid about things lately." He smiled into the darkness. "But we're here together now."

"And what I told you about Tony," she added. "I may be wrong. Everything after we left the brewpub is kind of hazy and mixed up." She tapped her head, wincing at the pain.

"Shh," he said again. "Tony isn't going anywhere. He's in a hospital room under police guard, so there's plenty of time to check it out." He reached out to gently touch the purplish knot on her forehead.

Amy winced again.

"Still pretty tender, huh?' Deacon asked.

Amy smiled. "I've had worse."

He gently took her hand. "How are you doing otherwise?"

Amy shrugged. "Mostly aches and pains."

Deacon kissed her scraped fingers, one by one. "Hope we didn't hurt you."

Amy murmured in reply.

"How are you—*otherwise*?" Deacon asked.

He could see her eyes open, glistening in the half-light.

He touched the top of her head. "How are you doing up here?"

Amy turned away and nodded. "I've had worse."

"Maybe we should have waited until you were more healed up. *Everywhere.*"

She gripped his hand and pulled it to her. "I couldn't wait."

She turned to him, her eyes glistening.

"I learned a lot while fighting for my life," she said. "Learned about myself. About my feelings." She stared into his eyes. "Learned that the biggest thing I'd miss was being with you." She gripped his hand harder. "Because I love you."

Deacon leaned in and kissed away her tears. "I love you, too."

Amy guided his hand to her breast. Then she leaned over and kissed him. She tasted salty but good. She tasted like love.

¢¢¢

Deacon lay awake, staring at the cobwebs in the corner. Amy snuggled beside him, her comforting funkiness wafting into his nostrils. His mind filled with many conflicting emotions—love, guilt, shame, anger.

He asked himself a thousand questions. How was he back in this mess? Why couldn't they leave him alone to drink himself into oblivion? Why did he feel duty-bound to fix their messes? Why did Amy have to love him? Why did he have to love her back?

The questions fled as quickly as they formed. In their place were faces flickering past his mind's eye like flashcards in some grisly classroom. Mayor Simon Bolivar Hernandez, his features going slack as the side of his head blew out. Lisa, his long-time friend turned traitor, her skull caved in by the barrel of his pistol. Cathleen Harris, beautiful in her evening gown, mouth open in shock as she gasped for life. His late fiancée, Liz, her face unlined in death, hands and breasts floating in a pool of Barbie pink.

He desperately wanted a drink. But before he could rise to see what was in the safe house cupboard, another image rose. Someone he hated more than he hated Harris, or Lisa, or even himself. Someone he thought was gone for good. Someone who epitomized the evil in politics and in all the alphabet-soup bureaucracies of government. He said the name softly through clenched teeth.

"Barzoon."

Amy curled deeper into the crook of his arm and murmured, "Penny for your thoughts."

"I was just wondering if all government safe houses have cobwebs on the ceilings."

She giggled. "Millions for defense but not one penny for cleaning cobwebs."

Deacon kissed her hair. "Go back to sleep."

"What *about* Barzoon?"

"Nothing. Go back to sleep."

"You said he was dead."

Deacon squeezed her shoulder. "Go back to sleep."

Yes, Barzoon should have been dead. Dead in Russia, not making mischief in Ohio. How could that be?

Amy turned dreamily on her side, sneezing as she did so. Deacon caressed her shoulder. "God bless you."

¢¢¢

Nelson Barzoon stared at the Makarov pistol he'd had since graduating from the Krasnodar military academy, a gift from his late father, the colonel. He and the Makarov had traveled together a long time. He'd had it through all his spy training, language immersion classes, and endless indoctrination sessions, in which a single slip-up would merit punishment. He had it still after his insertion into the West. He'd always kept the pistol hidden against this day. It was a trusted friend, as trusted a friend as his clandestine world allowed. He trusted it now to provide him with one last act of kindness.

The feel of the blued steel was cold and comforting, reminding him of the ice on Lake Ladoga near his family's dacha. He'd skated there often as a boy, playing hockey and racing his pals along the frozen surface. His life was all possibilities then, a future as bright as the winter sun reflecting off the ice. He'd risen high, almost higher than any KGB operative had ever risen. Even the fall of his beloved USSR had not dimmed his rise. It had only delayed it. He'd waited, bided his time through the long years until he stood at the brink of true greatness and power. But he had failed.

Barzoon nudged back the pistol's slide, reassuring himself that a hollow-point slug was in the chamber. He knew that to be already true, but he'd always been a careful man, and old habits died hard. He would die easier, although his death would not come as anticipated. There would be no blaze of glory for Nelson Barzoon. Instead, there would be only the burning agony of regret, knowing that all the years of training and biding had been wasted.

He placed the barrel under his chin, its hard edge making him swallow. His throat was dry. He considered getting some water to ease the discomfort but thought better of it. It was only a temporary irritation, and he wasn't worthy of having it relieved. No, failures didn't deserve creature comforts.

The comforts of the West had made him soft. Too much food, drink, luxury. Those years had also made him careless. He'd assumed he was the master, they the puppets. His was the foolproof applecart that no bumbling federal agent or bureaucrat could upset. Until someone did.

He snugged the ball of his finger over the trigger, gradually increasing the pressure. Death would be a relief, a balm for his self-loathing. His one regret at leaving that baggage behind was not seeing the agony on the face of the man who had foiled him. The look that said Creel had accepted guilt for Robbins's death. The pleading eyes that said Barzoon was doing him a favor by killing him. Seeing that would almost be worth all the other failures and disappointments. But with the now heightened security, it was doubtful. Barzoon had failed at that too.

His finger rode back with the trigger. He felt the hammer slip toward its apogee. Soon it would come crashing down. In an instant, he would be free of the regret, the guilt, the self-loathing. All the torments of life would end. Any second now.

The pistol clattered from his hand as the air buzzed with noise. Barzoon flinched, looking for the source of the sound that had startled him away from his last duty. His heartbeat slowed as he recognized the source and picked up the cell phone.

"Yes?"

The voice on the other end of the line said, "If you still want Robbins, there may be a way."

Barzoon's lips twitched into a smile. He pried the lid off the Xanax bottle and popped two pills into his mouth. He grabbed a pencil while he chewed. "Go ahead."

¢¢¢

Deacon knocked on the hospital room door.

"Come in."

Tony Movello was laying up in bed reading a paperback with a buxom blonde on the cover. "Hi, *Deke*." He smiled. "I didn't forget that time and call you Doctor."

Deacon smiled back. "I thought I'd stop by to see how you were doing."

"Good. I get to go home in a couple more days, which will be even better." He patted the bed. "Have a seat."

Deacon shook his head. "I've been sitting too much as it is." He glanced around. "Have everything you need?"

Tony shrugged. "I could use a six pack but other than that." After a couple of beats, he added, "Anything you want in particular?"

Deacon shook his head, then turned to face him. "Actually, there was a question I wanted to ask."

"Shoot."

"When you saw Barzoon outside the brewpub."

"You mean when he shot me?"

Deacon nodded. "What did you say to him?"

Tony looked startled. "Say?"

Deacon put his hands in his pockets and nonchalantly studied the artwork on the wall. "Yeah. Amy thought she heard you say something, but it's all kind of jumbled in her head. You know, with the trauma and all." He turned sharply to Tony. The injured cop looked guilty for just a moment before his boyish charm returned.

"Gee. I don't remember. I was kind of shook up as well." Tony pointed to his wounded shoulder, then shrugged. "Maybe "no, don't shoot?" Something like that."

Deacon walked closer and sat on the bed. "That's funny. Amy thought you might have said, 'No, you promised,' or something like *that*."

Tony blanched. "Geez. I don't, I mean, um, why would I say something like that?"

Deacon shrugged. "Whatever happened to your partner? What was his name, Lipsitz?"

Tony nodded. "Well, I don't know. I um, I haven't seen him since he called in sick a few days ago."

Deacon looked him straight in the eye. "I just learned a neighbor found him dead in his house. He'd been there a couple days."

"Oh my God," Tony said. But Deacon didn't think he looked too surprised. "Um, how did it happen? I mean the flu, COVID, what?"

"Suicide," Deacon said.

Tony gulped. "Oh. Jesus. That's too … I mean, I had no idea."

Deacon patted Tony's hand. The skin was clammy. "Yeah, you never really know what's going on with someone. Even your partner."

Tony swallowed. "Nope. I guess not."

Deacon rose. "The memorial service for Sergeant Lipsitz is in a few days." He stared hard at Tony. "Closed casket, considering the circumstances. You should be able to attend."

Tony paled. "Um, thanks for letting me know."

Deacon nodded. "I'll be seeing you."

"Thanks for stopping by," Tony said. Deacon didn't think the young cop's heart was in the statement.

In the hall, Deacon closed the door then walked a few steps away and motioned to the cop sitting guard.

The cop grunted from his folding chair and walked over.

Deacon stabbed a finger at the door and spoke in a half-whisper. "He doesn't leave without me knowing."

The cop looked at the hospital room door, then back at Deacon. "He's not going anywhere for a couple days."

"And anyone but his wife comes to visit, I want to know about it. He calls anybody or they call him, I want to know."

The cop dropped his hands to his belt. "And who are you that I gotta report to you?"

"You understand me?"

The tone of Deacon's voice and the look in his eye must have made his point. The cop answered, "Yes sir."

¢¢¢

Deacon and Terri Tremaine sat in the hospital cafeteria drinking coffee. The place was sparsely populated, just a few lab coats and visitors grabbing a late breakfast.

Tremaine put down her cup and squinted at Deacon. "So based on that, you think this Movello is a dirty cop?"

"I don't know," Deacon replied. "But he concerns me."

"Concerns you because Robbins thought she might *maybe* have remembered him say something suspicious? Said Ms. Robbins having been drunk, shot at, then knocked unconscious?"

Deacon sipped his own coffee. It tasted bitter, and not just from being industrial blend. "Listen, Terri. Amy is not your average hysterical female. She has nerves honed from combat. Those nerves saved my ass more than once. I trust them. And I trust her memory and her instincts."

Tremaine shrugged. "Okay. But she's also been through a lot, both recently and in the past, and not just overseas." Her smile suggested she knew at least something about Project Suicide. "I've read her file. And I've read Movello's file. That's standard operating procedure for anyone assigned to my security detail." She let that sink in. "Officer Tony may have taken a free donut or tickets to the ballgame now and again, but his record is clean. He graduated third in his class at the academy."

Deacon put down his cup and rubbed his eyes. "I'm just saying it should be checked into."

"And it will be," she replied. After a pause, she looked both ways and then lowered her voice. "But isn't it possible that you don't trust Movello because he was married when dating *your* Amy" She leaned back. "Not many of us are pure in that regard."

Deacon ignored the reference to his own infidelity, although the rebuke still bit. "Yes, that too. It speaks to truthfulness. Faithfulness. Character or lack thereof. So, yes. I don't trust that in a bodyguard."

Tremaine rose to take her empty cup to a nearby bin.

Deacon followed. "I want Movello checked out. And I want more security on the new safe house."

"Fine," Tremaine said. A guy dressed in scrubs smiled at her and she smiled back. "In fact, I'll head over there myself. I can ask Amy exactly what she heard then hang around until you get back." She thunked her mug into a grey plastic bin. "I'm assuming you're going into the lab today?"

Deacon nodded. "I should probably see how Howard is coming along."

"I'll drop you," Tremaine said. "Then head over to *your* Amy." The last was said with a hint of a chuckle that Deacon didn't particularly appreciate.

Chapter 17

Deacon doubted that much had been done in his absence. As he recalled, grad students and postdocs tended to play while the cat was away. As he expected, the office area was empty, a fast-food chicken box and an opened bag of Doritos marking adolescent progress.

He found Howard in the lab, snoring softly with his head in his arms on the table. The room smelled like a Habitrail, no doubt from the two white rats in techniplast cages squeaking beside Howard's recumbent form. The rats had been shaved above the shoulders, with small portals surgically implanted. There was no sign of Leon, Howard's partner in crime.

Deacon tapped Howard on the shoulder. "Howie?" The sleeping postdoc did not stir. Deacon tapped a bit harder. "Howie?" Still nothing. Deacon shook his head, then rapped hard on the stainless-steel table. "Corporal Threlkis. Rise and shine. It's another day in the corps!"

The rats squeaked. Howard sat erect, his eyes wide. He looked about. One of the rats wandered over to chew the bars. Then Howard noticed Deacon.

"Oh. Dr. Creel."

"Did you have a good nap?"

"What?" Howard asked, blinking. He rubbed his eyes. "What time is it?"

"Almost noon," Deacon replied, walking toward the office. "I'm gonna make some coffee. Want some?"

"Coffee? Ah, no." He looked about. "I have a Pepsi here somewhere."

Deacon saw an empty pint bottle next to the mini fridge in the office. "You *had* a Pepsi." He tossed the empty into the recycle bin, then took coffee and filters from their cabinet. "Big night yesterday?"

Howard walked into the office yawning. "What? Last night?"

Deacon scooped coffee. "I'm assuming that's why you're sleeping with the rats. Late-night partying."

Howard blinked. "What day is it?"

Deacon turned to him. "What *day*?"

"I mean, didn't you just leave me in charge here yesterday?"

Deacon poured water into the carafe. "That was *two* days ago, Howie."

"Huh. I must have …"

Deacon poured the contents of the carafe into the maker. "Get anything accomplished while I was gone?"

"Not much," Howard said. "Leon and I dosed two rats with the monoclonal antibody." He pointed toward the lab area. "As you can see, they're okay. Then I conjugated the monoclonal to a radioisotope." He scanned the room. "I had to get the isotope from Wright Patt—we don't handle radioactive materials here. Dr. Metternich called it in." He scanned again. "Now where did I put that?"

Deacon saw a vial of yellowish liquid sitting by where he'd found the empty cola bottle. He pointed. "Is this it?"

Howard nodded and came over to pick it up.

"Better put the lead gloves on first," Deacon said.

Howard snapped his fingers and headed toward the lab.

"Then label the vial so we don't forget what's in there and someone else makes the same mistake," Deacon called out.

Howard came out of the lab wearing oversized grey gloves. He grabbed the vial awkwardly but carefully. "I'll put it in the safe for now," he said, walking slowly back to the lab.

"So," Deacon called out as he added creamer to his coffee cup. "You tested the monoclonal *and* did the conjugation. In less than forty-eight hours." He shook his head and chuckled. "What did you do with all the spare time?"

"Well," Howard called out. "We dosed another pair of rats with the 606 suicide drug. I got some of the non-weaponized material from Dr. Metternich." He walked back in, taking off the leaded gloves. "They're anesthetized in the back lab." He thumbed over his shoulder. "I figured we could test the conjugate on them when you got back." He looked at his watch. "Should be good to go in about an hour."

Deacon stared at him in awe.

"Just a preliminary test," Howard said. "I know it probably won't work, but I figured …"

Deacon continued staring.

"What?" Howard asked nervously. "Was I wrong?"

Deacon smiled. "No, Howie. You're not wrong. You're amazing."

¢¢¢

Deacon watched as one of the rats blinked, its nose twitching. Then the other anesthetized rodent stirred and stumbled toward the water bottle. Déjà vu swept over Deacon as the rat began to drink, its tiny tongue moving the steel bearing in the tube up and down. He almost expected to hear Lisa Reilly pronounce the Christmas names she'd given them.

"Rudolph and ZuZu," he muttered.

"What?" Howard said.

Deacon shook his head. "Nothing important." He looked at Howie. "They've both been given the suicide drug *before* we applied the conjugate?"

Howie nodded.

The one rat continued to drink, no doubt thirsty after its long nap. Deacon watched it, waiting, expecting the worst. More déjà vu as his mind's eye called up imagery from a year ago. He thought again of Lisa, his heart stung by mixed feelings of betrayal and regret. Then the imagery collapsed amid the sound of a nearby crash.

Deacon flinched and spun around. The second techniplast cage had toppled to the floor. Its occupant, the male he thought of as Rudolph, hung from the wire. The rat whipped its head back and forth in ever more violent twists and jerks. Deacon waited for the crack of breaking cervical vertebrae. He didn't have to wait long.

Little Rudolph flipped like a trapeze artist, his gyrations increasing in intensity with each arc. Deacon watched, fascinated despite the grisly spectacle. Finally, the little rodent gave a herculean twist, its neck taking on a grotesque angle seen only among the dead. Life drained from the rat's body as it continued to sway back and forth from teeth locked firmly in the wire.

"Well," Deacon sighed. "I wasn't really expecting anything from this first attempt."

"But look," Howard said.

Deacon watched as the postdoc pointed toward the other cage. Deacon's eyes widened as ZuZu stopped drinking and wandered over to the food bin. The rat sat on her haunches calmly chewing pelleted feed.

¢¢¢

Deacon was tired and not in the mood to talk to Joe Metternich, even over the phone. His former boss wasn't his favorite person, but Deacon knew what the man had been going through. So, he tried to show some patience and understanding.

"It was just a preliminary test, Joe. I wouldn't get too excited."

"But it was successful?" Metternich shouted into his ear.

Deacon tried to dampen Metternich's enthusiasm. "Only *fifty* percent successful. And in rats, not people."

"But *one* of the rats lived? Even after getting the 606 drug?"

Deacon nodded. "So far." He held up a restraining hand. "But you should know that we ran the rat through a radial-arm maze and an object recognition test. Then compared the results to the baseline established in ZuZu's record."

"ZuZu?" Metternich asked.

"Just a nickname, not important. What *is* important is that the maze test took an additional minute twenty seconds over her previous runs." Deacon sipped coffee to get the coppery taste of stress from his mouth. "And she flunked object recognition."

"So?" Metternich said.

"So," Deacon replied, "instead of dealing with an intelligent rat, we now have the equivalent of a low-grade moron." He paused to let that sink in. "If it were a person, I'd guess a loss of 30 to 50 IQ points." There was silence from the other end of the phone. "Joe? Did you hear me?"

After another pause, Metternich answered. "But the rat lived?"

Deacon sighed. "Yes, Joe. It did. Just one out of two. And yes, we are in the process of repeating the procedure with a second pair for comparison."

Deacon thought he heard sobbing on the other end of the line. "You don't think I should come to Dayton to …"

"No need for that, Joe. You stay put and take care of Claudia." Deacon didn't know if that was the right thing to say, but the conversation was just as awkward for him as it was for Metternich.

"What do you think, that is to say, when do you think you'll have something ready for …"

"Human testing?" Deacon asked. He didn't wait for Metternich's response. "Impossible to say. I can't even tell you when we'll be done with animal testing." Deacon sighed. "Listen Joe, under a crash program, assuming we figure out why the one rat died, we might have something ready for people in a month or two. More likely, it'll be a year or two. I'm sorry I can't be more specific."

Metternich's anguish was clearly audible over the telephone. "Two *years*?"

"That's a guess," Deacon said. "Could be less … could be more." The sobbing on the phone increased. "We'll stay hard at it, Joe. Go from here."

"Please," Metternich replied, "please, um, keep me informed with further results as they become available."

"I will, Joe. You know I will." Deacon felt more sympathy for Metternich than he had since … ever. "Try and get some sleep." After a moment, the line went dead.

Deacon rubbed tension from his neck. For the hundredth time, he asked himself how he'd gotten back into the business of government bullshit and life-and-death decisions. For the thousandth time, he wished for a shot of bourbon—maybe ten.

¢¢¢

Barzoon was tired from the long drive. But sleep was not an option. Drifting off to sleep brought a loss of control, and he needed his control now more than ever. He still had a job to do. So, he popped a Benzedrine and waited in the dark living room.

It was a nice room, in a nice house; a large colonial common to places like Bethesda or Chevy Chase. Not quite opulent, but stately. The kind of home where higher-level bureaucrats set up shop.

Barzoon sniffed the air. It smelled stale. He wiped his hand along the end table next to his easy chair, then thumbed a layer of dust from his index finger. The place felt unoccupied, although that was not the case. He remembered picking the backdoor lock, noting how the shrubs had looked in need of trimming. No doubt the master of the house was oblivious to such domestic niceties, his mind preoccupied with other things.

Barzoon popped a Xanax and chewed, the bitter taste reassuring, almost as reassuring as his own thoughts of suicide. He heard the faint click as the front door opened and then closed again, a large squat figure momentarily silhouetted in the streetlamp. Then the room light flicked on.

Josiah Metternich shrugged out of his rumpled suitcoat and hung it on a coat rack. Then he saw Barzoon and froze.

"Hello, Joe," Barzoon said, pointing the Makarov pistol at his old colleague.

It took a moment for Metternich to recognize the now gaunt figure. Then he muttered, "You. You're, you're …"

"Dead?" Barzoon chuckled mirthlessly. "Why do you doubt your senses, Mr. Scrooge?"

"But, but …"

"As you can see, I am very much alive."

Metternich stumbled out of the hall and plopped his butt unceremoniously on the sofa.

"But, but, Creel told us what happened. The weaponized 606."

Barzoon nodded. "A blast full in the face. A death sentence by anyone's definition." He tapped his own chest with the pistol. "Yet here I sit." Barzoon leaned forward in his chair. "Which should give you pause to ponder why."

"But there is no antidote," Metternich gasped. "Not yet. How?"

Barzoon pointed the pistol at the ceiling for emphasis. "*Your* side has no antidote." He smiled. "Obviously, *our* side does." The pistol weighed heavily in his hand. Barzoon resisted the urge to place it against his own skull. Instead, his fake smile widened. "How else do you explain me?"

Metternich stared and blinked. "I can't."

Barzoon nodded. "No doubt. I suppose your agile mind has been involved with other, shall we say, pressing, personal matters. Matters that have dimmed your thinking. As they are dimming it now."

Recognition flashed across Metternich's face. "My wife."

Barzoon laughed. "Finally, it comes to him." He laid his gun along the armrest. Metternich was unlikely to be a problem now that he understood. "Yes. The lovely Claudia." Barzoon's smile changed to a frown. "Constantly sedated so that she won't end her own suffering." Even as Barzoon said it, the thought of doing the same was indescribably appealing. "Suffering that you are forced to witness day by agonizing day." He imagined Creel watching Robbins struggle for death. His smile was back, as genuine as the look of hope on Metternich's face.

"Yes, Joe. Creel could stumble along for months or even years, the cure still outside his grasp. Or Claudia could be smiling up at you soon, anguish replaced by joy, desperation by anticipation of a bright future." He raised his finger toward heaven. "If …"

Barzoon watched Metternich's Adam's apple rise and fall. "What do you want from me?"

Barzoon nodded, "To paraphrase Jacob Marley again—*much*."

¢¢¢

The sneeze came on suddenly, sending fine droplets into the air of the safe house. Amy pulled tissue from the pocket of her robe. She'd been dealing with a cold for the past couple of days. She chalked it up to stress and running around half-naked in the night air. In general, it left her feeling crummy.

"Bless you."

Amy looked over at Deputy Tremaine tapping away on her laptop. The deputy was beautiful in a black, tailored pants suit that accentuated her trim figure. Tremaine was part of the heightened security detail, which now included a deputy inside at all times, another one in front, and a state cop in the back. The county sheriff's deputies also made random drive-bys a dozen times a day. There was little danger of abduction and even less of privacy. To make matters worse, today's inside deputy was the ever-gorgeous Terri Tremaine.

"Thank you," Amy said, wiping her nose.

Tremaine frowned. "How are you feeling?"

Amy shrugged and pointed down the hall. "I think I'll go upstairs and lie down for a bit."

Tremaine nodded. "I was going to order food. You hungry?"

Amy shook her head.

"How about some chicken soup?"

Amy was about to say no, then thought better of it. "Some soup would be good. Thank you."

"I'll let you know when it's here." Tremaine smiled and went back to her typing.

Amy shuffled upstairs to the bedroom and lay down on the blue coverlet. She was generally an upbeat person who had worked through colds on many occasions in the Corps. But this one had her down in the dumps, for no reason she could think of. She knew she should be happy to be alive and safely reunited with

Deacon. That's how she'd felt overseas after surviving a firefight or rocket attack—happy to be alive and with her comrades. That was back in the days when she had a purpose, service to her fellow marines and to her country. Duty, honor, country, she thought. Those words used to mean so much. Now, lying around with nothing to do, she felt useless and depressed. She tried to chase away the feeling, but it wouldn't leave.

Even thoughts of Deacon failed to snap her out of it. Instead, she felt unworthy of him, holding him back somehow. Amy thought of Tremaine—beautiful, efficient, important. She was the type of woman he should be with, not the useless slug that Amy had become. She closed her eyes and tried to think of something else. Tried to clear her mind and get some rest as she always used to do after lights-out in the corps. But sleep wouldn't come. All that came were tears.

¢¢¢

Amy woke suddenly from a dream. It was one she'd had before, her mother hearing the news about her dad's death. Amy had been ten years old. She'd woken up late in the night as her mom answered the door. She remembered her mother's sobs as Uncle Bobby broke the news. Lying in bed, young Amy had started crying almost before she understood what the late-night visit meant.

The sadness of the event was always fresh and raw with each morphic reliving. Except for this time. This time, the sadness was sweetened with a kind of awe. A realization that her dad was the lucky one. That for him, all of life's pains and failures had ended. He'd joined the ranks of the honored dead. Amy found herself envying him.

There was a knock on the door. "Yes," Amy called.

"Soup's on," Tremaine said from behind the door. "Want me to bring up a tray?"

Amy paused for a moment then said, "I'll come down."

She didn't relish the idea of sharing a meal with Tremaine, but she never could eat in bed. Right now, she didn't want to, either. Her morbid thoughts had frightened her, not so much that she'd had them but because they were so appealing.

Amy shook off a shiver and got off the bed. She sneezed and wiped her nose. "Maybe the soup will cheer me up."

¢¢¢

Amy ate a spoonful of soup but didn't really taste it. At least it was warm.

"Sorry, but Wonton Palace didn't have chicken noodle, so I got you egg drop." Tremaine held up a white cardboard container. "Would you like some fried rice? Maybe an egg roll?"

Amy shook her head. "I'm not very hungry." She looked about the room. "Are we the only ones eating?"

"I took a plate out to Deputy Haggarty. Trooper Johnson brown-bagged it today." Tremaine frowned. "Feeling any better?"

Amy managed to smile. "A little." She hoped the deep purple of her mood would lighten with some food and company—even Tremaine's company. It didn't.

Tremaine forked up bean sprouts and rice. "Want us to take you to a doctor?"

"For a cold?" Amy asked.

Tremaine shrugged. "Could be the flu or COVID."

Amy lifted a spoonful of soup. "I'd have more than just upper respiratory sniffles with either. And the treatment would basically be rest and isolation." She managed another smile. "I think we have that covered."

Tremaine ate and nodded. "I was thinking about Dr. Creel. Testing would tell us if we should isolate you from him as well."

Amy looked down at her bowl and mumbled, "You'd like that, wouldn't you?"

"Pardon?" Tremaine asked.

Amy shook her head. "He didn't make it home last night. Problems."

Tremaine napkinned her mouth. "He was busy at the lab and slept there." She raised a hand. "Don't worry, we have increased security there as well." She smiled. "I'm taking good care of him."

"I'll bet," Amy muttered, still looking at her soup. She cleared her throat. "Is that where *you* were last night? Security at the lab?"

Tremaine raised her brows, then said. "Actually, I was at my hotel room catching up on some sleep."

Amy looked directly at Tremaine. "So, you didn't see Deacon yesterday?"

Tremaine paused, fork halfway to her mouth. She met Amy's gaze. "I saw him for a bit." Tremaine continued around a bite of food. "He *is* my responsibility." She sipped iced tea as she chewed. "He's quite a man. Brilliant. Very important to whatever hush-hush project Metternich has going on." She smiled. "That's why I'm seeing to it that he is well cared for." To Amy, Tremaine's smile meant more than business. "Just like we're taking good care of you. You're very important to Deacon."

Tremaine mumbled something else that Amy couldn't make out. But in her mind, she heard Tremaine say, "for the moment."

¢¢¢

Amy opened the medicine cabinet looking for a pain reliever. She'd had a headache off and on since her life-and death run-in with Barzoon almost a week ago. It seemed to be getting worse, rather than better, going from a minor annoyance to a preoccupying pain. Possible causes ran through her head, a gift from her corpsman training.

The most likely explanation was a sinus headache associated with her cold. Of course, it could also be psychosomatic, corporeal pain to match the deepening darkness of her mood, or some form of post-trauma stress reaction. More serious causes included a contrecoup injury or brain bleed from having been knocked unconscious only a few days ago. The latter was the least likely (the emergency room doctor had seen no signs when she'd examined Amy), yet it was the one Amy seemed to dwell upon. In her mind, she could see a blood vessel slowly leaking, pressure building on her cerebrum as the severity of pain gradually increased before stroke and sudden death. The persistent image fascinated her, not so much from worry that it might be true but from fear that it wouldn't be.

Amy tried to shake off this morbid fascination as she searched the cabinet's accumulated items left over from past safe house occupants. There was a comb, dandruff and tufts of hair still clinging to its teeth. Two toothbrushes sat sealed in boxes yellowed with age. There was a bottle of Brut splash-on cologne, a half-full tube of hemorrhoid cream, and a plastic bottle of acetaminophen that expired in 2016. Amy shrugged and grabbed the pain reliever. Hidden behind the bottle was a package of old-style razor blades, the double-edged variety in a steel dispenser.

Amy put down the pain pills and picked up the razor blades. She caressed the metal dispenser between her fingers, its cold edges soothing to the touch. The dispenser itself held tinges of rust, but the stainless blades shone as brightly as they had when they'd left the factory many years ago. Amy slid a blade into her hand. It gleamed in the glow of the bathroom lights. She found her mood lifting. The shiny blade seemed almost alive. As she stared at it, it spoke to her. She could hear it quite plainly in her mind's ear. "I am the way," it said. "The only way."

A sense of peace enveloped her. The cold steel seemed to warm in her hand. Amy rubbed her thumb along the beveled edge, producing a small drop of blood as it nicked her skin. There was no pain, only that peaceful feeling. She smiled.

She turned on the warm water to rinse away the blood. The sink stopper was already levered closed, so that the water rose up the sides of the basin. Blood from her thumb tinged the water pink. She thought the color beautiful, almost the crimson of a dying sky as the rays of the setting sun cast the horizon aglow. Soon it would be dark. Thoughts of darkness brought a sense of calm, peace, relief.

Amy put down the blade and dipped her hands up to the wrists in warm water. She studied the blood vessels pulsing just below the surface and thought of many things. She thought about how her life held little meaning without the Marine Corps and her work. How she was basically alone, her mother down in Florida, her sister out of touch in California. She realized she hadn't been much of a daughter or a sister. The corps had been her home. Now even that was gone.

Most of all, she thought about Deacon, the man she loved. But did he love her? Did she deserve him? He was an important man, one with much to give the world. He merited more than a has-been medic who was more encumbrance than helpmate.

Amy reached up, her hand leaving the gentle caress of the water. She snatched up the razor blade and plunged it into the water's warm embrace. The stainless blade shone even brighter than it had before, the water spinning its reflection into the myriad sparkles of a precious jewel.

After Project Suicide, she had sought out Deacon and found him. He stayed with her but one day. She spent the next year seeking him again. Now he was back with her but only because of the lure of the work, his sense of duty. She had hardly seen him the past several days because of this work. When that was over, would she see him at all? Would he return to drink and solitude, eschewing the love that wasn't worthy of him? Was she why he drank, to escape being chained to such a worthless woman? A woman so unlike the beautiful and successful Terri Tremaine?

Amy moved the blade toward her wrist. The running water had risen to mid-forearm. Its warmth caused her flesh to pinken and glow, the vessels dilating, the blood inside straining for release. Calmness as warm and comforting as the water settled over her. In her mind, she heard that voice again. "I am the way. The only way." It occurred to her that the voice was right. This was the way, the best way. It would free Deacon. It would free Amy Robbins as well.

Amy applied gentle pressure, gradually increasing it until a thin red line sent blood into the pinkening swirl. Her body relaxed. The decision was made. She smiled. For the first time in days, she was doing the right thing.

A knock on the bathroom door startled her. Amy dropped the razor blade and jerked upright, water from the full basin slopping onto her feet and legs.

"Ms. Robbins?"

Amy stared down at the tiny red line on her wrist, specks of blood already congealing against the shallow indentation.

"Ms. Robbins? Amy? Are you alright?"

The voice was Terri Tremaine. Amy grabbed a towel and wrapped it around her wrist. The previous calming warmth reverted to a cold shudder of nervousness and shame. "Um, yes?"

"You've been in there for close to an hour. Just wanted to make sure you are all right."

Close to an hour? Amy looked at the full basin. The still-running water gurgled down the overflow hole. Her gaze shifted to the mirror on the now-closed cabinet. The image that stared back from the foggy surface was wan and emptied of life. Another cold shudder traveled up Amy's spine.

"Ms. Robbins?" Tremaine's voice was insistent now. "Do you need help?"

"Help?" The spell finally broke. "No. I, um, no. I'll be out in a moment."

"Alright," Tremaine said. "I have some reasonably good news to relate."

"Good news?" Amy whispered. She didn't feel good. Mostly, she felt disappointment.

Chapter 18

Deacon woke from the dream. It faded quickly but not before he saw Liz's fingers bobbing in a sea of Barbie pink. Wiping sleep from his eyes, he grunted up from the old, sprung sofa in the office outside his laboratory. *His* laboratory, he thought. More Howie's lab these days.

Deacon took filters and coffee from the cabinet. He'd only meant to rest his eyes after lunch. He looked at the clock. He'd have to call Amy and say he might not make it home again tonight. Now that he knew she was safe, he and Howie had been working almost round the clock.

He couldn't get the talk with Metternich out of his head. There had never been any love lost between him and Joe, but the pity in the man's voice had touched Deacon deeply.

Deacon poured water into the coffee maker. So far, they had run two more rodent tests. In both, one rat had lived and the other died—violently. There must be a reason for the fifty-percent mortality, he thought, but his exhausted brain couldn't come up with it. It was probably something simple, but still it eluded him.

Howard came out of the lab, yawning and rubbing the small of his back.

"You fall asleep on the lab bench again?" Deacon asked.

Howard stifled another yawn. "In front of my computer."

"You want coffee?" Deacon asked.

Howard shook his head and reached into his pocket. "I'll get a Pepsi out of the machine." Howard turned his pocket inside out. "I could have sworn I had another dollar."

Deacon reached into his own pocket. "Allow me." He handed Howard a five.

"Thanks," Howard said. "I'll bring back your change."

"Keep it," Deacon said. "You've earned it."

Howard shrugged. "I don't see how. Four tests, four dead rats."

Deacon raised a finger. "But four *live* rats. *Dumber* live rats, but live nonetheless. Now we just need to figure out why."

"I've been thinking about that," Howard said.

"I should hope so," Deacon said. "*Live* is what we're shooting for."

Howard shook his head. "Not that. The dumb part. Look at this." He unfolded a paper from the pocket of his lab coat. "I ran this program comparing our monoclonal treatment to common neurotoxic agents."

Deacon held up a finger. "Threlkis-1, not *our* monoclonal treatment. You discovered it, so you get the credit."

Howard blushed then shoved the paper at Deacon. "The neurotoxins all have this side chain in common." He tapped the paper. "So does our monoclonal … I mean, Threlkis-1."

Deacon squinted. "You think removing the side chain should decrease the brain damage."

Howard nodded. "Without changing the basic structure. Efficacy should remain the same. Also …" He patted the pockets of his lab coat. "I had that necropsy report here somewhere."

"Just tell me," Deacon said.

Howard shrugged. "The histopathology report from OSU said that damage was primarily adjacent to the main arteries in the cerebrum."

"As we expected," Deacon said, clicking on the coffee maker. "That's where cognition takes place."

"Yes," Howard said. "But the human brain is over eighty-five percent cerebrum, the rat brain less than half that. So, rats have less to lose. People on the other hand …"

"Have cerebrum to spare. You think that maybe a person could compensate for the damage, like people do after a stroke?"

Howard smiled.

Deacon scratched his head. "You could be right, Howie. But that doesn't solve our main problem. Half of our test subjects are still dead."

Howard nodded. "Yeah, the males."

"Right," Deacon said, "they're still … What did you say?"

"What?" Howard stared at Deacon in surprise. "That all the female rats lived? You noticed that, right? The dead rats were the males."

Deacon blinked, mouth agape, then placed a hand on Howard's shoulder. "Where do you live, Howie?"

"I rent a room at a frat, Alpha Kappa Pi. But lately I've been staying here."

"You *sleep* here? The Science Center?"

Howard nodded. "There's a cot outside the locker room. Why?"

Deacon placed a fatherly arm around Howard's neck. "Because I want to assign you a security detail."

"Me?"

"Yep. You are far too important to risk losing. But first, I want you to set up for two more runs. One with two male rats and one with two females. Get Dion …"

"Leon."

"Right, get Leon to help you." They started walking toward the door. "Also, contact Joe Metternich about synthesizing more Threlkis-1, but this time without that side chain. Can you do that?"

"Sure. But even if the females survive, we've still solved only half our problem."

Deacon smiled. "That may be all we need to solve—for now." He patted Howard on the back. "Let's get your Pepsi."

¢¢¢

Deacon watched the two female rats munching pellets in their respective cages. "How long has it been?"

Howard checked his watch. "Thirty minutes, give or take."

Deacon nodded. "At one hour we'll call it a success. Did you send the males off for necropsy."

"Yep," Howard said. "Although I can tell you right now that causes of death were severe cranial trauma and a fractured neck."

"I'm more interested in brain histopathology," Deacon said. "If you're right, we should see Threlkis-1 tightly bound to neurons, probably at the juncture with the conjugated radioisotope." He sipped coffee. "When is Joe sending over the new batch without the side chain?"

"I meant to tell you," Howard said. "I couldn't get in touch with him."

"He didn't answer?"

Howard shook a negative. "I left a message, but that was almost four hours ago."

Deacon put down his cup. "That's odd. Joe is *very* interested in our results. He told me to call that number day or night."

Howard shrugged.

Deacon grabbed his mug. "I'll call Terri Tremaine. She should be able to get through to him no matter what." He started to leave, then looked around. "Where's Dion, I mean Leon?"

"I sent him home to get some sleep," Howard said. "We've been working the poor guy ragged."

"Well," Deacon said, "see if you can get him back here. I want to set up another run of female rats. We'll try the new Threlkis on them." He paused halfway to the door. "And tell Leon to bring a change of clothes, toothbrush, etc. I want him here under guard like you."

"*Threlkis*-1," Howard said, smiling. "I'll be famous."

Deacon smiled back. "This is hush-hush work, Howie. Nobody is supposed to know." He opened the lab door, then turned back. "But trust me, one day you'll be famous."

¢¢¢

Deacon retrieved Tremaine's card from his wallet. He felt a twinge of guilt about their night together—the night he couldn't really remember. He tried to chalk it up to too much booze and bad judgment. It was not his first time for either.

After the second ring, Tremaine answered.

"Hi Terri. I'm having trouble reaching Joe Metternich. Have you talked to him lately?"

"Not since he called with the good news," she said.

"Good news?"

"Right," Tremaine said. "You know, about Barzoon?"

"What about Barzoon?"

"That they caught him."

"They *caught* Barzoon?" Deacon said.

"Earlier today. Joe said he'd tell you."

Deacon blinked several times, then said, "Whoa. Let's back up. Joe called to tell you that they had captured Barzoon? When was this?"

"About noon. He said he'd call you, too."

Deacon looked at the clock in his office. "That was almost eight hours ago. And no, he didn't call me. Why didn't *you* call me?"

"Like I said, he said *he* would. And I've been busy closing up shop."

Deacon was past confused. "What do you mean?"

"I mean, we've been packing things up here at Miller Road, moving them back to the hotel. Now that Barzoon is out of the picture, I've sent home the security detail. I was just going to call headquarters to say they should send someone out to clean the safe house tomorrow."

Deacon had a very bad feeling. "Where's Amy?"

"Here with me," Tremaine said. "What's going on?"

"Just you and her at the safe house? The security detail is gone?"

"I just said that," Tremaine answered.

Warning bells sounded in Deacon's head. Something wasn't right. A dozen questions sprang to mind.

Metternich had told Tremaine that Barzoon was captured. How had he known? Why hadn't Tremaine known? She was more in the enforcement end of things. Why hadn't Metternich told Deacon? How was Barzoon even here? The man should be dead. The latter question haunted him most of all. How had Barzoon survived? A thought dawned, one that should have dawned when he first learned Barzoon was alive.

He remembered the anguish in Metternich's voice when Deacon told him a cure might be years away. It was the voice of a desperate man. But how desperate? Could that desperation be exploited? Deacon thought maybe it could, given the correct incentive.

"Deacon? You still there?"

"What? Yeah, I'm here."

"So," Tremaine said. "What should I do?"

"Give me a minute to think." Even as he said it, he knew he didn't need to take that long. "Listen, Terri, get …" A door knock carried through the phone.

"Just a sec," Tremaine said. "Let me see who's at the door."

The alarm bell in Deacon's head changed into a claxon. "Wait, Terri. Don't open the door!" He shouted louder. "Terri." In the background he heard the sounds of a struggle. The crash of a lamp. Someone screamed, followed by a single gunshot.

Chapter 19

Deacon popped out the cruiser door even before the car stopped. The cop at the wheel was on the phone, requesting back-up, but Deacon was too busy running to hear anything else. A few seconds later he hit the front porch. The door was ajar. The air still held a tinge of gun smoke.

The cop behind him was shouting about waiting for help when Deacon shoved at the door. It travelled only a few inches before thudding into an obstruction that groaned and rolled out of the way. Deacon paused before opening the door more slowly.

Terri Tremaine lay on the floor. Her tailored pant suit was wrinkled and covered with dust. Her forehead held a goose-egg bruise. Deacon dropped to one knee and held her shoulders. She opened her eyes, which were as deep blue as ever.

"Where's Amy?" he asked.

Tremaine blinked, then grimaced as she shook her head. "Not sure."

Deacon leapt over her and sprinted for the stairway. "Amy!" There was no reply. At the top of the stairs, he again shouted, "Amy!" Her bedroom was empty, the bedclothes slightly rumpled. In seconds, he had checked the other upstairs rooms, then pounded back down to the main level. Repeated calls of "Amy" produced no result. A quick scan of the downstairs rooms showed likewise. No blood. No signs of disturbance. Just empty.

The cop who'd driven him, Patrolman Janek, was helping Tremaine to her feet. Deacon tried to stay calm even as his heart pounded. He caught his breath and said, "What happened?"

Tremaine shook her head, again wincing from pain. She gently touched the knot under her bangs. "Barzoon."

"He was here?" Deacon asked.

She nodded. "Amy was in the kitchen when I opened the front door." She grimaced not in pain but in self-disgust. "I didn't check first. I figured it was the Highway Patrol. I'd asked them to drive Amy to the hotel."

Tremaine swayed and Deacon steadied her. "What happened?" he asked again.

Tremaine hesitated.

"I'll call for an ambulance," the cop said.

When Janek was gone, Tremaine continued. "Barzoon pointed a pistol at Amy. It was a small automatic, Makarov I think." Her eyes clouded and she stumbled again.

"Easy," Deacon said, leading her to the sofa. He swallowed. "Did he, did he shoot her?"

Tremaine shook her head. "I shoved his arm. The shot went wide." She pointed to where a bullet hole marred the plaster. "That's when I got this." She again touched the knot on her forehead. "Everything went hazy."

Deacon stood before her, numb. "What happened then?"

"Don't know," Tremaine said. She looked up with penitence in her eyes. "I'm sorry, Deke. Truly."

¢¢¢

Once again, Amy woke groggily in a strange bed, dressed only in bra and panties. A table lamp shone into her eyes. She tried to cover her face against the glare, but her arms were stretched wide by nylon straps securely buckled to her wrists. Her legs were likewise spread eagle. Small brass padlocks secured the wrist straps.

The place looked oddly familiar, but she didn't know why. Except for the bed and one bedside table, the room was empty. There were no pictures or recognizable furnishings. The sole window was covered with black paper that had been taped up to keep out light, so she couldn't see anything outside. Yet, she sensed she'd been here before.

As she moved her head slowly from side to side, she felt pain in her shoulder. Her vision cleared enough to notice a small red bruise on her left deltoid.

"Sorry about that."

Amy turned suddenly, the motion sending her vision spinning. When the topsy turvy ebbed, she was looking into the face of Nelson Barzoon. She tried to talk, but nothing came out. She swallowed and whispered, "How?"

Barzoon smiled. It was not the self-satisfied grin she had known during Project Suicide. This smile was strained, as if it was an effort to find joy in anything.

"A small dose of a knockout drug. The kind they use to dart animals."

"M99?"

"Very good." A bit of the old Barzoon tinged his smile, then left as quickly. "A diluted dose. *Very* diluted." His face clouded with concern. "Quite a tricky operation, really. If my calculations had been off by a fraction, you'd be dead instead of lying there so beautifully."

Amy's mind was in a fog, unable to recall what had happened at the safe house. She wanted to ask why he'd abducted her. How had he subdued her? What had happened to Tremaine? How had Barzoon escaped from Metternich? Instead, she said, "You should have let me die." This odd response shocked her. But even as she said it, she knew it was true. Knew it was what she wanted.

Barzoon's smile grew more genuine. "I know that's what you desire, but not yet. First, we are going to make some home movies, you and I." He pointed to a digital camera on a stand at the foot of the bed. "We'll send them daily to Dr. Creel." His eyes grew wide in appreciation. "You can tell him yourself just exactly what you want."

Thoughts of Deacon brought no joy. She could only think how she'd let him down, put him in danger, ruined his life. She shook her head despite the pain and spat, "I'm not telling anybody anything."

Barzoon bent down so that he was inches from her face. "But you will. Eventually, you will do anything I say. Anything if I only agree to give you what you want." His smile was back. "And I will." His face and smile retreated. He tsked a finger at her. "But you have to wait. After a week or two, when your beloved Deacon sees your suffering and experiences true suffering of his own, I'll grant your request." He held up the Makarov. "Then Deacon can join you." His smile grew warm, almost angelic in anticipation. "We'll all sit in hell and have a nice chat about it."

Amy felt helpless and afraid. But oddly, she didn't fear being killed. She believed Barzoon and knew he would keep her alive. That fact gnawed at her conscious mind like a hungry rat. The feeling again shocked her. She again tried to put on a brave face.

"You won't have a week," she said. "I'll refuse food and water. It should all be over in a few days."

Barzoon nodded, faux concern back in his eyes. "Yes, I thought that might be your attitude." He held up a finger and smiled. "And I'm taking measures to make you more comfortable."

Amy sneezed.

The old Barzoon smile was back. "God bless."

¢¢¢

Tremaine sat on a padded exam table holding a cold pack to her forehead. Deacon paced back and forth, shaking his head.

"How?" he asked for the tenth time.

"How did Barzoon find us?" Tremaine asked. "Why did he kidnap Amy? How did he escape after Metternich said he was captured? You're gonna have to narrow that 'how' down." She examined the cold pack for signs of blood and then replaced it on her head. "Better yet, was Barzoon even captured?"

Deacon stopped pacing. "What do you mean?"

"I checked with the FBI," Tremaine said. "Which is what I should have done after Joe's call. The Cincinnati field office didn't know anything about any capture. Neither did my headquarters." She met Deacon's stare. "It's still an active manhunt that has turned into a man and woman hunt."

"Metternich?" Deacon asked.

Tremaine nodded. "Looks that way."

"But why? He's got more interest in keeping us safe than anyone. His wife …" An astonishing thought struck home—one he'd had before but forgotten in the excitement.

"What about his wife?" Tremaine asked.

Deacon barely heard her over the implications pounding through his head. "Joe is desperate for a cure. Barzoon is alive."

"Cure for what?" Tremaine said.

"Of course."

Tremaine put down the cold pack. "Don't you think it's time someone told me exactly what's going on?"

"Where is Joe?" Deacon asked, still staring into space.

"That's the million-dollar question. No one has seen him."

Deacon nodded. "Of course."

Tremaine stood, swayed, then clutched the table. "Of course, *what*?"

Deacon turned to her, fire in his eyes. "There is *already* a cure. That would explain Barzoon." He frowned. "But why does Barzoon want Amy? Revenge? If there's a cure, revenge for what?"

Tremaine placed a hand on Deacon's neck and turned his head toward hers. "I might be able to answer some of your questions *if* I knew what the hell you were talking about."

"Fair enough," Deacon said. "What do you know about the events of last year surrounding the death of the newly sworn vice president?"

"I know that you and Robbins were implicated, hunted down, then ultimately released." She shrugged. "But I don't know why."

Deacon nodded. "Let me buy you a cup of coffee and tell you why."

¢¢¢

Barzoon waited alone in the darkened townhouse. Light might alert his quarry that something was afoot. Darkness, on the other hand, was his friend. It was soothing, eternally peaceful. It hid attractive temptations such as steak knives, scissors, and glass bottles. He popped a Xanax and chewed. Time enough for that later.

He scanned the room. Simpler and less impressive than Metternich's colonial. But then its owner was younger with less wealth, less to lose. Still, she had the one thing that everyone coveted—her life.

He touched the Makarov in his waistband. Like the knives and glassware, it was a temptation, but like the darkness, an old friend. Unlike modern plastic pistols, it was cold steel that had weight, gravitas, power. It was a friend he could count on. It was also a tool that he needed to exact his revenge. Then and only then would his friend lend him the peace he so desired. A friend indeed.

Barzoon tried to rub exhaustion from his eyes, but thirty-six hours without sleep was hard to expunge. The long round-trip drive to DC, Robbins's abduction, the Xanax; it was catching up to him. He closed his eyes and felt himself immediately relax. A quick rap of his injured hand against the chair brought him wide awake again. He would not sleep. Sleep brought dreams of an earlier time when his life was success and endless possibilities. Waking again brought the reality of his worthlessness and failure. He flexed the bruised hand, let the pain flare and subside. Pain was good, but it wasn't enough. With his good hand, Barzoon reached into his jacket for a pill vial. The bitter taste of the last pill was still in his mouth as he dry swallowed an amphetamine capsule. He smiled ruefully and thought of an old song. One pill makes you bigger and one pill makes you small. How many pills until you are nothing at all? "Go ask Alice," he whispered.

Just one idle, unguarded thought. But it was enough. An image broke into his mind with the speed of a battering ram and the power of an overriding compulsion. Without thinking, he dumped the remaining amphetamines into his palm. His mind counted them—thirteen. A magic number that should be enough. More than enough to do the job. He was on autopilot, his mind reduced to a fascinated observer watching his bodily actions. He shook his cupped hand like a crapshooter and prepared to pop the handful into his mouth. He got halfway there when the door lock clicked and the knob turned.

Barzoon's mind slipped back into his skin with a shiver of cold sweat. He shakily returned the pills to the bottle and deposited it into his pocket. The foyer light flared, and he could see his target removing her lab coat. He wiped sweat from his brow, then pulled the Makarov free.

"Good evening."

Dr. Isabela Sanford spun to face him, her eyes wide with recognition and panic. That was good.

"Or should I say good morning?" Sanford placed a hand on the doorknob, so Barzoon pointed the pistol. "Can't have you leaving yet, good Doctor. You've only just arrived."

"What?" Barzoon watched a lump travel down her throat. "What do you want, *exactly*?"

He pointed the pistol and smiled. "You *exactly*." Barzoon stood. "Now if you will be so kind as to face the wall, hands together behind your back."

He walked to her and removed a plastic tie from his pocket. He couldn't see her face, but her body trembled. All good. He cinched the tie around her crossed wrists and tightened. Sanford winced in pain.

"Sorry about the discomfort, but it won't be for long. Only until we reach our destination."

Sanford cleared her throat. "Where are we going?"

"Only a short drive. You see, you have a patient waiting."

¢¢¢

Tremaine put down her coffee mug. She glanced around the hospital cafeteria to see if anyone was watching or listening. No one was. "Is this on the level?"

Deacon raised scout's honor. "Technical name Project Seppuku."

Tremaine started to shake her head, grimaced and thought better of it. "I figured you were dealing with some bioterror threat, anthrax or something. But a suicide drug? No wonder they expunged that from the file." She glanced around again, then looked at Deacon. "And you're telling me that Harris, the VP, was a Russian agent? I heard she died choking on a piece of radish."

Deacon smiled ruefully. "Both true."

Tremaine looked at her cup as if some important answer was inside. "And that's what you're working on? A cure for this seppuku drug?"

Deacon nodded.

"And Barzoon? Another Russian agent?"

"Yes," Deacon said. "One to which I gave a full dose of the suicide drug."

"But he's not dead."

"Which is why I think there must be a cure that we don't know about."

Tremaine nodded in understanding. "So, why is Barzoon after you?"

Deacon sipped coffee that had gone cold. "I don't know. Revenge doesn't make sense. Revenge for what? And why kidnap Amy?"

"To get to you?" Tremaine said.

"To what end? If they already have a cure, what do they need a washed-up wunderkind who only started working on one a couple of weeks ago."

Tremaine smiled. "Don't be so hard on yourself." She swirled her cup; it was empty. "Maybe all this goes deeper. If Barzoon is a Russian plant, maybe he's looking for something else, something for the Kremlin."

Deacon shrugged. "Again, what?"

She shook a negative. "Whatever it is, he needs Robbins for some reason." She raised a finger. "He *took* her. He didn't kill her." She placed her hand gently on Deacon's. "Which hopefully means he'll keep her alive. Which gives us time."

Deacon met her gaze. "What's our next move?"

Tremaine removed her hand. "*My* next move is to search for our fugitive. Which means searching for Metternich. He shouldn't be that difficult to find, given what you've told me about his wife."

"Right," Deacon said. "You check out his residence in DC and the hospital where his wife is being treated. I'll check the hotel here. We'll need to question everyone we can…"

Tremaine snapped an iron grip on his wrist. "I said that was *my* job. Your job is back at your lab." Deacon started to protest, but she cut him off. "I may have screwed up with Robbins, but *your* safety is still my responsibility." She squeezed tighter. "Besides, we can't assume there's already a cure. You need to keep plugging away with your research."

"Fuck my research," Deacon said. "I'm the reason Amy is involved in this shitshow and I'm going to find her."

Tremaine gripped tighter. "Listen to me. This is nonnegotiable. *You* are my charge—mine. You stay where you can be protected. Besides which, you don't have the law-enforcement skills or the experience."

Deacon laughed. "I'll take my chances."

Pain flared in Deacon's wrist as Tremaine's nails dug into flesh. "I said no. We don't need amateurs mucking things up."

Deacon broke her grip and stood up, toppling his chair. "I have combat experience in Iraq. I won a medal for valor." He thumped his chest. "And this amateur, not law enforcement, managed to stop a plot to take over the government." Deacon stopped abruptly. Eyes were on him from several scrub tops and lab coats.

Tremaine smiled at the spectators but whispered to Deacon. "Why don't you shout a little louder? I think the people in the OR didn't hear you."

Deacon cleared his throat and sat.

"Listen to me carefully," Tremaine said. "There is a strong policy in the Marshal's service, in the FBI, in every other *legitimate* law enforcement organization. People with personal interest, people whose loved ones have gone missing, stay out of investigations."

Deacon started to protest before she stabbed a finger in his face. "When they don't, people get hurt." She paused to let that sink in. "Do you want Amy's death on your conscience? Don't you have enough there now?"

Deacon opened his mouth, then stopped himself. She knew just where to hit him, and the blow had landed.

She again placed her hand gently on his. "I'll find your Amy. I promise you. Okay?"

Deacon's eyes met hers. He nodded. "For now."

Chapter 20

Amy wasn't sure how long she'd slept or what time it was. She only knew that the lights had been out and that they were now turned on. Her head ached. The glare from the bedside lamp hurt her eyes so she turned toward the wall. The window was still covered, so she couldn't tell if it was night or day.

The spartan room still seemed oddly familiar, as if she'd been here before. She tried to figure out why when she was distracted by the sound of running water. Her body tensed, her aches and pains from the last week twinging to life. The running water stopped. Amy turned, expecting to see Barzoon enter from the attached bath. Instead, an African American woman of about her own age came in holding a washcloth. The woman was clad in green scrubs. She looked stressed and exhausted, a sad smile on her face.

"I see you're up."

It took Amy a moment to recognize Isabela Sanford. She tried to speak, but her lips and mouth were dry. Amy swallowed with difficulty and managed, "What are you doing here?"

Sanford wiped Amy's face with the damp cloth. The doctor was dressed only in green scrubs. Her face was haggard. "I've been asking myself the same question." Sanford placed the cloth on either side of Amy's runny nose. "Blow."

Amy blew her nose into the damp cloth. She tried to speak again but only croaked.

"Here, sip this." Sanford held forth a cup from the bedside table. It was one of those large, plastic cups with a lid and straw, the kind they used in hospital rooms.

Amy drank greedily before she remembered about Barzoon. She turned her head away, the room spinning.

"More?" Sanford asked.

"What are you doing here?"

Sanford's sigh filled the empty room. "Well, the best I can figure out, I'm supposed to be your personal physician."

Amy turned slowly to look at Sanford. "Barzoon *hired* you?"

"Hired?" Sanford's laugh bordered on hysterical. "Not hardly. I didn't exactly take this job on freely." Sanford placed her left foot on the bed, revealing a manacle around her ankle. The manacle was attached to a length of rubber-coated cable. Sanford hefted the cable, then threw it down. "To be precise, I am only *free* to travel from the bed to the bathroom." She jabbed a finger toward the far wall. "I can't even reach the window to see where the hell I am!"

The glare of the light combined with Sanford's yell upped Amy's headache. "Take it easy."

"Take it easy?" Sanford screamed. Her body shook with rage and fear. "I'm kidnapped by some nut, and then I'm chained to a bed in some strange house." Tears rolled down the physician's cheeks as she frantically gesticulated around her. "And this nut informs me that I am to be personal physician for a woman I barely know." She began to laugh again, hysteria only inches away.

"Get control of yourself," Amy said. "I don't understand you."

Sanford suddenly stopped mid laugh. She closed her eyes and clutched her arms. Amy saw her take a deep breath, then slowly let it out. She'd seen the same type of breathing during difficult surgery, when the cutter in charge needed to collect his wits enough to continue.

"Right," Sanford said. "Let me see if I can explain it." She looked at Amy, her eyes revealing barely restrained panic. "I had just finished a particularly grueling eight hours, including a cardiac arrest, when …"

Sanford stopped and spun toward the sound of a lock turning. Nelson Barzoon entered from the open doorway. In one hand, he held his pistol. In the other, a plastic grocery bag with "Melville Hospital Supplies" printed on it. He smiled his forced smile.

"Getting reacquainted, I see."

Barzoon tossed the bag casually on the bed. "Some supplies you'll be needing, Doctor."

"Supplies?" Sanford asked. Amy could see that the physician was frightened to the point of imbecility.

Barzoon nodded, then flicked the pistol toward the bed.

Sanford slowly picked up the shopping bag and reached inside. She withdrew a liter bag of sterile five-percent glucose solution and an IV kit. Sanford looked at Barzoon, her eyes puzzled.

Barzoon smiled and waved again with the pistol.

Again, Sanford reached into the bag, withdrawing another liter-sized bag of fluids. Unlike the clear bag of D5W, the solution in this second bag was hazy yellow. Amy couldn't make out the small print, but large block letters read "Nutritional supplement for IV administration."

"I'll bring more as needed," Barzoon said. "But that should get you started."

"Started doing what?" Sanford asked, still puzzled.

"I think it should be obvious, Doctor. Keeping your patient alive."

Jaw slack, Sanford looked at Amy. She then turned slowly to Barzoon. "You want me to put in an IV and feed her?"

Barzoon smiled in approval. He pointed the pistol at the grocery bag. "You'll find alcohol and iodine solution inside. Along with gloves, an IV catheter, syringes, and tape." He pouted. "I'm sorry I couldn't include scissors, but I'm sure an experienced physician is used to ripping tape."

Sanford again gaped at Amy, then Barzoon. He didn't seem to notice.

"I'll bring in an IV stand in a few moments, as well as a plastic …" He almost seemed to blush. "Well, something for elimination purposes. I'm afraid you will need to function as practical nurse as well as physician. I've taken the bedroom downstairs to give you your privacy for such matters." He turned to leave.

"Listen," Sanford blurted. "Let me go. I won't tell anyone. I'll, I'll leave town. Never come back. *Please*?"

Barzoon's face turned solemn. "Why, Doctor. What of your Hippocratic oath?" He pointed with the pistol. "You have a patient. Without you, she'll die."

"What's wrong with her?"

Barzoon scowled. "Just keep her alive."

Sanford looked at Amy, then frantically looked again at Barzoon. "Let us both go. I'll get her to a hospital."

He pointed the pistol for silence. His face was grim death, but with a hint of a Freddy Krueger grin. "I'll set you free in good time, Doctor." The grin brightened. "Set us all free. For now, just do your job." The grin was gone as quickly as it had arisen. "Or I'll have to provide incentives."

Sanford gulped. "Incentives?"

His hint of a smile was back. "Suffice it to say you wouldn't like them. But I'm sure you could do your job as well with nine fingers instead of ten. Perhaps eight, if it comes to that." He left and locked the door.

¢¢¢

Deacon realized he'd been reading the same page for ten minutes. He tossed the report aside and rose to get some coffee.

Tremaine said she'd keep him up to date, but that seemed hours ago. He looked at the clock and saw that she'd left him only forty minutes ago.

He couldn't stop thinking about Amy. How had this happened? He blamed Metternich. He blamed the Marshals service. He blamed Tremaine. Mostly he blamed himself. Amy had been safe and alive before she'd hooked up again with him. How had he allowed this to happen?

His cell rang. He almost dropped the coffee pot as he snatched up his phone.

"Hello."

"Deacon?"

He recognized Tremaine's voice. "Yeah, go ahead."

"So far, no sign of Metternich. Our people in DC have checked out the hospital where his wife is. The staff haven't seen him in over twelve hours, which is unusual. Typically, he spends the better part of the day there, either visiting his wife or sitting in the chapel."

"How is Claudia Metternich?"

"Heavily sedated," Tremaine said. "Listen, they've staked out his house, the hospital, and his hotel room in Dayton. I put out a BOLO for him or his car. Not sure there is much more to do on that front."

"What about Movello? Have you questioned him?"

"I kind of thought you might want to be present for that."

"I'll meet you downstairs in ten minutes."

Howard entered the office as Deacon was leaving. "Where are you going?"

"Out," Deacon replied. "I have to meet someone."

"The cop downstairs said we have a package. It might be that conjugate I ordered. I thought we could try it out on another set of rats."

"Good idea," Deacon said. "Why don't you get started? I should be back in a couple of hours."

"But …"

Deacon patted Howard's shoulder. "I have every confidence."

¢¢¢

Sanford used an alcohol swab to wipe away the iodine solution. "Okay, you're going to feel a little stick. Don't …"

Before she could finish her sentence, Amy swung her arm violently.

Sanford jumped back, dropping the IV catheter but snatching it midair with a gloved hand. "Are you crazy? A second later and I could have ripped open your vein."

"That was the idea," Amy said.

"What are you talking about?"

Amy caught her breath. "Listen, Dr. Sanford."

"Why don't you call me Izzie, and I'll call you Amy, okay? A nice cordial relationship." She repositioned herself next to Amy's outstretched arm. "So, Amy, let's try this again. Only this time, you lie still. Otherwise, I'll have to answer to that crazy man holding us prisoner, something I'm not looking forward to. Deal?"

Amy thought for a bit then nodded. "Listen, Dr. Sanford. I mean Izzie. I need you to do me a favor."

Sanford slid the catheter into Amy's vein, then released the tourniquet. Amy watched blood drip as Sanford taped the catheter in place. At the beginning of her corpsman training, the sight of blood made Amy queasy. She'd lost that feeling well before her overseas deployments. She'd set it aside, had willed away any distress. It was part of the job. But now, there was almost a longing at watching her life's blood drip. The feeling brought on panic, and she cast it aside.

"If I can," Sanford said as she hooked up IV tubing.

For just a moment, blood flowed up the tubing before it was pushed down by fluid flow. Amy felt the cold liquid entering her vein.

"You have syringes in that bag, right?"

Sanford nodded. "Three, five, and twelve mL. Why?"

"I want you to get one of the twelve mL syringes and fill it with air."

Sanford squinted down at her. "To what purpose?"

Amy nodded toward the IV. "Then stop the fluid flow and fill the line with air."

"What? Are you crazy, girl?"

"I know that won't be enough. But if you did it ten or twelve times, then started the flow again."

"Are you trying to kill yourself?"

Amy pleaded with her eyes. "You don't want to keep me alive, Izzie. As long as *I'm* here, he's going to keep *you* here. Maybe if you let me die, then he'll let you go."

Sanford slapped Amy's cheek hard enough to sting. "Shut your mouth with talk like that. Hear me?" Sanford placed her face inches from Amy's. "Now you get this straight. First off, I'm a doctor. I don't help people die. Secondly, you think that nut is gonna let me go just because I no longer have a patient to tend to?"

Amy saw the terror hidden behind the anger in Sanford's eyes. Those eyes softened. "Why are you talking like this?"

Amy could feel tears trickle down her cheek. "I've put you at risk. I've put Deke at risk. I've made a mess of my life and everybody else's." She turned her head away. "It's better that I die."

Chapter 21

Vanessa Movello added toiletries to a small vinyl bag while Tony adjusted his sling. The wounded cop was dressed in jeans and tee shirt, his feet in loafers instead of hospital booties.

"May we come in?" Tremaine asked from the open doorway.

"Oh, sure," Tony said. He turned to his wife. "Honey, you remember Deke Creel."

Venessa smiled and nodded.

Tremaine walked over to the younger woman, hand extended. "I'm Terri Tremaine. I don't think we've met."

"My pleasure," Vanessa said as they shook hands.

Deacon pointed to the small case. "Looks like you're going home."

Tony Movello smiled at his wife. "Yeah. Finally." Vanessa smiled back.

"Mrs. Movello?" Tremaine said.

"Please, call me Vinnie."

Tremaine smiled her patented smile. "Okay, Vinnie. I'm Terri." Tremaine pointed to Tony. "Mind if we chat with your husband before you take him home?"

"Sure," Vanessa said. After a pause, she realized they meant in private. "Why don't I go call the sitter, see how Chip is doing."

Tremaine nodded and smiled. "Won't be a minute."

When his wife was gone, Movello said, "I'm really anxious to get home, so if … well, what can I do for you?" He motioned to the chairs.

Deacon and Tremaine remained standing.

"We've got some bad news," Tremaine said.

"Amy has been kidnapped," Deacon added.

"Kidnapped? Who? Why?"

"The who is Nelson Barzoon," Tremaine said.

"We hoped you could help with the why," Deacon added.

Tremaine turned to Deacon. "Why don't you let me handle this." She smiled at Movello. "We're hoping that you can help us figure out why, and more importantly, where he took her."

Movello shrugged. "I don't know what I can tell you." He gestured around the room. "I've been right here."

"I don't remember anyone accusing you, Tony," Deacon said.

"What? No." Movello looked nervous and scared—more nervous and scared than an innocent man should. "I just meant, I've been out of the loop, so, you know." He shrugged and tried to smile, not quite pulling it off.

"Deke?" Tremaine glared at Deacon, then smiled again at Movello. "We understand that. But we're hoping you might have remembered something about that night when Barzoon shot you. Might he have said anything? Given any reason? Anything at all?"

Movello plopped on the bed. Deacon read relief on his face, mixed with something else—maybe guilt.

"Nothing more than I've already told you." He fiddled with his sling. "You know, it kind of, you know, happened fast, and you know, I was scared and, well, you know."

"Why so nervous, Tony?"

The wounded cop turned suddenly toward Deacon. "Nervous, I'm not nervous."

Deacon shrugged. "You act upset."

"Deke?" Tremaine repeated. "I said I'd handle it."

Deacon ignored her. "What you got to be upset about?"

Movello rose and paced the room. "Well, let me see." He flashed fingers into the air, one by one. "I get shot by some guy I've never met. I wind up in the hospital. I can't crap because of the pain meds. I find out my partner hanged himself. And now you tell me that Amy was kidnapped." He snarled at Deacon. "That enough for you?"

Deacon smiled. "I never said your partner *hanged* himself."

Movello blanched. "You, um, you said he …"

"Committed suicide." Deacon finished.

"I just assumed," Movello stammered.

Deacon nodded. "You assumed right." Deacon turned to Tremaine. "Don't most cops use their service pistol for that?"

Tremaine nodded in response but stared at Movello.

"Why did you assume hanging?" Deacon asked.

"I, um, I must have read it in the paper or seen it on the news or something."

"It wasn't in the paper," Deacon replied. "Or on the news or something." Deacon turned to Tremaine. "Why don't you step out for coffee, Deputy?"

Tremaine started to protest, but the look on Deacon's face made her stop. She turned to Movello. "Can I get you anything?"

Movello shook his head. When Tremaine left, he turned to Deacon. "Listen, Deke. I don't know what you're getting at but …"

"Sit down, Tony." Deacon stomped forward and jammed a hand against Movello's wounded shoulder.

Movello yelped in pain and flopped on the bed. "What the hell do you think you're up to?"

"I'm trying to find out what *you're* up to." Deacon jammed the injury again.

"Ow. Stop, okay?"

"When you tell me what I need to hear." Once again, he jabbed the shoulder.

"Okay. Okay. Just stop."

"So, how come you know that Hal Lipsitz hanged himself?"

"I told you," Movello said. "I must have read it or something."

"Wrong answer." Deacon jabbed the hurt shoulder.

"Shit!" Tears of pain rose in Movello's eyes. "Stop! You're going to start it bleeding again."

"I'll stop when you tell me what I want to hear." Deacon reached out, ready to jab again.

Movello slid off the bed, away from Deacon, then scrambled up to standing. "Alright. I saw him."

Deacon paused, hand raised. "Sergeant Hal? When? After he committed suicide?"

Movello rubbed his sore shoulder and nodded. "I stopped by his place and saw him." Movello grimaced and swallowed hard. "I guess he'd been dead about a day, maybe more. I'm not sure."

"Why lie about it?" Deacon asked. "Better yet, why keep it to yourself? Why didn't you call it in? Or at least, cut him down?"

Movello shook his head. "I don't know. It kind of shook me up. I didn't want to touch him. And I was in a hurry. I, um, I had to go pick up Amy and …" He trailed off, evidently recognizing how lame the excuse was.

"You're lying, Tony." Deacon stepped forward.

Tony flinched back onto the bed again. "Stop!"

Deacon balled his hand into a fist. "Come on, Tony. You find your partner hanging off his banister and you just skip out for a night of fun with Amy?" Deacon cocked his fist back, ready for a hammer blow to the injured shoulder.

Movello wrapped his good arm protectively over the injured one. "Barzoon said he just wanted her out of the way."

Deacon paused, fist cocked, features hard as stone. "Barzoon was there?"

Movello scrambled farther back on the bed, his head and shoulders scrunched against the headboard. "He had a gun. Said he was gonna kill me unless …"

Deacon spoke with the cold detachment of a man who had killed before and wasn't above doing it again. "Kill you unless what?" Movello was panting hard. His eyes held a look Deacon had seen before. A look that begged to live—at any cost. It was the look Barzoon must have seen.

"Kill you unless what?" Deacon repeated.

"Unless I …" Movello hesitated, then rushed ahead. "Drugged Amy." He held up his hand protectively even though Deacon's expression did not change. "He said it was a harmless sedative. It would just knock her out for a few hours."

"You believed that?"

"He wanted her out of the way so that …"

"So that what?"

Movello's Adam's apple bobbed. "So that he could deal with you. He didn't want her around for that."

Deacon could almost hear the sound of his own teeth grinding. "You *agreed* to that?"

"He said he'd kill me if I didn't."

"And *did* you drug Amy?"

Movello didn't answer. He just cast his eyes down.

Deacon flicked his hand into the injured shoulder.

Movello yelped, then started to cry. "He said he was going to go after my family if I didn't. He said it would just knock her out, and then I could …" Movello gasped at the implications of what he'd almost admitted.

"Then you could what?" Deacon asked, an icy smile on his face. "A little roll in the hay with a compliant babe?"

Movello didn't answer. He just whimpered, "Please? I got a kid."

"What did this knockout drug look like?"

Movello wiped his nose. "A brownish liquid—looked kind of like the vanilla my wife puts in cookies."

Deacon nodded. Then he cocked his fist back and drove it into Movello's face. He heard a satisfying crunch of nasal bones breaking. The injured cop's eyes rolled white, and he slumped onto the bed as rivulets of blood soaked into the sheets.

"Knock. Knock."

Deacon turned slowly to see Terri Tremaine standing in the doorway.

"You hear what that piece of shit said?" he asked.

"Enough," Tremaine said. "The guard heard the commotion and wanted to check it out, but I said I'd handle it." She smiled her killer smile. "How did I do?"

Deacon shook out his hand. The knuckles had already started to swell. "Not bad for government work."

Tremaine pointed to the unconscious Movello. "I'm assuming that liquid he gave Amy wasn't for baking."

Deacon flexed his swollen hand. "Doesn't sound like it was Ambien either."

¢¢¢

Barzoon chewed a Xanax as he replaced the pill vial in his pocket. The drug was losing some of its effect despite his ever-increasing dosage. The dreams came more frequently, the urges too. Only his iron will kept him from ending things right now. He tapped the Makarov in his waistband, its presence cold, hard, and reassuring. He began to reach for the pistol, his hand moving on autopilot. His other hand, the hand of his will, caught his wrist in an iron grip. He squeezed ever harder, the pain forcing his gun hand to release the pistol butt. A shudder passed through him as both hands relaxed. His breath steadied. He knocked gently on the door.

"Yes," a female voice answered. It was the doctor's voice.

"May I enter?"

"Do we have a choice?"

Barzoon chuckled mirthlessly and opened the door. "As a matter of fact, you do." He walked toward the camera set up at the far end of the room. "If you were in the middle of a medical procedure or if your nursing duties were involved: daily ablution, waste elimination, or the like, I would naturally wait."

"Aren't we the gentleman," Sanford sneered.

He stopped and stared at her. She held his gaze for a moment, then turned away. Barzoon walked toward her, his hand extended. "First things first."

Sanford raised her brows.

He smiled and motioned with his hand. "Deposit sharps here."

Sanford sighed, then reached into the pocket of her scrubs. She handed him the needles she'd used to administer vitamins to Robbins's IV.

He accepted the capped needles and placed them in his pants pocket before walking to the camera.

He eyed the viewfinder as he spoke. "How is our patient today?"

"Please," Robbins said. Barzoon placed her gaunt face in the center of the image and zoomed. "Let Dr. Sanford go. You can kill me, have your revenge, whatever, but let *her* go. She didn't do anything."

Barzoon nodded, his eye still fixed in the viewfinder. "Yes, I'm sure you would enjoy that. Have the death you feel you deserve while performing a heroic act. Almost martyrdom." He looked up and spoke coldly. "But what about the death I deserve? What of my heroic act?" His voice rose. "The heroic act denied me by your Dr. Creel. My just reward for achieving so much." His voice continued to intensify, its echo bounding off the walls. "Rising so high. Rising to heights deemed impossible."

He was screaming now, his face flushed, his skin pulled tight, blood pounding in his ears. "Only to have it come crashing down in failure." Suddenly the flood of words petered out into a quiet trickle. "Because of one smug, self-important, little man." He felt better—not good, he would never feel good again, but better. He smiled. "You ladies must forgive me. I'm not quite myself these days."

Sanford smiled back. "But you're still human, I see. With human weakness—like the need for revenge. So, you want your pound of flesh. Sounds kind of plebian for a man of your stature, Mr. Barzoon. I'd think you were above that sort of thing."

Barzoon eyed Sanford suspiciously.

The good doctor smiled and nodded. "I've heard all about you from our mutual friend here."

Barzoon turned to the prostrate Robbins. She held his gaze. He saw no defiance in her eyes, neither was there peace. Her look spoke a prayer for release, not from her bonds, but from this world. "A little *girl talk* to pass the time?" He turned back to Sanford. "Perhaps ways to end things for Ms. Robbins using your limited resources?" He saw Sanford blanch, and knew he was close to the mark. He returned his eye to the viewfinder. "Perhaps if Amy asks me nicely, I'll grant her request." He zoomed on Robbins's face, tears glistening in her eyes.

"Please," she whispered.

Barzoon pulled a digital disk from his pocket; it snagged on something for a moment then tugged free. He slipped the flash drive into the camera setup.

"That's right, my dear. Just speak what's in your heart." He pressed the record button.

Chapter 22

Deacon sat in his university office sipping his fifth cup of bad coffee and listening to Tremaine tell him no for the fifth time.

"Get it through your egghead," Tremaine said. "Your place is here." She rapped her knuckles on his desk. "This is what you do, what you are *trained* to do." She thumbed over her shoulder. "Out there, finding Amy, Barzoon, and Joe Metternich, that's what U.S. Marshals are trained to do." Her thumb jabbed one pert breast. "What *I* am trained to do."

Deacon chuckled. "Who found out about Barzoon? *You*?" He tapped his chest. "No, it was me and Amy." He looked about the room. "And who was fooled by Joe, leaving Amy unprotected? Oh wait, *that* would be you." He held out three fingers. "And who discovered that likable Tony Movello was really a scumbag mole in *your* security detail?" Deacon tapped his chest, then smirked. "So much for U.S. Marshals and their training." He downed the rest of his coffee, then slumped into his desk chair.

Tremaine's high cheekbones flushed. She closed her eyes and inhaled deeply. After a count of ten, she exhaled slowly and glared at Deacon.

"If we're going to set the record straight, let's include a few things you left out, Dr. Creel." She smacked fingers into her palm. "Who decided that this research should be done in some Podunk Midwestern university instead of the heightened security in Bethesda? Wouldn't that be the *same* guy who chose Movello and Lipsitz for *my* security detail? The same guy who kept this whole Project Suicide cluster fuck a secret from me, so I couldn't assess the threat properly." Tremaine slapped all five fingers in her open palm. "And who was it that got Robbins involved in the first place? I sure as hell didn't need her around." Tremaine turned away, then swung back for a parting shot. "And who is it that allowed Amy to go off on a date with Movello without ever notifying me or any of the marshals?" She shook her head in disgust. "Yep, Deke. You're batting a thousand."

Deacon clattered his empty cup onto the desk; the noise was thunderous in the silence. Tremaine's rebukes had struck home, especially the latter ones. Deacon had indeed insisted that Amy stick around, placing her in danger for his own vanity and personal comfort. Deacon had been the one who got drunk instead of going after her and Movello, or at least sending the marshals after them. Deacon was the one complicating security, the one pushing petulance and ego ahead of what was best. He sighed. Things hadn't changed. Same old know-it-all, even though he was now more has-been than wunderkind.

A quiet knock on the door broke Deacon's musing. He started to answer, but Tremaine beat him to it.

"Yes?"

The door opened a crack and Howie's bespectacled head poked in. "Um, Dr. Creel? Deke?" Deacon turned his way. "There's a package for you."

Deacon waved him off. "FedEx lab supplies? You handle it, Howie."

Howard cleared his throat. "Actually, it's not FedEx. It's someplace called Speedy Messenger Service. And the package is marked personal—your eyes only."

¢¢¢

"I think we should have it checked out first," Tremaine said. "Perhaps it's a bomb or virus of some kind."

Deacon examined the small flash drive. "What's someone trying to do? Destroy my laptop?"

Tremaine chuckled. "Very funny. I'm just saying, as a security matter, it should be checked out."

"I wouldn't worry. I think that Barzoon or whoever sent it is trying to communicate, not assassinate."

"Okay. I at least think I should be present when you see it."

Deacon put down the flash drive and used two fingers to pick up the mailer it came in. "It says for my eyes only."

"I think we can disregard that. Don't you?"

Deacon thought for a moment before saying, "No, I don't." He thrust the envelope toward Tremaine. "I think I should see whatever is on the flash drive while you check this for prints and trace evidence."

Tremaine started to protest, then gently grasped the edge of the envelope. "You can be a real pain in the ass. You know that, Dr. Creel?"

Deacon smiled. "So I've been told."

Tremaine shook her head and walked toward the door.

"Close that behind you, please," Deacon said. He smiled again when the door banged shut. "A slammed door is still a woman's most potent argument."

Deacon examined the flash drive again, then plugged it into his laptop. He looked about the little office while his virus software checked for problems. The room reminded him of the office he'd shared as a postdoc. This one was a little bigger and a little neater, but the institutional furnishings were much the same. He was reminded again of the passage of time. The many changes it brought, the many losses. He thought of Liz. He thought of his own wunderkind potential.

His trip down memory lane was abruptly halted by the shocking image on his screen. Amy stared up at him. It took him a moment to recognize her because her face carried an expression he'd never seen before. He'd known her happy, exhausted, frightened, determined, even rebellious. But her eyes had always held an underlying gentleness, a warmth that spoke of compassion, service to others, an inherent humanity. The eyes looking at him now were haunted. They were the eyes of a hunted animal caught in a snare. They were the eyes of abject despair.

¢¢¢

Tears streamed down Robbins's cheeks. Her eyes were red, spiderwebbed with conjunctival inflammation. Snot dripped down her nose, another upper respiratory sign that Creel was unlikely to miss. Her voice rasped with anguished weeping. "Forget me, Deke," she begged. "I'm no good for you. I'm no good for anyone." She momentarily closed her eyes, her head and shoulders twitched with sobs. She opened her eyes again. Her suffering was unmistakable. "Let me die. That's all I want now." She stared past the screen toward Barzoon. Her eyes pleaded. Her words came out as hitching gasps. "Please. Please let me die."

Barzoon started to zoom in further when a new face popped into the frame.

"This is bullshit!" Sanford screamed. "Deke, whoever you are, this is bullshit! Don't you listen to her! You hear me? Something very wrong is going on here."

Barzoon pressed stop.

"You know I can just edit that out, don't you, Doctor?"

Sanford ran toward him, her fists balled. Barzoon did not flinch. Instead, he smiled as her foot came up short against the plasticized cable. He heard the clack of her jaws as she dropped to the floor.

"Careful, Doctor. Such impetuosity is dangerous."

Sanford clutched an injured elbow and glared at him. "You bastard. I hope you rot in hell."

Barzoon's smile died. "No doubt. The sooner the better."

Chapter 23

Deacon ran down the stairs of the science building and almost knocked over Tremaine. She dropped the evidence envelope with the small mailer inside.

"Hey," she shouted. "Where are you going?"

"Out," he replied heading for the door.

Tremaine held up her hand and yelled, "Jablonsky." The big Montgomery County sheriff's deputy guarding the entrance stepped in front of Deacon.

Deacon paused, then pivoted back to Tremaine. "Tell your guard dog to knock it off, or I'll knock him *out*."

"You think so, huh?" the deputy said with a smirk.

Deacon balled his fist. "I know so."

"Okay," Tremaine said. "We don't have time for a pissing contest, either of you." She gently put a hand on Deacon's arm. "You want to tell me where you're going?"

Deacon shook her hand off. "First, I'm going to kill Tony Movello."

"He's our best lead, Deke."

"Then I'm going to find Amy."

"And how do you plan on doing that?" Tremaine asked.

Deacon closed his eyes and took a deep breath. When he opened them, Tremaine stared sympathetically back.

"Why don't you show me what's on that flash drive?"

¢¢¢

Tremaine pressed stop and looked up from the computer. "The suicide drug?"

Deacon pinched his eyes, holding back a tear. He nodded. "The upper respiratory signs are ..."

He turned away. "It looks like a common cold. That's one of the hallmarks."

"Couldn't it just *be* a common cold?" Tremaine asked.

"It could—but it's not," Deacon replied. "The look in Amy's eyes. The agony." He turned away again. He started to speak but had trouble getting the words out. "She, ah, the talk of wanting to die. It's 606. Movello must have dosed her—the son of a bitch."

"Then why is Barzoon or whoever doing this?"

"It's Barzoon," Deacon said. "It has to be."

"Okay. So why is he keeping her alive?"

"To punish me." Deacon pounded his desk. The pain radiating up his arm felt good. It was much less than he deserved, just a down payment, but he relished it, nonetheless.

"To what end?"

Deacon turned to her, his throat tight. "I don't know." He paced the room. "If they have a cure, which his being alive suggests, why does he give a flying fuck? Why isn't he living it up in Moscow or some dacha on the Baltic?" Deacon shook his head and raised his fist to administer a punch to the wall.

"Breaking your hand isn't going to give us the answer … or find Amy."

Deacon paused mid punch, then slumped his butt against the desk. Head in hands, he said, "I just don't know what to do."

Tremaine rose and patted Deacon's shoulder. "Well, let's look at this logically." Now she paced the room, ticking points off her fingers. "We know that Barzoon has Amy. We know that Amy has been given the suicide drug. We know that Barzoon is keeping her alive." She pointed to the laptop. "Evidently to send you love notes like this one." She paused in thought. "So, at least we know we have time. That Amy is safe."

"You call that safe?" Deacon shouted.

Tremaine held up her palms. "Safe enough for now. As long as Barzoon thinks he can get to you this way, he's going to keep her alive."

"But why is he doing it?" Deacon repeated.

Tremaine shook her head. "That's the sixty-four-thousand-dollar question."

Deacon rubbed the knot forming in the back of his neck. "What is Barzoon even doing here? Why is he risking his neck to make me suffer when he was safe, free and clear? If he's cured of the 606, why isn't he enjoying his well-known zest for living instead of …" It suddenly hit Deacon like a thunderbolt. "Zest for living." He nodded. "That was Barzoon's trademark when I knew him in DC. The good life. Good food. Good drink. Leisure." He turned to Tremaine, his jaw slack. "What comes with that?"

She shrugged. "Fancy clothes. Maybe a red nose from too much booze? A few extra pounds from goose-liver pate." Her eyes popped. "Wait a minute. Both Movello and Amy described him as thin and gaunt. Blue-collar clothes."

"Not exactly a Beau Brummel enjoying the good life, is it? Not if there is a cure and it took hold."

"But if there isn't a cure," she said, "why isn't Barzoon dead?"

Deacon raised a finger. "Maybe he just isn't dead, *yet*."

"What do you mean?"

Deacon tapped his finger on the desk. "I got the impression they really didn't know much about this suicide drug before they produced it. That is to say, it can't have gotten much human testing beyond Snyder Lab's initial patients and the handful of victims."

Tremaine smiled. "Not exactly going to be a crowd of volunteers signing up in exchange for free carfare and a gift card."

"Exactly," Deacon said. "The handful of cases that we know about committed suicide. But what if …"

Her blue eyes flashed in understanding. "What if everyone isn't affected the same? A range of efficacy? Some less affected than others."

"With Barzoon in the former group."

Tremaine sat down, her slightly shorter than regulation skirt riding up a nyloned leg. "So, maybe, just maybe, he *wants* to take his own life but he's forgoing that pleasure until he has his revenge."

"Revenge on me for taking away his good life."

Tremaine nodded. "Maybe he's using drugs to help keep temptation away. Mood elevators. During his interrogation, Movello described Barzoon as a little spaced-out, with eyes like a junkie's."

"That could just be fatigue, or maybe Officer Tony was blowing smoke," Deacon said.

She shook her head. "No, Movello may have told us some bullshit here and there, but I trust his judgment on that one. Uniformed cops see enough junkies to recognize the breed."

Deacon shoved hands in his pockets. He was exhausted. He hadn't gotten much sleep since Amy went missing. And he was worried. If Barzoon was fighting the effects of 606 while high on mood elevators, he could become dangerously unstable. On the spur of the moment, he might ditch his revenge fantasy, kill Amy, then kill himself.

But worry and exhaustion weren't Deacon's only burdens. The feeling that overrode all others, the old friend that preoccupied his waking thoughts and nighttime dreams, was guilt. He'd lived with guilt for a long time, ever since his mother's suicide. Over time, the weight of it grew. There was Liz, his fiancé who suffered and died because of Deacon's ego and arrogance. Lisa, his best friend, a victim of Deacon's misdirected anger. Politicians like Hernandez, Waters, and Lebel, who died because of Deacon's naivete in lending his mind to the evil that was Project Suicide. Now Amy, suffering because of Deacon's petulance and pride. Suffering and likely to … He couldn't bring himself to finish the thought.

"Deke?" Tremaine said.

He sighed. "Maybe I better have another chat with Officer Tony. See if I can get anything more out of him."

Tremaine shrugged. "If you want." She cleared her throat as she stood up. "But I have to warn you that we no longer are allowed to pursue interrogation methods that produce physical discomfort." She met his gaze. "I turned a blind eye once, but that's as far as I'm prepared to go."

Deacon smiled. "I promise I won't lay a hand on him."

Tremaine smiled back. "That's good. And I'll be right beside you to make sure you keep your word."

¢¢¢

Tony Movello sat alone in a cell at the Montgomery County Jail. When he saw the guard bring in Deacon and Tremaine, he jumped to his feet and backed against the far wall.

"Get that psycho away from me!" Movello yelled at the guard.

"Take it easy, Tony," Deacon said. "I just want to talk to you."

"I want my lawyer," Movello said. He pointed at Deacon. "I don't want to be alone with *him*."

"Deputy Marshal Tremaine will be here the whole time," Deacon said.

Movello scoffed as he caressed his injured shoulder. "Lot of good she did last time we met."

The guard opened the door and said, "You got fifteen minutes."

Tremaine smiled at the guard as he left. The guard smiled back. Deacon figured that smile may have bought them another fifteen.

Tremaine turned her smile on Movello. "I can get your union lawyer here if you want. It'll take a little time."

Deacon shook his head and chuckled. "You wanna lawyer up *now*, Tony? We just want to ask some more questions. The more you cooperate, the better it'll go for you. A smart cop like you knows that, right?"

Movello glared at Deacon.

"You want that lawyer?" Tremaine asked.

Movello paused, then turned from Deacon to Tremaine. "I guess not. Not if you're gonna be here and it's just questions." His eyes glared. "But that asshole touches me, I'm gonna scream bloody murder."

"No one's going to touch you, Tony," Deacon said. He pointed to the bed. "Mind if I sit down?"

Tony didn't answer. Deacon sat.

"I want you to remember back to your meeting with Barzoon," Deacon said.

"I already told everything I know about that."

Deacon smiled. "Humor me." He pointed to the corner of Movello's cell. "Your partner is hanging there stiff and blue, black tongue sticking out. You're trying to get him down when Barzoon speaks to you. That right?"

Movello nodded.

"When did Barzoon come in … exactly?"

"I already told everybody. I don't know. I was busy with Hal."

"And what exactly did Barzoon say to you?"

Movello sighed. "Like I said, he told me to leave Hal alone. That the fall killed him." Movello looked into the corner as if he could still see Sergeant Hal hanging there. "Then he told me to toss my guns on the floor."

"Did you?"

Movello glared. "He was pointing a pistol at me."

"What kind of pistol?"

Movello shook his head. "Jeez. For the thousandth time, one of those Russian jobs. A macaroon or something."

"Continue."

Movello leaned against the wall and spoke in a rush of words, as if pissed that he had to say it all again. "Barzoon told me he had caused Hal to kill himself. Then he said he could do the same thing to my family. He tossed me a vial of something."

"A knockout drug?" Deacon asked. "That's what he said?"

Movello smiled. "Actually, he called it a 'sleeping draught.'"

Deacon returned his smile. "Go ahead."

"He said he just wanted Amy out of the way for a few hours while he dealt with you."

"What exactly did he want with me?"

Movello grinned cruelly. "Revenge."

"What kind of revenge?"

"He didn't say. I didn't ask."

"Go on."

Movello shrugged. "I said go to hell or words to that effect and tossed back the vial. Barzoon said, in that case, I was no more use to him. He pointed the gun at me. I saw his trigger-finger tighten." Another shrug. "I agreed."

"Then you slipped the drug to Amy?"

Deacon saw the cop's Adam's apple bob. Movello nodded.

"Why didn't you just agree and then report it?"

"Like I said. He threatened my family."

"But it was okay that he threatened me?"

Movello laughed. "I don't even *like* you."

Deacon grinned. "We have that in common." Deacon waved his hand. "Then Barzoon just tossed you the vial and left?"

Movello hesitated, as if he was thinking about something he didn't want to say. "Yeah."

"He didn't say anything else? He didn't do anything else?"

"That's right …" Movello's eyebrows rose. "Wait a second." He raised a finger. "Actually, he stopped by the door."

"And?"

Movello stood up straight, eyes looking into the past. "His back was to me, so I couldn't see. But he stopped and reached into his pocket for something."

Deacon glanced at Tremaine, who was clearly interested. "Something what?" Deacon asked.

Movello shook his head. "I couldn't see. But I *heard* a pop."

"What kind of pop?"

"Like when you pop the top off a bottle. Then he leaned back a little and tossed something into his mouth. He turned to point the pistol at me one final time, and I noticed he was chewing."

Deacon glanced again at Tremaine, who was staring back at him. "What was in his hand, the one not holding the gun? The one he reached into his pocket with?"

Movello shook his head, his eyes coming back to the present. "I was staring down the barrel of the pistol, not looking at his other hand. I figured …"

"What?"

Movello shrugged. "That he was going to kill me anyway. He looked like he wanted to." He shook his head. "Then later, outside the brewpub, I *knew* he wanted to." Movello sighed again. "I should have known he wouldn't let me live. No matter what I did."

"Why is that?" Deacon asked.

Movello's shoulders slumped as he stared at his jailhouse slippers. "The way he looked. All, I don't know, twitchy. Like a junkie in need of a fix."

Deacon again met Tremaine's blue-eyed stare. "Describe how he looked."

Movello's shoulders rose and fell. "Like I said, like a junkie. His eyes were bloodshot, the pupils big. They had kind of a haunted appearance. And he looked … gaunt." Movello rubbed his jaw. "In his face, like when someone has lost a lot of weight from cancer or some sickness."

"What was he wearing?"

Movello looked at Deacon as if that was a stupid question. "A red jacket, one of the type like James Dean wore in that rebel movie." He motioned with his hand. "It hung loose on him, again like he'd lost weight or maybe just bought a size too big."

"No suit jacket, suit pants, spit-shined shoes?"

Movello shook a negative. "Chinos and a pair of knockoff sneakers."

Deacon and Tremaine stared at each other in understanding. "One last time, Tony," Deacon said. "Did he mention anything about what he wanted to do to me? Or where he might be taking Amy? Or any of his plans at all?"

Movello slowly shook his head from side to side. "Only that he wanted revenge on you. And that the drug would make Amy sleepy."

The guard came back. "You done?"

Deacon nodded, and he and Tremaine started to leave. Deacon paused at the cell door and turned back to Movello. "Did it?"

Movello's eyes clouded. "Did it what?"

"Did it make Amy sleepy?"

Movello thought for a moment, then shook his head.

"And you didn't think that odd?"

Movello studied his shoes again. "I was too worried about my family." He paused. "And my own life." He looked at Deacon. "I know what you're thinking, Deke. You're thinking that as a cop, I should have known he was lying, that he wouldn't let me live."

Deacon raised his brows.

Movello blushed and studied his slippers.

As they walked down the jailhouse hallway, Deacon said, "Looks like we're right. Barzoon is spaced-out on something to help keep suicidal urges at bay."

"You think Prozac or alprazolam?"

"Or Clonidine or bupropion or who knows."

The guard walked them through a double-locked entryway into a reception area. No visitors sat at any of the institutional tables. The only resident was the sergeant manning the desk.

"Maybe even amphetamines," Deacon said.

"Amphetamines?" Tremaine asked, showing her badge to the sergeant at the desk.

Deacon handed in his visitor's pass. "Mood elevators make you drowsy. Barzoon has been too busy to be sleeping all the time."

Deacon held the exit door for Tremaine. They headed onto Second Street and walked toward East Lot parking.

"You said that Movello was our best witness. Are there others? Someone at the brewpub?"

Tremaine shook her head. "No, they were inside. They dove to the floor when the shooting started. I meant Sinclair."

"Who?"

"Carl J. Sinclair. He's the one who found Amy."

Deacon was perplexed.

"Over on Clark Street? Near the brewpub? The night Movello got shot?"

"Oh," Deacon said. "Well, let's go talk to him."

"He's been talked to," Tremaine said. "He was a zero. See no evil, hear no evil. Described Barzoon well enough, but then …" Her shoulders raised. "He was worried only about his driving record."

They reached Tremaine's Lincoln. Deacon heard the door locks pop.

"Well," Tremaine said, "if Barzoon is mixing speed and downers, he's going to be unpredictably dangerous."

"I think we've already established that," Deacon quipped, getting into the car.

Tremaine unbuttoned her blazer and cinched on her shoulder harness. "Yeah, I know. But I meant, *highly* unpredictable. Mercurial. Liable to go against his own best interests."

"You don't know the half of it," Deacon said as buckled his own seatbelt. "This suicide drug, formula 606, acts on the brain. So do all the other drugs we mentioned."

"They interact with each other?"

Deacon shrugged. "Who knows? Like I said, there hasn't been a lot of human testing. The only effects they know for sure are initial cold-like symptoms followed by suicide."

Tremaine started the engine. "Movello didn't mention respiratory symptoms in Barzoon. Neither did Amy or Sinclair."

Deacon shrugged again. "Maybe they wear off after a while. No victim has ever hung around long enough to find out." As they drove forward, Deacon asked, "Where do you think he's getting the drugs?"

"What?" Tremaine asked, glancing in the rearview.

"The mood elevators and amphetamines," Deacon said. "They're not exactly over the counter."

"Probably black market," she replied, heading into traffic.

"Street drugs?" Deacon said. "Doesn't sound like Barzoon. I can't see him hanging around the ghetto to hit up the neighborhood pusher. Besides, he doesn't have the connections." Deacon shook his head. "No, white-collar junkies usually deal with white-collar sources. Doctor shopping, brother who's a pharmacist, something like that."

"Does it matter?"

"Maybe," Deacon said. "We might be able to track him through his source." He paused in thought. "You think the Russians are supplying him?"

Tremaine chuckled. "Don't you think that's a little far-fetched? They might meddle in an election every now and then, maybe a cyberattack or two. But why would Russia want revenge on you?"

Deacon tried to rub the strain from his eyes. "I don't know. All I do know is that we've got an unstable sociopath hyped up on uppers, downers, and a suicide drug. And this guy has got Amy."

Tremaine looked at Deacon. Their eyes locked in understanding. Tremaine nodded. "I think we need to find your Amy as quickly as possible."

Chapter 24

Amy watched Barzoon leave. She heard the click of the door lock. It was a sad sound. She didn't know when he would be back. She only knew that he hadn't answered her plea—she was still alive. Her sadness held one silver lining. She had been able to communicate with Deke, to let him know he should forget about her. She hoped this would convince him that she was unworthy of his love, that she could only be a burden not a partner. Part of her knew she hadn't always felt that way, but that wasn't the part in control. The controlling part, the overriding, commanding part said it was true. She wished she was dead.

Suddenly Isabela Sanford's face filled her vision.

"What's the matter with you, girl?" Sanford shouted. "Why are you doing what that bastard wants?" Sanford nodded toward the door. "Why are you giving him the satisfaction?"

New tears rose in Amy's eyes. She felt them run warmly down her cheeks and join the snot dripping from her nose. "So, he'll kill me. If I give him what he wants, maybe he'll kill me."

"Are you crazy?" Sanford nodded toward the door again. "He'll kill you alright. Just like he's going to kill me eventually. That's why we have to figure some way out of here, some way to call for help." Sanford's face disappeared. Amy heard the sound of running water. When Sanford returned, she rubbed a wet washcloth over Amy's face, then held it over Amy's nose. "Blow."

Amy blew. It relieved some of the congestion in her nose but not the anguish in her heart. She looked at Sanford. The doctor was eyeing her with compassion and curiosity.

"What is all this? Why are you so eager to die? Seems to me you have more to live for than most people. At least you have someone to love."

Amy shook her head and turned away. The tears started afresh. "No. I'm no good for him. It's best that I die. Best for everyone."

Even as Amy said these things, even as she believed them, some part of her said it wasn't so. It was a small part buried deep down, a part of her core being. The part that said life was precious; it was worth living. The part that made her want to be a corpsman, to save lives instead of taking them. The part that made her love Deke and want to be with him. Amy wanted to believe that part, but it was being shouted down by a louder voice, a voice that said it was all a lie. Life was a lie. Love was a lie. That only death mattered.

"I don't know this Deke," Sanford said. "But from what you've told me, I think he loves you, too. So, why are you so quick to ..." Sanford took Amy's face in her hands and turned it. The doctor's eyes beamed with understanding. "Is this that drug? The one you told me about? The suicide one?" Her understanding changed to concern. "Did you get a dose?"

Amy started to shake her head but stopped mid-turn. Had she? That deep little voice shouted yes. It all made so much sense. But when? How?

Amy's thoughts flew backward, remembering everything that had happened since Metternich's visit. There was Barzoon's first attempt to slip them the suicide drug in the hotel. She remembered the sweet, aromatic smell of the French fries. But that attempt failed. Deacon had seen to that. Her heart momentarily reached out to Deke before a mental shout said that his efforts were in vain. That she was fated to die. That she should die.

Amy shook off the melancholia and searched her memory further. Once they'd left the hotel, they were under the constant supervision of the marshals. Tremaine and her marshals oversaw the grocery shopping and food orders. They and the local cops like Tony Movello. Tony. Amy suddenly remembered his confrontation with Barzoon, Tony crying, 'No, you promised.' Her mind spun further back to the brewpub. Drinking beer with Tony. Laughing at his stories. Eating with him. The memory of their meal popped into her brain. The smell of the burger. The sweet, aromatic odor she'd assigned to the ketchup. Then the summer cold and the thoughts of ... It all made so much sense.

"What the hell is that?" Sanford said.

Amy came out of her musing. She twisted her head and scrunched her shoulders higher on the pillow, so she could see where the doctor was pointing. At first, she didn't see anything.

Then she noticed two small, blue specks against the beige of the old carpet. But she still couldn't make out what they were.

"Son of a bitch," Sanford muttered.

"What?"

Sanford crouched low and stared at the tiny objects.

"What?" Amy repeated.

"Sharps the man said."

Amy could now make out what Sanford was looking at, the two used 22-guage needles that Sanford had handed over when Barzoon came in to do the filming.

"They must have dropped from his pocket," Amy said.

Sanford looked at her, smiling. "When he pulled that flash drive out." Sanford got down on all fours and crawled toward the fallen needles. When she reached the end of the cable attached to her ankle, the needles were still several feet away. Sanford flattened against the carpet and stretched out her hand. A good one to two feet still separated her from her goal. "Shit. Almost, but no cigar. Still can't reach 'em."

"So?" Amy asked, thoughts of suicide forgotten. "What good would it do."

"Shhh," Sanford said, finger to her lips. "He'll hear you."

Amy shook her pinioned arms, then spoke more softly. "These straps are nylon. Your tether, steel. Knitting needles couldn't saw through, let alone thin syringe needles."

"No," Sanford said, stretching further. Her fingers were still a foot and a half away from the prize. "Shit. Not enough."

"It's hopeless," Amy said. "Why bother?"

"It ain't hopeless," Sanford said.

"You'll never be able to cut through heavy nylon and steel with two syringe needles."

"No," Sanford said, "but I might be able to pick locks with them."

"You know how to do that?" Amy asked.

Sanford showed all her teeth. "Sure. All us ghetto children learn to pick locks."

Amy found herself smiling back. She couldn't remember the last time she'd smiled. It felt strange but good.

Sanford rose to her knees and looked about the room. "Actually, my older brother got a lockpick set along with an instructional video for his birthday one year. He wanted to be an escape artist like Houdini."

"Did he become one?"

Sanford continued to glance about the room. "No. He's a general manager at Walmart. Shit."

"What are you looking for?"

"Something I can lasso those needles with. But there's nothing…" Sanford's eyes flashed as she snapped her fingers. "It might just work."

"What?" Amy was intrigued, thoughts of suicide temporarily forgotten. "What might just work?"

Sanford reached both arms behind and underneath her scrub top. "I tried not wearing one of these in med school, but the scrub material chafes." She undid the clasp of her bra. "And these tops don't leave much to the imagination when the girls get aroused. I found out the hard way that 'nips' is an embarrassing nickname." Sanford worked the bra straps off and out one sleeve. She held the plain, white undergarment up appraisingly. "This ought to do the trick."

Sanford stretched out again across the carpet, her neck craned toward the two needles. She swung the brassiere over her head like a lariat, then launched it. It landed just to the right of the needles. "Shit."

"I can tell you were never a cowgirl." It was the first joke Amy had cracked in a week.

Sanford chuckled. "Not much call for it growing up in Cincinnati." She swung the lingerie again, one cup covering the needles. "Gotcha."

"Easy does it," Amy said.

Sanford looked her way and nodded. Then the doctor slowly tugged on the bra strap. The cup slid across the carpet, revealing the two needles still out of reach. "Shit."

"But you moved them," Amy said. She found herself caught up in the excitement. "They were near that stain on the rug before, now they're several inches further away."

Sanford nodded, then swung again. The lasso landed; Sanford tugged it gingerly toward her. Amy could no longer see the needles on the floor. As Sanford snatched up the bra to reveal her prize, Amy heard the doorknob turn.

¢¢¢

It was déjà vu all over again. Once more, Deacon sat in his office listening to Terri Tremaine read him the riot act. He was in no mood for it and was barely listening. His entire being was focused on Amy. His mind's eye kept seeing the look on her face as she spoke those pathetic words, the words that his late fiancé, Liz, might have spoken to him if he'd been listening. Now Amy, beautiful Amy, with Linda Ronstadt eyes much like Liz's.

Amy was in the depths of despair, imprisoned by a madman. And it was Deacon's fault. That's what it always came back to. Everything was his fault. He longed for a drink, but the thought simply brought more guilt. He couldn't lose himself in the serenity of booze until he'd found Amy. Then what? Unless he also found a cure for 606, her fate was sealed. He placed his head in his hands. Like an alcoholic, he needed to take things one at a time.

"Are you listening to me?" Tremaine asked.

Deacon only sighed.

"My job," Tremaine continued, "the job of the Marshals service, the job of the FBI, is to find Amy and catch Barzoon." She gesticulated around the room. "Your job is here. You're the genius who uncovers the cure for this, whatever it is."

Deacon thought for a moment that she looked beautiful even when angry. Then his thoughts snapped back to Amy and guilt.

Tremaine put her hands on her hips. "Am I getting through to you, Dr. Creel?" Before Deacon could say anything, she raised her palms. "And I don't want to hear about how you were the hero last year."

"Me and Amy," Deacon said.

"Fine. You and Amy, the two-person wrecking crew. And I don't want to hear about how you guys foiled the plot and brought the bad guys to justice, while the intelligence community and cops didn't."

"But they didn't." Deacon looked up. "Maybe I should talk to the other witness, this Sinclair guy."

"I said that he's already been questioned."

"Yeah. But maybe I could get more out of him. Like I did with Tony."

Tremaine didn't say another word. She just stared at him. Then she pointed at the door.

"I'm going to post a guard right outside your lab. That guard is going to be told that you don't leave here except to go to the safe house. Is *that* understood?"

Deacon looked up. "Do I have a choice?"

Before Tremaine could answer, there was a knock on the door. "Enter," she yelled.

Howard sheepishly poked his head in. "Um, I don't mean to interrupt."

"It's okay," Tremaine said. "I was just leaving." She grabbed her purse off the desk. "You can come in and keep your boss company. He's going to be here for a while."

"Terri," Deacon called.

Tremaine turned, hand on the door.

"Promise to keep me in the loop?" Deacon said.

Tremaine thought for a moment, then nodded. She smiled at Howard as she left.

"Something, Howie?"

Howard slowly turned around. "Yeah. We've got two more rats about ready to wake up in the lab. Leon and I dosed them with the 606 and then the new conjugate, the one without the neurotoxicity side chain." He smirked. "I guess we could call that Threlkis-2."

Deacon rubbed his eyes.

"I figured you might want to check on them," Howard said.

Deacon looked over at the closed office door. He heard Tremaine speaking to someone. She spoke loudly enough to be overheard. He shook his head in despair.

"Is that a no?"

Deacon turned to Howard and managed a wan smile. "That's a yes, Howie. Let's go see how they're doing."

¢¢¢

Nelson Barzoon stopped walking down the hall. He thought he'd heard something, so he stepped quietly to the door. Inside were muffled voices. Had he remembered to lock the door? He jiggled the knob and the voices stopped. Or had he heard them at all? His mind was playing tricks. The stress of fighting the suicide urges combined with the mood elevators and uppers fogged his brain. His thoughts were blurred and hazy, like looking through scratched glass.

He knocked twice. Silence. He took the key from his pants pocket and unlocked the door. He opened it slowly, pistol drawn. Paranoia was evidently another side effect of his condition. He poked his head inside expecting the worst, but all was as it should be. Robbins was where he'd left her. Sanford stood at her side, her hands suspiciously tucked behind her back. Barzoon stepped inside. He watched Sanford swallow hard.

"What do you want?"

In lieu of an answer, Barzoon motioned with the pistol. "What do you have behind your back?" He signaled again that she should show him. Tentatively, she held out a brassiere.

He smiled. "Getting comfy, are we?"

"You try wearing one of these all day."

He nodded as he wandered over to the video camera. "Time for another little love note to your Deacon, Ms. Robbins." He withdrew a flash drive from his jacket and inserted it into the camera. Robbins once again grew large in the viewfinder. He noticed again how beautiful her eyes were. No wonder Creel lusted for them. Robbins glanced toward Sanford.

"Look at *me* please, Ms. Robbins."

Her visage once again faced the camera. "Just like last time, say what's in your heart."

Robbins glanced once again at Sanford, who muttered something.

"No kibitzing from the gallery, please. I only want Ms. Robbins in this shot." He zoomed. "Go ahead."

Robbins stared straight at the lens and said, "Fuck you." Her eyes still showed fear but with a newfound determination.

"Come now," he said. "You can do better than that for your Deacon. Tell him what you want."

Her lips trembled. She licked them. Then she said, "Hi Deke. I want you to kill this crazy bastard."

¢¢¢

Isabella Sanford watched Barzoon turn off the recorder and slowly raise his head. He was not a happy man. "That kind of talk will not do." He spoke slowly and coldly, with a threat underlying his icy words. "There are consequences for not playing your part, my dear." He withdrew the ugly black pistol and pointed it at Amy.

Amy chuckled. "You going to shoot me? That's a threat? Unlock these shackles and I'll do it for you."

Now Barzoon pointed the pistol in Izzie's direction. The barrel trembled, but the bore looked big and dangerous. Izzie doubted even a trembling hand would miss at this distance. She swallowed again. "You're gonna kill me anyway. Might as well be now."

Barzoon seemed confused, as if the plan was going wrong. He lowered the pistol and tried to smile, but his face couldn't quite come up with one. "There are methods of inflicting pain short of death. Methods that would make you beg for its sweet release."

Izzie hadn't considered this. She didn't know how much pain she could handle, especially when inflicted by a master of the art. She felt her legs weaken. The world around her dimmed. Her breathing grew shallow, her thoughts airy. Then, as if from far away, Any spoke again.

"But that's not your style, is it, Nelson? You're a big shot. You let others do the wet work."

Barzoon stiffened. His gun hand slowly rose again. Izzie was sure their captor would turn the gun on Amy, revenge or no revenge. Instead, she watched in awe as Barzoon pointed the pistol toward his temple. The ugly black gun rose about halfway, then stopped, the hand holding it trembling noticeably. Then, without a word, Barzoon spun around and stumbled from the room.

¢¢¢

He stood outside the door; his body shaking. The desire to raise the pistol was strong, but he used his bruised weak hand to wrestle it back into his waistband. He stood there, trembling, listening to his own harsh breath. He faced the door and strained to hear any sound from his guests. There was only silence.

He was a trained Russian agent. He'd accomplished the second-greatest infiltration ever achieved by a Russian agent. He should have known what to say to Robbins, how to turn her words against her. But he hadn't. He was in charge, not her. Yet her rebuke struck home and left him feeling a plethora of emotions. Confusion. Emptiness. Frustration. Anger. And most of all, exhaustion.

He bent his head and tried to rub fatigue and stress from his neck and temples. Then he reached into his pants pocket for the Benzedrine bottle, before thinking better of it. More drugs would only strain the mental fabric that was already thinning to the point of transparency. He took a deep breath, then let it out slowly. He needed rest. He needed time for his feverish thoughts to settle. Perhaps a few hours of sleep. Perhaps the dreams and waking urges wouldn't be as strong this time. Perhaps when he woke up, he'd know what to do. He rubbed his fatigued eyelids.

Just hang on, he thought. Only a few more days. Days needed to heighten Creel's suffering. Barzoon thought of Robbins's quip about doing the job herself. He smiled weakly. That would be perfect. He could record it. A final gift for Creel. They could share a quiet visit watching it together. Then, when Creel's anguish was at its height, a single gunshot. With Creel dead, Barzoon's vengeance complete, he could find the sweet oblivion he desperately sought.

Thoughts of Creel's suffering brought some measure of peace. Barzoon's hand unconsciously touched the butt of the Makarov, but he willed it away. Instead, he sent his trembling fingers to the door and turned the key, locking in his guests if not locking out his confusion. Then he walked slowly toward the master bedroom.

¢¢¢

Izzie held a finger to her lips and waited for what seemed an eternity. All was quiet in the hall but still she waited, holding her breath. Finally, she heard the key turn in the lock and footsteps move quietly away. When she heard the footsteps recede into the distance, she exhaled deeply and flopped on the bed. She started to wipe sweat from her brow, then realized she was still clenching her bra. She threw it down.

"Good for you, Amy. Don't give that bastard the satisfaction." She turned and could see that Amy was crying.

"I'm not so sure," Amy said. "If I give him what he wants, he has a reason to keep you alive. If not …"

Izzie pulled a tissue off the bedside bureau and wiped Amy's eyes. "Don't count us out yet." She smiled and showed Amy the two needles in her other hand. "We got a chance."

"That's never going to work," Amy said.

"Not with that attitude." Izzie uncapped the two needles, then opened the drawer of the bedside bureau. She placed one needle barrel in the gap. She then closed the drawer and gave the trapped needle a twist. When she removed it, there was now a ninety-degree bend on the flattened end. "That ought to do it."

"Do what? Ruin the needle?"

"No, provide me with a tension wrench." Izzie grabbed the padlock attached to Amy's outstretched arm and inserted the needle into the keyhole. The needle flexed as she applied pressure. She smiled at Amy. "See?"

"Do you really know what you're doing?"

"To quote the Wolfman, if I'm lyin' I'm dyin.'"

"Who's the Wolfman?"

Izzie set down the bent needle and picked up the second one. "Some white DJ in an old movie. My brother loves old movies." She popped the cap off the second needle and pushed the point against the table. When she held it up to the light, it had a nib pointing up from the end. "Good. Got me a rake."

"Even if you free us, we're still locked in a room. We still don't know where we are. We still have an armed madman to deal with."

"One thing at a time. Now hush while I see if I still got the knack." Izzie sat on the bed, her foot resting beside her on the mattress. She placed the tension wrench in the lock on her ankle, then inserted the needle with the nib on the tip. She looked toward the door, then returned attention to the lock. "You just lie still while I work here."

She held the tension wrench and small, brass padlock with one hand, then began raking the straight needle back and forth within the lock. Her face scrunched in concentration as she worked. Sweat beaded on her face and hands. She dropped the raker needle but caught it in the air. "Shit!" She held her finger to her mouth and sucked. "Damn thing bit me." She went back to work.

Izzie wiped her palms on her scrubs, then glanced at the door and resumed working on the lock. There was no clock to tell how many seconds ticked by, but it seemed forever. Stiffness developed in her neck and fingers, but she kept working. She'd been able to pick locks as a girl, often racing her brother, sometimes winning. But that was another much younger version who practiced with a real lockpick. This Isabella Sanford wasn't as confident. But she had to try. They had nothing else.

Izzie kept working the raker pick, pausing now and then to ease pressure on the tension wrench. Her fingers, so adept in surgery, now seemed dull as a butter knife. She paused again, twisting stress from her neck and stiffness from her hands. She felt a pin click into the sear line of the lock. Then there was another. The third pin started binding so she eased off on the tension wrench, only to feel the first two pins drop down. "Shit."

Izzie wiped sweat from her hands, shook out her fingers, took a deep breath, and started again. The first two pins clicked into place easily. The third one started to bind but she eased slightly on the tension wrench and heard a click. The padlock was small, so there was probably only one pin to go. She tried to relax and manipulate the rake more casually. She blinked sweat from her eyes and took another relaxing breath. "Come on, you bitch."

"Why don't you give up?" Amy asked. "This isn't going to …"

Izzie heard a final soft click and the hasp popped open. She smiled. "You were saying?"

"I'm sorry I doubted you." Amy shook her tethered hand, sending her IV line whipping against the stand. "Now do me."

Izzie started to remove the padlock from her ankle, then froze at the sound of a key turning in the door lock.

Chapter 25

Nikolai Belikovsky trod along, his footsteps squeaking on the snow. The icy wind bit into every inch of skin not covered by his coat, gloves, and fur ushanka hat. He knew that wind, knew it well. They were old friends, even older than he and the Makarov. He reached for the pistol, but it was gone. In its place were a pair of skates hung about his neck. Nikolai thought this odd, given that he hadn't skated on Lake Ladoga since he was sixteen. He would go with friends to play hockey, sometimes coached by his father on those rare occasions when the colonel was at the *dacha*. The colonel was a stern taskmaster who did not countenance either laziness or failure.

Nikolai scanned into the distance. He saw the ice of the frozen lake, snow crystals dancing along its surface on their way to the horizon. He also saw a lone figure, his body as tall and straight as a Sarmat missile. The man wore a sheepskin greatcoat and a large, black ushanka like the one that Nikolai himself wore. Was it possible? After all these decades? Love flooded Nikolai's heart. Fear flooded in as well. He stopped walking. He stopped breathing. One word escaped his lips. "Nana." Then Nikolai ran.

He ran as a boy runs, not as an old man who has been beaten down by disappointment and disgrace. His feet danced over the snow, never slipping. The whistle of his breath replaced the squeak of his footfalls, both lost in the beating of the heart within his ears. As the tall silent figure grew in his vision, Nikolai became more and more certain. Somehow, the colonel was here. Some trick of time and space had brought them together again, the young boy entering the Krasnodar academy reunited with the stern, old warrior who had been his lifelong role model.

Nikolai covered the distance in moments, then slid to a stop as his father turned to face him. Nikolai opened his mouth to greet the great man, but the words froze in his throat. The look on his father's face was nothing like the mask of love that beamed from

Nikolai's. Colonel Belikovsky's features were cold and devoid of affection. He stared harshly at Nikolai, eyeing him up and down. Then he spoke, his words registering more in Nikolai's mind than in his ears.

"Skating, Nikolai?"

Nikolai self-consciously clutched the long blades of his Russian skates.

The colonel tsked his head slowly. "Skating is not for you, Nikolai. Skating is for boys growing into manhood and success." The colonel's steely eyes glinted with shame and condescension. "No, Nikolai. Failures don't play bandy or rise to be hockey greats. Miserable failures like you don't rise at all." The colonel pointed. "They sink."

The blood drained from Nikolai's face as his eyes followed to where his father pointed. The cold, white surface of the frozen lake stretched on and on, broken by only one speck of black in the distance. Nikolai walked toward it, his trembling feet moving inexorably forward as if in a dream. The speck grew with each footstep, grew out of proportion to the distance traveled. Soon Nikolai was standing beside it. It had grown to a dark rectangle cut into the ice, a one-by-three-meter hole into the black, frigid waters of the lake.

His father spoke in Nokolai's mind, as if standing beside him.

"A fitting gravesite for a miserable failure."

Nikolai stared at the blackness of the eternal lake. His shame was replaced by a feeling of peace. His father spoke again, his voice seeming to rise from the freezing water.

"Make your atonement, Nikolai. It is the only way."

Nikolai Belikovsky nodded in understanding. Then he jumped.

¢¢¢

Nelson Barzoon awoke shivering. His face and hair were bathed in icy sweat. He clutched the coldness of the Makarov to his chest. The imagery of the dream had already departed, but it left behind an indelible imprint. He knew what he had to do. He knew it as surely as he knew that the sun would no longer rise in the sky. Today was the last day. He clutched the pistol in his hand and rolled out of bed.

¢¢¢

Deacon stared at the two rats drinking water but didn't really see them. His mind was filled with thoughts of Amy. He saw the sorrow and pain on her face as she pleaded to die. He thought again how he'd never seen such anguish in her large, brown eyes. The eyes that reminded him of his late fiancé. He loved those eyes. He guessed he loved Amy. Now she was most likely going to die, just like so many women he'd known. Another chalk mark on his tally of guilt.

He felt that he needed to do something. Tremaine said that wasn't his job. She said that talking to this Sinclair person would do no good. But she'd said the same thing about talking to Tony Movello, and that had given them new information. He thought back on his interrogation of Tony. Something about it nagged at him, but he couldn't put his finger on it. He tried to remember their talk, word for word, something his eidetic memory used to be able to do before stress, booze, and age took their toll. He concentrated and it started to come to him, rising from the murky depths of his subconscious.

Someone tapped Deacon on the shoulder. He looked up with a start. Howard was smiling at him.

"I said, good news, right?"

"Huh?"

"The rats both made it. The new conjugate, I mean Threlkis-2, reversed the suicide drug. Aren't you happy?"

"Oh." Deacon nodded. "Sure."

"I mean, it's rats, not people, but still." His eyebrows rose as he asked, "Should I run them through the RA-maze and object recognition tests?"

"Huh?"

"I said, should I run them through the rodent intelligence tests? Since they survived, I mean. So, we can gauge the amount of brain damage."

Deacon shrugged. "I guess."

"Are you all right, Deke?"

Deacon sighed. "No, but it's nothing you can …" The ringing phone in the outer office interrupted him."

Howard trotted off, saying, "I'll get it."

Deacon tried to recapture his concentration. What was it about his conversation with Tony that nagged at him? Before he could come up with it, Howard returned.

"It's for you, Deke." The young postdoc leered. "My dream woman."

Deacon knew who that was as he walked to the office and picked up the phone.

"Hi, Terri."

"Hey. I thought you'd want to know that Dr. Sanford has come up missing."

"Who?"

"Isabella Sanford, MD. The emergency doc who treated, then helped rescue Amy."

Deacon slumped into his office chair. "How do you know she's missing?"

"Boyfriend reported her missing for forty-eight hours." There was a pause, then Tremaine spoke again. "Guy named Ellsworth Stackhouse. He was supposed to have a date with her, and she never showed. He went by her house; no one was home."

Deacon was confused. "How do you know all this? I mean, who reported it to the Marshals service?"

"It was a fluke," Tremaine continued. "A cop originally involved with the clinic shooting overheard Stackhouse filing his report. He remembered the name and called us."

"So, are we going to check this out?"

"No," she replied, "*we* aren't. The Marshals Service and the FBI are checking it out."

"Fine. While you're doing that, I'll talk to Sinclair. He was probably one of the last people to see her." Deacon could hear Tremaine's long exhale through the phone.

"Let's go through this again. You scientist, me law enforcement. I'm only letting you know about Sanford because I promised to keep you in the loop."

"Come on, Terri. I need more than being "in the loop." I need to be actively involved."

"For the last time, Deke, you *need* to work at the lab."

"But I …" The phone went dead. "Shit." Deacon raised the receiver high, took a deep breath, then gently placed it in the cradle.

"Problem?" Howard asked.

Deacon flinched. "We need to put a bell on you, Howie."

Howard smiled sheepishly. "Sorry. I just heard the yelling. Thought maybe I could help."

Deacon snapped his fingers. "You can." He rose and put an arm around Howard's shoulder. "I want you to run the behavioral tests, and record results for these two female rats. I want those tests run again tomorrow on the same rats."

"To see if any neurological deficits are temporary?"

"You catch on fast. And no matter what the outcome is with those two, I want you and Deon …"

"Leon."

"Right, I want you and Leon to repeat the process with at least three more pairs of females."

Howard grimaced. "That's gonna take a few days."

Deacon patted his back. "That's okay. I want a database of at least ten, so we don't go chasing random chance."

"Anything else, boss?"

Deacon smiled. "Yes. Do you have a car?"

"Huh?"

"A car. You know, those things with wheels, rubber tires, use them to drive around town?"

Howard's eyebrows rose. "Yeah. Over in the parking lot off Stewart, by Anderson Center."

"What's it look like?" Howard just stared at him. "You know, make, model, color?"

Howard scratched his head. "It's a 2006 Honda Civic. Red, but the trunk is just primer. Why?"

"Excellent. Give me the keys."

"Huh? Why?"

"I'm going to borrow it for a couple days."

"But …"

"Don't worry. I'll bring it back with some gas in it."

"But, but … what about the deputies … the guard at the door."

Deacon winked. "That's where you come in. Here's what I want you to do."

¢¢¢

Barzoon didn't bother knocking. The dream had shown him the time for quaint propriety had passed. He simply turned the key, then burst into the room. His hackles rose. Something in the room seemed different. He couldn't place what, and that fact bothered him more.

Things appeared just as he'd left them. Robbins was on the bed. Sanford stood beside her. Both seemed properly restrained. The windows were still curtained. His video equipment was where he'd left it. He studied his two guests and finally realized it was their attitude that had changed. Before, there had been quiet resignation. Now, a heightened energy like static electricity filled the room. Robbins's face was flushed, her body tense. The doctor seemed flustered, her respiration rapid. He stared into her eyes searching for the reason.

"What do you mean barging in like this," Sanford stammered. "I thought gentlemen knocked first."

Barzoon relaxed. They were only startled. That explained it. Or maybe the perceived sense of tension reflected his own hyper state brought on by the dream. The heartbeats drumming his ears almost masked his own harsh, rapid breaths. He tried to calm himself.

"My apologies." He wiped a hand across his feverish brow; it came back slick with sweat.

"Well," Sanford said. "What do you want?"

Barzoon knew what he had to do, but was suddenly hesitant to do it. He slowly withdrew the Makarov from his belt. His gun hand shook so he used his bruised one to steady it. He had a strong desire to place the pistol against his own skull but instead pointed it at Sanford.

"I must apologize for this as well, Doctor. But it's time to end our little game. I know you are only a pawn, but pawns are meant to be sacrificed after all." He watched Sanford's brown eyes grow in size. "If it's any comfort, I'll be joining you momentarily." His finger tightened on the trigger, the hammer rising about a quarter way.

Sanford held up her palms as if they might stop the bullet. "Wait!" she shouted.

The hammer rose to half.

"What about your revenge?" Robbins spoke calmly and quietly.

Barzoon hesitated. "Yes. Well, I guess your death will have to suffice, Ms. Robbins. I've been made to understand that failures don't deserve revenge, at least not the full measure I had planned."

The hammer rose further. Any moment now, it would come crashing down. He wouldn't be crossing the Rubicon with that first shot. Even with the good doctor dead, he might still keep Robbins alive for several days. Not as long as he'd anticipated, but long enough to send Creel several more gut-wrenching videos. But Barzoon knew in his heart that, once begun, he'd be unable to stop. Once that first long, double-action trigger pull was accomplished, the pistol shot reverberating in his ears, he'd pull again, and then again. He knew now that he had been foolish to plan otherwise. Foolish and unworthy.

"Again, my apologies."

As his finger tensed for the final, inevitable plunge, Robbins spoke. Her voice was relaxed and unhurried. "Don't you want to record it?"

His brows rose. He turned to Robbins, his eyes locking with hers. "Pardon?"

"The great moment." Robbins seemed unconcerned as she nodded to the video camera. "When you kill me. One final message to Deke. Let him watch me die."

Barzoon stood for a moment, puzzled with indecision. Her suggestion made sense, although he didn't know why she was making it. He could record the event for Creel, even include a little personal note that told him where to find the three bodies. He lowered his gun and patted his pocket with his other hand. "I seem to have forgotten to bring a flash drive."

"We'll be happy to wait," Sanford said.

Barzoon turned to face the doctor. Her dark color had paled, and her eyes remained the size of saucers, but she seemed calmer. She shrugged as if to say, 'why not.' Barzoon thought for a moment, then nodded in return. "Why not?"

¢¢¢

Izzie felt the color drain from her face. Her legs were suddenly made of over-cooked pasta. She collapsed on the bed in a sea of cold sweat. She raised her hand to wipe her brow and realized it was shaking. She held it with her other hand, and both shook. She inhaled for a sigh of relief before realizing that Barzoon would soon be back.

"You okay?" Amy asked.

Izzie nodded. "For the moment." She turned to Amy. "That was good thinking, but I doubt you bought us much time."

"Enough. I wanted to tell you something, and I didn't want him around."

Izzie removed the brass padlock and tossed it and the improvised lockpick tools under the bed. "What?"

"If you survive and I don't, I want you to tell Deacon something." Her voice was calm, resigned. The kind of voice Izzie had heard from hospice patients entering the last mile. "Tell Deacon not to worry. No matter what he sees or hears, he should know this is all for the best."

Izzie gazed about the room searching for a weapon. "Sees or hears what?"

"Never mind. Just tell him I love him and that he's better off without me."

Izzie knelt down and swept her fingers under the bed, hoping to find something with which to fight Barzoon. "Shit." She held her finger to her lip, sucking where the lockpick had pierced it.

"And Izzie? This is important."

Izzie rose with a grunt. "What?"

"Tell Deke that this, none of it, was his fault."

Izzie looked curiously back at Amy. She saw sadness in her eyes. She saw love there as well.

Amy smiled. "He has a heightened sense of responsibility."

Izzie shook her head as she turned away.

"Promise you'll tell him," Amy said.

"You'll be telling him yourself if you just keep quiet and let me think." Izzie scanned the room again, when her eyes fell on the video camera. She pointed and snapped her fingers. "Got you."

At that moment, the doorknob turned. Izzie panicked and ran back to the other side of the bed, trying to look natural.

Barzoon entered, holding a flash drive in one hand, his pistol in the other. He walked unceremoniously to his video camera and inserted the memory stick.

Izzie tried to keep her breathing regularl as she casually moved her foot, hoping that Barzoon wouldn't notice that the end of the steel cable now lay under her shoe instead of locked to her ankle.

"Mr. Barzoon," Amy said.

Izzie stiffened as Barzoon looked up.

"I have a proposition for you."

His gaunt face half smiled. "A last request?"

Izzie wanted to rush Barzoon but didn't want to risk it while he was looking at them. Why didn't Amy shut up so the crazy bastard would look down to his viewfinder?

"Something like that," Amy said.

"I'm listening."

"What would you give if I did what you asked?"

Barzoon titled his head like a beagle watching a bug. "How's that?"

"If I cooperated. Did what you wanted. Poured my heart into your videos. Like the first time, but even better. Pleaded. Begged to die. Begged to end my suffering." Amy paused. "What would you give if I did that?"

Barzoon's face was a blank of curiosity. "What do you ask?"

Just shut up, Izzie thought. If Barzoon put his head down to the viewfinder, Izzie could charge him. If she could catch him by surprise, they had a chance. The video camera sat on a tripod of metal legs, legs that might make a good bludgeon. A few hits and he was sure to drop the pistol, maybe even lose consciousness. They had a chance if Amy would just shut up.

Izzie watched as Amy turned toward her and said, "Let Dr. Sanford go."

Barzoon studied Izzie and began to speak, but Amy cut him off.

"You don't need her. I promise to take in nutrients orally. Water, soup, milkshakes, whatever you say. You can place down incontinence pads for the other." Barzoon looked at Amy queerly, apparently unsure how to process this new information. Before he had a chance to do so, Amy continued speaking. "She can't hurt you. She doesn't know where we are any more than I do."

Barzoon tilted his head again and lowered his pistol. "But she will know when she leaves."

Amy raised her eyes to heaven, as if she couldn't understand why this intelligent man was being so obtuse. "Not if you bind and blindfold her. You can drop her off somewhere. Someplace where someone will eventually find her and set her free."

Barzoon turned toward Izzie. His eyes were still wild but with a hint of understanding in them, perhaps even compassion. Then he looked at Amy. "How do you know I won't just drive her off and kill her? Then she is sure not to be a problem."

"Because," Amy said, "I don't think you'll go back on your word once you've given it." Amy locked eyes with Barzoon. "I've dealt with a lot of people in my life, Mr. Barzoon, in lots of desperate situations when all they have is their basic natures. I've learned to read characters. I think your character is to keep your word once you've given it."

"Wait a minute," Izzie said. She spoke to Barzoon, but her eyes strayed to the tripod. If Amy was serious about trusting this maniac, Izzie would rather take her chances now, with a physical fight. At least she would be free, not hogtied and helpless.

She knew that statistics said once a nutjob had you powerless in a secure location, your chances of a long life were nil. "I've got a stake in this, and I say …"

Barzoon kept looking at Amy but pointed his gun directly at Izzie. She had no doubt he'd use it. When all was quiet, he lowered the gun slightly and said, "How do I know you will keep your end of the bargain, Ms. Robbins? I could turn the good doctor loose as you suggest, only to have you clam up, refuse to speak or eat." He smiled. "Am I to accept your word as you profess to accept mine?"

Amy met his gaze and slowly shook her head. "No. That is not in your nature. Even if you believe me, and I can see in your eyes that you do, you will still require added assurance of my sincerity." Amy smiled wanly. "You're a belt-and-suspenders kind of man, Mr. Barzoon."

His smile dimmed. "So, unless there is some other assurance that you can give me?" He began to raise the gun again.

Izzie tensed. This was it. Now or never. Her heart raced. She held her breath and crouched slightly, her legs storing energy. She prayed to God that her leap would knock Barzoon down and disorient him. She prayed for a chance to seize the tripod. Her hearing dimmed to only the beating of her heart. Time seemed to slow, the gun rising in increments like the ticks of a wall clock. Now or never. Then Amy spoke again.

"Dr. Sanford has picked her lock and is going to jump you."

Barzoon spun to face Izzie, stopping her in mid-leap. His eyes bore into her, her eyes could see only the muzzle of his pistol and his two-handed grip behind it.

"On your belly, facing me," Barzoon said. His voice was cold and final. Still, Izzie hesitated. "Now," he snapped, his thumb cocking the pistol's hammer.

Blood again left Izzie's face as her legs gave out. She dropped, first to her knees then her chest.

"Hands behind your back."

Izzie complied as she watched Barzoon walk toward her. She heard the whoosh of leather on fabric. A belt looped around her crossed wrists and cinched cruelly tight.

"How?" Barzoon asked to no one in particular.

Amy answered "She used syringe needles as lockpicks. You dropped two earlier." There was a pause before Amy added, "They're under the bed."

Izzie felt the carpet give as Barzoon stepped over her to reach under the bed. Then she heard footsteps enter the bathroom and return. Without any notice or apology, Barzoon lifted Izzie by her elbows and pulled her to her feet. She grimaced but did not cry out from the pain. She turned her head to Amy, wanting to look in her eyes and ask why she had betrayed them. But Barzoon rudely wrapped a hand towel over her eyes and snugged it down. The darkness was complete.

"You are resourceful, Doctor," Barzoon said. "I respect that." He turned Izzy toward the door. "And you, Ms. Robbins, are honest. I respect that also. And I accept your proposition."

Izzie found herself thrust roughly toward the door.

"Dr. Sanford?" Amy called out.

Barzoon stopped. "What?" Izzie asked.

"Tell Deacon that when I see the cobwebs in the corner, I think of our last time together and long for death."

¢¢¢

Amy watched Barzoon shove Sanford through the bedroom door. She felt stupid not realizing where they were all along. But then, she'd had other things on her mind. Things like guilt, shame, and thoughts of the peace that came with death. But when she averted her gaze away from the betrayal on Sanford's face, her eyes lit on the cobwebs in the corner. Just like that, she knew. Of course, she couldn't tell Sanford that. Telling the doctor would have defeated the whole reason for the betrayal. If Barzoon knew that Sanford knew where they were, he couldn't let her live. So, Amy had blurted out the ham-handed clue. She didn't know why she bothered. She was already lost, past saving. And truth be told, she didn't want to be saved. She just wanted to die.

Chapter 26

Deacon watched the cop through a crack in the office door. The guy was young, maybe twenty or twenty-five. He was fair-skinned with freckles, which made him look even younger. So much the better, Deacon thought. He turned to Howard and nodded. Howard nodded back and began to moan.

Deacon flung the door wide. "You! What's your name?"

The Dayton cop looked both ways, then pointed at himself.

"Yes, you. Who else is out there?"

"Um, Obrien."

"Get in here, Obrien. Now!"

The cop rushed in, then froze, his eyes locked on Howard moaning in the office chair. "Something wrong?"

"Of course, something is wrong," Deacon yelled. He pointed at Howard. "Don't you know a sick guy when you see him?"

The cop bent his knees, arms akimbo, and studied Howard. "What's a matter with him?"

Deacon thought for a moment, hand on chin. "I'm not sure. It came on suddenly. Intense pain on the *right* side. Could be appendicitis."

Howard shifted his hands from the left side of his belly to the right. "Ohhhh!"

Deacon raised his eyes to heaven and thought it was a good thing Howard was a brilliant biologist, because he sure wasn't an actor.

Obrien straightened up and said, "I'll call for a doctor."

As the cop started to leave, Deacon signaled to Howard.

"Ooooh," Howard moaned. "I think I'm going to throw up."

Deacon hurried to his side then cast a steely eye on Obrien. "Help me get him to the bathroom."

Obrien rushed to the other side of the postdoc and they both helped him up. "It's okay, Howie. Everything is going to be alright."

Howard remained hunched over as the three of them shuffled out the door toward the men's room. When they were about halfway, Deacon pinched Howard's bicep. His assistant looked up and Deacon nodded.

"Hurry," Howard moaned as he doubled up.

They walked faster, Howard hunched over, Obrien holding his right arm, Deacon his left. "You get him to the bathroom," Deacon said. "I'll call for an ambulance."

Obrien nodded. The cop's Irish complexion paled as he put an arm around Howard's waist and hurried off. Deacon smiled and ran for the stairs. He looked back once to make sure they'd gone into the lavatory, then hurried down to the lobby.

The front door of the science building was still manned by Deputy Sheriff Jablonsky, the big cop with proportions like Jack Reacher. He stepped in front of Deacon, arms crossed.

"Where do you think you're going?"

"My assistant is sick," Deacon panted, pointing to the second story. "You better go check on him while I get a doctor."

Jablonsky held Deacon off with one meaty palm. "Not so fast, tough guy. You wait here. I'll call it in." Jablonsky reached to the microphone sitting on his belt. He looked down to adjust the squelch.

Deacon cocked his fist then tapped Jablonsky on the sleeve. "Hey."

Jablonsky looked up in time to see five knuckles traveling at thirty miles per hour. The cop's head snapped back from the blow and then straightened. He looked quizzically at Deacon for just a moment, before his eyes glazed and his knees gave in.

Deacon caught him halfway and eased him to the floor. "Sorry about that, Jablonsky. But you can't say I didn't warn you."

¢¢¢

It was nighttime when Deacon got to Clark Street. There was a car parked in Carl Sinclair's drive, but his house was dark. No one answered the door. When Deacon was walking back to Howard's Civic, he noticed the curtains creep open on the house across the way. He recalled Tremaine describing the nosy neighbor who seemed to know everyone's business. Deacon smiled and crossed the street.

The curtains dropped back into place even before Deacon stepped onto the lighted porch. There was no initial response to his knock, so he knocked again. "Ms. Forgeron?" After a pause, the door opened as far as permitted by its security chain.

The woman visible through the crack in the door looked mid-seventies. She was dressed in an old-style cotton housecoat with flowers printed on it. Her head was covered by the kind of netting worn by short-order cooks.

"What do you want? I have a gun."

Deacon smiled. "Well, you won't need it. I just want to ask you some questions."

She eyed him up and down. "You don't look like a policeman or government agent."

Deacon continued smiling. "I'm not. But I am an associate of the government woman who spoke with you before."

Recognition seemed to hit her. "That pretty one."

"That's right. Deputy Marshal Terri Tremaine. May I come in?"

"Show me your badge first."

Deacon rubbed his neck. "I don't have a badge. I'm not a deputy marshal. But Deputy Tremaine sent me here to talk with your neighbor, Carl Sinclair." Deacon pointed across the street. "He isn't home. Might you know where he went?"

Forgeron seemed to relax. She still didn't undo the chain, but she nodded in understanding. "I should have known it had something to do with him. This was a quiet neighborhood until he moved in." She leaned into the crack and whispered. "Do you know that only a few days ago I saw him with a lady of the evening?" She pointed through the crack in the door. "Right out there. She was half naked."

Deacon leaned in and whispered back, "I know. Shameful. You, um, haven't by chance seen that lady since then?"

Forgeron straightened and clutched her robe tighter. "Goodness no. Once was enough." She leaned in close again. "Is that why you're here?"

"Something like that," Deacon said. "We think Mr. Sinclair is involved in something well …" He looked both ways and lowered his voice even more. "Illegal. That's why Marshal Tremaine sent me to find him. You wouldn't happen to know where he is?"

Forgeron's face took on an evil grin. The door closed and re-opened a moment later without the chain. She did not invite Deacon in, but she motioned him closer. "Maybe I shouldn't tell you this, but he's a drunk."

Deacon raised his brows. "*Really?*"

She nodded vigorously and pointed to Sinclair's car. "Comes weaving in here at all hours." She looked both ways, then held her hand to her mouth conspiratorially. "I don't think they allow him to drive anymore." She pointed to Sinclair's car again. "The police put that on yesterday."

From this angle, Deacon could now see that there was a police boot on the passenger-side tire of Sinclair's car. "I see." He turned back to Forgeron. "So, where is he? Was he arrested?"

"Not this time," Forgeron said.

Deacon shrugged. "Did he call a cab? Somebody pick him up?"

She looked both ways again, as if to make sure no one was eavesdropping, then said, "I shouldn't tell you this, but I was looking outside earlier." She raised her palm. "I'm not a snoop, you understand.

"Of course not. You're a concerned neighbor."

"Exactly." She grinned slyly again. "I saw him walking down the street about eight o'clock." She pointed toward Main.

"Where do you think he was going?"

Her grin widened. "Well, there's only one place serves alcohol within walking distance."

Deacon nodded in understanding. "Yes. I passed it on the way in."

¢¢¢

The Pier 27 Brewpub was packed. Deacon parked near the ally in what wasn't really a spot, although he didn't think Howard's car would get towed. He went inside to look for Sinclair. He didn't have to look far. The bar was only about twenty feet long, and Sinclair was perched on a stool in the near corner talking loudly to some guy in paint-stained clothes. Deacon recognized Sinclair from the driver's license photo Tremaine had shown him.

"I'm talking Cleveland Indians baseball," Sinclair said. "Before they were the frickin' Guardians. Back before nineteen-ninety-five, in fact." He finished a shot of whiskey with a grimace. "They couldn't buy a win. They must have gone thirty years without playoffs. Of course, part of that time there were no playoffs. Either you won the pennant or …" He slashed his hand across his throat, then gulped some beer. Sinclair shook his head, then looked confused. "What was I saying?"

The painter picked up his beer mug and turned away. "How the hell do I know?"

Deacon wedged in to stand beside Sinclair. He wasn't technically in a legitimate spot by the bar. just as he hadn't technically parked in a legitimate spot. But this wasn't a night for technicalities.

Deacon caught the barmaid's attention with a smile and a wave. She was a bleached blonde of middle age who might now be called handsome instead of cute.

"What's yours, sweetie?" the barmaid beamed.

"Let me have an IPA," Deacon said. He pointed at Sinclair. "And another beer for my friend."

The blonde winked and left.

Sinclair eyed Deacon blearily. "Thanks, partner." He squinted. "Do I know you?"

Deacon shook his head. "I'm just a baseball fan. Go on with what you were saying."

Sinclair started to answer, then stopped in confusion.

"Something about the Indians' losing streak," Deacon said.

Sinclair nodded. The beers arrived. He downed a third of his pint. "Yeah. Back when I was a kid, they lost *all* the time. It was a constant, like the speed of light." He gulped more beer. "So, you're an Indian's fan, huh?"

Deacon sipped his own beer. Something in his brain asked, 'how about a shot with that?' but Deacon closed it down. "When they're winning."

Sinclair eyed Deacon up and down. "Yeah. You're too young for the lean decades. The *Major League* years. You know that movie?"

Deacon shook his head.

"It was kind of comforting back then. The Indians losing. You could count on it." Sinclair smiled a drunken smile. "The only unknown was how much they'd lose by, and if there'd be the excitement of a fight on the field."

Deacon smiled back. "Speaking of excitement, that was some excitement around here last week."

Sinclair stared at him. "Huh?"

Deacon sipped beer. "Right here." He thumbed over his shoulder. "Out in the parking lot. Some guy got shot." Sinclair's face went cold. "About a week ago. Didn't you hear about it?"

Sinclair shook his head. "Nah." He downed most of his beer. "I gotta go." Sinclair almost fell getting off his stool.

"Whoa," Deacon said, steadying him. "I better drive you home."

"No. Thanks." Sinclair pushed Deacon away and staggered toward the door.

Deacon stopped him with a hand to the chest. "I insist." He signaled to the barmaid. As she rushed over, he check marked the air, then drew forth his wallet. "How much on my friend's tab?"

"He pays by the drink." She shrugged. "Manager's orders."

Deacon threw a twenty on the bar. "That'll cover the last two, and the rest is for you."

The barmaid beamed. "Thanks, sweetie. Come see us again— *soon*."

Deacon winked, then grabbed Sinclair's arm. "Shall we?"

Sinclair resisted being pulled toward the door but was too drunk to be effective. As they exited into the night, he said, "Listen. I don't need a ride. I just live a couple of blocks from here."

Deacon tightened his grip. "I insist. I'd hate to see you fall down in the dark. Or get mugged." He tugged Sinclair along. "Or get shot like that poor guy in the parking lot … or the staff at that emergency clinic."

Sinclair froze. "The emergency clinic?" His face paled. "Who are you?"

Deacon spun him face to face. "The name's Creel. Deacon Creel. And you're Carl Sinclair. Now that we've been introduced, I want to ask you a few questions. Chiefly about that night and the current whereabouts of Amy Robbins and Dr. Isabella Sanford."

Sinclair shook free and staggered back, raising his palms. "I don't know anything. I already told you cops that."

"I'm not a cop," Deacon said.

"Fine. FBI, U.S. Marshals, whatever." He stood up straight but swayed like a tree in the breeze. "I already told you guys everything. Which wasn't much. I didn't know those people. I didn't know why some guy named Vavoom was shooting at them."

"Barzoon," Deacon corrected, leaning closer. "Listen, Carl. I'm not the law. You might say, I'm an interested bystander who wants to rehash everything from that night." Deacon viced Sinclair's forearm, "So, how about it?" He jerked the cringing Sinclair toward the ally and Howard's waiting Civic.

When they got to the car, Sinclair broke free again. "If you ain't the law, I don't have to talk to you." He straightened up and brushed down his shirt. "Why should I answer your damn questions?"

Deacon wrapped an arm around Sinclair's shoulder, pulling him in tight, his mouth inches from Sinclair's ear. "Because if you don't, I'm going to beat the living crap out of you."

Sinclair broke free again. "Are you threatening me?"

Deacon smiled. "Not at all. I'm *promising* you."

As Deacon stepped forward, Sinclair backed up and looked around the crowded lot. "Help! This maniac is attacking me!"

"I wouldn't do that if I were you, Carl."

"You ain't me. Help!"

A guy exiting the bar stopped and looked toward them. Sinclair was facing away from the guy, so he didn't see him at first. Then Sinclair followed Deacon's eyes and looked behind him. He waved his hand and took a deep breath to scream.

Deacon clutched Sinclair's shoulder with his left hand. "Sorry about this, Carl," He cocked his right fist as he spun Sinclair around. In the reflected glow of parking lot kliegs, he saw the look of confusion on Sinclair's face. A second later, that look was replaced by Deacon's fist.

Sinclair's eyes went white, and he stumbled toward the front bumper. Deacon grabbed Sinclair about the body to hold him up. The exiting bar patron started walking their way. Deacon waved him off. "It's okay." He pointed to Sinclair dangling in his arms. "My buddy had a little too much to drink and wanted to drive." Deacon shrugged. The bar patron smiled and okayed his fingers before heading toward his own car.

Deacon grasped Sinclair about the waist, draping the man's arm over his shoulder. "This way, Carl." They both stumbled around the front bumper, heading for the passenger door. After a few steps, Deacon's foot caught on something soft and alive. There was a muffled groan, and then both he and Carl Sinclair fell onto a body lying on the pavement.

Deacon released Sinclair, who landed with a whoosh of air from his lungs. Deacon's fall was broken by the body lying in the space between the building and Howard's car. It was too dark to see who that body belonged to, but Deacon knew immediately it was a woman. He'd spent enough time in bedroom rodeos to know a breast when he grabbed one. The body grunted again; the sound muffled in his ear as Deacon rolled to one side.

"What the hell," Deacon muttered, scrambling to his feet. As his eyes adjusted to the gloom, he could see that the woman was lying in the traditional hogtied position, her arms pinned behind her, her ankles tucked together and back. A strip of strapping tape was stretched across her mouth. She was dressed in scrubs, like a doctor, and she smelled of BO.

"Who are you?" he asked.

The woman muffled a reply and struggled from side to side.

"Take it easy," Deacon said. He felt along the tape gag and found the edge. "This is going to hurt." He tugged the tape free in one swift motion.

"Ow!"

"Sorry. Now who are you and how did you get here?"

The woman coughed. "I'm a doctor. And it's a long story. You wanna untie me?"

She was bound with zip ties, but Deacon didn't have anything sharp to cut them with. He looked about the lot and saw a beer bottle lying against the alley wall. "Just a sec," he said, bounding over to retrieve the bottle. Holding it by the neck, one quick tap was all he needed to produce a jagged edge. "This next part is a little tricky," he said, heading back to the bound woman. "Keep very still."

"Freeze!"

Deacon was suddenly bathed in bright light. He raised the hand holding the bottle to shade his eyes.

"Drop the weapon. Now!"

Deacon recognized the authoritative voice of John Law. He couldn't see past the glare but knew from experience that the cop was pointing a pistol at him. He tossed the busted bottle, shattering it, then raised his hands. "Don't shoot. This isn't what it looks like."

The cop's flashlight travelled lower to the Black woman lying on the ground. Her scrub top had pulled up during their struggle, revealing one breast gleaming in the flashlight beam.

"Well," the cop said. "It *looks* like an attempted rape." The beam was back in Deacon's eyes. "Now on your belly, facing me. Hands behind your neck."

Deacon closed his eyes to stop the glare, then knelt down. He started to place his hands on the pavement, but the cop yelled, "Keep 'em up."

Deacon shook his head and rolled forward, the rough pavement giving him a fat lip. "Ow. If you'll just let me explain."

"You'll get a chance for that back at the station, after I cuff you and read you your rights."

Deacon saw the cop walk past him, then felt the cold click of steel bracelets on his wrists.

"You have a right to remain silent."

The woman on the ground cleared her throat and groaned. "Would someone untie me? Please?"

The cop shone his light on the woman. "Wow, Maybe we can add attempted kidnapping to the list." Then he swung the flashlight left to where Sinclair was struggling to stand up. "Who the hell are you?"

Sinclair blinked his eyes into focus. Then he stumbled forward and threw up on the cop's shoes.

Chapter 27

Deacon sat in an interrogation room holding a cold pack to his fat lip. He once again watched as Terri Tremaine paced back and forth. Her color was high, which added a sensuality to her classically good looks. At another time, he might have said, 'You look awfully purty when you're angry.' But he was not in the mood for quips. He wasn't thinking about Tremaine. His thoughts were on Amy.

This déjà vu was losing what little appeal it ever had. They were wasting time. He'd gone after Sinclair to gather information, tease out bits and pieces that detectives might have missed; use some interrogation techniques forbidden to law enforcement. But Carl Sinclair was a minor witness unlikely to know Amy's whereabouts. Sanford was a prize. She'd been with Amy, interacted with her and Barzoon. She was the key. And instead of interrogating her, he was stuck enduring another tirade from agent beautiful.

"Just what the fuck did you think you were doing?" Tremaine yelled.

"Well," Deacon said, "this woman was tied up, so I was untying her."

"You and that Harry concoct this fake illness."

"Howard."

She stared daggers at him. "You and *Howard* concoct a fake illness, then you coldcock a sheriff's deputy and disappear. Next thing I know, the cops are bringing you in on attempted rape of a woman who just happens to be the doctor kidnapped by Barzoon." She stopped pacing and scowled at him, arms akimbo. "You want to tell me how you knew where to find her?"

"That's easy to explain; I *didn't*. I was taking drunken Carl Sinclair to my car, I mean Howard's car, for questioning, and we literally stumbled over her." He scratched his head. "Who called the cops into it?"

"Anonymous tip," Tremaine said. "By the way, Sinclair wanted to file assault charges against you, but I persuaded him otherwise."

"I'm surprised he can remember anything."

"I'm surprised Barzoon left Sanford alive.

There was that déjà vu again, but of a different sort. Why was Barzoon leaving people alive? First Tony, then Tremaine, now Sanford. Tony was a useful tool, but …

"Are you listening to me?"

Deacon was startled out of his reverie.

"Sorry?"

"I said," Tremaine continued, "You didn't answer my first question. What the fuck did you think you were doing?"

"I *think*," Deacon said, rising to confront her, "I was trying to ask Sinclair some questions about Amy, after you told me to mind my own business. But considering that Amy *is* my business, I chose to ignore you."

Deacon glared at Tremaine. She glared back and through gritted teeth, said, "I told you that investigating her kidnapping, finding Metternich, finding Barzoon was law enforcement's job, not yours." She stabbed a finger into his chest. "Your job is finding this cure, whatever it is. A job you're neglecting."

Deacon fisted her finger. "A job that is being handled by Howard Threlkis, one of the best minds in the country." He released her and turned away. "I should know, I used to be one, too." He paused, then turned back. "Anonymous tip? What, a bar patron?"

"No," she replied, rubbing her neck. "Barzoon. That's what Sanford told us anyway."

Deacon's jaw dropped. "He released her and then called it in? Did she tell you why?"

Tremaine shook her head. "She was suffering from dehydration and post-traumatic stress. She's at Soin Medical Center. I was just heading over to debrief her."

Deacon stared coldly at her. "You don't think you're doing that without me, do you?"

"Listen," she said, "I already told you…" She threw up her hands. "I quit. Fine. You want to come along to see what Sanford knows, okay. Trust this Howard kid to do *your* work. What do I care, I'm not the one who has to live with himself if Metternich's wife commits suicide. Or if Amy …" Tremaine's eyes grew softer.

She pointed at him. "On one condition. I take you to question Sanford, then you go back to your lab and let us follow up. Agreed?"

Deacon paused. He thought of Tremaine's unfinished statement about Amy. Her fate if they didn't find a cure. The barb hit home. "Agreed."

¢¢¢

Deacon and Tremaine followed a nurse in scrubs to Sanford's treatment bay in the emergency service of Soin Medical Center. The nurse pulled back the curtain and said, "Dr. Sanford? I have some visitors from the police. Do you feel up to answering questions?"

The young Black woman in a hospital johnny looked up from her bed and smiled. "I guess."

An IV line fed into Sanford's left arm. Her color was good, but there was a light rash where Deacon had pulled the tape off her mouth. She held up her hand to rub the area and Deacon could see a red welt where the zip tie had bit into her wrists.

Deacon smiled reassurance. "You look a little better than the last time I saw you." He touched above his lips. "Sorry about ripping the tape off like that. But I always heard that's the least painful way."

Before Sanford could answer, Tremaine stepped in front of Deacon. She held up her credentials. "I'm Deputy Marshal Tremaine." Her smile was less genuine. "You can call me Terri, and I'll call you Isabella. Okay?"

"Make it Izzie," Sanford said.

Tremaine nodded, then pointed to Deacon. "This is Dr. Creel."

"Call me Deke."

Tremaine shot him a look that said, 'stay out of this,' then smiled back at Sanford. "Okay if I ask you a few questions?"

Sanford shrugged. "Sure." She pointed around the treatment bay. "I'd ask you both to sit down, but there's only the one chair."

"We're fine," Tremaine said, pulling out her cellphone. "Okay if I record this?"

Sanford suddenly pointed at Deacon. "Deke? Are you Amy's Deke?"

"Guilty," Deacon said.

Sanford reached over and took his hand. "I'm so sorry." She began to weep. "I'm so, so sorry that you had to see her like that." She let go of his hand and cupped her face.

Deacon sat beside her on the bed. He patted her head. "It's not your fault. And we need your help to find her."

Tremaine cleared her throat. "Yes, could you tell us where she is being kept?"

Sanford laid back and sighed. "I wish I knew. It was just a room. A bed. A table. A lamp. An adjoining bath. No different from any of a million rooms from Barstow to Boston. I couldn't even look out the window to see where it was."

"How about when he took you to the pub lot? What did you see when you left the house? What did the street look like?"

"I didn't see anything. I was blindfolded."

Tremaine cleared her throat again. "Perhaps you should let me ask the questions, Dr. Creel?"

Sanford looked up plaintively. "Actually, I'd like to talk with Deke alone for a minute, if you don't mind." She paused before adding, "It's kind of important."

Tremaine's jaw dropped. She started to protest, then held up her hands. "Sure. Why should I mind? I'm only a cog in this investigation. Not as important as Deacon Creel." Tremaine spun to leave, then turned back. "But when I return, I hope you will answer *my* questions."

"Sure," Sanford said. "But I need a minute alone with Deke first.

Tremaine stomped out of the treatment bay, whooshing the curtain closed behind her.

Sanford watched the quivering curtain, then she turned to Deacon. She reached out and took his hand. "Amy is alright." She looked down and added, "At least for now." She looked up into Deacon's eyes. He saw the concern and compassion that no doubt made her a good doctor. "She wanted me to tell you something. I promised I would."

Deacon felt his own eyes tearing up but did not wipe them. Instead, he squeezed her hand. "What is it?"

"She said …" Sanford pointed. "Can I have a drink?"

Deacon handed her the cup from a nearby tray. She sipped, then stared back into his eyes. "Please remember that she's not herself. She's been given that drug." She looked around, as if someone might overhear. "You know the one I mean?"

Deacon nodded. "Go on."

Sanford licked her lips. "She said not to worry. It's all for the best." She looked down at her hand gripping his. Deacon felt a tear plop against his wrist. "She said that she loved you and that you were, um, better off without her." Sanford looked up suddenly. "But she didn't mean it. I mean, she, she wasn't herself, and … Whatever you see on those videos. Whatever you hear Amy say, she's not herself." She broke his grip and covered her face.

Deacon gently stroked her hair. "Was there anything else?"

Sanford shook her head. "The rest was gibberish. Something about wanting to die, seeing cobwebs in the corner." She cried into her cupped hands.

Deacon held her in his arms. "Shh. It's alright."

"She was out of her head, Deke," Sanford sobbed. "She didn't know what she was saying. And she's made a deal with Barzoon."

"What kind of deal?" Deacon asked. Before Sanford could answer, he heard the sound of the curtain opening. He glanced over to see Tremaine looking down at him, her eyes flashing.

"Is it alright for *me* to interrogate the witness now?"

Deacon wanted to tell Tremaine to piss off and give Sanford a minute. Instead, he met her gaze and nodded. Time was short and Tremaine was a professional investigator, Deacon only an amateur. But amateur or not, he was smart enough to know that time was the enemy. The longer they took to ask the questions, the less likely they'd get the answers they needed. Memory ran down like a clock, and the good doctor's memory was all they had to go on right now. That and the borrowed time Amy was living on.

¢¢¢

Deacon sat glumly beside Tremaine as she drove back to U of D campus. He recalled everything Sanford told them. The dark, crazy words Amy had said. Her death for the best? Cobwebs in the corner? He wished that his eidetic memory would fail him so he wouldn't have to dredge it up over and over. Each word brought a vision with it. Imagery of Amy helplessly bound, pouring out her soul—a soul that had become hopelessly corrupted by the suicide drug. The same drug that had blackened the spirits of several high-profile politicians, his colleague Ray Treadaway, Claudia Metternich, FBI agent Paul Carstairs, his own beloved Liz. All but one now dead. All but two, if you included Amy. But for how long?

Maybe Tremaine was right. Maybe Deacon should stay in the lab. A cure was their only hope. But that was false hope unless they found Amy before Barzoon felt satisfied with his pound of flesh. How many more videos would arrive by messenger until one held the ghastly image of Amy taking her own life. And in the background, behind the camera, Nelson Barzoon smiling, relishing it all.

Deacon glanced at Tremaine behind the wheel of her government SUV, staring straight ahead. He was expecting another lecture about how he was a scientist not an investigator, how he had been allowed to debrief Sanford as a favor, nothing more. Tremaine surprised him.

"What did you think of what Sanford had to say?"

Deacon looked at the road. "Are you actually asking for *my* opinion?"

Tremaine turned into the left lane to pass a truck. "Yes. I'm *actually* asking your opinion."

"Even though I am just a scientist ignorant in the ways of investigation."

She smiled. "You are many things, Dr. Creel, but ignorant is not one of them. And you know Amy Robbins better than I do, perhaps better than anyone other than her family."

"You notify them yet?" Deacon asked.

Tremaine shook a negative. "Didn't see what good it would do at this point. Why worry them?"

Deacon nodded, then yawned. He hadn't gotten more than a dozen hours sleep in the last four days, and most of that was catnaps. His mind was fuzzy.

"So, Deke? What's your opinion of Sanford's observations?"

He waited a moment, then said, "Not very helpful."

"I was afraid that your opinion was gonna agree with mine."

He rubbed sleep from his eyes. "She was tethered inside a locked bedroom with an adjoining bath. No distinguishing characteristics. No way to look outside. No traffic noise that suggests a major highway. No bell tower. No airport noises. Nothing that could help us pin down a location." He shook his head in disgust. "The room sounded too big to be a hotel or motel, so we're probably dealing with a private residence. But which one?"

Tremaine sighed. "Yeah, we can't search every house in the state of Ohio. Even within a hundred-mile radius, we've got to be dealing with more than a million houses." She laughed. "Even if we limited it to bedrooms with adjoining baths, it's still a million."

"Don't forget those with cobwebs in the corner." Deacon's chuckle morphed into a gasp. "Cobwebs!"

"What?"

It hit Deacon like a ten-pound sledge. He clapped his hands. Could it be that simple? "*Cobwebs*. I thought Amy was just talking crazy. That she was referring to some dark recess of the mind. But what if she was giving us a clue."

Tremaine stared at him in stunned bewilderment. "What the hell are you talking about?"

"I'm talking about the safe house."

"You want to go to the safe house on Miller Road?"

"No," Deacon shouted. "The other one, off Nutt Road!"

Tremaine had slowed to take the exit onto Route 35. A horn honked behind her. She waved the other driver around then looked at Deacon. "What about it?"

"What would have happened to it, after we left, I mean?"

Tremaine put on her blinker for the turn. "The cleaning crew would have come in, straightened up, replenished supplies. Why?"

"After that."

Tremaine shrugged. "Nothing after that."

The crazy idea was making more and more sense to Deacon. In fact, it was perfect, diabolical even. It was just the kind of thing Barzoon would think of. An in-your-face contempt. "So, it would be vacant? I mean, until you needed it for another witness?"

"Yeah." Tremaine's eyes grew wide. "What are you saying? You think …"

Deacon slapped the dash. "It's perfect. A vacant house that Barzoon knew about. Sparsely furnished to start with. And the two upstairs bedrooms are connected by an adjoining bath."

Tremaine merged onto Route 35. "Listen, lots of houses connect bedrooms by an adjoining bath."

"No, they don't," Deacon shouted. "The *master* has an adjoining bath. The way Sanford described it, this room wasn't a master. It was a spare room. They usually put a separate bath on the same floor for the spare rooms, so people don't risk walking in on each other. And what about the cobwebs?"

Tremaine slowed and pulled onto the shoulder. She popped the trans into park and looked at Deacon the way a psychiatrist studies a patient. "What the hell are you talking about? What about these cobwebs?"

Deacon unbuckled his harness so he could turn to her. He pounded his palm with the back of his other hand. "The bedroom at the safe house. The one Amy and I used when …" Tremaine raised her brows. "The one Amy and I used. It had cobwebs in the corner by the ceiling, lots of them. Amy laughed about billions for defense but not one penny for cleaning the ceiling." He snapped his fingers. "And the walls were the same drab beige as in the video Barzoon sent me."

Tremaine shook her head as she checked her seatbelt, then glanced into the rearview mirror. "I think you're nuts, but I guess it's worth a shot." She put the car into drive and pulled out.

Something clicked in Deacon's brain. Call it a logical connection, call it intuition, call it what you will. He knew he was right. For the first time in a week, he saw a light at the end of the tunnel. He felt relieved but only for a moment.

He'd just rebuckled his seatbelt when he heard a screech of tires and a loud horn blast. From the corner of his eye, he saw another SUV. This one was dark grey, like a shark's head. The big car was almost on top of them, its plastic grill shining like so many rows of angry teeth. This imagery filled his mind as he was jerked into his shoulder harness by the sudden impact.

¢¢¢

"Are you alright?"

Deacon patted himself down. There was no blood on his hands. He could see clearly. His only injury would seem to be bruising where his shoulder harness had jerked him back. "Yeah. Good thing I got my belt buckled before you decided to play demolition derby." He glanced at Tremaine, who seemed unruffled except for a slight flush of excitement that only made her more attractive. "They teach you to drive like that at marshal school?"

Her blue eyes shot daggers. "Shut up." She unbuckled her harness then hit the emergency flashers. As she popped her door, she said, "Stay inside. I'll check on the other car and phone for help."

Deacon clicked open his own door latch.

"I said stay in the car."

His door groaned open a crack. "Not going to be a problem. Your defensive driving skills sent us into the guard rail, so my door is jammed by the fender."

Tremaine shook her head and carefully exited onto the freeway shoulder. Deacon saw a cell go to her ear before she'd taken two steps toward the charcoal-colored SUV.

He popped his own harness, taking pressure off the injured area, then leaned painfully into the driver's seat to shout through the open door. "Be sure to tell them to surround the safe house. But be careful. Amy is in there with Barzoon."

His intuition had solidified into certainty. Amy was being held at the first safe house, off Nutt Road. Tremaine was right, it could be any one of a thousand bedrooms that looked similar. But in his heart, Deacon knew it wasn't. He knew because he was getting to know Barzoon. No matter what the man had been through, whatever devils were plaguing him, he was still trying to prove his superiority. The elite. The master spy. The superior gamesman. Wilier than all those who would pursue him. So, he'd hidden Amy under their very noses while he took his revenge on the one man who'd beaten him.

Deacon looked up to see Tremaine talking on the phone by the back fender of the other car. The driver started to get out, but she waved him back in with a flash of her credentials. She spoke quickly with someone before putting her phone down and walking toward the other car. She seemed calm and collected as she tapped the driver's window. She said something to the driver that Deacon couldn't hear, then started walking back toward Deacon. But when she got halfway, she ducked into the safe space between the two vehicles. Again, she dialed her cell and spoke with someone. Deacon heard bits and pieces of what sounded like a call for roadside assistance as Tremaine assessed the damage on the passenger side of the car. When she reentered the car, she dropped the cell into her blazer pocket, then shook her hair over the collar.

"This must happen to you a lot."

Her eyes darted daggers again. "*Excuse* me?"

"You don't seem shook up at *all*."

Her mood softened. "Training."

Deacon pointed toward the other car. "Who did you call?"

"Triple A. They give government agencies priority." She snapped on her harness and started the engine. "Buckle up."

Deacon grabbed his seatbelt. "Are we leaving the scene of the accident? What about the roadside assistance?"

"That's for the other car. We're drivable." She checked her mirrors, then pulled into traffic.

Deacon fastened his safety belt. "Who else did you call?"

For the first time, she looked startled. "What do you mean?"

Deacon rubbed his bruised shoulder. "The first call. Before you talked to the driver and called the auto club. Was that about having somebody check out the safe house?"

"Oh, that. Yeah, that was for backup." She smiled. "Let's go check out your hunch on the safe house."

¢¢¢

They parked on Nutt Road, fifty feet from the drive that led to the safe house. Deacon couldn't see the house or all of the driveway, but what he could see was devoid of marked or unmarked vehicles. "I thought you called for backup."

Tremaine snapped open her seatbelt. "I did. We must have been closest."

"Closer than the county sheriff or the Centerville Police?"

Tremaine ignored him and kept her eyes on the empty driveway. As she opened her door, she said, "You stay here."

"Shouldn't we wait for the backup?"

"I'll just check it out," Tremaine said.

"Then I'm coming with you." Deacon started to open his own door, before realizing he was still trapped. "Shit!" He tried climbing over the console but was caught short by the pain in his bruised side.

"I said stay *put*." Tremaine left her door open as she dropped into a shooter's crouch behind it. "I'll call your cell if it's clear." She drew her Glock, then crept around the door and down the drive.

"Wait for backup," Deacon whisper shouted. "Amy's in there."

Tremaine ignored him and jogged forward in a crouch. She stopped beside a clump of bushes at the head of the drive. She was breathing hard, her face flushed. Why wasn't she waiting for backup? As if she heard his thoughts, he watched her retrieve the cell and punch speed dial. She spoke into the phone for a few seconds before returning it to her pocket. She looked at him watching her, gave a wave with her gun hand, then sneaked a look at the house. She paused for just a moment before sprinting down the drive out of his field of view.

Deacon couldn't take it anymore. Pain or no, he began to leverage himself into the driver's seat. He tried to bring his leg over the console first, but that was too awkward. So, he took a deep breath, grabbed the console with one hand, his seat back with the other, and lofted his body up and over. Despite the spacious cab, his head hit the ceiling with a jaw-jarring clunk. His ass found the driver's seat, but his back kept going toward the open door. Fireflies flitted before his eyes as he fell backward into space.

Deacon landed on the macadam with a whoosh of breath, leaving him winded and dazed amid the dancing fireflies. When his vision cleared, he rolled onto all fours, panting for breath. Tremaine was nowhere in sight. Deacon rose unsteadily and staggered after her.

Chapter 28

Amy clenched and unclenched one fist, then the other. She next compressed the muscles of her forearms. Since her promise to cooperate in exchange for Sanford's freedom, Barzoon had unbound her legs and loosened her arm tethers, allowing better range of motion. But her inability to change position still plagued her with numbness and muscle cramps. The isometric exercises helped. Eventually, there would be bed sores, but Amy didn't think she'd live that long.

Thoughts of death were never far off, but her promise kept them at bay. Odd, she thought, how she could worry about keeping her word to a foreign agent recently dedicated to the overthrow of her government. She thought of her marine credo: duty, honor, country. Perhaps if she were duty bound by a clear threat to her country, she could sacrifice her word of honor. But she didn't see Barzoon as such a threat. He wanted revenge, not world domination. So, she would keep her word, as he had kept his.

Amy didn't really know if Barzoon had indeed kept his promise to release Sanford. But part of her did know he had. She couldn't explain how she knew, but she did. Maybe it was female intuition. Maybe a side effect of the suicide drug Sanford said she'd been given. Maybe it was just her knowledge of her enemy, her growing surety that although Barzoon was ruthless, he was not unscrupulous.

For the second time, her thoughts were interrupted by her captor entering unannounced, but this time was different than the last. Before, he had seemed highly agitated, emotionally disturbed, as if some mental demon were pursuing him. Now, he was calmer and more determined, his eyes with less of a feral glaze. His pistol was tucked into his waistband. In his hand was a roll of duct tape.

Barzoon closed the bedroom door with a soft click. "I apologize for once again entering so boldly. But I have received news that our time together is short." He tore a strip from the tape as he strode toward her. "Cavalry is on the way, your knight in shining armor. So, we must soon part." Before Amy could say anything, he slapped the tape across her mouth. Ignoring her muffled protests, he managed an almost genuine smile and said, "I shall grant your wish for death."

He tossed the tape on the bed beside her, then drew the pistol. The cold, black steel seemed to come alive, a tiger released from the confines of its cage. She could almost hear it speak to her. Instead of a roar, it whispered. She could hear the words in her mind's ear. Peace. Eternity. Her heart lifted. She would die without sacrificing her honor. Best of all, Deacon would be spared more needless suffering. There would be no more videos, just her lifeless body. He would grieve for a time, but in the end, he would see that it was for the best. And his life would be better without her.

Barzoon's features twisted into a look of regret. She met his eyes, which were soft and forgiving. "You have been an honorable woman, Ms. Robbins, a loyal soldier. I bear you no ill will." His eyes suddenly darkened. "That I reserve for Dr. Creel." A hint of a smile returned, one tinged with an evil glint. "Be succored that he shall precede you." His eyes took on a far-away stare. "Then I shall follow." Amy could see his gun hand twitch in anticipation. "We shall share eternity together."

Amy's gut dropped. For the first time, she saw Barzoon's master plan. She cursed herself for not seeing it sooner. It was that obvious. She'd been busy wallowing in self-pity and self-loathing and had ignored her captor's ultimate motive. Yes, watching her suffering would make Deacon suffer. But that wouldn't be enough for Barzoon. Such a man couldn't die knowing that his nemesis lived. His goal all along had been to ramp up Deacon's misery, to look into his eyes and declare victory. Then, and only then, would he kill all concerned, Deacon first.

Duty, honor, country—these were what Amy had lived by, first in her marine father's home, then during her own time in the corps. This is what had made her keep her word to Barzoon. But there was more than these three. There was also love. As long as Deacon was safe, she could sacrifice all but her honor. Now, Deacon was walking into a deadly trap, with her as the bait. A trap that she was duty-bound to foil—if she could.

There was a noise outside, as if something thudded against the siding of the house. Barzoon flinched in the direction of the sound.

Amy tried to scream a warning but emitted only a muffled grunt. She watched in horror as Barzoon slowly pointed the pistol at the bedroom door. He looked as determined as any soldier Amy had ever known. She needed to do something—and quickly.

¢¢¢

Deacon stumbled toward the driveway, his eyes directed at the macadam, then ducked behind the same bush where Tremaine had stopped. He took a few moments to catch his breath and quiet the stitch in his bruised side. As he panted, he dreaded to hear the gunshot signifying that Barzoon had already seen Tremaine and had taken it out on Amy. Deacon mentally cursed the deputy marshal for running off half-cocked, not waiting for backup. But the deed was done. All Deacon could do now was pray that they still had surprise on their side. His time in Iraq, his time in the shitshow that was Project Suicide, had taught him that surprise could make the difference. It also taught him that delay was the ally of failure, and failure meant the death of the woman he loved. He was increasingly certain that she was captive less than a hundred yards away, held hostage by a crazy man who was unpredictably dangerous. With that thought, Deacon took a deep breath and ran for it.

The safe house seemed deserted, no cars in the turnaround, no light leaking from the curtained windows. It looked as if it hadn't been touched by human hands since he and Amy had vacated. But none of that changed his certainty that Amy was inside. Barzoon would want to keep the place looking deserted. Any car would be parked in the detached garage or on a nearby road. He ran on.

Tremaine was against the side of the house, her back pressed to the clapboards. She paused for a moment, looking both stunningly beautiful and crisply professional, then spun toward him as he pulled up short, his eyes staring down the bore of her Glock 19.

"What the …" Tremaine grabbed his arm and pulled. She was deceptively strong for a woman, slamming the unsuspecting Deacon into the side of the building. "I told you to wait in the car—that I'd call you."

Deacon managed to rip his arm from her grasp. "Keep your voice down. Someone might hear."

Tremaine holstered her pistol. "Who? This place looks deserted." The deputy pointed. "No car in front or back. Curtains drawn. No lights." She flicked her wrist. "Deserted."

Deacon looked around. Everything she said was true, but his gut still told him that Amy was inside. "How can you be so sure? I mean, Barzoon wouldn't advertise. He'd keep it dark and deserted looking. Maybe his car is in the garage."

Tremaine's blue eyes seemed to consider this, then looked toward the front of the house. "Tell you what. I don't think they've changed the keyless entry code, so you stay here while I go in. Give me a couple of minutes to check things out." She started walking around front, then turned back. "Stay put."

Deacon watched her steal away, his mood darkening with each of her steps. Why was she being so brash, not waiting for backup, sacrificing caution? His gut was still sure he was right. The safe house was the answer. It *felt* right—the cosmic tumblers clicking. But Tremaine was the cop, the one trained for these things. Was her training stronger than his sixth sense? Maybe, maybe not. But if not, she was walking into a trap. A trap that could get her and Amy killed.

Tremaine was smart and beautiful. She was used to getting her way. That sometimes led to arrogance and lapses in judgment. Deacon knew that sensation well, had experienced it firsthand. His monster intellect fed a self-satisfied certainty that he was always right, all others wrong. Could he be wrong now? His gut said no, but could he trust it?

Time ticked by, he wasn't certain how long. He wiped sweat from his eyes, then slicked his palms against his pant legs. Deacon looked toward the front of the house for any sign of movement. There was none. He looked toward the back of the house, seeing the single-car garage at the end of the drive. The garage door was solid, but there was a window on the side of the building. He decided to check if there was a car hidden inside. He took two steps toward it, then heard a loud grunt from the front of the house. It might have been a woman. Moments later there was a thud, as if a body fell to the floor. He waited for several seconds, then whisper-shouted, "Terri?" Nothing. He spun quickly and sprinted toward the front entrance.

¢¢¢

Amy heard another sound, this one from inside the house. Pinioned on the bed, unable to speak, she closed her eyes, stretching out with her hearing alone. She recognized the distant click of a door being opened and closed. Someone grunted—from inside the house. Moments later, there was a thud, as if a foot had stamped on the wooden floor of the entry foyer. Amy tensed, listening. At first, nothing. Then there were more faint sounds, perhaps the soft tread of someone stealthily moving up the stairs. The cat-like steps grew steadily, then stopped completely. Amy strained to hear more. At first, she heard only the thudding of her heart. Then there was another soft double click, the front entrance again opening and closing. She opened her eyes.

Barzoon stood directly next to the bed, his pistol pointed at the bedroom door, his intention clear. Amy grunted into the tape and struggled against her nylon straps, anything to make a noise that might warn Deacon. The sounds were weak. She doubted anyone but Barzoon could hear. She looked at him, his gun steady, his features set. Then she stared at the door, trying to peer beyond its wooden panels. She waited. For several seconds, she heard nothing. Then there was a metallic clunk from downstairs. She looked at Barzoon. He remained rock still, staring at the bedroom door.

Amy thought she could hear movement downstairs, but it was faint, wavering in and out. Suddenly, she heard definite footfalls groaning on the stairs. She continued staring at the door, willing it to open, dreading that it would. The footsteps were in the hallway now. Then they stopped. Someone whispered, "Terri?"

Amy recognized Deacon's voice. She grunted and struggled but the sounds were weak even to her own ear. She continued to stare at the door, her vision tunneled onto the worn brass knob. Time slowed, its reality broken into a series of disjointed moments. Something thumped against the bed. Amy flinched. Barzoon had bumped into the mattress, using it to support his shooter's stance. Another soft click, and her eyes pivoted back to the knob. The worn brass began to turn. Behind her, she heard another click, the hammer of Barzoon's pistol being thumbed back for an easy, single-action pull.

Amy struggled, grunted, pounded her legs up and down on the mattress. Then a realization struck like a sudden bolt from above. Her legs. Barzoon had removed the leg restraints as a courtesy to his prisoner. Now, perhaps she could use it to her advantage.

Barzoon stood directly opposite her right leg, but he was too close for an effective kick. She'd need to rely on her left one. She didn't know how much energy she could generate with her non-dominant leg, which had grown weaker still from days without use. But she'd have to try.

Amy moved her leg slowly and carefully away from Barzoon. His attention remained focused on the turning knob. She tensed her leg muscles, praying they wouldn't cramp. She held her breath. She could hear the door creak open. It was now or never.

Chapter 29

Deacon flinched as he opened the door. The click of the knob was like a gunshot to his ears. He didn't like it. Someone had grunted earlier—he was sure he'd heard it when he was outside. He was less sure that it was Tremaine. Could it be Amy? If it was the marshal, why had she grunted? And what was the thud that followed?

In his mind's eye, Deacon saw Barzoon hammering a pistol across Tremaine's silken hair, her trim body dropping. But the inside of the safe house was dark, quiet, and empty. There was no Terri Tremaine. There was no one. He paused, listening, wishing he had a gun, a knife, even a club. He looked about for some weapon, his eyes settling on a fireplace poker. He grasped it, grimacing at the metallic clank as he lifted the cold metal. The scuttle shovel beside it teetered, then fell away. Deacon snatched it before it hit the ground. With a sigh of relief, he lay the shovel on the hearth. He hefted the poker once, twice, satisfied with the solidity of his weapon. Then he shuffled forward.

The living room was empty, as was the kitchen. It looked as if no one had occupied them since he and Amy had left. As he crept slowly, he thought he heard a grunt from upstairs. This noise was weaker than the previous one, but it didn't sound like the house settling. It sounded human. He looked down the hall leading to the master bedroom, wondering if he should clear the downstairs first. But the memory of the faint grunt sent him up the steps instead.

Deacon moved as stealthily as he could but still cringed at each creak of the old stairs. It seemed to take forever to cover the nine treads. When he reached the top landing, he thought that the upstairs looked as vacant as the down. Still no sign of Tremaine. No sign of anyone. Then he saw a thin ray of light coming from under the first of the two guest rooms. It was the room he and Amy had occupied, where they'd made love the last time.

He held the poker high as he dashed forward and grabbed the knob. He listened, now sure he heard muffled movement from inside the room. "Terri?" he softly said. There was another muffled grunt. Deacon took a deep breath. His body tensed. He raised the poker high and turned the knob.

¢¢¢

Amy had eaten little for days and exercised even less. But though her flesh was weak, her spirit was willing. After days of despondent malaise, she was finally motivated. Deacon would be coming through that door, and she was his only chance. She swung her leg with all the force she could muster. The rest was a series of broken images that went from bad to worse.

As Amy arced her leg, the bedroom door swung open, causing Barzoon to flinch back. This lengthened the distance between them and robbed Amy's kick of its force. Instead of a solid round-house to the ribs, her foot thudded weakly against Barzoon's thigh, pushing him further back into the corner. Then, from out of nowhere, a fireplace poker whooshed through the air, aimed for the space Barzoon had occupied moments before. The black iron thumped ineffectually into the mattress, missing Amy's foot by inches. Deacon suddenly appeared, the strength of his misdirected blow tumbling him atop Amy's outstretched leg. She grunted with pain, then grunted again as an explosion sent an icepick through her ear. Then, all action ceased as quickly as it had started.

Deacon lay atop her leg, blood seeping from a hole in his left bicep. Amy instinctively reached for him, her wrists coming up short against her restraints. The air smelled of burnt powder and copper. Her leg felt warm from Deacon's blood. Deacon looked at her through shocked eyes. Then his head turned unsteadily toward Barzoon.

"Well, Dr. Creel," Barzoon said. "We meet again, after so long." Barzoon raised his pistol and smiled, the first genuine smile Amy had seen on her captor's face. "But as the saying goes, revenge is a dish best served cold." Amy watched as the pistol centered on Deacon's face, then swung further toward her. "As you watch Ms. Robbins die, know that her fate is your fault." Amy stared down the black bore of the pistol. "Take that knowledge to your grave." Barzoon's genuine smile turned to genuine hate. "And know that I have beaten you."

The muscles in Barzoon's hand tightened. Amy stopped breathing, her mind numb, her ears still ringing. Then a second shot hammered her aching ears and broke her heart.

¢¢¢

Amy's gaze was glued on Deacon. In her mind, his head exploded into grey and red mush as his eyes rolled lifeless white. But in reality, her lover's eyes remained alive, if shocky, his forehead whole, if ashen.

She tore her vision from Deacon to Barzoon. Her captor's face registered surprise as his head and body slunk down the wall and onto the floor, leaving behind a slug-like trail of blood. Barzoon's polo shirt turned red as more blood seeped from a neat, round hole several inches below his Adam's apple.

Amy saw all this as if through a haze, her brain unable to fully comprehend what was happening. Then a new figure broke through the fog. She recognized Terri Tremaine immediately.

"Deke," Tremaine shouted as she rushed to Deacon's side, dropping her Glock upon the mattress. She whipped the belt from her slim suit pants, tumbling her holster and associated law enforcement gear onto the floor. Tremaine cinched the belt tightly around Deacon's shoulder. She held Deacon's face in her two hands and stared at this pale flesh. "Don't worry. We'll get you medical attention." Then she finally noticed Amy.

Tremaine hopped over and ripped the tape from Amy's mouth. Amy yelped in pain as Tremaine grasped her arm restraints.

"Barzoon has the key," Amy said, jingling the locks on her wrist bindings.

"Shit." Tremaine cursed, snatching a switch knife from the jumble of her gear. Even before the blade popped free, Tremaine was slicing through the nylon wrist straps.

Amy rose quickly, her head spinning from the sudden movement. She stood still until the room stopped swimming.

"Stay with Deke," Tremaine shouted. "I'll call an ambulance."

Amy dropped down beside Deacon. She glanced around for something to bind the wound and spied her pillow. Crawling back to the bed, the ratty carpet scraping her knees, she slipped the case from the pillow and pivoted back to Deacon. Once she'd tied the makeshift bandage tightly around his bicep, she released the tourniquet. The pillowcase did not immediately fill with blood, so she checked Deacon's pulse. A bit fast, but he would live. She looked into his eyes. He smiled at her. She smiled back and squeezed his good arm. Then she turned to Barzoon.

Amy had learned triage as a marine corps medic. The rule was—treat the most life-threatening injuries first, regardless of whether it was friend or foe. Barzoon was definitely the latter but definitely the most serious. His pulse was barely perceptible. His skin was growing cold. She opened one of his eyes and the pupil slowly constricted. He wasn't brain dead—yet. She gently leaned him down onto the floor, cradling his head to prevent sudden movement. Then she checked his wound.

Tremaine's nine-millimeter hollow-point had punched through the centerline just above the clavicle. The wound in front was small, the one behind the size of a silver dollar. Her fingers came away slicked with blood and bits of grit that could only be crushed vertebrae. If he lived, she doubted that Nelson Barzoon would ever walk again, or even move his arms. But he was still alive, so she needed to act.

The most immediate problem was that he wasn't breathing. The bullet had severed the trachea. Instead of a steady stream of air, Barzoon's lungs were filling with blood. Amy marveled that he wasn't already dead.

Snatching the switch knife from where Tremaine had dropped it, Amy sliced through Barzoon's shirt, using its remains to swab blood from the wound. Before the hole could fill again, she cut into it, widening the wound. A large bubble of air burst to the surface. She'd established a patent airway but needed to keep it open. She glanced about and spied Tremaine's mag flashlight. Ripping out the batteries and lens gave her a makeshift tube. Tearing off more of Barzoon's shirt, she sopped up blood, exposing the hole. With all the force she could still muster, Amy pressed the end of the flashlight housing into the hole and pushed. At first it wouldn't move but then sunk an inch into the flesh. Amy pressed down on Barzoon's chest and heard a wheeze of air through the tube. She released then pressed again; her efforts were rewarded by a second wheeze. She was about to repeat the process a third time when his chest rose and fell on its own.

Amy cut away more of Barzoon's shirt and packed it around the flashlight tube. She nodded, satisfied that she had done all she could. Then her adrenaline ebbed, and she collapsed next to him. She felt numb but good. Remarkably, she did not feel the need to kill herself.

<h1 style="text-align:center">Chapter 30</h1>

Deacon woke with a yawn. He started to roll over until the pain in his left arm reminded him that this was a bad idea. Thanks to the Percocet tablets he'd been given, there was only a twinge when he adjusted his sling. An IV still adorned his right hand, but the line had been removed, the end of the catheter capped off. The swift actions of Tremaine and Amy had shut down the bleeding quickly, so the emergency staff hadn't needed to administer whole blood, just a couple liters of fluid. Now he felt the need to pee.

He threw the sheet off the bed and swung his feet over the side. The world tilted for a moment, then righted itself. Deacon rose slowly, his vision steady, and took a step toward the toilet of his private room.

"Hold on a minute."

A pair of strong hands gripped his right arm. Deacon turned. "Come on, Dr. Sanford."

"You can call me Izzie," Sanford replied.

"Come on, Izzie. I appreciate you patching me up, but I think I can take a piss by myself."

She maintained her grip. "I'm your doctor, so why don't you let me make that decision?"

Deacon looked her in the eye. "I've been peeing by myself for thirty plus years, Izzie. I don't mean to stop now."

Sanford shook her head and sighed. "Just because you're being discharged tomorrow doesn't mean you get to travel willy-nilly. You're supposed to ask for help. That's why they put that buzzer by your bed." She led him to the bathroom. "Need me to help you sit?"

Deacon shook his head as he grabbed the stainless bar beside the toilet. "I've also been doing that by myself for years now."

Despite his bravado, sweat popped out on his forehead as he dropped onto the plastic seat.

"Everything alright in there?" Sanford asked from outside the door.

Deacon smiled. "Right as yellow rain." He enjoyed the feeling of release. "I was surprised to see you when they brought me in. I thought you worked at that urgent care in Centerville."

"You mean the crime scene that still has yellow tape around it? Too many bad memories."

Bladder satisfyingly empty, Deacon grasped the metal bar and stood. The hospital johnny flapped closed behind him as he flushed the commode. When he turned, Sanford was at his side again.

"Now let's lie down."

They were halfway to his bed when Deacon froze. "How is Amy?" He felt guilty that he hadn't thought of her earlier.

"She's sedated," Sanford said, leading him on. "We have her on fluids and IV feeding. Her vitals are stable."

Deacon plopped onto the bed. "Any sign of the …" Deacon had trouble saying it.

Sanford smiled sadly. "She's on suicide watch. A nurse present twenty-four seven."

"Can I see her?"

"She's unconscious, Deke."

He repeated. "Can I see her?"

Sanford's eyes softened. "Rest up a bit first."

Deacon leaned back, marveling that he was exhausted from a trip to the toilet. He closed his eyes. "What about Barzoon?"

"Still unconscious," Sanford said. There was a pause. "Amy saved his life."

"Duty, honor, country," Deacon murmured. He dozed off thinking of brown eyes that seemed to fill his mind forever.

¢¢¢

Deacon opened his eyes and peered into smiling blue ones. Terri Tremaine looked a bit tired but otherwise as beautiful as ever.

"Hey there, sailor. How you doing?"

Deacon started to speak, but his mouth was glued dry. He reached for the water cup on the nightstand. Tremaine beat him to the punch and held the straw steady while he sipped. He nodded and leaned back. "Good as new."

Tremaine laughed. "Don't tell me. You can't function until your morning coffee. Or in this case, sip of water."

Deacon yawned. "It's the pain pills. They dry the mouth. And I'm a mouth breather when I sleep."

"Well, you've had enough of *that* the last couple of days." Tremaine yawned.

"How much sleep have *you* had?"

Tremaine waved him off. "I've got news about Metternich."

"Joe? Did they find him?"

Tremaine sat on a bedside chair and crossed her legs. She reached back to massage her neck as she nodded. "Holed up in a hotel outside Falls Church. Housekeeping found the body."

Deacon tensed. "How?"

Tremaine mimed a pistol to the head.

Deacon swallowed hard. "Did he leave a note?"

Tremaine nodded again. "Two words printed in marker. 'I'm sorry.'"

Deacon reached for the water cup, waving off Tremaine's attempt to help. He drank deeply, which helped relieve the knot in his throat. "What about his wife?"

Tremaine took his cup and went into the bathroom to refill it. "Someone at Parkside General removed one of her wrist restraints while the nurse was called away. When the nurse returned, Claudia Metternich had managed to drive a pen through her eye into grey matter."

Deacon felt faint. He closed his eyes. He lay back and the lightheadedness vanished as quickly as it had come, replaced by a feeling of resignation. "At least their suffering is over. Joe paid the price for his part. Hope to God that's the end of it."

Tremaine offered him the cup again; he declined. He managed to smile. "If you give me a second to buzz for the nurse, you can join me in that morning cup of coffee."

Tremaine shook her head, once again reminding Deacon of amber waves of grain. "Afraid I can't. I just stopped by to see how you were doing. And to say goodbye."

"You leaving us?"

"Yeah. On my way to the airport."

"Where's the Marshal's Service sending you this time?"

She wagged a finger at him. "Secret Service, not Marshal's service. My transfer came through."

"Congratulations."

"Thanks." She looked at her watch. "In a couple of hours, I'm catching an eastbound plane. They've got me on presidential detail for his trip to Dallas tomorrow."

Deacon smiled. "Hopefully, he won't be traveling in an open car through Dealy Plaza."

Tremaine grimaced.

"Sorry. I guess it's still too soon. Anyway, try and get some sleep on the plane. You look all in."

Tremaine yawned again. "Yeah. A long few days."

She started to leave, when a sudden flash of memory lit Deacon's brain. "Where were you?"

She turned, startled. "Beg pardon?"

"At the safe house." It was all coming back now. "One minute, I thought that Amy and I were goners, then Barzoon was sliding down the wall with a hole in his neck." He met her gaze, which still seemed startled. "Where did you come from?"

Tremaine swallowed and recovered some composure. "Oh, that. I was in the bathroom."

Deacon squinted his lack of understanding.

"I noticed the light under the door in the first bedroom, so I snuck past to the second. I'd just eased my way into the connecting bath when I heard the shot. When I got to the doorway, Barzoon was ready to shoot you again, so I …" She pantomimed a finger gun.

"Saved our lives. Thank you for that."

Tremaine's cheeks gained color. After a pause, she said, "How's Robbins?"

Deacon sighed. "Amy's resting."

Their eyes met in silent understanding. Tremaine walked over and kissed him on the lips. "Goodbye Deacon." She turned to leave."

More memories flooded Deacon's mind. "What was that thump?"

Tremaine turned, perplexed. "What thump? I didn't hear anything."

"Not now," Deacon said. "At the safe house. I heard a groan and a thump. That's why I came in, to see if you were in trouble."

Again, the sure-tongued deputy seemed uncertain what to say. Finally, her face lit up. "Oh, that. I, um tripped when I searched the kitchen."

Deacon eyed her oddly. "*You tripped*?"

She laughed. "Yeah." She pointed to her casual pumps. "Damn heel caught on a snake-head crack in that old safe house linoleum." She raised her palms in surrender. "I know, not my finest hour in law enforcement." She cupped hand to mouth in clandestine pantomime. "Don't say anything, or you might put the kibosh on my transfer. Can't have clumsy people around the president."

Deacon smiled. "Your secret is safe with me. Sure I can't buy you that cup of coffee before you go?"

Tremaine looked at her watch again. "No. I really have to run. I still need to double-check some details and finish my report before I hit the airport." She kissed his cheek. "Take care of yourself, Deke."

"You, too."

When the door clicked closed behind her, Deacon lay in thought. Something puzzled him. It was ill defined, like a shred of memory from a dream. It would almost come to him, then vanish. It wasn't the first time he'd felt this way over the past few days. "Déjà vu all over again." He shrugged and sat up. "I guess it's time I get dressed and blow this pop stand."

¢¢¢

Deacon nodded to the nurse on duty as he left the room. Amy had been resting comfortably and didn't seem to be in any pain or anxiety, but he knew this was an illusion. Once they allowed her to regain consciousness, the suicide drug would descend as it always did, ramping up her distress until self-destruction seemed like the only answer. Then the restraints would come out. She'd be trussed up like an animal, as Barzoon had trussed her. Her days would be waking torment, her nights sedative-induced oblivion.

Deacon felt a pang of guilt that he wasn't striving for a cure back at UD. The feeling left quickly. Howie was doing remarkable work, more than Deacon could have done at his age, perhaps any age. But even under the best of circumstances, with brilliant researchers and millions devoted to the problem, cures usually took years. Often, they never came.

He slumped back into the wheelchair. His uncomplicated wound was on the mend, but he still tired easily. He was now clad in Walmart sweats and knockoff sneakers. The personal effects he'd been shot in were still with the police. Casual attire suitable for cocktail hour, he thought. And that's all he wanted right now. Just to find himself a bottle and seek his own oblivion.

"Let's go, Barney," Deacon said.

The orderly assigned to him wheeled the chair down the hall. They approached a room with a bored cop out front reading *Sports*

Illustrated. Deacon raised his good hand. "Hold it a minute, Barney. I'd like to stop in here."

"See a friend of yours?" the orderly asked, stopping the chair.

"More an acquaintance," Deacon said, grunting up.

"Need a hand?

Deacon waved the orderly off.

Barney nodded and smiled. "Okay, but not too long. My job is to get you safely off the premises so you're no longer the hospital's responsibility.

Deacon smiled back. "I won't be long."

As Deacon stepped forward, the guard rose and raised his brows.

Deacon read the cop's nametag. "Hey, Jim. I'm Dr. Creel." Deacon held up the temporary credentials he'd been given by the late Josiah Metternich.

The cop didn't seem to know what to make of this casually clad wounded man with official-looking ID. He peered at Deacon's credentials for a moment, saw that the face matched the one on the card, then shrugged and held the door open.

Barzoon lay on the bed, eyes closed, face smooth and pale, his breathing slow and regular. An IV dripped into his left arm, his right lay uselessly at his side. A stiff brace kept his neck vertical. A bandage was visible above the hospital sheet, in its center sat a tracheotomy tube, a replacement for the makeshift one Amy had fashioned. Deacon heard air hiss from the tube with each of Barzoon's exhalations.

Deacon went forward a few steps and looked at the face of the man who shouldn't be alive, yet was. The man who'd tried to kill Deacon and had forced Amy to suffer just to make a point. A man who was dangerously disturbed, yet now looked helpless and harmless.

Deacon glanced up to the whiteboard on the wall. Barzoon was on cephalexin and dexamethasone administered into his daily two liters of D5W. The packing around the tracheotomy tube was cleaned and changed twice daily. This was done by a pair of nurses evidently named Diane and Bryan, their names in blue on the whiteboard, a smiley face next to the former.

Deacon stared back down at Barzoon and froze. The injured man was staring back at him. Barzoon's eyes were rimmed with red but nonetheless fixed and determined. Hatred shone through those eyes, hatred that appeared undimmed by recent events. Something else shone through as well, almost desperation.

Deacon stepped forward. "Can you hear me, Nelson?"

Barzoon's tongue moistened his lips, then those lips formed the word 'yes.'

Deacon didn't know what to say. He wanted to castigate this man who had done so much harm, caused so much unnecessary pain. But that seemed inappropriate. No matter what, Barzoon was still a human being who was destined to be a human vegetable. Despite everything, Deacon felt more compassion than hatred. "Can I do anything for you?"

Barzoon's eyes sought his, anguish behind the pale lids. His lips moved again, frantically forming words that Deacon couldn't make out. Deacon leaned closer, as if to hear, before realizing this was ridiculous. No air moved past Barzoon's voice box, so no words moved past the man's lips. Still, Barzoon struggled to be heard. His mouth moved, his eyes pleaded. Deacon tried to read lips, but they moved too quickly. Finally, Barzoon paused, then slowly mouthed the single word 'tube.'

Deacon looked at the tracheotomy tube sticking out of Barzoon's chest, then looked back into Barzoon's eyes. "Blink once for yes, two for no. Understand?"

Barzoon managed a thin smile and blinked once.

"Do you want to tell me something?"

Another blink.

"If I cover the breathing tube, do you think you can speak?"

Barzoon held his eyes closed for several seconds then opened them just once.

Deacon leaned in close to the man's lips and then placed his hand over the trach tube. He could feel air pressure against his palm, pressure that slowly built until it bubbled up past Barzoon's lips. The words were soft and guttural, but Deacon could just barely make them out.

"End it."

Deacon removed his hand and air once more hissed from the tube. He looked at Barzoon and shook his head. "Sorry, Nelson. You'll have to get another executioner. I've had my fill."

Barzoon's lips frantically moved again. Deacon leaned down and plugged the tube. Once again, the words were faint. Deacon could make out only the last few.

"Worth your while."

Deacon released the tube and felt the rush of air. "How so?"

Barzoon paused, gathering strength, then mouthed a single word that looked like 'soul.' Deacon plugged the tube and strained to hear.

"Mole."

Deacon released the tube and met Barzoon's gaze. "Mole? You mean a spy?" Deacon smiled. "That's old news, I'm afraid. We already know about Tony Movello, the mole you planted."

Barzoon blinked twice, paused, then blinked twice again. Deacon plugged the tube and heard a single word.

"Another."

The word was faint and difficult to hear but unambiguous. Deacon plopped on the bed and stared at Barzoon. "There's another mole? Another spy?"

Barzoon blinked once.

Deacon gasped in surprise. Without thinking, he grabbed Barzoon's face and turned it toward him. His fingers felt grating as the man's neck cranked to the left, as if bone was grinding on bone. "Who?" he said. "Who is it?" Barzoon only stared. Deacon took Barzoon's head in his hands and shook it. "Tell me who." Barzoon's eyes rolled white. Deacon jammed his hand over the breathing tube and pressed his ear to Barzoon's lips. Two faint words were audible. "Thank you." Deacon released the tube and heard one long exhalation that went on and on.

¢¢¢

The guard looked up from his magazine. "Everything alright in there? I thought I heard something."

"Fine," Deacon said, flopping into the wheelchair. Sweat poured off his brow. His vision spun, his mind spun as well. He'd need to contact Tremaine, tell her what had happened. They'd need to check out everyone.

"Ready to go home now?" Barney asked.

"Huh?"

"I said, is it okay if I take you to discharge now?"

Deacon shook his head. "Give me your cell phone."

"Sorry. I don't carry a cell when on the job."

"Shit," Deacon said. "I need a phone—now."

"We're on our way to admissions," Barney said. "They can get you an outside line."

"What are we waiting for?"

As they rounded the corner of the corridor, Deacon could see the admissions desk in the distance. Beyond was a wall of glass, two sliding doors in the middle. The desk was occupied by a female staff member in a blue smock, talking on the phone. An elderly man with a four-pronged cane leaned in to get her attention. Beyond the glass entrance doors, a police car was parked, its gumball lights flashing. A portly, middle-aged cop was busy helping a man in handcuffs exit the back door.

Deacon lurched up from the chair before Barney had even stopped it. He sped forward and tapped on the desk.

"Excuse me," Deacon said. "I need to make a call."

The receptionist, Cora by name, waved to him but continued talking on the phone. "Yes, ma'am. Visiting hours end at 8:30." Cora grimaced and held the phone away from her ear. Deacon could hear that the person on the other end of the line didn't like that answer. "Be that as it may, ma'am …" Cora held the phone at a distance again and shook her head. "Perhaps a special arrangement can be made. I'll put you on hold and transfer you to the administration office." Cora punched a button, and another phone line began flashing.

Deacon raised his voice. "Beg pardon, but I need an outside line."

Cora raised her palm in a stiff-armed salute. "One moment, sir. This gentleman was next." Cora punched more buttons, and the flashing light on her phone changed to steady. Then she beamed a smile as phony as a starlet's chest at the old man, "May I help you?"

Before Deacon could interrupt, the doors slid open, and the middle-aged cop led in the handcuffed man.

"Is this really necessary?" the prisoner said. "All I did was…"

"Go through a red light and almost cause an accident."

The prisoner's voice sounded familiar, but Deacon was focused on getting the attention of reception. "Excuse me?"

Cora gave him another Nazi salute. "In a minute."

"Okay," the prisoner said, "I can explain."

"Why you were driving drunk at two o'clock in the afternoon?" the cop asked.

"I'm not drunk. I just had a couple of beers at lunch."

"Then refused a Breathalyzer®, which means we draw blood at the nearest medical facility."

"Can you at least take the cuffs off now?"

"I'll take them off, if you promise to shut up."

"Deal." The prisoner turned his back to the cop and the cop undid the cuffs, then pointed. "Now go sit down." The cop stepped past the old man with the cane. "Excuse me. I'll need a nurse to draw a blood sample on this guy."

Cora slid a form to the cop. "Fill this out."

The prisoner rubbed his wrists. "We just can't leave my car on the street."

The cop grabbed a pen and began filling out the form. "My partner is parking it just outside." He pointed over his shoulder. "Then the wrecker will take it to the impound lot."

The double doors whooshed open again, and the cop's partner came in. This cop was younger, probably a rookie. Deacon thought he saw peach fuzz on the kid's chin.

The reception area had grown from Cora and one old man to a noisy crowd. There was the cop filling out his form, the prisoner complaining, the old man trying to be heard, the young cop looking confused, Deacon trying to get an outside line, and Barney trying to get Deacon to sit down. It was starting to take on the trappings of a Marx Brothers movie. All that was missing were Margaret Dumont and an order of hard-boiled eggs.

"Excuse me," Deacon said.

"I'm still waiting," said the old man with the cane.

"Quiet," shouted the older of the two cops. Silence reigned. The older cop slid the form and pen at Cora, then hitched up his pants and pointed to the right-side corridor. "I'm gonna hit the can." He pointed at the chairs. "Watch him."

The younger cop grabbed the prisoner's arm.

"Take it easy," the prisoner muttered, still rubbing his wrists.

Deacon finally put the prisoner's voice to the face. "Carl?"

The prisoner turned to Deacon, his face bewildered.

"Carl Sinclair?" Deacon asked.

Sinclair still looked perplexed.

Deacon pointed to himself. "Deacon Creel. Remember? You and I ... *chatted* about Amy Robbins a few nights back."

Sinclair blanched and bumped up against the younger cop.

"Watch it," the cop said, strong-arming Sinclair toward the chairs.

Deacon walked toward the pair. He pointed at Sinclair's face. "Sorry about that, Carl."

Sinclair touched the shiner under his eye as he scurried behind the younger cop. "Keep that psycho away from me." He jabbed his finger repeatedly at Deacon. "I want him arrested. He assaulted me the other day—I mean night."

Deacon extended his open hand. "No hard feelings, Carl?"

Sinclair ducked further behind the cop. "I mean it. This guy knocked me out. I'm lucky he left me alive."

"Take it easy, Carl. I'm not going to …" Deacon froze. The thought that had been nagging unexpressed at the corner of his mind suddenly revealed itself. Carl had just said it. So had Tony Movello. And so had Terri Tremaine. "Alive. Why would Barzoon leave somebody alive?"

At the mention of Barzoon's name, Carl started shouting. "I mean it! Get him away from me!"

As the cop pushed Sinclair toward the chairs, Barney grabbed Deacon's arm. "Take it easy, Dr. Creel. Come sit down in your wheelchair."

Deacon shook him off. He no longer needed Barney's support. He was no longer tired. His wounded arm was forgotten.

The younger cop pushed Sinclair toward the chairs and turned to Deacon. "Who the hell are you?"

Deacon glanced down at the kid's uniform, then flashed his credentials. "Officer Davis, I'm Dr. Deacon Creel from NIH. I'm currently on detached service to Homeland Security on a top-secret project of national importance." With a flourish, he closed the ID and stowed it in his pocket. "I need you to drive me somewhere immediately."

The young cop gaped, his mouth wide open.

"Now," Deacon shouted.

Davis flinched. "But … I, I … um, I can't just drive off." He pointed to the restrooms. "I need to get an okay from Sergeant Hendershot."

Deacon nodded and spun on his heels, as Barney stared on in disbelief. "Fine," Deacon said. "Then I'll need to commandeer Mr. Sinclair's car."

Davis's jaw dropped again. "But, but … this man is our prisoner. We just arrested him."

Deacon cut him off. "Federal emergency. It takes priority over your traffic stop." Deacon presented his open palm. "Keys, if you please." The cop just stared, so Deacon snapped his fingers. "Now."

The cop pointed hesitantly outside. "The keys are in it."

Without another word, Deacon stalked toward the sliding doors.

"Hey, Doc," Barney yelled as he started after Deacon. "You have to be signed out first."

Deacon thumbed over his shoulder. "Officer Davis, arrest that man for impeding a federal investigation." Deacon tensed, expecting someone to grab him. No one did. Before the glass doors hummed shut behind him, he heard Carl Sinclair yell, "Wait a minute. That's *my* car."

Chapter 31

Amy slowly opened one eye. Whatever sedative they had given her was wearing off, at least enough to rouse her to the nearby noise and movement. Through fuzzy vison, she saw the nurse use a large-gauge needle to inject a yellow nutrient solution into the IV bag. The nurse placed the used syringe and needle on the nightstand, its sharp, steel point glistening in the room light. The point looked dangerous, perhaps deadly. Amy's hopes rose.

A nylon restraint not unlike the one Barzoon had used on her lay inches from Amy's wrist. Its glistening metal hasp was less comforting. It spoke of restriction. She'd had enough of that. Agonizing days of it while Barzoon tormented both her and Deacon. Now Deacon was safe. Amy's corpsman's brain knew his wound was not life-threatening, even as she'd bandaged it. So, her duty was done. She looked again at the syringe and needle. She knew exactly what she would do with them.

Duty, honor, country. She had kept her word of honor to Barzoon. With him out of the way, her country was no longer in danger, if it ever had been. Deacon was alive; she had done her duty by him.

The nurse turned toward her, sending thoughts of Deacon to flight. Amy snapped her eye shut and tried to keep her breathing slow and steady. If the nurse realized she was awake, Amy knew that the restraints would be applied immediately. Playing possum she could gain time, perhaps enough to do what needed to be done, what she now felt free to do.

Duty, honor, country. Amy had only one duty now. She had to do the honorable thing. To do what was best for Deacon, her country, and herself. To put an end to the pretense that she had worth, that she deserved Deacon. She thought of Deacon lying there, his boyish face smiling even as she applied the bandage to his bullet wound. He would survive. His love would survive to be directed elsewhere, a more worthy target than lowly Amy Robbins.

The nurse placed a cloth across her forehead. Amy tried not to tense up. The cloth was barely damp. After a moment, it was lifted from her brow. Amy heard the nurse's footsteps heading to the bathroom. Then there was the sound of running water. She had a brief window in which to act.

Amy's eyes shot open, and her hand reached for the syringe. Part of her wanted to impale herself with the needle, but that would only be painful, not deadly. The water continued running in the distance as Amy held the barrel of the syringe in her left hand, the plunger in her right. It was a fifty-milliliter syringe, the kind used to place a lot of material into IV bags, or to bolus a large volume of drugs during shock treatment or cardiac arrest. She pulled the plunger all the way back to the fifty-mL line, then sought her IV access port. Her fingers were still unsteady from the sedative, but after several tries, she was able to shove the large bore needle into the port.

Amy was well aware of the old Hollywood trope concerning air in IV lines. According to tinsel town, a single bubble injected into a vein could collapse the heart into sudden arrest. Amy was just as aware that this was a myth, one used to flesh out thriller movies and murder mysteries. She knew from her training that the heart could easily cope with a bubble of air, even a few milliliters. But she didn't think it could handle fifty.

The sound of running water ceased. She needed to do it soon. If she acted quickly, the nurse would never even know. Amy held the syringe in her trembling hand, her thumb on the plunger. Do it now, she thought. It's the best thing. Best for you. Most of all, best for Deacon. She applied thumb pressure to the plunger.

¢¢¢

Sinclair's Kia rocked as Deacon pulled away from the hospital. He heard the door slam shut behind him. Glancing into the rearview mirror, Deacon smiled.

"Hey there, Carl. I'm surprised to see you here."

Carl looked into the mirror. "It's *my* car."

"Sure it is," Deacon said. "But I'm a psycho nutjob, remember? Aren't you afraid I'll run it into an abutment and kill you?"

"You almost did, driving off like that while I was still getting in."

"Lighten up, Carl. I got you out of a DUI, didn't I? And I'm guessing it's not your first. Am I right?"

Deacon watched Sinclair's mirror image brush down his clothing as if he'd just jumped from a moving train. Sinclair looked up. "*Are* you planning on running into an abutment and killing us both?"

Deacon smiled again. "I like you, Carl. And if you do what I say, you may come out of this in one piece." He turned and looked Sinclair directly in the eye. "Understand?"

Sinclair hesitated before nodding sheepishly.

As Deacon turned his eyes back on the road, Sinclair held up two fingers. "On two conditions."

"Shoot."

"Tell me where we're going."

"We're headed to a house off Nutt Road."

"Why?"

"I need to check out the kitchen floor."

"The kitchen floor?"

Deacon nodded. "What's condition two?"

"You tell me what the hell this is all about."

¢¢¢

Police crime scene tape was draped across the drive so Deacon parked the car on Nutt Road and walked down. When he left, Carl was dozing in the back seat. Deacon knew from his own run-ins with the law that adrenaline lasted only so long when your blood alcohol was well over the limit. Just the same, Deacon had pocketed the keys in case Carl woke and decided to take a hike.

Deacon could see more yellow tape streaming from the front door, one end having given up the ghost. He headed toward it. He no longer felt exhausted, although his arm pained him with every few steps. He was on a mission and didn't have time for fatigue and pain. He tucked the injured wing into his body and walked on.

He didn't know safe house procedures between guests, but Tremaine had said they hadn't yet changed the keyless entry code. Tremaine had also said other things that needed checking out before Deacon could be sure.

Deacon creaked up the wooden steps and peered into the side-light window. The place looked deserted, just as it had the last time he'd been here. His eidetic memory recalled the keyless code and he also remembered that you needed to push in on the knob with one hand while you entered the four digits with the other. He gently removed his arm from the sling, his wound sounding a silent alarm. As he reached for the keypad with his injured hand, he turned and pushed the knob with his good one. To his surprise, the door clicked open. He chuckled. "Whoever put the tape across the front door must have also been in charge of locking it."

He passed inside reverently, as if entering a tomb, which wasn't a bad description. The air smelled of dust and the accumulated lives that had resided here. He closed the door quietly behind him and scanned the living room. During the time he and Amy had lived in the safe house, he'd probably spent less than forty-eight hours total here—and most of that was sleeping. Nevertheless, he was swept by an odd nostalgia. There was nothing homey about it, but it felt like home. Like home, it held good and bad memories and a longing for things that can no longer be. He took in the familiar setting: the cheap, serviceable furniture, the hotel-style prints on the walls, the fireplace tools in their hanger, except for the scuttle still resting on the hearth where he'd laid it down.

A few weeks before, he'd never seen this place. How much things had changed during that time. Barzoon was dead. Amy might soon follow him. Deacon himself was injured and confused. What he was thinking was unthinkable, but it also made a strange, perverted sense. He gingerly replaced his arm in its sling. He longed for a drink, maybe twelve.

Deacon headed for the kitchen. Very little of the forty-eight hours he'd lived here had been spent in that room. Yet, he could still see it in his mind's eye. That's what bothered him now. Bothered and excited him. The nicked appliances in their white enamel. The scratched butcher-block table. The sink dulled by too many spoons and forks carelessly tossed onto its stainless-steel surface over the years. All as well used as any temporary housing he'd ever inhabited. Everything as old and dog-eared as a motel directory. Everything except the vinyl floor covering, which Deacon remembered thinking was the only thing that looked …

Deacon suddenly stopped, his arm singing again at the jerky movement. There, in the doorway to the kitchen, stood Deputy U.S. Marshal Terri Tremaine.

Tremaine was as beautiful as ever, resplendent in her dark, tailored suit. Her high-boned cheeks were aflame, as if from surprise or embarrassment. She looked like a kid stealing from the cookie jar as she suddenly removed her hand from the pocket of her slacks,

"What are you doing here?" Tremaine asked.

Deacon's heart started beating again. "I could ask you the same question."

She smiled, which seemed more from nervousness than humor. "Like I said, checking out a few details for my report." She cleared her throat and brushed back her blonde locks. "Now how about you answer my question?"

Deacon smiled. "I'm doing kind of the same thing. I saw the tape across the drive and assumed no one was here."

She nodded. "I replaced it after I drove down." She thumbed over her shoulder. "I parked in back."

Deacon smiled. "But not the front door, huh?" She seemed confused. "The tape is off there."

"Oh. Yeah. I was going to reattach it when I left."

He pointed with his good hand. "What are you hiding there in your pocket?"

Again, she resembled that mischievous cookie thief. Her cheeks flushed anew as she withdrew a pocketknife from her slacks.

Deacon thought he understood. "What were you doing with that?"

Tremaine giggled. "While I was here, I thought I'd fix that snake head snarling up from the linoleum." Her color dropped a bit as she regained some self-assurance. "Wouldn't want anyone else to trip like I did."

"Very commendable," Deacon said as he walked around her into the kitchen.

"You okay? Shouldn't you be resting?"

"I'm fine," Deacon said, as he clicked on the light. He panned the room quickly and found where a gouge snaked up from the linoleum. He pointed. "Looks like it still needs mending."

Tremaine followed him inside, nodding vociferously. "Yes, I was just about to fix it when I heard you in the other room." She whipped the knife from her slacks, the blade flashing open in the fluorescent light. With the grace of a jungle cat, she slunk over to the snag and removed it with a flick of her wrist. "There." She smiled her beautiful smile. "My good deed for the day." She sighed as she replaced the blade. "Well, as I said, I have a plane to catch. Can I walk you out?"

Deacon bent down to examine the gouge in the floor. "Was that what you tripped on?"

Tremaine nodded. "You know about these places and their old floors."

Deacon grinned. "Yes. Millions for defense but nothing for safe house maintenance."

She chuckled as he squatted down and examined the gouge. "Odd, isn't it, that this *old* snake head seems freshly made?" He swirled his good hand around the room. "In fact, this *old* floor looks in remarkably good shape except for this *old* snake head and a few recent scuff marks." He swiped his hand across a spot, rubbing off the dirt. He pointed to her shoes. "*Very* recent scuff marks."

Tremaine paused in indecision, then shook her head and smirked. "I don't know what you're getting at, Deke. Are you accusing me of something?"

Deacon shrugged. "It just seemed odd to me that Barzoon spared your life."

Her neatly trimmed eyebrows rose. "Excuse me?"

"When he kidnapped Amy. He supposedly knocked you out but didn't kill you."

"Supposedly?" She touched her bruised forehead. "You think I got that goose egg from walking into a door?"

Deacon ignored the question. "I was stumped for a while. He left Movello alive, but that was a slip up. He was going to kill him, but Amy intervened. Same with the urgent care clinic. He killed the staff there. Sanford and Sinclair escaped with Amy, but she said he took shots at them as well. He didn't mean to leave any survivors." Deacon scratched his head. "But you? He had you knocked out, dead to rights. Why did he leave you alive?"

Deacon met her gaze. Her eyes seemed afire, almost feral. In that moment, he knew he was seeing behind a mask, one maintained from long training and practice. In that moment, he was sure who and what she really was.

She turned away, no longer able to hold his gaze. "I don't know what you're talking about, Deke. I don't think you do, either."

"It's odd for someone as thorough as Barzoon to leave a loose end, don't you think?" Deacon snapped his fingers. "Joe Metternich." He pointed at her back as she faced away. "That loose end got tied up rather nicely." He pointed a finger gun at his own head. "A closeup bullet to the temple. Suicide note sloppily printed in marker." Deacon flipped his good hand nonchalantly to the side. "Joe's wife was even easier. Just undo a restraint at an unguarded moment." He paused. "Was that Barzoon or you?"

Deacon watched her stiffen at the question. Tremaine normally exuded confidence as well as a sultry femininity, her body relaxed and self-assured. But when she turned to him, he saw none of that. He was now looking at a cold, calculating machine. Pure business. A terminator holding a Glock 19 pointed directly at his head.

She shook her head. "Deacon, Deacon. Deacon. You are becoming a nuisance."

"I can see why you killed Joe. His suicide leaves a conveniently dead fall guy. But why Claudia Metternich?"

Tremaine acknowledged him with one shrug. "Insurance in case anyone got nosy about Joe's state of mind. Scientist turns traitor to help his wife. She commits suicide. Now he's lost his job, his freedom, his wife, his … everything." She winked. "Besides, after settling with Joe, I was in the neighborhood."

"Hence your fatigue of late. You certainly are thorough."

Tremaine tipped him a salute with the barrel of her Glock, then again aimed the pistol at his skull.

Strangely, Deacon didn't feel frightened. He was standing in front of a trained killer pointing a gun at him. His wounded arm was in a sling. No rescue was likely because no one knew he was here. Yet, Deacon felt curiosity more than fear, intrigue more than anxiety. He looked into Tremaine's eyes and no longer saw warm, beautiful blue. Now they were the cold, steely eyes of a spy, a trained killer. He thought of Cathleen Harris, another beautiful spy who had wormed her way into government service. He found himself smiling. Beauty was the most valuable commodity for women who sought power in a man's world. Beauty, properly applied, turned men into tools, even fools.

"What are you smiling about?" Tremaine asked.

"Myself, I guess. My own stupidity." Deacon pointed at her with his good right hand. "Do you think Mata Hari ever tripped on a vinyl snake head?"

Her return smile was as cold as her eyes. "Yeah, not my best hour in espionage either. Spy 101, never come up with an alibi that can be proven false." She shrugged, but her gun hand didn't waver. "But you surprised me with your non sequitur about shooting Barzoon. So, I came up with the first excuse I could think of." She yawned. "I was tired and had a lot on my mind. Like I said, not my finest hour."

"Then you had to come back here to put paid to the lie, just in case I got curious." He squatted down and nonchalantly massaged the linoleum gouge. He looked up at Tremaine. "If you were working with Barzoon, why kill him?"

She laughed. "Let's say I was working *for* Barzoon, not with him."

Deacon straightened up. "I don't understand."

She motioned toward the table. "Have a seat."

Deacon pulled over a kitchen chair and straddled it.

"Barzoon was not part of my mission. He was a complication." She laughed again. "Truth be told, he was a pain in the ass. Him and his revenge fantasies. Demanding help. Blackmailing me. Threatening to divulge my true mission if I didn't go along."

Deacon snapped his fingers. "Your transfer to Secret Service. *Presidential* detail."

She tapped her nose. "You didn't think Barzoon and Harris were the only irons we had in that fire, did you?" She rotated a kink from her long neck, her gun hand as steady as ever. "By shooting Barzoon, that loose end kind of tied itself."

"You left him alive, though. Another screwup?"

Her steely eyes flashed. Her words came in a short staccato burst. "It was a kill shot. One in a million survival."

"But you didn't count on a trained medic being there. Someone you couldn't kill without a lot of explaining. Just like you couldn't kill me."

Tremaine saluted the pistol to her brow once again. "My compliments, sir. You are clever. Now, what to do with you?"

Deacon raised his brows. "Another suicide? Loose-cannon scientist is despondent over his girlfriend's state and shoots himself? Where did I get the gun?"

She chuckled. "No, that's not your style, Deke. Suicide yes, but not a gun. No, you are a suicide in slow motion. Have been for years." Keeping the gun trained on him, she reached into the cupboard next to the fridge. "Ah. I thought there still must be some stock available." She pulled out a half-full bottle of Maker's Mark.

Now it was Deacon's turn to laugh. "I drink myself to death? You're going to need more than that. I've built up quite a tolerance. And you're going to need something else … a willing participant." His laughter faded. "Like that night when you got me drunk to get me into the sack."

Tremaine sniggered. "Don't flatter yourself. I didn't sleep with you. I just fed you booze until you passed out, then let your imagination fill in the rest." She winked. "Men are predictable, very predictable."

She gripped the pistol two-handed, knees slightly bent in a true shooter's stance. "Now, Dr. Creel. I'll need you to get up very slowly and walk toward the refrigerator." She moved to his left, gliding around and behind him, her gun steadily pointing at his head.

The extremity of his situation was finally making its way past the curiosity. Deacon glanced about the room for a weapon, his eyes settling on a carving knife holder. Smooth handles rose from its wooden surface, held in place by the knife blades, no doubt dull but serviceable for such an emergency. But the knives were a good fifteen feet to his right, on the other side of the sink. On a good day, he couldn't outrun a bullet for fifteen feet, and today was not a good day. The adrenaline and excitement that had kept him going were gone, exhaustion taking their place.

"I said now, Deacon."

Deacon rose unsteadily, the day's exertion wearing thin his fragile condition. Several faltering steps, and he was leaning against the counter next to the fridge. He turned to face her. "Now what?"

She smiled; he thought of a grinning cobra. "Now, have a drink."

"If I refuse?"

Her eyebrows rose. "Then we wait." Her smile broadened. Her aim remained rock steady. "You move like a long-retired librarian. Your face is pale, and I believe I see sweat gleaming from your upper lip."

Deacon self-consciously wiped his lip.

"And I'm guessing your wounded arm is singing the Hallelujah Chorus about now. I give you maybe sixty seconds before you pass out."

Deacon placed a hand on the bottle. It felt smooth and comforting, the wax below its cap soft and forgiving. "May I take it to the table and sit?"

Tremaine backed up a few steps as she nodded.

Deacon picked up the whiskey bottle by the neck. He had to tuck it to his chest to keep from dropping it. The table seemed miles away as he stumbled forward. The world tilted and took on the sepia tones of an old tintype photo. He felt like he was moving through a mountain pond, cold and clammy, his movements sluggish. He fell more than sat, thudding onto the kitchen chair. The room regained some color. His face beaded cold sweat. The bottle clunked from his arms onto the table.

"Careful not to break it, please."

Deacon righted the bottle. He turned to Tremaine. "May I have a glass?" He tried to smile. "I'd get it myself, but as you can see, it's a long way to the cupboard for me."

Her expression looked part amusement, part annoyance. She angled toward the glasses.

His fingers closed gently around the waxed neck of the bottle, as if fondling a lover. With his vision averted, he sensed more than saw her move toward him. He was centrally positioned in the room, so she'd have to cross within several feet of him to get to the glasses. He tried to appear helpless, which was easy to do; his recent exertions left him panting and sweat soaked. But he had a weapon. Not exactly a gun or a knife or even a club, but if she got within arm's reach, he had a chance.

Deacon kept his eyes focused on the bottle, hoping she couldn't read his thoughts, surprise his biggest ally. The amber liquor spoke to him soothingly, as it always did. She moved closer; he could hear her cat-like tread, feel the warmth of her, smell the subtle fragrance she wore. The latter was mixed with fresh female sweat, arousing him despite everything. He smiled inwardly; men were indeed predicable.

The long moment dragged on. Any second now. He sensed her passing, her eyes now focused on the glasses in the cupboard, not him. Another moment and she would be out of reach. He marshalled his remaining strength in one deep breath. He gripped the bottle tightly. It was now or never.

¢¢¢

Amy pressed gently against the plunger. She watched the rubber stopper leave the fifty ml mark. Slow and steady, lest excess pressure blow the vein. Amy saw the air bubble form and begin its lazy circuit down the clear plastic tube. Forty-nine. Forty-eight.

Just a few inches of tubing before the catheter. Then the air would reach her vein. Forty-seven. Soon it would all be over. Her final duty completed. Forty-six. Soon she could be at peace. Soon, Deacon would be shed of her. She loved him more than her life. She knew she was not worthy of his love. Forty-five. He was too good for the likes of a miserable failure.

She stared in fascination as the air grew into a long, clear bubble that moved lazily down the river of her life. She was reminded of reading *Huckleberry Finn* in junior high; two drifters off to see the world—floating down the mighty Mississippi. The air bubble rounded a bend—my Huckleberry friend, just like in the theme song from "Breakfast at Tiffany's", one of her mom's favorite movies. Amy's mind drifted to that night so long ago when Uncle Bobby knocked on the door, awakening them with middle-of-the-night news that was never good when your father was deployed to a war zone. Forty-four. News that changed her world, sending it off in a new direction. In many ways, that night almost twenty years ago had been the beginning of Amy's life journey—one that was now ending. Forty-three. She thought again of Deacon.

Dr. Deacon Creel. He was too noble for the likes of her. Noble, but flawed, as all men of substance invariably are. A man of greatness, with the guilt that goes along with it. Much as her father had been. But Amy fell short of her mother, just as she fell short of Deacon. He deserved better. Now, he would have someone better. Someone who was more than a failed medic, a shiftless nomad on a sham government pension. Her thirty pieces of silver.

The rubber stopper neared forty. The air bubble had grown to six inches as it disappeared under the tape holding tube to wrist, then out the other side. It moved more quickly now, the leading edge almost at the maw of her catheter.

Deacon would now be free of the millwheel that was Amy Robbins. He could pursue other women. Women of substance like himself. Scientists. Doctors. Career women. A beautiful face framed in golden tresses filled Amy's mind. Terri Tremaine. Amy ceased all pressure on the plunger. Tremaine was a woman of substance, a woman on the rise. She wanted Deacon, that was plain. Amy began to press the plunger again but couldn't. The image of Tremaine was too strong. Her pretty but predatory smile. A smile that Amy had seen on too many pretty faces of too many scheming women. Self-centered women. Women who used instead of nurtured, disposing of the remains like an empty pizza box, only scattered crusts left to mark their passing. Would this be Deacon's fate. Anger flared through Amy. No, she thought. This must not happen.

"What are you doing?"

The nurse snatched the syringe from Amy's hand and pulled it out of the IV port. She held it to the light, noted the air filling its barrel, then looked down at the long, blank trail in the IV line. As Amy watched in dumb bemusement, the woman flung the syringe away. Amy felt a stab of searing pain as the nurse ripped the IV line out of her arm, tape, bloody catheter and all. The nurse pressed her thumb over the blood rising from the puncture site, then snatched a microphone from the side of her smock. "Assistance needed in Room 206. Stat!"

Before Amy could do more than blink, the nurse had cinched the restraining strap around Amy's wrist. Then the nurse's weight was on her chest as she straddled Amy, wrestler fashion, to secure the other wrist as well. Amy did not put up a fight.

Chapter 32

Deacon kept his eyes on the bottle as he tightened his grip on its neck. He'd only have one shot at this, and it had to be now. Tremaine was gliding past him, the heat and scent of her filling his senses. He tensed, marshaling his remaining strength, and swung.

The rest happened fast, basically a jumble of kaleidoscopic images. Before he'd raised the bottle off the table, Tremaine had slunk cat-like out of the way. Deacon realized he was going to miss her but could not stop his momentum. He rose, almost knocking over his chair. The bottle whooshed through empty air, spinning him around with it. As it arced back toward the table, Tremaine sidestepped into him, using an elbow shot to drop him back into the chair, the bottle thunking harmlessly onto the table.

Deacon's neck ached where she'd hit him. His ass stung from falling into the chair. His wounded arm ached just because.

"Men are predictable," Tremaine panted. She was behind him now. "You in particular. I saw what you were planning even before you did."

Deacon laughed, more from release than humor. "My compliments."

"Now that we have that out of the way," Tremaine said. "How about you have that drink?"

"How about you get me a glass?" Deacon could not see Tremaine, but he knew she was smiling, still the cunning cobra.

"I think not. Out of the bottle. I'm sure it's not your first time."

As he unscrewed the cap, Deacon thought of the many times he had done just that. It was awkward one-handed, but he held it to his chest to get the job done. He grasped the neck again.

"Go ahead. Take a long pull."

Deacon held the bottle but didn't lift it. "And then? After I've had my final drink?"

He could sense her grinning again. "Then, a very unfortunate series of events will unfold. To wit. Having been discharged from the hospital, the very place where his beloved Amy suffers under continual sedation and suicide watch, Dr. Creel returns to the safe house, knowing there is liquor inside. Predictably, he drinks too much, spilling in the process. For some reason, we may never know why, he turns the burner on the stove. His bourbon-soaked shirt catches fire. The fire spreads. The government loses one safe house. The world loses one drunken genius. How does it sound? Loose ends nicely tied?"

"Indeed. Unless Dr. Creel has told others his suspicions. What then?"

He could feel that wicked smile boring into his neck. "No. If that were the case, you wouldn't have come alone. You wouldn't have even needed to check to confirm your suspicions. No. You told no one."

"You're willing to bet your life on that?"

"No. Yours. Now drink."

Deacon pushed the bottle away. "Sorry, but I'm not thirsty."

She laughed. He once thought her laugh musical. Now, it was sinister. "Drunks are always thirsty. Drink."

He shook his head. "If I refuse? What are you going to do about it?" He waited. She said nothing. "You can't afford to put a bullet into me. That would be very hard to explain given your neatly concocted story."

She sighed audibly. "True enough. A gunshot wound might be discovered, even in a body that had been badly burned. But I doubt that a lump on the head would be noticed or even thought unusual in a drunk." He felt cold steel tap his skull. "Is that the way you want it? Or do you want that last drink?"

Deacon reached for the bottle. He had run out of options and was running out of choices. He grasped the graceful neck and felt the warm, smooth wax that had been used to seal the cap. He stared at the rich, caramel-colored liquid. He'd always found comfort there. No, that wasn't quite right—he had always *sought* comfort there. Temporary comfort. A moment's peace. Reprieve from guilt, bad memories, nightmares. True comfort was harder to come by. Deacon smiled inwardly. He doubted if he'd felt real peace since Liz died—since he had failed her, just as he'd failed Amy, just as he'd failed his mom. He lifted the bottle halfway to his lips. He could smell the liquor now, hot and tangy. He could almost feel it melting down his throat, spreading its warmth. He touched the bottle to his lips, ready for the sweet kiss. Ready for oblivion.

"Can I come in?"

Deacon almost dropped the bottle as he snapped his head toward the kitchen door. The familiar head of Carl Sinclair was looking in.

"I heard talking about drinks and ..." Sinclair finally saw the gun. "Jesus. What the ..."

Deacon could feel Tremaine tense behind him. Without looking, he knew that her attention had shifted; the gun was now pointed at Sinclair. Deacon could sense her mind working, calculating a cold equation. In a moment, and it would be no more than that, she'd act. She might order Sinclair inside to share Deacon's fiery fate. She might shoot the poor guy. She might shoot them both and concoct a new cover. He wasn't sure which way the spy would jump. He only knew he had to jump first.

Deacon gripped the bottle tighter, his fingers pressing into the hardened wax. Having heard Tremaine speak from behind him, he had a general idea of where she stood. He flipped the bottle like a burger on the grill, catching it again by the waxed end. Bourbon sloshed onto his hand and sleeve. He ignored it, just as he ignored the pain of his injured arm shifting in its sling. He didn't have time for pain now. He didn't have time for thought. The world distilled down to his own cold calculation. He swung his good arm back, feeling the weight of the bottle in his hand. He tensed his legs. He'd gained a little strength resting in the chair. He hoped it was enough. Either way, he didn't have time to worry about it.

With a grunt, Deacon thrust both legs down, using those muscles to strengthen his swing. The bottle arced to his right as he stood. He heard the chair topple behind him. The world turned agony grey as his wounded arm flung free of its sling. His vision condensed into the sweep of the half-full bottle. He made his best guess, adjusted the arc, and pivoted. Through hazy vision, Deacon could see the look of surprise on Tremaine's normally confident features. The gun was still pointed at the kitchen door, but her attention was back on Deacon. Her Glock spoke twice as she swung it with predatory speed away from Sinclair toward Deacon. The first bullet hit dry wall by the kitchen door, the second popped past Deacon's ear. But the booze bottle had already found its mark. Tremaine blinked once before the bottle made contact with the bridge of her nose, then shattered. Her look of surprise changed to one of dull stupidity as Deacon followed through. The jagged edge of the bottle sliced open one lovely cheek, then continued, as if on its own, to her graceful neck. The last thing Deacon saw before the room greyed out was a spurt of red, arcing into the fluorescent glow.

¢¢¢

Deacon's eyelids flapped open like a window shade. The haze was replaced by the brightness of the overhead fluorescent. He blinked against the glare, then remembered about Tremaine. Rising, he clutched his wounded arm and spun onto his knees, the world dimming again from the pain. When his vision cleared, he was staring at Carl Sinclair standing near the kitchen door. The poor guy looked comically like a cartoon character, eyes bugged from his pasty grey face, pink lips outlining the black of his gaping mouth.

Deacon's eyes followed Sinclair's stare to the body lying on the floor. Tremaine lay as if crucified, one outstretched arm still clutching her Glock. Her flaxen hair was spread like a halo within a pool of red blood. More red lines streaked away from her neck into a several-foot swirling pattern, almost like the strokes of a Jackson Pollock painting. Her cheek was flayed neatly to the bone, a flap of flesh bulging forth from the jagged cut that extended to her lovely neck. Her staring, steel-blue eyes were startling bright against the almost translucent marble-like sheen of her flesh. Deacon thought of some statue, perhaps Saint Joan, its beauty marred by a vandal's hand.

"Is she, is she dead?"

Sinclair was now pointing shakily. Deacon looked at Tremain's prostrate form and nodded. Then he turned back to Sinclair. "What are you doing here?"

Sinclair didn't appear to hear, his attention still focused bug-eyed on Tremaine.

"Carl?" Deacon yelled.

Sinclair flinched, then turned his glassy eyes toward Deacon. "I needed to get into the trunk, but you …" He cleared his throat. "You had my car keys."

"The trunk? What did you need in the trunk?"

"I, um, well I had a bottle, you know for emergencies, stashed behind the spare tire."

Deacon sunk onto his heels and laughed. The release felt good, but he stopped himself before it turned into hysteria. "Well, Carl, I guess this qualifies as an emergency."

"I heard someone talking about having a last drink, so I came into the kitchen." He pointed again. "Who is she? And why did she shoot at me?"

Deacon sighed, suddenly exhausted. He gingerly tucked his injured arm back into its sling. "Her name was Terri Tremaine. She was a U.S. Marshal. But that wasn't what she really was. Below the surface she was something else."

"My God," Sinclair said. "She was beautiful."

Deacon nodded. "That was superficial, too."

¢¢¢

Deacon spent almost two hours answering questions at the safe house. First the pair of uniforms questioned him about what happened. Then he'd had to explain it again to the sergeant who was manning tac-one. The bullet holes and recently fired Glock still gripped by Tremaine backed up his story, as did Carl. But still, a homicide had been committed, and Deacon appeared the likely perpetrator. They were just leading him to a patrol car for his trip downtown when two guys in suits arrived. They flashed credentials from Homeland Security. The tac sergeant scratched his head, and Deacon was released into their custody. Instead of taking him downtown, the new arrivals, Agents James and Bond, had driven him to the hospital. Deacon approached Room 206 slowly. He longed to look inside, to see her again. But he feared what awaited him. If she was asleep, lying there peacefully, he could at least pretend she was going to be alright, although he knew in his heart it was pretense only. He feared more that she would be awake—loneliness and despair in her eyes. The same despair he'd seen on the video Barzoon had sent. The same despair that had filled Claudia Metternich. A knot formed in his gut as he reached for the knob.

"You should be resting."

He turned to face Dr. Isabela Sanford. Deacon tried to smile but knew it was forced. He raised his arm in its sling, the pain now manageable. "Almost as good as new. They didn't even admit me this time."

"You were never officially discharged," Sanford said. "That means you're still my patient. So, go home and rest."

Deacon nodded toward the door. "Can I see her?"

Sanford met his eyes. He saw empathy there and a little pity. "She's restrained and heavily sedated. We were going to try and switch her to only mood elevators, but that was before the incident."

She didn't say it, but her eyes spoke the truth. It was the hard truth, the one doctors have known since Hippocrates but have had trouble communicating for just as long. It was Cassandra's truth, one never completely believed but truth nonetheless. Truth summed up in one word—hopeless. A word synonymous with another—helpless. Sanford didn't know how to say she was helpless to save Amy. Deacon knew the feeling.

"Can I see her?"

Sanford smiled. It was a sad smile that spoke of shared understanding. "Just for a minute."

Deacon stared into Sanford's eyes for another moment, then flipped the knob. The knot in his gut flipped as well.

Chapter 33

Deacon tossed papers out of his bottom drawer, nicking his finger in the process. "Shit." He sucked the injured digit, then went back to rummaging through the desk.

Sanford had told him to go home. But where was that? The safe house? A hotel room he wasn't even sure he still had? With Joe Metternich dead, Deacon was in persona-non-grata limbo. But he was apparently still assigned security, so he told the cop guarding him to head his squad car to the University of Dayton. Deacon's office was as good a place as any to get shit-faced, and he knew he had a bottle in his desk. Only now he couldn't find it.

On the ride over, he'd had time to think, which was why he need-ed the bottle. As it always did, his sober mind wandered down mem-ory lanes full of ruts and potholes. Top of the list were all the women he'd failed. All dead. His mom. His fiancée, Liz. His best friend, Lisa. Amy, soon to be next. All gone because of his self-absorbed, self-righteous, self-pity. Self. Self. Self. That was Deacon Creel, the boy wonder rapidly growing into middle-aged disappointment.

"Dr. Creel? Where have you been?"

Deacon recognized the voice of his savant postdoc, Howard Threlkis, but kept sweeping the desk drawers. "It's a long story." Deacon turned to check behind the desk.

"Jeez! What happened to your arm?"

"It's an even longer story." Deacon swept a folder to the floor in disgust.

"Dean Shirmer's been looking for you. The semester is start-ing soon, and he wants to know when he'll get his science build-ing back."

"Tell him to check with Joe Metternich." Deacon kicked the desk, then turned to his assistant. "I had a half bottle of Maker's Mark in here. Do you know what happened to it?"

Howard tugged his collar and looked sheepish. "I, um, I mean *we* kind of drank it."

Deacon plopped his ass on the desk. "Who is *we,* and why did you drink my bourbon?" He watched Howard's Adam's apple bob.

"We is me and Leon. The um, *why* is we were kind of celebrating." He smiled. "It makes a good mix with coke from the machine down the hall."

Deacon massaged his shoulder. His pain meds were wearing off, and the ache had started up again. "You mixed premium bourbon with … Never mind." He stared at Howard. "Celebrating what?"

"Completing what you told me to do." Howard ran over to search the desktop. He scanned the mess and said, "It was here somewhere. There it is." He snatched up the folder Deacon had knocked to the floor. "Just like you said." He handed the file to Deacon.

Deacon eyed the folder suspiciously, then did the same to Howard. "You mean, you're done?"

The postdoc beamed. "Yeah, we finished a couple of days ago. That's why we had the little party. Sorry about your whiskey."

Deacon rubbed the back of his neck and chuckled. "That's okay. I guess we should get started on the neurological testing." Howard blanched. "Is that a problem?"

The young man held up his palms. "I didn't know you wanted to be a part of that, so we already ran them."

"You already did *all* the neurological testing on the rats?"

"Well, yeah, me and Leon."

"Object recognition *and* radial arm maze?"

Howard shrugged.

"Pretest and posttest, both?"

"I didn't know I wasn't supposed to. We already had the results from the early rats, so I figured, why not? I didn't know that you wanted …"

Deacon held up his palm to stop the boy's stammering. "No need to apologize, Howie. In fact, I'm going to go out on a limb and say *you* probably *never* need to apologize. Not scientifically, anyway." He handed the file back. "And your findings, Dr. Threlkis?"

Howard blushed again. He cleared his throat then opened the folder and handed a printed sheet to Deacon. "Ten live female rats."

Deacon scanned the page. "How long did they live?"

"Until necropsy. That is, at least 24 hours."

"No signs of self-destructive behaviors? Even though they'd been dosed with the suicide drug?"

Howard nodded again. "All healthy."

Deacon cocked his head and raised a brow. "No side effects at *all*?"

Howard's good mood dampened. He handed another page from the file to Deacon.

"What's this?"

"The results of the neurological testing." Howard crossed to look over Deacon's shoulder. "As you can see, Threlkis-2 still produced some neurological deficits, although there were no statistically significant differences on paired t-tests."

Deacon nodded. "I see. P values of about 0.25." He smiled at his assistant. "Looks like Threlkis-2 was a success." Howard's face brightened again at the mention of his name. "Were there any other major defects?"

"The lab said the necropsies were all normal."

Deacon tossed the printout on his desk and slumped into his chair. He rubbed his shoulder, which was as close as he could get to assuaging the ache in his wounded arm. He felt a glimmer of hope. "Ten rats and all survived without major side effects." His hopes dimmed almost as soon as they had glimmered. "But that was rats, not people."

"Are human trials planned? You mentioned before that Dr. Metternich could set that up."

"You have a good memory, Howie." Deacon leaned back and closed his eyes. He suddenly felt very tired. Tired and hopeless. "No, I don't think Joe Metternich will be setting anything up. Not anymore."

"How long does that usually take? Human trials I mean?"

"You mean, by the book?"

He could sense Howard nod.

"Well," Deacon said, eyes still closed, "first you have to find volunteers for a phase one trial. A few healthy people who are willing to have an experimental drug injected into their spinal canal." He held up a finger for emphasis. "A drug known to be associated with brain damage." He chuckled humorously. "You also need an institutional review board to sign off on that, which is unlikely." Deacon held up a second finger. "Then you run those people through a series of pre-study and post-study tests."

"Like with the rats."

Deacon nodded. The immensity of their problem was adding to his fatigue and his need for a drink. "Only more extensive." He held up a third finger. "Then the big kicker, you need to find people who agree to be dosed with both the suicide drug and Threlkis-2." He laughed. "I don't think there is enough money in the government to get somebody to agree …" Deacon opened his eyes and bolted upright. "Unless there was someone already suffering from the suicide drug."

"Is there such a person?"

Deacon didn't answer. "Then you'd only need to find someone for the phase one trial." An idea was forming in his mind, one that was as awesome as it was perilous. "At least *one* someone." Deacon stood. He was no longer exhausted. He no longer wanted a drink. His arm no longer hurt him. All his focus was on the enormity of the idea taking root. If it worked, it could solve a lot of problems. Shortcut a possible cure for Amy. Lift a ton of guilt from Deacon's shoulders.

"I don't understand." Howard looked curious but confused. "I figured that maybe somebody somewhere was afflicted with this suicide drug. Otherwise, there wouldn't be such a rush to find a cure. And I figured that maybe Dr. Metternich could pull strings to get approval for human subjects. But I still think it's going to be hard to find people to agree to receive an experimental drug that has caused brain damage in rats."

"*Mild* brain damage only," Deacon said, tapping the desk for emphasis. He'd heard and understood Howard's words, but his mind was scrambling on ways to make this crazy idea work. "Mild decrements in recognition and memory wouldn't necessarily translate to noticeable loss of life skills in people." He jabbed a finger at his young assistant. "And the human brain is more complex than the rodent one, with more redundancy and a capacity for remediation of deficits. Who's to say people would even experience the same level of loss?"

"Who's to say it will *even* work in people?"

Deacon shook him off. "I'm willing to take that chance to save her life."

Howard crossed his arms and looked sternly at Deacon. "Whose life are we talking about, here? And who exactly is going to volunteer for this phase one trial?"

Deacon sunk onto his chair, his burst of energy drained. He met Howard's gaze. The postdoc no longer looked like a kid. Deacon could now see the brilliant scientist and good man Dr. Howard Threlkis would become. "The life we're talking about saving is a young woman who I happen to love." Howard's eyes showed surprise and empathy. "As for the volunteer?" Deacon tapped his chest. "You're looking at him."

Howard's jaw dropped. When he closed it, he shook his head. "You can't do that, Dr. Creel. It might kill you. It killed some of the male rats."

Deacon tossed the folder back to him. "But they died from the suicide drug. I'm immune to that."

"You're immune how?"

Deacon waved him off. "Not important. Suffice it to say that I've been exposed, and it doesn't affect me."

Howard sighed deeply and dropped onto the edge of Deacon's desk. "Listen, Deke." It wasn't Dr. Creel anymore. "You've said yourself that drug development is littered with dry holes. Most drugs that are successful in rat studies still never make it to market. Rats aren't people, and people aren't rats."

Deacon smiled. "With a few exceptions."

Howard didn't smile back. His eyes locked onto Deacon's, wisdom beyond their years hidden in his gaze. "You could end up crippled." He paused. "Or just plain dead."

"It's my life, and I can do as I *damn* well please with it." Deacon saw Howard blanch from his outburst, so he softened his tone. "I've made up my mind, Howie."

Howard looked down at his hands clutching the folder. His shoulders drooped. He shook his head and opened the folder. He shuffled through the papers, retrieved a printout, then handed it to Deacon.

"What's this?"

"Something else you need to consider." Howard pointed, his jaw set. "While you were gone, I was looking for things to do, so I ran additional statistical analyses."

"Why?" Deacon asked. "The t-tests already showed there were no longer significant neurological effects from Threlkis-2."

Howard ignored him and bulled ahead. "This printout holds the results for regression models using the pre-injection test times as a variable. Notice anything interesting?"

Deacon didn't know where his assistant was going with this, but he looked down at the paper. "Well, there's moderate correlation, but it's still not statistically significant."

Howard stabbed at the paper. "Moderate *negative* correlation." He gave this a moment to sink in. "The smarter the rat at the start of the study, the more neurological deficits it experienced."

Deacon looked up. The young postdoc was looking back with genuine affection and concern.

"What's your IQ, Deke?"

Deacon finally understood. The rats with moderate intelligence were relatively unaffected by Threlkis-2. But the top performers, the wunderkinds of the rodent world, took a measurable hit. It was logical when you thought about it. The brain has a great capacity for adaptation. The average person with moderate brain damage, from say a mild stroke, returned to relative normalcy over time. But what about an exceptional mind, a one-in-a-million Mozart or Einstein? Their normal was abnormal to begin with. Could such a highly tuned instrument be expected to return to full capacity? If you cracked a Stradivarius, would it ever play such beautiful music again? In science, it was known as regression toward the mean. Outliers tended to drift toward the middle.

Deacon had never been in the middle. All his life, he'd soared in the rarified atmosphere of the gifted. It had been his rock, the pedestal that supported his ego and his self-confidence. It had also been his curse, the potential to live up to, the need to diminish others to heighten his own self-worth. He thought back on the number of times his ego, his feeling of superiority, had led him down a garden path to poisonous fruit, gotten in the way of his personal relationships, caused him to neglect those he'd cared about until it was too late. The weight of his guilt pressed him like a stone. He thought of his mother, Liz, Lisa. He thought of Amy.

"I'll take my chances, Howie."

Howard tossed the folder on the desk. Papers fell, scattering across the floor. The normally sedate postdoc stomped away, his back to Deacon. When he turned around, the look on his face spoke of anger and concern, especially concern. Deacon had liked the kid from the beginning, his brilliance and enthusiasm reminding Deacon of his own early career. But the concern on Howard's face made Deacon like him even more. No, it was more than concern, perhaps it was even affection. Deacon was touched.

"It's alright, Howie."

Howard's eyes widened and his face flushed. "Alright? It's not alright. It's absolute *lunacy*." Howard stabbed a finger at Deacon as he yelled. "You're crazy, you know that? Stark staring off your nut."

Deacon only smiled. "It's alright, Howie."

Howard grunted and turned away, clenched fists pumping the air. After a moment, he stopped his well-meant tantrum. His shoulders slumped. He turned to Deacon.

"Even if you go through with this craziness, what doctor in his right mind would inject you?'

Deacon considered this for only a moment. "I think I know someone. But it's a she, not a he."

¢¢¢

Deacon leaned against an exam table while Dr. Isabella Sanford paced the treatment room they'd used as an office. He recognized the expression on Sanford's face as the same mixture of concern and anger he'd recently seen on Howard. But unlike the postdoc, anger—not compassion—held center stage. The kind of anger that arose when an idealistic medico was asked to violate her oath and maybe the law.

"You want me to do what?"

"I know it's a lot to ask, but I would consider it a personal favor."

Sanford's laughter reverberated off the walls. She picked up a surgical pack, hefted it as if testing its weight, then tossed it back down. "You would, would you?" She put a hand to her chin and squinted up at the ceiling. "Which part would that favor be? The part where I violated my ethics by injecting a healthy man with an experimental drug, or the part where I broke the law by doing so?"

"It wouldn't be illegal," Deacon replied. "You'd have my signed permission."

She laughed again. It was a nice laugh, almost musical. Under other circumstances, Deacon would have found it attractive, just as he would have found her attractive.

"So," she continued. "It would only be *unethical*. I'd only lose my license to practice medicine." She turned to him, arms akimbo, face set in disapproval. "And as far as owing you any favors, I don't think I do."

"How about Amy? Do you owe her any favors? The woman who saved your life?"

"That's a low blow, Dr. Creel."

He could see he'd struck paydirt. "Make it Deke … please."

Sanford sighed. Her shoulders slumped. She shook her head. When she looked at him now, the anger had left her face. Deacon could see the kindness of a doctor who cared about people.

"Listen, Deke. We're doing all we can for Amy."

Deacon nodded. "I'm sure you are."

"We're giving her fluids and NPO nutrition. She's on mood elevators. We're seeing to her general nursing needs. She's on suicide watch, monitored around the clock."

"I know. But it won't be enough."

Sanford looked at him quizzically. "How can you be so sure?"

Deacon met her gaze. "Let's just say, I am sure. Perhaps I'm the only one around right now who really is. The others are gone. Barzoon. Carstairs. Joe Metternich."

Her quizzical expression deepened. "Who?"

He held up a hand in lieu of an answer. "Sooner or later, somebody will screw up. Amy will be in good spirits or seem like she's sleeping, and they'll let their guard down. And then, she'll take her own life."

Sanford shook her head. "She's under constant watch, Deke, and …" The physician paused, as if remembering something unpleasant.

Deacon raised his brows. "What?"

Sanford stared off without answering.

Deacon recognized the expression. "It's already happened, hasn't it?"

Sanford flinched. "*No.*"

Her answer was too loud, feeding Deacon's intuition. "Tell me."

Sanford paused, that pained expression back. She shook her head. "It was nothing. Just something one of the nurses reported. I'm not even sure …"

Deacon stepped over and placed a finger on Sanford's lips. "Let me guess. This nurse removed one of the restraints while Amy appeared to be unconscious. This nurse stepped away to get an incontinence pad or something. When she returned … what?" Seeing the startled expression on Sanford's face, he added, "Tell me."

Sanford shrugged. "The nurse had just finished administering a parenteral injection into the IV bag. She'd undone the restraints to adjust the IV catheter and change some bedding. Amy seemed to be zoned out, so the nurse set the syringe and large-gauge needle down and stepped away for a moment."

"And?"

Sanford hesitated to answer, then rushed ahead. "And when she came back, Amy was injecting air into the IV." Sanford raised a hand to cut off Deacon's reply. "But the nurse caught it in time. And that nurse was taken off the case. Everyone else has been talked to. It won't happen again."

"Yes, it will," Deacon said. "You know it will. And next time, we won't be so lucky."

Sanford rubbed the back of her neck. Then she shrugged. "In that case, maybe we just go ahead and administer this cure you mentioned and hope for the best."

Deacon slowly shook his head.

"But if what you say will happen, then …"

"No!" Deacon shouted, slamming his fist on the exam table. He lowered his voice. "No. I can't be the cause of her death. I've caused too many. I'll not make her a guinea pig. I chose that role for myself."

Sanford only stared at him, her dark eyes radiating compassion. "Well, Doc. What do you say?"

Sanford started to answer but instead turned away. She brushed hair off her forehead. Her shoulders sank. "I'm sorry, Deke. I know you want to help, but I, I just can't do it."

Deacon placed a hand on her shoulder. "I'm going to do this, Izzie. One way or another. I've already gotten clearance from Washington, and they're ready to assign a doctor to perform the lumbar puncture." He was lying. He'd spoken to no one in DC.

She turned back, question marks in her eyes. "Then why me? I'm no neurologist who performs CS taps several times per week. I've done it only a few times."

As Deacon thought about his answer, he studied the look in Sanford's eyes. He saw compassion there. Concern as well. Not just concern for Deacon and his welfare. Not just concern for Amy. But concern about doing the right thing. A look that was the embodiment of 'first, do no harm.' A concern about duty. He'd noted that same look in Amy's eyes from time to time. To Deacon, that look was more important than proficiency or clinical skill. And there was something more.

Deacon was a scientist. He'd never thought of himself as a superstitious man. But just lately, he was starting to believe in some higher power. Call it God. Call it fate. Call it what you will. Something that guided and controlled him. The thing that brought him to Amy. The thing that guided Amy's hand when she administered Creel-1 to him over a year ago. The thing that guided them both against impossible odds pitted against Barzoon and Harris during the Project Suicide fallout. The same thing that brought Sanford and Amy together. The force that ultimately defeated Barzoon. Not religion really, but definitely faith. He had faith in Isabelle Sanford.

"Because I trust you," Deacon said. "And to me, trust is more important than qualifications." He raised one finger before she could answer. "And because I think you were fated to do it."

Sanford slumped into a chair, defeated. "You know that this is a thousand-to-one shot, right? Even if it doesn't kill you or turn you into a human vegetable or low-grade moron, the odds that this experimental drug will cure Amy are slim."

Deacon smiled. "I'll take those odds."

Sanford shook her head with a snort. She paused, looked at Deacon, then sighed deeply. "I'll need to see something from some higher up. Somebody in Washington or somewhere, giving the official go-ahead for this craziness."

Deacon's smile deepened. "Let me make some calls."

Chapter 34

Amy saw light. At first, it was as dim as the dawn cresting a hill. Then it grew into the outline of a window, the morning sun smiling at her. She smiled back. She felt rested. She felt good, as good as if she was experiencing pleasure for the first time. Good to be alive. She also felt tired, the kind of fatigue that came with battling a long illness. Her forehead was clammy, the hairs stuck to it as if from fever that had recently broken.

She wasn't sure how long she'd slept. But she was sure that she'd dreamed. They were crazy dreams. She smiled again. Deacon was in the dreams. And there were doctors. They were telling her about some vague procedure meant to … she couldn't remember what. It would involve anesthesia and a spinal tap. In the dream, she'd told them to just let her go, to deepen the anesthesia until she was gone. What an odd thing to say. A shiver ran through her at the thought.

She tried to lift her hand to cover a yawn, but it wouldn't move. This seemed both strange and not. The fatigue descended on her like a comfortable old sweater. She closed her eyes. Maybe she would dream of Deacon again.

When Amy opened her eyes again, the sunshine was higher in the window, its rays blinding her. She blinked against the glare until a shadow fell across her face. She saw Deacon smiling down at her. She smiled back.

"Hey cutie. How you doing?"

The sight of him made Amy stop breathing, as if her breath might blow away her illusion. Fatigue fled as she reached to take him in her arms, but those arms moved only a few inches. Startled, she looked to see her wrists buckled into nylon straps. She turned back to Deacon.

"What's this all about?"

"Don't you remember?"

She thought hard. Nothing. She concentrated harder. A vague recollection of something rose to her mind. It had to do with restraints like these. Her face flushed. "A bondage game?"

Deacon's laughter filled the room until his arched spine brought him up short. He grimaced and reached toward the small of his back.

"Are you alright?"

He nodded. The pain left his face as he straightened up. "Just some lower back pain from my lumbar … ah, from not lifting with my legs." He smiled.

"That's funny. My back's a little sore too, It's almost like a dream followed me to waking." Amy shook her restrained wrists. "What's with the …

"What *do* you remember?"

Amy thought again, but her mind was fuzzy. "I don't know. I mean, I'm not sure."

Deacon sat on the edge of the bed, another twinge of pain arching the scar on his forehead. He sighed. "Let me ask you this. What's the *last* thing you remember?"

Amy concentrated. An image of a fat, bald man flashed into her head. "Metternich," she blurted. She locked eyes with Deacon. "Dr. Metternich. He came to see me." She looked around at the unfamiliar surroundings that screamed hospital room. "Not here. At my apartment in … Columbus?" She looked back at Deacon, seeking his approval.

Deacon nodded. "What did he want?"

"You," she said. "He wanted to find you." She scrunched her forehead in concentration. "Or wanted me to go see you. I can't remember why." She shrugged as much as her restraints allowed. "It's all kind of hazy."

Deacon's brows rose. "What about Barzoon?"

"Who?"

"Nelson Barzoon," Deacon said. "Do you remember him?"

"Of course. Him and that Harris woman." Her mood dropped as she lowered her eyes onto the sheets. "I let her die."

Deacon leaned over and stroked her cheek. His touch was soft and tender.

"You did the right thing," he said.

Amy tilted her head to kiss his hand. "It didn't feel right. I'm a corpsman. I mean I *was* a corpsman. I was supposed to save lives. It was my duty to save her."

Deacon placed fingers to her lips. "Shhh. Water under the bridge." He paused, a questioning look on his face. "And you don't remember Barzoon after that?"

Amy thought this an odd question, but she answered anyway. "How could I? You said yourself that he'd died. Another victim of the suicide drug. Why do you ask?"

Deacon shook his head. "No reason."

After all they'd been through, Amy could read his moods. She saw relief behind his smile. Her stomach rumbled. "Any chance of getting something to eat?" she asked. "I'm hungry enough to eat a vegetable, as my dad used to say." Deacon laughed again. "I think that can be arranged." He rose, then bent down to kiss her.

His lips were warm and soft. He smelled of maleness and just plain Deaconness. The kiss stirred her as if it were her first. "On second thought," she murmured with a grin. "Why don't you lie down and join me?"

Deacon shook his head, his grin matching hers. "First, let's get some food into you." He straightened up with a slight groan of pain, then reached for her wrist restraints. "I don't think we'll be needing these anymore."

¢¢¢

Deacon signaled to the nurse waiting outside the room. "Can you please get Ms. Robbins something to eat?"

The nurse nodded. "I'll call down for a milkshake."

The nurse turned toward the wall phone, but Deacon stopped her. "I think she's ready for solid food that she can eat with a knife and fork."

The nurse looked shocked. "Knife? But what about …"

Deacon patted her arm. "I think it'll be okay. I've removed the restraints." He nodded toward the door. "Why don't you order the food inside and keep Amy company?"

The nurse still looked skeptical as she scurried into Amy's room. "How's the patient?"

Deacon turned to the familiar figure of Dr. Sanford approaching down the hall. He pressed a hand into the small of his back. "Amy or me?"

Sanford smiled. "Either. Both."

"We'll live."

Sanford pointed toward the door. "Does she remember much?"

"Thankfully, no," Deacon said. "I think it's like a bad dream to her."

Sanford nodded. "By the way, there's a government-type fellow waiting for you in the business office."

"What's he want?"

"He didn't say. Just flashed his badge."

"I better go see him." Deacon turned then flinched as pain stabbed his lumbar spine.

Sanford took his arm. "Are you alright?"

Deacon nodded, massaging his lower back. "It just sneaks up on me every once in a while."

Sanford grimaced. "I guess my technique could have been better."

Deacon smiled. "You did fine."

"Any other side effects?" Sanford asked.

Deacon thought for a moment, then shook his head. "None worth mentioning. *Considering.*"

¢¢¢

The business office consisted of a couple of desks and a collection of filing cabinets. The occupants were off at lunch, except for one man in a dark suit that had GOVERNMENT AGENT written across it in block letters. The man looked up when Deacon entered.

"Dr. Creel?"

Deacon nodded.

The man opened a bulky folder and took out a glossy photo. He studied the picture, then looked at Deacon. "Yes." He replaced the photo, then flipped open his badge. "Special Agent Horrigan, Department of Homeland Security."

Deacon massaged his lower back. "What can I do for you, Agent Horrigan?"

Horrigan motioned Deacon to a seat.

Deacon shook his head and continued rubbing his back.

"I've been sent down here," Horrigan said, "to oversee the collection and archiving of all pertinent data and materials related to … well, the matters at hand vis-a-vis the biological agents you've been working on."

Deacon plopped his butt on the edge of a desk and waved. "All that material is at UD. You'll need to see my assistant, Howard …"

"Threlkis," Horrigan continued. "I have spoken with Mr. Threlkis."

"*Dr.* Threlkis."

Horrigan nodded. "Dr. Threlkis. He was reluctant to turn over materials without your say so, but we *convinced* him to cooperate." Horrigan's smile suggested a crocodile. "A crew is currently cleaning out your laboratory."

Deacon shrugged. "So, what do you need from me?"

Horrigan rummaged through his folder. "Naturally, the department is hesitant to rely solely on the statements and materials in possession of a mere graduate student."

"Postdoc," Deacon corrected.

"Regardless, I'd like for you to confirm that this is the correct formula for this antidote or whatever." Horrigan found what he was rummaging for and handed Deacon a sheaf of papers stapled in the corner. "Threlkis tells us that this is the summary sequence for the chemical synthesis, and I just wanted to get your confirmation on that."

Deacon took the papers. He recognized Howard's signature below a three-paragraph summary. He flipped through the papers, the pages filled with arcane chemical formulas and equations that were so many hieroglyphs to the uneducated. Some of them looked familiar, as if seeing an old friend out of context. Others were undecipherable to Deacon. He knew he should know them, that he used to understand them. Now?

"Well, Dr. Creel?"

Deacon handed back the papers. "I'm sure they're fine."

Horrigan took the pile. "So, you confirm the authenticity of these materials?"

"If I were you," Deacon said, "I'd accept the word of Dr. Threlkis." Deacon smiled. "It's all Greek to me."

THE END

About the Author

John Bukowski is an accomplished writer of both fiction and nonfiction. His short stories have been published in numerous notable venues such as Dark Secrets, Makarelle, and Land Beyond the World. In a previous life, he wrote hundreds of medical publications, including handbooks, websites, and radio scripts, translating technical topics for the general public. As with his first two novels, *Project Suicide* and *Checkout Time*, he has lent his scientific expertise to *Bad Pennies*, blending technical authenticity with fiction for an exciting ride.

When he isn't tapping his computer keyboard, he's tapping his feet to music, singing pop, Broadway, and opera — in multiple languages. Originally from Detroit, he and his wife now reside in Eastern Tennessee.

www.ingramcontent.com/pod-product-compliance
Lightning Source LLC
Chambersburg PA
CBHW060708190726
48289CB00002B/592